# — TEARS OF DARKNESS —
## TRAGEDY AND HOPE

# 1

## SOPHIA LIDDELL

**TEARS OF DARKNESS**
     **Volume 1: Tragedy and Hope**

# TEARS OF DARKNESS

## VOLUME 1: TRAGEDY AND HOPE

## SOPHIA LIDDELL

TEARS OF DARKNESS, Volume 1: Tragedy and Hope
SOPHIA LIDDELL

Artwork by
VERONICA LIDDELL

TEARS OF DARKNESS, Volume 1: Tragedy and Hope
© SOPHIA LIDDELL 2018

Check out my blog and get updates @
sophialiddellbooks.webs.com

First Edition

Soft Cover ISBN# 978-1-7323049-1-8

## PROLOGUE: THE HOUR OF DESPAIR

Five-year old Michael was playing on the monkey bars. Every Saturday, barring bad weather, his mother would take him to the same park so that he could play. He loved to play on the monkey bars and to climb to the top of the wooden tower that contained a small wooden box fort.

Michael dropped down to the sand from the monkey bars and climbed up the ladder to his special tower fort. He stood higher than everyone else as he stood on top of the tower. It was from that point that he could get the best view of the big city on the other side of the river. The tall skyscrapers reached up into the sky.

After looking at the big city, Michael turned around to see the smaller suburb in which he lived. Michael noticed a strange black object that was approaching them high in the sky.

Michael pointed to the object and yelled out to his mom, "Mom, look, an airplane!"

His mother looked in the direction that he pointed at and noticed the odd shape as it continued to grow closer to them. She then directed the attention of other parents who were in the park. Adults began to talk among themselves about what it could be.

As the object grew closer, they could see that it had a thin diamond shape to it. It looked like one of those old spear heads that ancient people once used long ago before guns were invented. The object was definitely black and did not seem to have a typical engine located on it like earthly air planes would. It also lacked any wings that were visible so to call it an airplane, as we understand it, would have been wrong.

As the object continued to approach them, an ominous low humming could be heard. The sound seemed other worldly and penetrated through their bodies.

Michael continued to stare at the approaching craft in amazement. He began to jump up and down yelling, "Airplane! Airplane!" His mother saw him doing that and called to him, telling him to get down from up in the tower fort. He sighed and said, "But I want to see the airplane from up here!"

His mother yelled, "I want you down here now!" Michael took the hint and climbed down, running into his mother's waiting arms. She bent down and scooped him up, holding him in her arms as they continued to stare at the approaching craft in amazement.

The unknown craft finally reached above the park where they stood. It seemed not to notice or care about the people below but continued moving on at a constant pace toward the big city of Portland. As it passed over the area, everyone felt a strange energy that caused every hair on their body to stand up.

As the craft went over them, half of the people began to run away. Michael and his mother stayed more out of shock than anything else. The remaining people gazed on as the craft passed over head toward the big city of Portland.

As the craft headed toward the center of the city, three United States Air Force jets screamed overhead and began to approach the unknown craft aggressively. Michael heard someone nearby say, "Are we under attack?" Another person said, "I don't know, I've never seen anything like that."

The unknown craft ignored the Air Force jets. Since that tactic failed, the Air Force jets launched two missiles at it. Instead of hitting their target, the missiles suddenly veered off in a strange random path striking a nearby building. Michael heard another voice yell out, "Oh my God, we are under attack!" Michael could hear the footsteps of people running away.

Two more Air Force jets passed overhead, their engines screaming in hot pursuit. More missiles were launched, which continued to be ineffective as they also veered off course randomly and exploded into another building.

At this point, the people who were still standing there gazing at the scene began to comprehend the seriousness of the situation as well. Michael's own mother also cried out, "Oh my God, we are under attack!" She turned around and began to run back home while Michael viewed the scene from over his mother's shoulders.

The Air Force jets turned around and began to make another pass at the invading craft. They began to lay down strafing fire with their rotary cannons. The shells bounced off the armor of the unknown craft. Then, just like with the missiles, the jets began to move erratically and they crashed into nearby buildings too. Black smoke began to rise from the buildings that had been hit by the missiles and jets. Soon the area was engulfed in flames.

The unknown craft finally reached the center of the city, which appeared to be its intended destination. It came to a complete stop, hanging there in the sky.

A loud crunching noise echoed throughout the region as the craft seemed to split open in the front. It was so loud that Michael's mother had stopped running to look at the source of the sound. Michael began to cry and said, "Mommy, what's happening?" His mother kissed him on top of his head and said, "I don't know Michael. I don't know,"

Light began to bend around the tip of the craft and a dark sphere of energy began to form. A loud sound began to echo in the air as this dark sphere of energy formed. The sound was nearly indescribable but would sound something like that of a vacuum cleaner sucking in the air.

As the dark sphere got bigger, it seemed to absorb the light around it. The sound got louder and louder until it was deafening. The sphere then suddenly dropped and descended to the ground as if it were an apple that fell from a tree.

When the sphere hit the ground, it began to expand rapidly in a matter of seconds until it had completely engulfed the city in a black dome of energy. Then, as quickly as the sphere came, it vanished.

When the sphere had vanished, what had once been a city was no more. It was completely gone. Where the city of Portland once stood there was now a large crater in the ground. It was completely erased. Not one piece of building rubble remained. Not one person or part thereof remained. It was all gone in an instant.

With its inhuman work done, the unknown craft reset itself to its original form and continued on its way.

Portland was not the only city that had been hit that day. In fact, almost every city across the world with a population of over a million people had been utterly erased into nothingness.

There was no warning.  There were no demands.  There was no other invasion.  The strange crafts viewed all over the world, left the earth as quickly as they came.  The attack was complete within the space of an hour.  June first in the year 2050, from two-thirty to three-thirty, became known as the Hour of Despair.  Their only purpose seemed to be to annihilate cities with a population over a million people.  With their work now done, these strange invaders were never seen again.

Though this event was horrific, it seemed to be the thing that finally allowed the nations to put aside their petty differences and unite together into one.  This day, July twenty-first, 2050, became known as Unity Day.  With the world united under one banner the earth began to pool together their resources and technologies in an effort to prepare for the next time an alien menace would come.  In only a matter of months, new weapons and vehicles began to be produced in the hope that they could fight off another alien assault.

In addition to the positive events that happened since the catastrophe, another strange thing happened.  About a year after the world united under one banner, a percentage of girls began to be born with strange eye colorization.  For every one thousand girls born, one of these girls were inflicted with the odd eye colorization.

What made these girls so strange was that the irises in their eyes were colored in ways not seen in normal humans.  These girls were born with either solid red, yellow, or blue irises.  The blue color was a bright shade of blue that was not seen in other humans.

Doctors and scientists performed various tests but could find no reason for their abnormal eye colors.  The only thing that could be ascertained by study was that this condition could only be present in the duel X chromosome of females.  Genetically speaking, these girls were no different from other girls.  It also did not seem to be the result of any virus.  They were unable to find any solution to this question presented to them.  In the end, people tended to think that it was a mark left behind by the alien destroyers as a sign that they would return.

As these girls with the odd eye colors grew older, more strange things began to occur.  The girls with red eyes began to show signs of significant strength differences then other children their age.

The first recorded case was a girl with red eyes in her kindergarten class.  The girl, named Sally, was playing with a toy.  A classmate named Greg came to her and tried to take the toy away from her.  She became angry and the whites of her eyes began to glow red. She ripped the toy out of Greg's hands and then sent him flying across the room, being stopped only when his fragile body hit the wall. The poor boy suffered a severe concussion, multiple broken bones, as well as permanent brain damage.

For the girls with the bright blue eyes, it was shown that they could manipulate a field of energy around them that could protect them from harm. In one reported incident, one of these girls with blue eyes, named Anushka, was accidently left without supervision which led to her wandering into traffic.

If Anushka had not contained this special ability within her, she would have most likely been killed. As she was running into the street, a car came rushing toward her. Instinctively, the whites of Anushka's eyes began to glow blue and a barrier of energy formed around her. The car began screeching to a halt but did not stop in time causing it to hit the energy barrier. The car rolled over the barrier and to the amazement of onlookers ended up landing upside down behind the girl.

The strangest ability by far was seen in the girls with yellow eyes. They seem to have developed the ability to rapidly heal themselves. They could heal others as well with focused touching, but this seemed to drain their own strength. Even stranger yet, only a small percentage of them developed a deadly ability that was able to absorb the energy of another life form. This ability could even lead to the death of the life form being drained. They could steal the energy from anything living and then use that energy to heal another person with no consequences to their own energy levels.

The first recorded instance of a yellow eyed girl using her power was after a car accident. When emergency workers arrived on the scene, the parents of the girl were already dead and the girl herself was in critical condition. Upon removing her from the vehicle, the whites of her eyes began to glow yellow and the cuts and scrapes on her body began to heal immediately. There was no scarring at all.

Of course, with these reports and others, it was decided by the World Government that, in the future, these strange girls would prove to be valuable soldiers to defend humanity from another alien attack.

Seven years after the horrendous unprovoked attack that exterminated half of the earth's population, an even worse enemy appeared from the stars. An asteroid, about ten miles wide, appeared in the view of astronomers heading straight for earth. This started a panic across the world as a new and unprovoked disaster was about to affect the earth again. Scientists predicted that the asteroid would make landfall somewhere between Saudi Arabia and India.

Much to the surprise of the world, the asteroid began to shift its own course dramatically. The apparently self-propelled asteroid, which later proved to be more like a colony ship, ended up crashing into the city of Nanping, China utterly decimating the region in a blast of heat, fire and rocks. Those who survived the initial impact in that region were faced with annihilation by the most horrendous creatures that the world has ever seen.

The creatures, or rather, aliens, became known as the Harvesters for their desire to harvest humans as a food source. These Harvesters did not seem to have intelligence as we would describe it. How they reached earth was beyond the ability of the scientists to understand as the Harvesters seemed to not know how to create or use technology.

The Harvesters were an insectoid race, looking somewhat similar to the stag beetles of earth except they tended to be a little larger than a typical family van. They had an exoskeleton that was as hard as steel. The color of it was so deeply purple that it looked almost black. The exoskeleton had a sheen to it that made it glisten in the sun.

On their heads they had four black eyes that allowed for a full frontal view as well as to the sides of their head. Along the sides of their mouth were two extremely powerful mandibles that could crush a human in two with no difficulty. Two arm like appendages also hung on the sides of the mouth that the Harvesters used to dismember their prey and bring food to their mouth.

Swarms of Harvesters quickly spread throughout China, Russia, India, and all the surrounding regions. The Earth Defense Force quickly took action but it was almost meaningless. As more and more territories began to fall to the Harvesters, the Earth Defense Force retreated, and the world began to build large walls around its remaining city centers.

The walls proved to be a somewhat effective deterrent to Harvester attacks but occasionally wall breaches would occur. If the Earth Defense Force could not hold the Harvesters back long enough for the wall to be fixed, another city would fall to the Harvesters.

Soon enough the world was divided into two areas: inside the walls where humanity lived and outside the walls where the Harvesters lived. After five years from the arrival of the Harvesters, another half of the remaining population of earth had been exterminated.

As the girls, with the strange eye colorization got older, it was discovered that around the age of eight or nine, they could begin to control the electrical energy that produced their unique powers. This allowed them to activate or deactivate their powers at will. The Earth Defense Force quickly took notice of the military advantage within these girls as their energy proved to be extremely effective against the Harvesters. It seemed that the girls were born specifically at the right time to meet the challenge of the Harvesters on purpose. No one had the ability to explain it except to attribute it to a miracle from God. Perhaps it was even payment from the first aliens that slaughtered so many innocent people before.

It was expected that, when these girls grew up, they could be used by the Earth Defense Force as weapons against the Harvesters. In reality, as the girls with these special powers reached menarche, their first period, their energy went out of control and tore apart their bodies in a gruesome explosion. Not one of these girls lived a year past their first period. It was also discovered that overusing this energy also caused the girl's bodies to be torn apart prematurely.

The only way for these girls, who became known as Spirit Wielders, to be of use to humanity was to force them to use their powers when they turned nine years old and use them till they self-destructed between the ages of twelve and fifteen.

It became a long and drawn out argument in the World Governing Congress. Arguments of morality versus need lasted for weeks. In the end, humanity's government decided that the only way the Harvesters could be defeated was to use the powers of these Spirit Wielders before they self-destructed.

The World Congress created the Wielder Registration Act, which required that all girls born with this eye color attribute be registered with the Earth Defense Force upon birth. At nine years of age the girls would be taken and forced to use their powers to protect humanity from the Harvester menace.

To maximize effectiveness, the Spirit Wielders were put into special squads of three, each containing a red Wielder, a blue Wielder, and a yellow Wielder. In addition to the three Wielders, each unit was led by an adult Lieutenant, who would also serve as their guardian and caretaker.

With the Wielder Squads in action in 2064, humanity struck back at the Harvesters, but with almost endless Harvester numbers it seemed that humanity would be in an endless stalemate. Even so, humanity has no other choice then to continue to struggle against the Harvesters or be wiped off the face of their own world.

- 1 -

Lieutenant Michael Snyder stood on the front porch of the house listed in the file that he carried.  Out of habit, he brushed the shoulders of his white dress uniform that had black stripes along the front and edgings of it, which indicated that he was a squad commander in the Wielder corps.  He then straightened his black tie.

Lieutenant Michael hesitated for a moment as he stood there on the porch.  He sighed before knocking on the door.  This was the part of his job that he hated the most but somebody had to do it.  He understood the necessity of it but it was still hard to be the one to do it.

If everything was going as planned, there should already be two conscription officers inside already preparing them for what had to happen.  They were also there in case the parents resisted and had to be detained.  A moment later he breathed deeply, exhaled and knocked on the door.  One of the officers that was inside the house opened it for him and saluted.  He saluted back and said, "Is she ready?"

The officer nodded and replied, "As ready as she'll ever be I suppose."

Lieutenant Michael ran his hand through his short dark blonde hair and stepped inside of the house.  The officer led Lieutenant Michael into the front room where a little nine year old girl sat in the middle of the room on a chair.  Her parents were sitting inside the room on the couch trying to put on brave faces. Despite that, there was an air of gloom inside the room. The second officer stood at ease in the opening archway of the front room. Lieutenant Michael stood in the entryway and assessed the situation.

The girl was wearing a white dress with spaghetti straps over her shoulders. Several images of monarch butterflies rose up to her waist line starting from the hem. Her platinum blonde hair extended just below her shoulders. A monarch butterfly clip held the right side of her hair back behind her ear. She was sitting with slumped shoulders leaning forward with her hands tightly squeezed between her thighs. Her head was down cast as she stared intently at the carpet beneath her. A small suitcase sat on the floor beside her.

Lieutenant Michael was used to dealing with girls of this age. He understood how difficult this transition would be for her. He knelt down in front of her on both knees and smiled as he tried to look into her eyes. The irises of her eyes were a deep shade of yellow.

Lieutenant Michael then spoke gently to her, saying, "Hello, my name is Michael Snyder. I am going to be your commanding officer. What's your name?"

The girl looked up nervously and said, "My ... my name is ... is Valerie."

Lieutenant Michael smiled again and said, "It's nice to meet you, Valerie. Do you know why I am here?" Valerie nodded.

Lieutenant Michael said to her, "Can you tell me why I'm here?"

Valerie reluctantly replied, "I ... I turned nine and since I have yellow eyes I have to go and fight the Harvesters."

Lieutenant Michael said, "Yes, that's right, you have a unique power inside of you that makes you special. We need you and others like you to help protect the world. Only you can protect your mom and dad. Do you understand?"

Valerie nodded her head. She then looked up toward her parents, saying, "Yes, I understand. Will I ... will I be able to ever see my mom and dad again?"

Lieutenant Michael nodded his head, and said, "Of course! I will personally take you to see them when there is time. At other times you can face time them on the vidcom."

Valerie then said, "Will I be alone?"

Lieutenant Michael immediately replied, "Of course not. There are two other girls waiting to meet you who are just like you. I will be with you too. I hope that we can be friends. Are you ready to go with me?"

Valerie started to get teary-eyed. Her voice seemed to be on the verge of crying, "I ... I'm afraid ... I don't want to go. I ... I wish I wasn't born this way."

Lieutenant Michael took her by the hand and held it dearly, saying, "I know. I promise you that I will do everything I can to help you not be afraid. If I didn't have to take you, I wouldn't. Will you go with me anyway?"

Valerie nodded and said, "I will go. I know I have to. You want me to say that I'll go so that you don't have to rip me away from here. Can I at least say goodbye to my parents?"

Lieutenant Michael nodded and said, "You're right. Whether you want to go or not, I'll be forced to take you. The World Government forces me to do this. I ask you that question because I really do hope that you'll be coming with me on your own choice. It would be a lot easier for your own self if you choose to come with me. And, of course, you can say goodbye to your parents. I wouldn't let you leave without saying goodbye."

Valerie slid off the chair and hugged each one of her parents saying goodbye. She walked over to Lieutenant Michael and took him by the hand, saying, "I can't tell whether you are a monster or just a really nice guy."

He nodded his head and said, "Well, I can tell you that I'm a nice guy, but I'll let you decide that for yourself. Let's go before it gets too hard on you." He picked up her suitcase and led her out of the house to his car that was parked on the street. Her tiny hand seemed to tremble in his palm.

He opened the back door for her and she crawled in. She sat down on the side behind the passenger's seat and buckled her seat belt. As she sat there, she began to cry again.

Lieutenant Michael opened his own door and heard her sobbing. He sat down in his own seat and then said to her gently, "Valerie, that was very brave of you." He turned around and placed his hand on her shoulder and smiled lovingly at her. His eye were filled with compassion for her. He then turned back around and started the car. He drove down the street away from her house. She continued to sob for the next ten minutes until she calmed down.

She stared blankly out of the window of the car as various images passed by her sight. She saw a government sponsored bill board with an image of three girls, each one having the red, blue, and yellow eye colorization. Below them in big letters read: "Don't forget to register your Wielder child. It's the Law!"

Lieutenant Michael spoke to her, saying, "I know that it was hard to say goodbye to your parents. I meant what I said that I will take you to see them when we have the time. When I was young, I lost my parents in a Harvester attack. I know what it is like missing your parents. If you ever need to talk about it, I'll listen."

Lieutenant Michael could feel that she had calmed down quite a bit and had accepted her fate. It was always hard on these girls but some handled it better or worse than others. Valerie seemed to be handling it better. He said to her, "I told the two other girls all about you already. They are looking forward to meeting you. Their names are Mary and Sarah. Mary is thirteen years old and a red Wielder. Sarah is eleven years old and a blue Wielder. Mary is a little rough around the edges. But, she's really nice when you get to know her. Sarah is always friendly and calm. I think you will all get along just great."

Valerie continued to stare out of the window but she repeated their names, saying, "Mary and Sarah." As she stared out of the window another government sponsored billboard passed by that read, "Religion is a myth of the old world. Embrace the New World."

Lieutenant Michael responded, saying, "Yes, Mary and Sarah. They'll help you get all set up in your new place. We all live in one apartment but we all get our own separate rooms."

Valerie then said, "Where exactly are we going now?"

Lieutenant Michael replied, saying, "We are going to the military airport where we have a transport helicopter waiting for us. It will take us to the Sacramento Wielder Complex. It's about a two hour ride from here."

Valerie looked forward and looked into the rear view mirror, she met the reflection of his eyes. She brushed back the hair over her left ear, saying, "You said that you lost your parents, can I ask you what happened?"

Lieutenant Michael met her gaze for a moment in the mirror and then said, "I was five years old when the Hour of Despair occurred. I was twelve years old when the Harvesters attacked earth. At the time, my family was living in the small town of Beaverton in Oregon. The World Government constructed an anti-Harvester wall around our city sector, which became known as New Portland.

When I was fifteen the Harvesters finally crossed the North Pole into North America. If we hadn't constructed all those anti-Harvester walls already, the death toll would have been unimaginable.

About a year later, on my sixteenth birthday, the Harvesters managed to make a breach in the wall. In an hour, they began pouring into New Portland slaughtering the people in that area. My dad worked in the area where they breached. I never saw him again. So, I can only assume that he was murdered by the Harvesters.

When the sector government realized what had happened, they sounded the breach alarm. My mother and I attempted to reach the evacuation zone. As we were running for our lives, I didn't realize that my mom had tripped and fallen. When I realized that she was not with me, I turned around to find her. A few moments later, I stood there and watched her get torn apart by a Harvester. I was so scared, all I could do was run away. I felt ashamed of myself that I did not realize sooner that she was not with me."

Lieutenant Michael stopped speaking and he could not hold back the grief from his face. Valerie saw the look of deep pain in his eyes and regretted asking him about it. She said, with as much care in her voice as she could muster, "I'm sorry. I probably shouldn't have asked you that. I'm sorry I called you a monster."

Lieutenant Michael shook his head and said, "No, it's alright. You and I are now a team so I want you to know everything about me and I want to know everything about you. Do you know our team's name?"

Valerie shook her head and said, "No, I didn't think about that at all."

Lieutenant Michael, slightly chuckled and said, "I suppose you wouldn't know about that stuff, being so young. Our unit's name is the Phoenix Guard, we are unit three of five. Do you know what a phoenix is?"

Valerie shook her head and said, "Nope, I haven't heard that name before."

Lieutenant Michael pointed to a patch on his right arm. The patch contained a bird made of fire with wings lifted upward. In between the wings and above the head was a black number three in Roman numerals.

Lieutenant Michael then said, "The phoenix is a mythical bird that people used to believe in. Its feathers were made out of fire. The phoenix would live for a long time and then, when it got old, it would die and turn to ashes. A new phoenix would then be reborn from the ashes of the dead phoenix."

Valerie, seeming not to care about the story, said dispassionately, "That's interesting." Her gaze returned to the window.

Lieutenant Michael, not wanting to agitate her, decided to change the subject back to what he was talking about earlier. He said, "The reason I joined the military and became a Wielder Guardian was so that I could be part of the teams that destroy the Harvesters. I guess you could say that I am seeking revenge. Maybe it's also a way to redeem myself. I suppose you could also say that I want to make sure that nobody else would lose their parents the way that I did. Together, you, myself, Mary and Sarah will work together to protect the people of earth so that, what happened to me, won't have to happen to others. "

Valerie sighed and said, "I know ... are you one of those people who are afraid of silence?"

Lieutenant Michael was taken back by this comment, he stuttered, saying, "Uh ... no, I ... uh, no, I am just worried that you will get depressed."

Valerie looked back at him and said, "I was just teasing you."

Lieutenant Michael breathed a sigh of relief and said, "I'm glad that you feel comfortable enough to joke around with me."

Valerie didn't say anything but smiled at him with a big grin through the mirror, her eyes still a bit red from crying. She then looked back out the window and continued to watch the images pass by. She pointed at a small airport and said, "Is that where we are going now?"

Lieutenant Michael relied, "Yep, that's right. That's where our helicopter is waiting for us."

The helicopter was an older military dual rotor model. It was the standard olive drab color of the army but contained the logo of the World Government, which was merely copied from the old United Nations logo. The helicopter's propellers were already spinning when they arrived.

Lieutenant Michael got out of the car and opened the door for Valerie. She hopped out of the open door and stood on the tarmac. He extended his hand to her and said, "Do you want to hold my hand?"

Valerie stared at his hand questioningly and then took his open hand into her own without saying anything. Lieutenant Michael smiled at her and said, "Have you ever been on a helicopter or airplane before?"

Valerie shook her head and said, "Nope."

Lieutenant Michel then said, "Well, this will be fun, being your first time. I'll let you have a window seat if you want."

Together, they then walked to the helicopter where a sergeant in field dress stood waiting for them. A rush of wind began blowing over them as they approached. Valerie shielded her eyes with her free hand.

The Sergeant saluted Lieutenant Michael, saying, "Welcome, Lieutenant." Lieutenant Michael returned the salute, saying, "Thank you, Sergeant." The Sergeant then opened the door of the helicopter.

Lieutenant Michael let go of Valerie's hand and then pushed her gently forward with his hand on her back toward the door. She took the hint and began entering the helicopter. As she stepped forward the Sergeant saluted her and said, "Good luck, Wielder." Valerie, unsure of what she should do, saluted him back to the best of her ability, and said, "Thank you, Sergeant." She nervously smiled at him and continued up the ramp and into the helicopter.

Lieutenant Michael followed behind her and the Sergeant shut the door behind him. He then pointed to the passenger area and said, "Feel free to sit wherever you want." Valerie looked around for a moment and then sat down on the padded bench along the middle section next to a window. She bounced a few times as she felt the softness of the padding. Lieutenant Michael then proceeded to sit down next to her but giving her a little space. He set her suitcase between his feet on the floor.

A voice echoed from the intercom, saying, "Cargo is loaded, prep for takeoff, one minute."

Lieutenant Michael spoke after the intercom went silent, "Have you ever seen over the wall?"

Valerie shook her head and said, "Nope, I never even got close to the wall. I was too afraid."

Lieutenant Michael pointed to the window and said, "Feel free to take a look, if you want to, when we get up in the air."

Valerie jumped up on her knees and knelt on the bench with her face looking out of the window beside her. She watched all the workers running back and forth performing their assigned tasks.

The helicopter started shaking and Valerie's body felt heavy as the aircraft lifted itself off the ground. She watched the houses below her get smaller and smaller. The people below her looked like ants.

As Valerie watched the scenery below, she muttered, "I wonder if the aliens look at us the same way we look at ants."

Lieutenant Michael was a little stunned by the maturity of this statement and said, "Who knows what the aliens thought about when they attacked us. They never tried to communicate with us."

Valerie replied, "Have you ever tried to talk to an ant? When I look at all the people below us they are no bigger than ants the way I see them. If the aliens look at us this way, why would they bother trying to talk to us?"

Lieutenant Michael sighed and said, "You certainly have an ability to grasp concepts that other children don't usually understand yet."

Valerie then said, "May I ask why I was put in your group, or, was it just random?"

Lieutenant Michael said, "When an opening becomes available, a Lieutenant, like myself, is given the files of available Wielders. I get to select the Wielder that I think would best suit the unit. I also get input from the other team members so I know what they think."

"So, then," Valerie said, "when you looked at my file, you saw something in me that you thought would be best for your team.  Can I ask what it was about me that made you want me?"

Lieutenant Michael smiled and chuckled, saying, "It was your maturity and perceived ability to grasp difficult situations.  And, might I add, that from what I can see so far, you certainly are intelligent."

Valerie stopped looking out the window and looked back at Lieutenant Michael.  He could see in her face that she wanted to ask another question but hesitated within herself.  He said, "It's okay to ask me anything that you want.  I promise I won't get mad."

Valerie sighed and said, "Did the girl I'm replacing die?"

Lieutenant Michael's face became downcast as he remembered the horrific incident that led to that girl's death.  He nodded and said, "Yes, she did.  She suffered structural collapse of her body due to her age.  Most replacements are because of death, though if a Wielder really wants to, they can transfer to a new unit, though that is rare."

Valerie's face turned grim and said, "Am I going to die like that."  She already knew the answer but asked anyway.  It was a topic that was always on the minds of these Wielder girls since they knew it was inevitable.

Lieutenant Michael replied to her, "Yes, unfortunately, there is no way to prevent eventual structural collapse.  No Wielder has ever lived a year past their first period.  Every week I will give you an injection that will help your body to endure the vast amounts of energy you will produce.  But, eventually, like all the others, your body will reach its limit and collapse on itself.  Fortunately, you still have many years so try not to worry about it.  Okay?"

Valerie looked back out the window and stared at the buildings below her again.  She said, "What was her name?  Did you love her?"

Lieutenant Michael tried to hold back the tears that wanted to come but his eyes became watery nonetheless and he said, "Her name was Susan.  I loved her as if she was my own daughter.  I love all my girls as if they were my own daughters.  It's very hard not to."

"So," Valerie said, "will you love me too?"

Lieutenant Michael forced a smile and wiped the water that had started to pool in his eye, "Of course, I already think that you are great.  I bet we will soon become good friends."

Valerie smiled and then pointed out at the window excitedly, saying, "Look, it's the wall!"

The wall around Reno sector was massive considering the five million citizens that were forced by the harvesters to centralize into one area. The wall was thirty feet high and ten feet thick. It was made of hardened concrete blocks reinforced with steel rebar. On top of the wall, guard towers were placed every few miles where soldiers kept watch by sight and by video monitoring.

The land area around the outside of the wall was scorched from a recent fire bombing, which prevented plants from interfering with the maintenance or strength of the wall. Helicopters would drop bombs of napalm from time to time. It was safer than risking people's lives to do it manually. The scorched area made it easier to see what the Harvesters were up to near the wall.

As the helicopter passed over the area, Valerie could see the ruins of the old suburbs that once were the homes of people. In addition to the old ruins, the forests that once surrounded the city had overtaken the region since there was no one there to prevent it from over growing. "This is horrible," Valerie muttered under her breath.

Lieutenant Michael, nodded and said, "You're right. It is horrible. That's why we have girls like you in our unit. Without you, we're not strong enough. This dead city looks like this because we were not strong enough." Valerie continued to stare out the window.

Lieutenant Michael said, "Have you ever seen a Harvester before?" Valerie shook her head and said, "I've seen pictures but nothing in real life." He pointed out in the window and said, "Look." A pack of six Harvesters were down below them.

Valerie slid down from kneeling on the seat and sat on the bench normally. Her eyes were wide in shock. Lieutenant Michael shook her shoulder gently and said, "You okay?"

Valerie just kept her gaze forward and said, "Do I really have to fight those things?"

Lieutenant Michael nodded his head, saying, "Yes, but try not to worry. I will be with you. Mary and Sarah will be with you too. You don't have to do this alone. You can't do it alone."

Valerie sat there calmly on the bench and never again looked out the window for the rest of the trip. Lieutenant Michael didn't push her. He knew that she needed time to get used to the absolute horror of the Harvesters. He knew that the true horror of the Harvesters would come when she would confront them face to face for the first time. She would have to get used to it.

- 2 -

The helicopter landed on the roof of what looked like either an office complex or an apartment building. Valerie couldn't tell which. A sign above a doorway read *Phoenix Guard Wielder Complex*. The whole complex itself was an extension of the local military base even though it was geographically separate from it. It was designed to house the local Wielder units for this region.

Another soldier opened the door to the helicopter. Lieutenant Michael and Valerie stepped out. By the door, another man, in an identical white dress uniform with black stripes, stood there as if he were waiting for them. The man had two silver colored bars on each shoulder strap.

Lieutenant Michael took Valerie's hand again and walked toward the man that appeared to be waiting. As they walked away, the helicopter door was shut, and the soldier who opened it made some hand signs to the pilot. The helicopter took off back into the air and rushed away. The area quickly became silent once again as the helicopter flew away over the ridge of skyscrapers.

The older man began to walk toward them as they also walked toward him. When they were close enough to shake hands, Lieutenant Michael straightened his legs together and saluted the man and said, "Captain, I have brought Wielder Valerie Bennet as ordered."

The Captain returned the salute and said, "At ease, Lieutenant Snyder." Lieutenant Michael let go of Valerie's hand, spread his legs slightly apart, and squared his arms behind his back. The older man, who appeared to be in either his late thirties or early forties, then directed his attention to Valerie. "Wielder Valerie Bennet, I am Captain Edward Faust. I am the commander of the Phoenix Guard Wielder Company. That means that I am this man's boss. So, if he gives you a hard time, you can talk to me and I'll show him a thing or two."

He jokingly slugged Lieutenant Michael in the arm and then said, "Though we are technically a military unit, we don't expect you to act all formal like other soldiers. Your rank is Wielder, which is below your Lieutenant's rank, but is above all the non-commissioned officers. This means that, in joint exercises, you may be called upon to direct troops, but I guess you don't really need to worry about that kind of thing yet. For now, I want you to just focus on the training that Lieutenant Snyder will give you. I know he's young, but he is really good at what he does. Do you have any questions?"

Valerie brought a finger to her lips as she thought for a moment, "What should I call you, sir?"

Captain Faust said, "Feel free to just call me Captain like most of the girls do if you want. If you would prefer, a couple of the girls have even called me Uncle Ed."

Valerie smiled and giggled, saying, "Okay, Captain. Thanks." She gave a childish salute and the Captain saluted her back, saying, "Get this girl a bunk below and a uniform, Lieutenant."

Lieutenant Michael nodded and saluted saying, "Aye, Captain." He took Valerie by the hand and walked with her to the door. He opened the door and together they walked down the stairs that were before them. The stairway had plain concrete walls and metal grilled steps so that you could see beneath them.

Lieutenant Michael spoke as they started to descend the stairs, "This facility has everything that you could want in a home. In addition to having our own squad apartment, you each get your own room. I think I said that before. There is an exercise room and a training room. There is a recreation room and there is even a pool." Valerie did not reply but continued staring down the stairs.

The building was six stories and included a storage basement. The first floor was dedicated to bureaucratic offices. The second floor was a recreation room, which contained the indoor pool as well as gaming platforms. The third floor was the training/exercise room. Floors four through six contained the apartments and officer rooms. Lieutenant Michael and Valerie walked down to the fifth floor from the roof top.

Lieutenant Michael opened the door and said, "This is our floor." He held the door open and allowed Valerie to enter first. She entered into the hallway and noticed that there was only one door on each side of the hallway in the middle. There were no other doors as far as she could see.

Lieutenant Michael seemed to understand her confusion and said, "Each floor is divided into two apartments that are used for each squad. Since we are squad three, our door is marked with the number three."

As they started to walk down the hall together, the door suddenly opened up behind them, and three young girls walked in wearing white uniform dresses each with its own yellow, red, and blue color stripes. They wore small ties with their color type around their necks. The girls stopped their chatter and stared at the new girl that was with Lieutenant Michael.

The girl with red eyes and the red striped uniform pointed at Valerie and said, "Oh, you must be the new girl." She had long dark brown wavy hair that extended over to her mid chest area. She parted her hair into two equal parts and had a tie wrapped near the bottom of each part. She had light-olive colored skin.

Valerie shyly said, "Good to meet you."

The three girls then approached her and the red-eyed girl said, "My name is Giana; I'm thirteen. This is Tina and Elsa." Giana, Tina, and Elsa formed a half circle as they stood in front of her. Tina had the blue eye colorization and blue strips on her white uniform. Her hair was black, straight, and was cut evenly around her head. It extended just below her jaw line. Her skin tone was very pale. Elsa had the same yellow eye colorization that Valerie had. She had straight blond hair that she pulled back into a ponytail behind her head that extended just below the base of her neck. Her complexion also seemed pale, but not as pale as Tina's.

Valerie shyly said, "M-M-My name is Valerie."

Giana replied, "We'll look forward to working with you, Valerie. We are with Squad four. Feel free to come see us anytime, especially if you want to challenge us."

Giana then looked at Lieutenant Michael and said, "See you Lieutenant." She smiled at him. Giana and the two other girls then started walking away. As they passed Valerie, Tina nodded her head and said in a melancholy tone, "Hey." Elsa smiled and patted her on the right arm as she walked by.

As Giana passed by Lieutenant Michael, he grabbed a hold of her shoulder, and said, "Wait a minute Giana. What have you been doing? Your back is covered in dirt." She turned around and said, "I was just practicing with Tina outside."

Lieutenant Michael then began to brush the dirt off of her back and Giana stood there allowing him to do it. When he finished, he patted her on the back and she said, "Thank you, Lieutenant, this can be our little secret from Mary." She smiled mischievously at him. Lieutenant Michael looked at her confused and replied, "Why would I care about that?"

Giana and the two other girls then walked into their own apartment across from Squad three's apartment. Lieutenant Michael shook his head as the girls left the hallway and said out loud to himself, "Why do those two like to make fun of me like that?" He brushed off the incident and smiled, looking at Valerie, saying, "Welcome to your new home, Valerie."

Lieutenant Michael opened the door and walked in first this time. Valerie followed behind him. They entered into an open room where she could see the kitchen, dining area, and what looked like a television sitting room.

Another red-eyed girl in the same type of white uniform with red stripes like Giana was wearing, stood near the door with a huge grin on her face. She had long black hair that she pulled into twin tails on each side of her head and had a fair complexion. She stood there smiling at Lieutenant Michael with arms wide open. She said, 'Welcome home, darling!"

Immediately Lieutenant Michael put the palm of his hand over her mouth and started rocking her head back and forth, saying, "How many times do I have to tell you to knock off that stupid joke. I'm not your darling, stop being a goofball. I've brought your new teammate with me." He then walked past her with Valerie trailing behind him.

The red-eyed girl, pretending to be annoyed, placed both her hands on her hips, squaring her arms, and said, "Why'd you have to go and bring another girl home when you already got me?"

Lieutenant Michael sighed and said, "Mary, could you go easy on the new girl? It's just her first day and she don't know you yet. She'll probably take you seriously."

Mary walked up to Valerie and crossed her own left arm over the top of her stomach and rested her other elbow on her arm while stroking her chin. She looked Valerie up and down with a look of deep thought. Mary then began to walk around Valerie while still looking her up and down. Valerie stood there with a confused look on her face, saying, "What's wrong, is there something wrong with me?"

Mary then stood in front of her and said, "Well, you certainly are cute. I'll give you that."

Valerie still confused said, "Thanks?"

Mary then pointed right at Valerie and said, "You may be cute, but remember this: Lieutenant Michael has already promised that when I'm old enough we're going to get married!"

Valerie's eyes widened and her jaw dropped. She said, "You two are getting married?'"

Lieutenant Michael sighed again and wiped his face with his hands, saying, "No, she's just making fun of you. Don't take her seriously. She thinks this joke is really funny when it's not!" He then turned to Mary, saying, "Mary, will you PLEASE cut it out for today!" He put a lot of emphasis on the 'please' part.

Mary giggled and started to act all friendly as if she had not been making fun of anybody, saying, "Welcome, Valerie, my name is Mary. I guess I can accept you as a new teammate." Mary extended her hand with a smile.

Valerie looked at her hand and then slowly extended her own with a look of distrust on her face. Mary took it and shook it with both hands, saying, "I'm going to show you all the ropes so don't hesitate to ask for help."

Another girl entered the main room from another part of the apartment and yawned. She looked like she had just woken up from a nap. She had light brown hair that she also pulled back into a pony tail. She had the blue colorization in her eyes. She wore a similar white uniform as the others all wore but with the blue stripes. She smiled at Valerie and said, "Oh, the new girl is here. My name is Sarah. I'm eleven years old."

She walked up to Valerie and gave her a big hug saying, "We're going to be good friends. I just know it." Valerie responded by returning the hug and saying, "I hope so too."

Sarah let her go and stepped back giving Valerie some space, saying, "Where are you from?"

Valerie replied, "I'm from the Reno sector. Where did you come from?"

Sarah tilted her head and looked upward. A look of deep thought came upon her face and then she said, "Well, I'm from the old Salt Lake sector. I can't remember which part though. It's been so long I haven't even thought about it."

Valerie gave a look of surprise and then quickly glanced at Lieutenant Michael. She then returned her attention to Sarah and said, "Don't you visit your family?"

Sarah nervously laughed and said, "They all died when I was seven after that wall collapsed, I've been with the military since then. It's been about four years now. I don't really think about them that much anymore."

Valerie looked downward, embarrassed, saying, "I ... I'm sorry. I probably shouldn't have asked."

Sarah rubbed Valerie on the right arm and said, "Please don't worry about it. It doesn't bother me talking about it anymore."

Lieutenant Michael then said, "Why don't we show her around the apartment together girls."

Mary gave a sarcastic salute and said, "Aye, aye, Lieutenant! I'll do it!" She quickly took Valerie by the hand and began pulling her through the open area of the apartment.

Mary first led her into the kitchen and said, "This is the kitchen where you can get all the yummy food that you want. Don't worry, the government pays for it so basically you can get whatever you want. Our Lieutenant tends to cook for us but some of his dishes ... how should I say it ... could use a little work."

Mary leaned over to Valerie's right ear and cupped her hand around her mouth and whispered into it, saying, "I think he does it on purpose so that I will make it for him." She winked at her and then looked toward Lieutenant Michael with a mischievous grin. Lieutenant Michael returned her gaze by looking confused and she batted her eyes at him. He then rolled his own eyes at her and then shook his head, saying, "Geez, what are you telling her now?" Mary acted innocent and said, "I don't know what you're talking about Lieutenant."

Mary then led her into the dining area and pointed at the table, "This is where we usually eat, unless something good is on TV." Mary then pointed at a chair on one side and said, "See that chair? That's my chair. This way I get to sit next to the Lieutenant."

Lieutenant Michael interjected, saying, "There is no saved seating here Valerie. It's first come, first served seating."

Mary then pointed at Lieutenant Michael and said, "Soooo, Lieutenant, what you are really saying is that you would rather I sit across from you so that we can gaze into each other's eyes?"

Lieutenant Michael sighed again and placed a hand over his eyes. He shook his head and said, "Mary, that joke is starting to get really old quick. It's not funny. Knock it off!"

Mary grunted and rolled her head back, "Geez ... fine Lieutenant, I'll give it a rest!" She arched her left eyebrow and smiled mischievously as she quietly ended her statement, saying, "... for today."

Mary took Valerie's hand again and led her into the sunken in area of the living room. It was sunken in two steps, which acted like a bench. A huge flat screen television hung on the wall in the back. There was a couch and two recliner chairs angled perfectly with the television.

Mary led Valerie down the two steps and flung herself onto the couch from over the back side. She rolled onto her back and put both her hands behind her head, saying, "This is where we waste time and watch TV. Do you got any favorite shows?"

Valerie walked around to the other side of the couch and said, "Well, I really like Magical Girl Squad."

Mary jumped up from the couch and excitedly grabbed Valerie's arms from both sides, shouting, "Really? Me too! See, I knew I'd like you. Who's your favorite character?"

Valerie, who was beginning to forget her distrust of Mary, said with excitement, "Really, you love them too?! My favorite is Asteria because she is really strong and can read the future in the stars!"

Mary began to jump up and down and yelled out, "Me too! I also love Maia. Her outfit is so pretty. Uh ... wait one moment." Mary jumped back over the couch and ran into a room down the hallway. Valerie looked questioningly at Lieutenant Michael. He responded by shrugging his shoulders. Sarah stood there and yawned again. She then rubbed the sleep out of her eyes and seemed a little more alert.

Suddenly Mary came running back carrying something in her hands. She jumped back over the couch and handed Valerie a rolled up piece of clothing. Mary said, "This is too small for me now, so you can have it. I'm almost fourteen now."

Valerie unrolled it and stared at it in delight with her mouth open wide. It was a midnight blue dress with silver sparkles that had a slightly gothic style to it. The arms were exaggerated drapes that would have come down to just below her knees. The skirt of the dress would have gone down to just above the knees on her size. It was also string-laced along the back and front.

Valerie held the dress up in amazement and said, "This ... this is a Magical Girl Asteria costume dress. I've always wanted one of these! Are you really just giving it to me?"

Mary waved her hand like it was nothing and said, "Sure, like I said, it's too small for me. I just couldn't bear to get rid of it though. But, since you're a fan too, I wouldn't mind if you had it." Valerie ran to her and hugged her tightly, saying, "Thank you!"

Mary took Valerie by the hand again and led her toward the rooms in the back side area down the hallway. The rooms were on both sides of the hallway and there were two doors on each side. Mary pointed out that the first two rooms belonged to her on the right side and to the Lieutenant on the left. The next room on the right belonged to Sarah and the one on the left belonged to Valerie. At the end of the hallway was another door, which Mary had stated was the bathroom.

Mary opened the door for Valerie and led her into the room and began to point at various objects in an exaggerated way, saying, "This is your room, Valerie. This is your bed. This is your closet. These are your drawers. This is your desk and your computer terminal. Everything in here is yours now."

Mary motioned for her to sit on the bed. She then opened the closet door and pulled out a similar white uniform that both she and Sarah wore. She handed the uniform to Valerie and said, "They expect us to wear this most of the time. It's not too stylish but it's comfortable and strong. This is what we wear when we go out on missions as well. That's why we are supposed to wear it most of the time so that we can be ready to deploy quickly."

Valerie stood up and stripped off her civilian clothing. She tossed it on the bed and reached for the uniform. The dress uniform consisted of a dress that went down to the top of her knees. There was a yellow stripe that ran down the length of the dress along both sides. It went down to within half an inch of the hem. A ring of yellow also ran along the bottom of the dress leaving half an inch of white at the bottom. The dress had no sleeves but was like a dress shirt with a pointed collar. Over the dress they wore a thin dress jacket that consisted of three large black buttons. From the center of the shoulders, on each side of the dress jacket, was a colored stripe based on the type of Wielder that the wearer was. Since Valerie was a yellow Wielder, the stripes on her jacket and dress were yellow. She also had a yellow tie.

Valerie put on the dress and the jacket. Mary pulled up the collar on her dress and helped her put the tie on over her head. Mary then tightened the tie and pulled her collar down, saying, "It looks really good on you, girl. Now you're really part of the team."

Valerie sat back down on the bed and straightened the skirt of her dress along her thighs, feeling the fabric. It was smooth to the touch but felt rather strong. She looked at Mary and then looked downward at her hands on her thighs. Mary noticed this too and said, "What's wrong? You can tell me anything you want."

Valerie looked back up at Mary and said, "Are you afraid to fight the Harvesters?"

Mary sat down on the bed next to her. She placed an arm around her shoulders and said, "Everyone's afraid to fight. That's just normal."

Valerie slumped forward and slid her hands underneath her thighs, "I'm afraid to fight."

Mary pulled Valerie close to herself and held her tight, "I know, I was really afraid to fight my first time too. That's normal. None of us really wants to fight but it's something that we just gotta do. No one else can do it but us. Tomorrow we'll start your training. Just stick with me and you'll be alright."

A tear began to roll from Valerie's eye as she struggled to not let her body shake from sobbing. Despite that, Mary could feel her shaking and continued to hold her, saying, "Why don't you lay down and get some rest. The Lieutenant and I will be making dinner soon. You can just relax and get used to your new room. If you need me or Sarah, just let us know."

Mary helped Valerie to lie down on the bed. She smiled at her caringly, and stroked her platinum blond hair. She then turned around to leave. As she closed the door behind herself, she watched Valerie and smiled at her again.

Valerie's door clicked shut and Mary sighed looking down cast. She turned around to see Lieutenant Michael waiting for her just outside. He put a hand on Mary's shoulder and said, "Thanks for helping her out. Is she okay?"

Mary put her hand on top of his hand on her shoulder and said, "She started to cry, so I told her to lie down and get some rest. You know, it's not like I'm some heartless bitch ... she is me just four years ago. "

Lieutenant Michael said, "I know, you are a really sweet girl. Just a little rough on the outside, but that's why I like you."

Mary smiled mischievously and said, "So ... you are admitting that you like me, Lieutenant?" She held her hands behind her back and leaned towards him.

Lieutenant Michael then pulled her close to himself and hugged her tight, saying, "As if you were my own daughter."

Mary allowed him to hold her and she began to cry into his chest. She said out loud, her voice muffled by his uniform, "Michael, I miss Susan."

Lieutenant Michael whispered into her ear, "I do too."

- 3 -

Mary and Sarah sat down at the dining table as Lieutenant Michael entered into the kitchen. He opened a drawer and pulled out a wine colored apron and hung it around his neck. He tied the sashes together behind his back and brushed the front with his hands. He put his hands on the counter and leaned forward saying, "So, girls, what do you feel like eating tonight?"

Sarah raised her hand excitedly and yelled out, "Spaghetti and meatballs! Spaghetti and meatballs!" Mary stretched out an arm and gave him a thumbs up with a huge smile. Lieutenant Michael nodded his head and said, "Okay! Spaghetti and meatballs it is."

Lieutenant Michael unbuttoned the cuffs on his shirt and rolled up his sleeves. He began to rummage through the cabinet above his head and pulled out a box of dried spaghetti and a jar of pasta sauce. Next, he searched through the fridge and pulled out a package of ground beef, an onion, and some fresh herbs. He hummed a tune as he began to work his kitchen magic.

Lieutenant Michael grabbed a bowl, placing it on the counter, and a frying pan, which he set on the electric stove. When he looked up, he saw Valerie standing in between the dining table and the living room. She not only had on her new uniform, but she also had managed to find the knee length white socks and her black combat boots that went up to the middle of her calves.

Lieutenant Michael squared his arms on his waist and said, "Well hello, Valerie, don't you look great in your new uniform."

Valerie hesitated for a moment and then said shyly, "Is it alright if I join you at the table?" She tugged at the bottom of her dress jacket as she spoke.

Sarah pulled out the chair beside her and said, "Of course, this is your house too, so you don't even need to ask. We're all friends here." Valerie climbed up and sat on the chair next to Sarah.

Sarah turned in her chair to face Valerie. She placed an elbow on the table and rested her head on her hands, saying, "So, do you like your new room?"

Valerie nodded and said, "Yes, I like it. It's much bigger then my old room but it is missing all my stuffed animals and stuff that I used to have."

Sarah replied, "Yeah, they don't let you take too many personal belongings except for like photos and paper, maybe a toy or two if you can squeeze them in your suitcase. The good news is, that since you are getting a pay check, you can buy all the stuff you want and keep it here now."

Valerie gasped and a look of surprise fell on her face, "We get paid?!"

Mary giggled and said, "Of course we get paid, it's our job!"

Sarah said, "Well, it's not really a paycheck, we get a monthly allotment of funds. We only get three hundred dollars a month. It's not much, but, when you consider the fact that they pay for everything else, it really adds up. They pay for our housing and our food and for everything else that we need. It's more like fun money so we can do what we want with it."

Valerie looked at Lieutenant Michael and said, "Lieutenant, when do I get paid?"

Lieutenant Michael paused from cooking and came out of the kitchen. He pulled a plastic card out of his pants pocket and handed it to Valerie, saying, "You've already been paid. This is a debit card that is linked to your account. It is already filled with this month's allotment for you. I was going to give it to you tomorrow but since you're asking."

Valerie took the card and looked at it. Her name was written on it in capital letters beneath a string of numbers. A huge grin began to form on her face as she began to think about the things that she wanted to get but her parents wouldn't let her. The World Government logo was on the front side.

Mary leaned forward, rested her head on her hand, and sighed, saying, "I'm sure the Lieutenant won't tell you this, but if you don't use all your money in a month they only refill your account till it reaches three hundred again. That means that if you want to build up some money you got to pull it out of your account and stash it secretly in your room."

Valerie looked at Lieutenant Michael for confirmation and he nodded his head and said, "Yep, that's true. I was waiting for you to tell her, Mary, since I knew you wanted too."

Mary rolled her eyes and sarcastically said, "Sure you were."

Valerie looked back to Sarah and asked, "Do we have to go to school still?"

Mary gave a sarcastic laugh and said, "Why should we go to school?"

Sarah put a hand on Valerie's shoulder and said, "No, we don't have to go to school anymore. This is a full time job so we don't really have time to go to school."

Lieutenant Michael said from the kitchen, "Well, you could technically attend some classes if you really wanted too. Most of the girls though don't bother with it."

Mary leaned back in her seat and kicked her feet up onto the empty seat beside her. She then rudely picked her nose and made a flicking motion with her finger, saying, "Why should we go to school? The reason you go to school is so that you can get a good job when you grow up. Number one, I've already got a really good job. And two, I'll be dead probably by the time I'm fifteen so I ain't going to grow up much more than this. That means I'm already an adult." She then rested her hands behind her head and smiled at Valerie.

Sarah squinted her eyes in disgust and shook her head, saying, "You're so disgusting sometimes."

In response, Mary picked her nose again and flicked her finger, saying, "Ah, bite me. I like to enjoy what little adult life I've got left."

Lieutenant Michael, still engaged in his cooking project, said, "Come on girls, no fighting at the dinner table please. Save it for the training room tomorrow. And Mary, you are not an adult even if you think you are."

Mary gave another sarcastic laugh, "What are you talking about, Lieutenant. Since I'm going to die soon that should mean I'm already an adult. I should be allowed to do adult things."

Lieutenant Michael replied, "But Mary, whether you think you are an adult or not, you are only thirteen and a half. The law says that you are not an adult until you are eighteen and that means I can't let you do adult things."

Mary sat up from her slouched position and said, "But Lieutenant, I want to be able to experience what it's like to be in love and to be a mom. I want to be able to drink alcohol and go see a rated R movie."

Lieutenant Michael said, "It's true that adults do that kind of stuff but that's not what makes you an adult. Being an adult means that you are responsible for yourself and for the society around you."

Mary retorted, "Lieutenant, that's exactly my point. I'm responsible for myself and for the lives of all the people in this area. By your own definition that should make me an adult."

Lieutenant Michael began to laugh and he said, "Mary, you are certainly not responsible for yourself. Who's the one making your dinner? Me. Who cleans your bathroom? Me. Who does your laundry? Me. All this while you're sitting there picking your nose, and watching kiddie shows like Magical Girl Squad."

Mary's face began to pout and she slumped forward saying, "I help sometimes."

Lieutenant Michael said, "That's true; you do help sometimes and I am grateful for it. Let's stop talking about you wanting to be an adult and talk about maybe you and Sarah having a fight tomorrow."

Mary said, "Pfft ... no point in fightin' Sarah. I'm still a thousand times stronger than her. Now that Giana over there; that would be a good match tomorrow. I'd show Valerie how I kick butt!"

Mary's face lit up as her expression showed that a good idea came into her mind. She jumped up out of her chair and ran out the front door, slamming it shut behind herself. Sarah, having the same thought, clapped her hands together and excitedly said, "Just wait till you see those two go at it. They are both among the older Wielder's here and they can really go at it good."

A few moments later Valerie could hear some girls yelling at each other, or maybe it was some laughing, or even both. She couldn't understand what they were saying. A moment later, Mary walked back into the apartment with a big smile on her face and slammed the door shut behind herself again. She pounded her fist into her other hand, saying, "Okay, Lieutenant, it's on! Tomorrow I'm going to kick Giana's butt again!"

Lieutenant Michael, putting cooked food into a serving bowl, said, "Again? Don't you two usually tie?"

A look of offense appeared on her face and she said, "We don't always tie! I've beaten her butt before. I feel particularly motivated today."

Lieutenant Michael, not sounding impressed, said half-heartedly, "Great, I bet Valerie would love to see that. Right Valerie?"

Valerie shrugged her shoulders and said, "I don't know. I've never seen two Wielders fight before so I don't know what to expect."

As Mary sat back down, Sarah said, "You are a soldier now, so you got to train your brain to think about fighting."

Valerie's face started to show a little fear, but she swallowed it back down inside of her. As she was about to speak, Lieutenant Michael put a large bowl of spaghetti and meat balls down right in front of her. Sarah got up and grabbed a few plates and forks. Mary grabbed some glasses, filled them with water, and put them on the table too.

Valerie leaned forward and breathed deeply the smell of the pasta before her. She smiled and said, "It smells so good. I love spaghetti and meatballs!"

Lieutenant Michael smiled and replied, "Thanks, dig in!"

Valerie put some of the pasta on her plate and then pushed the bowl to Sarah, who proceeded to do the same. Valerie looked at her food and then looked at Lieutenant Michael and said, "Do we say a blessing on the food here?"

Lieutenant Michael leaned toward her and said, "Well, not really, but if you want to, we can."

Valerie then folded her arms and said, "Dear God, thank you for this food and for my new friends. In Jesus' name. Amen." Lieutenant Michael and Sarah both said, "Amen," while Mary was already stuffing her face. She looked at both of them with her mouth full of food and then mumbled, "Uh-mem." Some of the chewed pasta fell out of her mouth and landed back on the plate.

Another expression of disgust fell on Sarah's face and she rolled her eyes, saying, "That was gross. Don't you have any manners?" Valerie started laughing. Sarah said, "Well at least you can entertain one person." Mary, still stuffing her face stretched out an arm and gave Valerie a thumbs up.

Lieutenant Michael said, "After dinner, you girls can take a bath if you want too. I'll take care of the dishes tonight so that you girls can have more time to get to know one another."

Mary, whose plate was now empty, said, "Good idea! Sarah, Valerie, let's take a bath together tonight."

Valerie, confused, said, "Do we always bathe together too?"

Lieutenant Michael shook his head and said, "No, you don't have too, but you can if you want too."

Sarah gently shook Valerie's shoulder and said, "Come on, it'll be fun. We're all girls so it shouldn't be a problem."

Mary said, "Yeah, come on Valerie, we can have some real girl time in the bath. Haven't you ever bathed with others before?"

Valerie shook her head and said, "Well, no, I don't have any sisters."

Sarah clapped her hands together again and said, "Oh, it's really fun to bathe together, give it a try."

Valerie nodded her head and said, "Okay, I'll give it a try."

Mary suddenly sighed out of nowhere and said, "I wish I could bathe with Lieutenant Rachel, then maybe some of her assets would rub off on me."

Sarah turned to Valerie and said, "Lieutenant Rachel is the Lieutenant of Fourth squad. She has a really big chest. Mary on the other hand has a really small chest."

Mary suddenly gasped and covered her chest with her arms. She mournfully said, "They're going to get bigger."

Lieutenant Michael shook his head and rubbed his face with his hands, saying, "Could you girls not talk like this in front of me, please."

Sarah said, "But Lieutenant, it's true. Lieutenant Rachel ..."

Lieutenant Michael said, "Sarah, Lieutenant Rachel is my best friend. I already know everything about her. You don't have to say anything else. Don't say another word about it."

Mary jumped out of her seat, slammed her palms on the table, and yelled out, saying, "It's not fair that she's overly endowed! It's like she stole something from me!" Mary lifted her hands from the table and began to clench her fists so hard that her arms began to tremble. Her eyes and fists began to glow with red light as she released her Wielder power into them.

Lieutenant Michael immediately jumped up out of his chair and grabbed her shoulder, yelling, "Calm down, Mary! You're going to break the table again!"

Sarah jumped up and grabbed her plate off the table, saying, "Not again."

Valerie, a little stunned, jumped up as well and copied Sarah, picking her plate up off the table. She waited to see what Mary and the others would do next.

Slowly the red glow began to fade from her eyes and fists, she lowered her hands down, and dropped herself back down on her chair. She gave a loud sigh for show and said, "Geez, sometimes that woman makes me so angry I could just smash something."

Lieutenant Michael, calming himself down, sat back down slowly in his chair, and said, "What have I told you about releasing your power inside the apartment?"

Mary crossed her arms and rolled her head back, saying sarcastically, "Don't release your power inside the apartment because you always break something. But I don't always break something. I didn't this time."

Lieutenant Michael replied, "This is our sixth table, Mary, I really don't want to buy a seventh one. They'll probably start to charge you for it eventually."

Mary, still crossing her arms, began to swing her feet, saying, "You two are always flirting with each other! It makes me sick to watch it."

Lieutenant Michael rolled his eyes and shook his head, saying, "You know, Mary, there is nothing going on between me and Lieutenant Rachel. Lieutenant Rachel and I have been friends for a long time. If there was something between us it would have happened a long time ago. Besides, even if we were together, there's still no reason for you to get so angry."

Mary gave a "humph" sound and then went silent. She brought her chair closer to the table, and finished what was left on her plate; she sat there quietly waiting for the others to finish what was left of their dinner. She sat there looking frustrated.

Valerie finished her plate next and then Sarah did. Sarah said, "Lieutenant, are you sure you don't want us to help you with the dishes?"

Lieutenant Michael shook his head and said, "No, that's okay, tonight is special since Valerie is here now. Why don't you three head into the bath now and I'll clean up everything here tonight by myself."

Mary, Sarah, and Valerie headed to the bathroom. Mary opened the door for Sarah and Valerie and then shut it behind herself. Valerie stood there in amazement with eyes wide open, saying, "Wow, this bathroom is huge! And look at the size of this tub. When I thought of us taking a bath together I pictured the three of us crammed into a little tub."

Sarah giggled and said, "Oh no, they take good care of us here. We get the best stuff."

Mary said, "Yep, gotta keep the ones saving their butts all the time happy."

Sarah began to unbutton her jacket, saying, "The truth is this bathroom is only for us. There are three toilets over there, and there are also three standing showers over there. We also each get our own sink." She tossed her jacket into a basket near the door.

Valerie, still amazed, said, "I never would have thought that it was this big and that they would give us each our own stuff like this. Does the Lieutenant use this bathroom too?"

Mary said, "Nope," she waved her hand in dismissal, "something to do with the military's child protection laws. He's got his own bathroom in his own room."

Mary then turned on the water for the bath and said, "You can put your dirty laundry in that basket over there that is marked with your name." Mary then stripped off all her clothing and tossed it in the basket marked with her own name. She struck a pose in the mirror and sighed, saying, "I wish I was an adult like Lieutenant Rachel."

Sarah stripped off the rest of her outfit and tossed it into her own basket, saying, "So you think Lieutenant Michael likes Lieutenant Rachel?"

Mary rested a hand on her hip and pointed to Sarah with the other, saying, "Of course he likes her. We've both seen how he stares at her. Can't say I blame him when she looks like that. It's so vulgar."

Sarah imitated Mary by resting a hand on her own hip and pointed right back at her, saying, "Yeah, I think you're right. There's no way that you'd ever catch up to her."

Mary shook her fists and stomped once on the ground, yelling, "Oh, let's just drop it! I don't want to talk about that woman anymore!" Mary then pointed to Valerie and said, "The bath is getting full now, Val, get your clothes off so we can all get in."

Steam began to fill the bathroom. As Valerie began to take off her own uniform, Mary stuck her hand into the bath to test the temperature. "Just right," she said as she slipped into the bath and rested her arms along the top of the sides. Sarah slid in next and sat down on the other side of the corner, saying, "Come on Valerie; it feels really good."

Valerie finished taking off her uniform and laid it over the edge of her basket since it was still relatively clean from being worn only a few hours. She then took off her underwear and tossed it into her own basket. She walked up to the bath and stuck her own hand into the water to test it herself first. She then climbed over the edge and sat down on the side next to Sarah and across from Mary. Valerie leaned her head back, sighed, and said, "This is really nice."

As Lieutenant Michael finished putting the clean dishes away, a knock came at the door. He yelled out, "One moment please," and quickly took off the apron he was wearing, tossing it onto the counter.

Lieutenant Michael opened the door and a beautiful woman with brown eyes and long brown hair pulled back into a ponytail braid, was standing in the doorway. "Ah, good evening Lieutenant Rachel, what can I do for you?"

Lieutenant Rachel leaned forward, looking inside the apartment, and said, "I wanted to see how you are doing, Lieutenant Michael. Do you mind if I come inside and sit down for a bit with you?"

Lieutenant Michael stepped aside and motioned for her to come in and sit down at the table. He shut the door behind her and said, "Would you like me to make you some herbal tea?"

Lieutenant Rachel sat down at the table in the chair closest to the door and said, "Sure, that sounds nice."

Lieutenant Michael quickly pulled out a tea kettle, filled it with water, and put it on the flame of the stove. He then took an empty teapot, spooned an herbal blend of his own make into it, and set it aside.

Lieutenant Michael then walked into the dining area and sat down at the table next to Lieutenant Rachel. He leaned forward, rested his arms on the table, and looked down at his clenched hands, "I used to think that it would get easier over the years, but it seems to get harder every time it happens. When Susan self-destructed right in front of me, I ... I ... I ..." a tear began to form in his eye as he struggled to hold them back. His arms began to tremble.

Rachel quickly put a hand over Michael's own clenched hands, saying, "You don't have to say it, I understand how you feel."

Michael's arms stopped trembling. He released one of his own hands and put it over Rachel's hand, "I know, we all go through it. It has only been two weeks and already I'm putting another girl in that position. Logically, I know that it is something that has to be done. I know that those girls are the most effective way to fight the Harvesters. But still, I feel like a monster forcing those girls into the most dangerous of circumstances. I mean, I think of those girls as if they were my own daughters and yet I still push them into a battle that could tear their fragile little bodies apart. Do you know what Valerie said to me shortly after I picked her up? She said that she wasn't sure if I was a really nice guy or a monster. I couldn't really say much because the truth is I'm not so sure myself."

Rachel's eyes began to tear up some but she held them back too, saying, "Michael, those girls don't think of you as a monster. From what I've seen they sincerely love you and trust you. I don't think of you as a monster either. You're still the same good guy that I knew back in the academy."

Michael sat up and leaned back in his chair, saying, "I suppose that's what makes it worse. It's that they all do trust me and when it comes down to it, I'll just use them up till they are expended. Then, I throw a new one into the mix and the whole process just begins again. If only I could obtain that power that they have, then I would make sure that not a single one of them would be forced to fight ever again!"

Michael slammed his fist onto the table and harshly said, "Damn those Harvesters! Damn them to hell for making a monster out of me, who uses up these little girls' lives! They should be playing and going to school, not going up against creatures that are trying to murder them."

Rachel put a hand on his shoulder and said, "Michael, your anger is proof that you are not a monster. If you were a monster you wouldn't give a second thought to those little girls. Trust me, I've been your closest friend since our days at the academy. I know a thing or two about you."

Michael lightened up and rubbed the tears that were forming in his eyes, saying, "That's true. You and Josh are my closest friends. You always know how to cheer me up."

Sarah pushed Valerie's chest with her foot and said, "So, Valerie, what do you think of the Lieutenant?"

Valerie waved her hand in the water, feeling the flow of it through her fingers. She said, "I think he is a very nice man."

Sarah replied, "He is. He is a good Lieutenant too. He really does care about us."

Mary added, "Yep, that's true. I'm glad that I was chosen to be here with him. I've heard of squad leaders that do their job but don't really care about us Wielders. To those types, we're just weapons that are disposable."

A look of despair fell upon Valerie's face again. She glanced down into the water and said, "What's it like fighting the Harvesters?"

Both Sarah and Mary looked down toward the water but said nothing. Valerie held her hands up and waved them in dismissal, saying, "I'm sorry, I didn't mean to ask you something like that."

Mary dunked her head under the water and then quickly brought it up again. She flattened her hair back with her hands and said, "No, that is a valid question. It's just hard to answer it. We also don't want to scare you too much before you get there. The truth is that the first time you go up against the Harvesters is absolutely terrifying. It's just something that you have to get used to."

Sarah nodded her head and said, "The fear gets replaced by trust. I trust Mary and the Lieutenant with my life, and I know that Mary trusts me with her life as well. I'm sure the Lieutenant trusts both of us with his life too. When we go out together on the battlefield I am going to trust you with my life and I hope that you will trust me with your life. When you can do that, then you won't be afraid anymore.'

Mary then interrupted and said, "Well there is always a little fear. If you weren't afraid at all, then you wouldn't value your own life. The fear helps us to stay alive when we use it properly."

Valerie then said, "So, it's okay that I'm afraid right now to fight?"

Sarah scooted over next to Valerie, placed an arm around her neck, and said, "Of course you're afraid to fight. Both of us were afraid the same just as you when we first started."

Mary then came closer to Valerie and took her right hand with both of hers, saying, "It's okay to be scared, Valerie. That's just normal, but you don't need to worry about it anymore, Val. I promise that I'm going to protect you, so you don't need to worry. Okay?"

Valerie nodded and said, "Okay, I'll try not to worry."

Sarah removed her arm from around Valerie's neck and took her left hand. She held Valerie's hand in both of her hands as Mary did and said, "I promise you too. I won't let those Harvesters touch you."

Sarah let go of her hand and stood up. Her eyes began to glow blue and her hands began to radiate with the same color. She placed her hands together and slowly moved them apart until they were stretched straight outwards. A fist sized ball of light appeared out of her chest and began to expand until it engulfed the entire bathtub.

Valerie reached out and touched the sphere of light. It felt hard and repulsed her finger with a slight electric shock. She quickly pulled her hand back out of reflex and said, "Ouch!" She shook her hand from the slight shock. Valerie then said, "What is this? Is this your power?"

Sarah smiled and said, "Yes, this is my shield ability that nothing can penetrate. It is only one of my abilities. As a blue type Wielder I can manipulate this light into a shield barrier or I can condense it into a powerful beam that can hit enemies from afar. I can also cause this energy to surround objects and then use those objects as a weapon. When I go out to fight, I like to bring two metal sticks that I use as a base to cover with my power. I then use them like swords."

The sphere of light then shrunk back into a tiny ball and disappeared inside her chest. The blue light that radiated from her hands vanished and the light of her eyes dimmed. Sarah then sat back down.

Mary then held up her two arms and her eyes began to glow again with red light. Both of her hands also began to radiate with the same red light. Mary said, "This is part of my power. Unlike Sarah, my power only concentrates on my body but it causes me to become really strong. If I wanted too, I could smash this tub into pieces. If I concentrate my power on my feet, it will cause me to jump really high and far. I'll show you more of my power tomorrow when I kick Giana's butt!"

The light radiating from Mary's hands vanished and the light of her eyes dimmed. She put her hands back under the water and said, "Your turn, Val. Let's see what you got."

Valerie lifted both of her hands out of the water and her eyes began to glow with a yellow light. Her hands also began to radiate with the same yellow light. Valerie said, "This is my power. With this light I can heal both myself and others. Though you probably already know that."

Mary began to karate-chop the air and said, "Do you have a name for your special moves yet?"

A look of confusion fell upon Valerie's face and she said, "What do you mean 'a name'?" The light faded from her hands and eyes.

Mary said, "You know, like how the Magical Girl's Squad calls out their magic spell before they use it?"

Valerie said, "Nobody ever told me I was supposed to do that."

Sarah giggled and said, "You don't really have to do that. Mary just does that for fun."

Mary sarcastically said, "I don't do it for fun, it helps me to focus my power." She threw a couple of punches into the air, saying, "Oh, I can't wait for tomorrow. I'm going to pound that little snot into the floor with my thunder hammer punch!"

Mary suddenly went quiet with a look of shock on her face. Valerie, worried, said, "What's wrong?" Mary brought a finger to her lips as she stood up and hushed her to be quiet. Mary then cupped her hands around her ears and listened.

Mary dropped her hands and then began to shake her fists again, saying, "I can't believe it! Not again!" Mary then jumped out of the bath and began to dry herself off with a towel. She then wrapped another towel around her body and stomped out of the door.

Valerie looked back at Sarah and said, "What's going on?" Sarah shrugged her shoulders and said, "Don't know. Perhaps we should get out too."

Lieutenant Michael took a tea cup for himself and Rachel. He handed it to her and then poured the herbal tea into her cup; he then poured a cup for himself. Rachel blew the steam off the hot tea and then took a sip.

Michael said, "How is your squad handling it?"

Rachel put down her cup of herbal tea and said, "Oh, they're doing okay. They're still sad about Susan but they're ready to be your backup till your new girl is up to par. I hear they already met her."

Michael took a sip of his own tea and said, "Yep, that's right. Thanks, for letting Mary and Giana fight tomorrow. It will help get Valerie situated."

Rachel said, "Sure, no problem; it can be fun to let the girls go at it once in a while. Helps them blow off some steam too. Those two certainly are a handful."

Michael rolled his eyes as he took another sip of his tea, saying, "Yeah, those two like to make fun of me too much. It can get annoying sometimes. I think Mary's going to win this time. She's going to be extra motivated tomorrow since Valerie is here. With Susan gone, Mary's now the oldest so she's going to step up and be Valerie's mentor like Susan was for her and Sarah."

Rachel laughed and said, "I don't know if Mary can win this time. Giana's getting really good. You should have seen her at the last sortie. She grabbed a half-sized Harvester by the mandibles and then flung it on its back. She then punched its head clean off and tossed it at another Harvester which knocked that one back."

Michael leaned back in his chair with eyes wide open, "Wow, that is pretty impressive. On that last sortie that we went on, Mary jumped at a half-sized Harvester from thirty feet away. She jumped onto its back and then ripped its head off with her hands while breaking its back with her feet. I was pretty impressed by that. But, yes, tossing a Harvester over is still pretty impressive. We'll just have to see how it goes tomorrow."

"I knew it!" The loud, shrill voice of a girl echoed throughout the room. Lieutenant Michael and Rachel both looked toward the voice in surprise. Mary stood there in nothing but a towel wrapped around her wet body. Her feet were spread apart and her finger was pointing angrily at Lieutenant Rachel. Drips of water fell from her hair.

Lieutenant Michael shook his head and said angrily, "For the love of God, Mary, put on some clothing before you come out of the bath!"

Mary ignored him and stepped closer to Lieutenant Rachel, "I knew it! As soon as I leave that woman comes sneaking in here to flirt with you again."

Lieutenant Rachel leaned back in her chair, took another sip of her tea, and then said, "Mary, what are you talking about?"

Lieutenant Michael arched backward in his chair and gripped his hair with both of his hands. He let out a loud groan and sat straight back up in his chair, saying, "Mary, would you cut it out and go put some clothing on please!"

Lieutenant Rachel sat there quietly and continued sipping her tea as if nothing was going on. Then she stated calmly, "Mary, were adults, so it's okay if we flirt a little."

Lieutenant Michael interjected, saying, "Mary, we weren't flirting. Like I said before, we're just friends."

Lieutenant Rachel turned to Michael and said, "It must be hard to be a teenager. Not being able to do all the things that you want to do because you're too young."

Mary took another few steps forward and stated loudly, "You two flirting makes me sick! It's no fair! My life sucks! I'll be dead by the time I'm fifteen assuming I don't get killed by a bug. I'll never get to flirt with someone like a normal person. I didn't ask to be born this way!"

Lieutenant Rachel finished what was left in her cup of tea in one gulp and placed it back on the saucer. She then stood up and walked over to Mary and put her hands on her shoulder, saying, "We know that Mary, but, there is still plenty of stuff going on for you. You should count yourself lucky that your Lieutenant puts up with your jokes and your attitude. If you were in my squad, I'd transfer you the hell out. He puts up with it because, you know why Mary? It's because he loves you like you are a part of his family."

Lieutenant Rachel then walked over to Lieutenant Michael, kissed him on the cheek, and said, "Good night Michael; I'll see you tomorrow." She then smiled at Mary and proceeded to let herself out of the door in silence.

Mary then turned her attention to Lieutenant Michael and said, "I thought you said that there was nothing going on between you and Lieutenant Rachel!"

Lieutenant Michael shrugged his shoulders and said, "There is nothing going on. Believe me, if she was actually interested in me, we'd already be together. Besides, a little kid like you shouldn't worry about my dating life. Also, I can't believe how rude you were to her just now. I have half a mind to make you go over there and apologize to her. And you still haven't put on any clothes like I asked you to."

Mary stood there quietly. She then spun around and marched into her room, slamming the door behind her.

Lieutenant Michael, leaned over the table and rested his face in his hands, sighing. He said aloud to himself, "Why does she have to act like this all the time."

Lieutenant Michael stood up from the table. As he stood up, Sarah and Valerie came out into the room in their pajamas. Sarah wore a light blue and white pajama shirt that extended to her knees. Valerie wore a white and pink pajama top and bottom with buttons on the front of the shirt. A dark pink silhouette of a butterfly was on her right chest pocket.

Lieutenant Michael looked at his wristwatch and said, "You girls got out just in time. Your favorite show is going to start in five minutes."

Sarah stood there and said, "Is Mary okay?"

Lieutenant Michael said, "I'm sure she's fine."

Valerie said, "But she was crying when we passed her."

Lieutenant Michael said, "She'll be okay, just go ahead and turn on the TV. I'll go tell Mary that Magical Girl Squad is on." Valerie and Sarah headed for the couch as Lieutenant Michael went back into the hallway.

He knocked on Mary's door and said, "Mary, is it alright if I come in?"

Mary yelled through the door, "No, go away!"

Lieutenant Michael said, "I'm sorry, Mary. We didn't mean to get you so upset. Please don't take it so seriously."

There was nothing but silence. Lieutenant Michael then said, "I just wanted to let you know that Magical Girl Squad will be on in a few minutes. I thought you might want to watch it with Sarah and Valerie. It's a new episode if I remember correctly."

Suddenly the door opened wide and Mary came out wearing her own red and black checkered pajama top and bottom. She glared at Lieutenant Michael and then thrust her head sideways mumbling a loud, "Humph" as she walked past him toward the couch.

Mary walked over to the couch and forced herself between Valerie and Sarah. The spite gone out of her voice, she excitedly said, "I've been waiting for this new episode. Asteria, Maia, and Gaia are finally going to stand off against the Dark Lord. Hey Lieutenant, is it okay if we have some popcorn?"

Lieutenant Michael, said, "Sure thing, I'll put it in the microwave right now." He then went into the kitchen to make it.

After the show was over, Mary yelled out, "Geez, not another cliffhanger! What am I supposed to do if we get called out to sortie next week?"

Sarah said, "What are you talking about Mary? There's a cliffhanger just about every week so you'll want to watch it the next week."

Mary retorted, "I know that. What I'm trying to say is that they're going to put out an episode and then I'll have to miss it one day."

Valerie said, "They'll play it again mid next week."

Mary said, "I know that but then everybody else will have seen it except for me and, you know, somebody is going to spoil it for me."

Lieutenant Michael came over to the couch with a small case in his hand. He opened the case and said, "Alright girls, it's time to get ready for bed. It's Friday so it's time for your weekly injection."

Mary rolled up her sleeve and Lieutenant Michael pulled out a small device that looked like a stunted gun from the case. He took out a small vial of liquid and shoved it into the base of the injector unit. He then held the injector unit up to the base of her bicep and pulled the trigger. There was a small click and Mary winced from the slight prick. She then rubbed the spot with her other hand and said, "I think you like doing that too much."

Lieutenant Michael sarcastically said, "Yeah, yeah, now get some rest." Mary stood up from the couch and said, "Good night, Lieutenant, girls, see you in the morning."

Sarah then rolled up her own sleeve and Lieutenant Michael pulled out the old vial from the injector unit and replaced it with a new one. He then pressed the injector onto Sarah's arm and again pulled the trigger. Again, there was a slight click and then Sarah stood up and said, "Good night." She then walked back to her room too.

Next, Valerie rolled up the sleeve on her arm and said, "Is it going to hurt."

Lieutenant Michael said, "It is only a slight prick so only a little, but this shot will help your body be able to endure the energy that you'll need to produce to fight the Harvesters."

Valerie held out her arm and closed her eyes tight. She felt the needle press against her skin. There was another slight click and she felt the needle puncture her skin for a split second and then it was done. She rubbed the spot that felt like it had been slightly pinched. Valerie then got up and said, "Good night, Lieutenant."

Valerie went into her room and opened the small suitcase that Lieutenant Michael had carried for her. Inside she pulled out a picture of her parents and placed it on the nightstand beside her bed. Next, she pulled out a small pillow that was in the shape of a monarch butterfly. She hugged it tightly and then crawled into bed, turning off the lights. As she laid there, she said a silent prayer before going to sleep.

Lieutenant Michael sat there alone on the couch in silence. Again he thought about what Valerie said to him, "I can't tell if you are just a really nice guy or a monster." He said to himself, "I hope I can prove that I really am a nice guy." He stood up and headed into his own room after turning off the lights in the apartment.

- 4 -

The morning sun began to peak through the shades of Lieutenant Michael's windows and he felt the warmth of the glow on his face. He tried to roll over but felt a heavy weight on the side of his body that hindered him from moving. He opened his eyes and tried to focus on the clock by his bed. It was six-twenty, only ten minutes before the alarm would go off.

Lieutenant Michael tried to reach for the alarm clock, but, again, he felt the familiar weight holding his arm down. "Geez, not again," he blurted out. "You have your own bed you know." He slipped his arm out from under Mary's still sleeping head and turned off the alarm.

Lieutenant Michael sat up and rubbed the sleep out of his eyes. He then shook Mary, who was still asleep beside him, saying, "Come on Mary, it's time to get up."

"Good morning, Lieutenant. Uh, what's going on?" A familiar voice came to him as he looked toward the open door of his room. Valerie stood there still in her pajamas with a questioning look on her face, saying, "How come Mary is sleeping in your bed?"

Lieutenant Michael began to wave his hand in objection, saying, "Nothing's going on. She often sneaks in here without my permission."

Suddenly, Mary sat up and yawned deeply. She raised her arms and stretched, saying, "Good morning, Lieutenant."

Lieutenant Michael shook his head and said, "Good morning, Mary. You do know you're supposed to sleep in your own bed, right?"

Mary rubbed her eyes and then looked at Valerie, saying, "Good morning, Val. You're up early."

Valerie shook her head and said, "Not really, this is when I normally get up. My mom always said I was a morning person."

Mary said, "Why do you look so embarrassed, Valerie?"

Valerie shyly said, "I-I'm just wondering why you are sleeping in the Lieutenant's bed?"

Mary wrapped her arms around Lieutenant Michael's left arm, and said, "It's okay Valerie. We're engaged after all, so it shouldn't be a problem. Right?"

Valerie's cheeks turned red in embarrassment. She began to stutter and said, "I ... uh ... I don't know."

Mary began to laugh at her joke. Lieutenant Michael pushed Mary off the bed as she was laughing. She crashed onto the floor head first with a loud thud and her laugh ended in an "umph".

Lieutenant Michael shook his head and said to Valerie, "Don't believe a word she says, Valerie. She's just making fun of both you and me again."

Suddenly, another head popped up from Lieutenant Michael's bed. Sarah yawned and rubbed her eyes, saying, "It's too early to be so loud you two."

Lieutenant Michael looked backward and said, "Sarah, you were in here too? Can't I get a moment's rest without one or both of you popping into my room for the night?"

Sarah crawled out of his bed, saying, "I'm sorry, Lieutenant. I couldn't sleep because I had another nightmare. When I sleep in here, I'm not afraid, and my nightmares go away."

Lieutenant Michael sighed and said, "Okay, okay, I understand that." He reached over and hugged Sarah, letting her rest her head on his chest. He said, "Do you want to talk about your nightmare?"

Sarah said, "No, it's okay. It was just the same nightmare."

Mary's head popped back up from the floor and she said, "Geez, Lieutenant, can't you take a joke?"

Lieutenant Michael bopped her on top of the head and said, "You're jokes aren't that funny, you know. Don't forget what Lieutenant Rachel said last night."

Mary, pretending to be innocent, tilted her head and batted her eyes at him with a smile. He shook his head and stood up. He rubbed a hand through his bed head and said, "Okay, why don't you girls get into your uniforms now and then we can make breakfast together."

Mary jumped up from the floor, rubbed her forehead, and said, "I want French toast!" She then ran out of the room as Valerie jumped aside to avoid getting run over by her.

Sarah then said, "That sounds good." She then walked out of the room taking Valerie by the arm. She shut the door behind her and Valerie as they left.

Lieutenant Michael stood there watching the girls leave as the door closed. He yawned again and began to put on his uniform. "I suppose they would have nightmares," he said to himself, "after all, I still get them too. I guess if they were still at their parents' houses they would run into their parents' bed too."

Sarah continued to softly hold onto Valerie's arm as she approached Valerie's room. She leaned her head toward Valerie's ear and whispered, saying, "Mary and I get nightmares a lot during the night. When it is too much, we both sneak into the Lieutenant's room and lay with him till we pass out. It helps us go back to sleep and we feel safer."

Valerie nodded and said, "I understand. It's like when I get a nightmare and would crawl into my mom's and dad's bed at night too. It also helps to talk about it; I'll listen if you want to talk about it."

Sarah opened Valerie's door and stepped inside. She sat down on her bed and said, "There's not much to talk about. I was just fighting Harvesters and I was all alone and couldn't find anybody. It's the same nightmare over and over. I don't know how to make it stop."

Valerie shivered as she remembered seeing the Harvesters from inside the helicopter and said, "Sounds scary."

Sarah replied, "It's just a dream. The doctor told me that it is just my mind working out my situation in the field. I wake up and remember that I got all of you here, so I'm not really alone. I guess my subconscious is afraid that I'll be left alone one day."

Valerie sat down beside her and said, "Does Mary have nightmares like that too?"

Sarah nodded her head and said, "I know she does but she won't talk about it." She stood up and said, "Well, I guess it's my turn to get ready for today."

As Sarah was walking out of the room, Valerie called out to her, saying, "Am I going to have those nightmares too?"

Sarah stopped walking and stood there silently. She held onto the door knob of Valerie's room as she stood there. Without turning back she said, "Everybody gets the nightmares." She then walked out of the room and shut the door behind her. She leaned herself against the door. She folded her arms across her chest and sighed, saying to herself, "Everybody has their own nightmares."

Valerie sat back down on her bed and stared at the shut door. She shuddered again and reached for her butterfly pillow. She held it to her chest and hugged it tightly saying to herself, "I hope I don't get those kind of nightmares."

Valerie put her butterfly pillow back down and then lightly slapped her cheeks with both hands. She jumped up off of the bed, smiled, and said, "Guess I'll get ready too!" She stripped off her pajamas and folded them nicely, placing them back into her drawer. She then put on her knee length socks and closed the drawer back up.

Valerie then opened the closet and pulled out today's uniform and began to dress herself. The dress was a perfect fit for her, which made sense. She could remember some military personnel taking her measurements the week before she was required to leave. She raised the dress over her head and let it fall down over her body. She slipped her yellow tie over her head and tightened it around her neck and straightened her collar. She then took the outer jacket and put an arm through each sleeve as she put it on. Again, it was a perfect fit. She closed the jacket and buttoned the three buttons that held it together.

Her combat boots were next to her bed. She pulled out the chair to her desk and put a boot on each foot. She tied them after she raised her foot to the seat of the chair. The boots were somewhat heavy, but they felt sturdy and strong to her.

For the first time since coming here, she felt a little excited about what she would do today. Today would be her first full day as a member of the Spirit Wielder squad. Today, she would begin her training.

Valerie left her room. She could hear that the Lieutenant was already in the kitchen and seemed to be smacking pans around. She walked down the hallway and into the bathroom. Both Mary and Sarah were already standing there brushing their hair in front of their own sink and mirror.

Valerie stepped up to her own sink and mirror and opened a drawer there that she did not notice before. Inside of it there was a comb and brush as well as other important toiletries. She said, "Wow, they really thought of everything didn't they." She pulled a brush out of the drawer and shut it.

Mary, who was brushing her hair into twin tails, said, "I said this before, but I'll say it again, they take good care of us since we're the ones saving their butts all the time. If you complain enough they'll pretty much get you anything you want."

Sarah, who was putting her hair into a ponytail, said, "Well not anything, but yeah, that's basically true."

Valerie began to brush her own hair. She pulled her monarch butterfly clip out of her pocket and placed it over the right side of her hair, pulling her hair on that side back behind her ear.

Sarah said, "That clip is really cute."

Valerie smiled and said, "Thanks, my dad bought it for me."

Mary said, "So, do you really like butterflies?"

Valerie nodded her head and said, "Yeah, I like them. They're so beautiful and gentle."

Mary sighed and said, "If only the Harvesters could be so beautiful and gentle."

Sarah said, "I had a clip one time that had a flower on it. I wore it to battle one time and lost it in the field."

Mary laughed and said, "That's what you get for bringing something so nice onto the battlefield. If you want my advice Val, if you truly value that clip, don't wear it when we sortie for a mission. It can get pretty messy out there."

Valerie nodded and said, "Okay, thanks for the warning." She then put her brush back into the drawer and shut it.

Mary glanced at Valerie with a smile as she stroked her chin. She then jumped at Valerie and embraced her in a big hug. Valerie, who was too weak to break her hold, could do nothing but stand there as Mary grasped onto her as if for dear life. Valerie managed to turn her head and to mumble saying, "Mary, I … I can't breathe!" Mary loosened her tight grip a little and said, "I'm sorry, I can't help it. You are just so cuuute!"

Valerie began to blush a little and said in an embarrassed tone, "Th-Th-Thanks, but could you let me go now."

Mary sighed and then let her go. She took a step backward, gripped her hands behind her back, and smiled at Valerie again.

Sarah reached over and ran her hand through Valerie's hair, saying, "I have never seen anybody with platinum blonde hair in real life before. Is that your real color?

Valerie ran her own hand through her hair, fixing it from Sarah's intrusion, saying, "Yep, that's my natural hair color. Just like my mom."

Sarah sighed and said, "My own hair color is so common, it's boring."

Valerie replied, "But your hair is beautiful too in my opinion."

Sarah said, "You think so?"

Valerie nodded and replied, "I do. Isn't it the same color as Lieutenant Rachel's hair? She has really beautiful hair like you. I can see why the Lieutenant likes her."

Mary interrupted her by flinging out her right hand and began to wave it back and forth, shouting, "Alright! Alright! Alright! Let's not bring that woman up right now. We're done here so let's go help the Lieutenant with breakfast."

Valerie giggled and said, "Okay, okay, calm down. I'm just teasing you, Mary."

Sarah then laughed and said, "Val's already starting to get the hang of it!"

Mary scrunched her face and stuck her tongue out at Valerie. Then she strutted past them and walked out of the bathroom with both hands squared on her hips.

After Mary left, Sarah said, "Wait a minute. Have you even seen Lieutenant Rachel yet?"

Valerie turned to Sarah and said, "Well, no, but that hair color is common so I guessed that she was likely to have it. I hope I didn't make Mary hate me."

Sarah patted her on the back and said, "Hate you? Are you kidding me? She enjoys taunting games like this. Feel free to zing her whenever you think of something. After all she does it to everyone all the time. And, you're right, we do have the same hair color. You were pretty lucky on that one. Let's go out there now and help make breakfast too!"

When Sarah and Valerie entered the dining area, Mary was already at the counter next to Lieutenant Michael beating a batch of eggs. As she beat the eggs she softly swayed her head from side to side.

The scent of heated butter already was wafting through the kitchen. Lieutenant Michael stood there next to Mary, wearing his wine colored apron, waiting for her to finish beating the eggs.

Sarah walked into the opening, with Valerie right next to her, saying, "Lieutenant, is there anything I can help with?"

Lieutenant Michael looked at her and stroked his chin in thought. He said, "I'll have you flip the toast when they're in the pan." Sarah then nodded and jumped up to the stove. She smiled and picked up the spatula waiting for the first piece of French toast to be cooked.

Valerie held her hands in front of her dress and shyly said, "Is there anything I can do too?"

Lieutenant Michael looked at her and stroked his chin again, saying, "Have you ever cooked French toast before?"

Valerie nodded her head and said, "I helped my mom make it before."

Lieutenant Michael gave her a thumbs up and said, "Excellent, you can dip the bread into the egg mix and put it on the pan."

Valerie nodded and walked up to the stove next to Sarah. Her head slightly reached above the stove top. She turned to Lieutenant Michael and said, "I think I'm too short for that."

Lieutenant Michael looked at her again and laughed, saying, "No problem." He turned around, bent over, and picked something up that she couldn't see. He then turned back around and revealed a stepping stool in his hands, saying, "Here you go Valerie, now you can reach the stove with this."

Valerie smiled and accepted the stepping stool. She brought it over and stepped onto it, bringing her to the perfect height for cooking on the stove.

Mary laughed and said, "Looks like the shorty's having shorty problems!"

Valerie gave a loud "hah!" and then said, "I may be short, but you're flat!"

Mary put down the bowl of eggs, turned around, squared her hands on her hips, and loudly said, "Wha ... what are you even talking about? You're flatter then me!"

Valerie retorted, "True, but I'm nine; you're almost fourteen, and from what I've seen of other thirteen year olds here, you got the short end of the stick!"

Mary stood there with mouth wide open in shock. Sarah began to laugh and Lieutenant Michael, also in shock, said, "Valerie, I'm surprised at you."

Mary turned to Lieutenant Michael and said, "Are ... are you gonna let her talk to me like that!" She pointed at her as she stared at him, waiting for his response.

Lieutenant Michael laughed and said, "Mary, you started this by calling her short."

Mary turned back toward Valerie, stepped towards her, and pointed her finger in her face saying, "Alright, Val, you've got guts; I'll give you that. But, you went too far on that one."

Valerie stared back into Mary's eyes and said, "If you take back what you said about me being short, I'll take back about what I said about you being flat."

Mary squinted her eyes and her lips went as straight as they could go. She said, "Alright, alright, I'm sorry I called you short. There, you happy?" She leaned back and folded her arms across her chest with her head stretched upward.

Valerie smiled and said, "I'm sorry I called you flat for a thirteen year old. I didn't mean it."

Lieutenant Michael said, "There you go, girls. There's no need to fight anymore." He looked to Mary again and said, "Mary did you finish those eggs yet?"

Mary spun back around to Lieutenant Michael and said, "Yep, they just need some milk now." Lieutenant Michael took some milk out of the fridge and poured some into the beaten eggs. Mary began to stir it again with vigor.

Lieutenant Michael then turned toward Valerie and said, "Now Valerie, though Mary started it, I don't want you girls fighting in here, okay?"

Valerie's smile of victory went away and was replaced with embarrassed regret, saying, "I'm sorry, Lieutenant."

Lieutenant Michael said, "You girls are supposed to be a team. I don't want you girls starting fights with each other all the time. Okay? It could interfere with your teamwork. Then what are we supposed to do? If you really need to fight it out, we'll do it during a training session."

Lieutenant Michael rested his hand on Mary's shoulder and said, "Mary, you are the oldest one here, so I expect you to set a better example for Sarah and Valerie, okay?"

Mary nodded her head and said, "I know, I'm sorry. I was just trying to lighten things up, but I know I tend to go too far."

Lieutenant Michael smiled and said, "I know, let's not worry about this anymore. Okay? Today's your big fight. I'll be rooting for you." He then rubbed the top of Mary's head and she lifted up her head and smiled, returning to her old jolly self. He then rubbed the top of Valerie's head as well. She lowered her gaze and blushed.

Mary then handed the bowl of egg mix to Valerie with a big smile. Valerie said, "Thank you" and took it from her. She put the first slice of bread in and dropped it into the frying pan.

Sarah gripped the pan's handle and then let it go as she gasped in pain, yelling, "Ouch! It's too hot."

Lieutenant Michael went over to her and said, "Did you burn yourself again?"

Sarah nodded her head and said, "Yes, I forgot to test it first again."

Lieutenant Michael took her hand and looked at it. Redness began to form in her hand and what looked like a blister started to surface. Lieutenant Michael then turned to Valerie and said, "Now's your chance Valerie."

Valerie looked at him confused and said, "What do you mean, Lieutenant?

Sarah held her burned hand to Valerie and said, "Well, you are a healer aren't you?"

Clarity fell upon Valerie and she said, "Oh, yes, that's right!" She began to activate the power within her and her eyes began to glow with a yellow light again. She took Sarah's hand into her own and her hands began to radiate with yellow light. As she focused on healing Sarah's hand, a gentle warmth replaced the burning sensation. Valerie let go of her hand and Sarah withdrew it from her.

Sarah looked at her hand and smiled, saying, "Look, all better! Thank you Valerie!"

The yellow light that radiated from Valerie's hands withdrew back into herself and her eyes stopped glowing yellow. She said, "Sure, no problem. I'm glad I can help."

Lieutenant Michael rested his hands on Sarah's shoulders and gently rocked her back and forth from behind her, saying, "You need to be more careful when you cook, Sarah."

Sarah turned around to face him and said, "I'm sorry, I just wasn't thinking." She then knocked herself on top of the head with her own fist.

After breakfast, Lieutenant Michael and the girls did the dishes together and put them all away. When the last dish was put away, he said, "Alright, girls, who's ready for some training?"

Valerie raised her right hand and said, "I suppose you are talking about me."

Lieutenant Michael nodded, and said, "You got it, but we're all going to do it together."

Mary began punching the air again and said, "Are we going to fight first or later?"

Lieutenant Michael said, "You were the one who set it up. What did they say?"

Mary blushed and looked embarrassed, saying, "Oops, I forgot to talk about that."

Lieutenant Michael patted her on the head and said, "Gee, you would forget an important detail like that, wouldn't you. Alright, let's go ask them." He opened the door and all three girls followed him outside to the door on the other side of the hallway. He knocked on it three times.

A moment later Lieutenant Rachel opened the door and said, "Oh, I've been expecting you."

Lieutenant Michael rubbed the top of his head and said, "Mary says she forgot to ask what time the fight will take place."

Lieutenant Rachel turned her head back into the apartment and yelled, saying, "Hey, Giana, come over here for a moment." She then looked back at Lieutenant Michael, smiled, and said, "She'll be right out."

A moment later, Giana came out from under Lieutenant Rachel and said, pointing at Mary's face, "What do yoooou want? Come here to forfeit already?"

Mary shoved Giana's hand out of her face and said, "No, you idjit, we forgot to talk about what time!"

Giana said, "What do you mean? We always fight at nine. That gives you an hour to warm up since I know you're going to need it."

Mary shook her fist at Giana, saying, "If I were you, I wouldn't act so confident. You're only going to embarrass yourself later when I kick your little butt."

Giana leaned back and rested her right hand on her hip, saying, "Pfff ... If you are so confident, why don't we put a little friendly wager on it. Say ... whoever wins gets to go on a date with Lieutenant Michael."

Lieutenant Michael shook his head and said, "I'm not doing that so you can wager with something else." Nobody seemed to notice what he said though.

Mary also leaned back and rested her right hand on her hip, imitating Giana, saying, "Geez, you're always trying to get in my way! He's already engaged to me, so go find your own."

Lieutenant Michael again spoke up, saying, "I'm not agreeing to this agreement."

Giana laughed and replied, saying, "Where's all your confidence now Mary? Now that it's gettin' interesting, you're backin' down."

Mary stepped forward and said, "I never said I was backin' down. Fine, you're on! Whoever wins this match will get to go on a date with Lieutenant Michael, but there's no way I'm going to let you go out with him. I'm kicking your butt in an hour!"

Lieutenant Michael sighed and said, holding a finger up, "Did nobody hear what I just said? You can't win a date with me. I'm not going along with it."

Giana slammed the door and Mary turned around toward Valerie, saying, "Come on, Val! Let's go do some warmups before I kick her butt." Mary then grabbed Valerie's and Sarah's hands and took off running with them down the hall. Lieutenant Michael shook his head and sighed, saying to himself, "What am I going to do with those two?" He then took off jogging behind them to catch up.

Mary ran down the stairs to the third floor still clutching Valerie's and Sarah's hands. Lieutenant Michael continued to jog behind them but he was a full floor behind them. At the third floor, Mary let go of their hands and opened the door to enter the training area.

When Valerie entered, following Mary, she could see a bunch of exercise equipment, mats, and a large open area with a polished wooden gym type floor. Mary jumped in front of Valerie waving her hands, saying, "This is our training area. You can use it whenever you want to and have the time."

Lieutenant Michael then entered behind them, saying, "Okay, girls, let's do some stretches."

Valerie ran her hands down along the front of her uniform and said, "Aren't we supposed to change into exercise clothes?"

Lieutenant Michael said, "There's no need for that, your field uniform is designed to withstand intense use so it's perfect for exercise wear. You can take off your jacket if you want."

Valerie took off her jacket and hung it on a hook near the door. Mary and Sarah also took off their jackets and hung them on a hook as well. Lieutenant Michael followed suit and took off his jacket, putting it on a hook, saying, "Alright, time for stretches."

Mary and Sarah went straight for the square padded mat and sat down on one of the four sides. Lieutenant Michael pointed to them and said to Valerie, "Go ahead and sit on the mat with them like they are doing."

Valerie nodded and went over to the mat and sat in one of the open spots. Lieutenant Michael then came over and sat down in the last open spot. He began leading the girls in doing various stretches. He would often pause to help Valerie to correct her posture. Mary and Sarah were already familiar with these daily stretches.

After about twenty minutes, Lieutenant Michael clapped his hands once and said, "Alright girls, let's do some jogging now that we're all loosed up." He jogged over to the large open area and began to run around the edges. Mary and Sarah followed after him. Valerie followed, running after them.

Another twenty minutes passed and Lieutenant Michael slowed down to a stop with the rest of the girls stopping behind him. He stopped to catch his breath and the girls did likewise. Valerie was panting heavily as she leaned forward and rested her hands on her knees.

Lieutenant Michael said, "Valerie, are you okay?"

Valerie nodded her head and said pausing after each word, "Yeah … I'm … just … not … used … to this."

Lieutenant Michael rubbed the top of her head, smiled, and said, "I know, we're going to bulk you up soon enough, and get you ready for the field." He then squared his hands on his hips and said, "Alright girls, free exercise time!" He pointed to Valerie and said, "Do whatever you want as long as you are exercising."

Mary ran off to the bench weight sets. Sarah went off to a leg exercise machine. Valerie stood there and looked at the different machines. Lieutenant Michael noticed her hesitation and said, "You can do whatever you want, but to start with, I would suggest you lift some of the dumbbells."

Valerie, who was now breathing normally, wiped the sweat from her forehead, and said, "Dumbbells? What are those?"

Lieutenant Michael patted her shoulder and said, "Come on, I'll show you." He walked over to the rack of dumbbells and Valerie followed behind him. Once there, he pointed to them, and said, "These are dumbbells. Have you ever seen these before?"

Valerie nodded her head and said, "Oh, yes, my mom says they're called paperweights. My dad had a couple of them, though he never used them."

Lieutenant Michael laughed and said, "Well, a lot of people have workout plans but never follow through. Let's find a good weight to start you off with."

Lieutenant Michael folded his left arm across his chest and then began stroking his chin with his right hand. He stared at Valerie and said, "Well, for your age, we'll start you off at ten pounds. Go ahead and grab the weights marked with a number ten."

Valerie strained to pick up the ten pound dumbbells. She stood there with the two weights hanging straight down the sides of her body. Valerie said, "These are heavy."

Lieutenant Michael replied, "Are they too heavy for you?"

Valerie lifted the weight and brought it to her chest while exhaling. She said, "I guess not."

Lieutenant Michael nodded and said, "Yeah, that looks about right to start with. You want them heavy enough to give your muscles a little strain, but not so heavy that you can't lift it." He began to show her various exercises she could do with them to strengthen her upper body. When Valerie got the hang of it, Lieutenant Michael walked away and left her to do it alone.

Valerie continued to do the multiple sets that Lieutenant Michael had shown her. She noticed Mary, whose eyes were glowing red now, and that she was bench pressing a lot of weight. Valerie walked over to her while she was still carrying the ten pound dumbbells, saying, "Wow, that seems like a lot of weight."

Mary, who was still lifting her own weights said, "Well, I only put three hundred on there today. I wanted to keep it light so I don't tire myself out before the fight."

Valerie her eyes wide open in shock, said, "Three hundred! How much can you lift?"

Mary set the bar down and sat up, saying, "Well, I'm not too sure, but this stupid set will only let me put six hundred on it." She set the weights down and then the red light of her eyes dimmed.

Valerie, still holding her own weights, said, "Wow, you are really strong!"

Mary shrugged her shoulders and said, "Well, I am a red Wielder. We're known for our strength."

Suddenly, the door was thrust open. Giana appeared in the room shouting, "Let's do this!" She ripped off her jacket and dramatically tossed it on the floor next to the door. Tina, Elsa, and Lieutenant Rachel followed behind her.

Giana pointed at Mary from across the room and yelled at her, saying, "Alright, Mary, I'm ready to kick your butt so that Lieutenant Michael can take me out to dinner!"

Mary jumped up and shook a fist at Giana, yelling back at her, saying, "Like hell you are! You ain't goin' anywhere with my Lieutenant!"

Mary and Giana stood on opposite sides of each other in the open area of the training room. Lieutenant Michael sat down next to Lieutenant Rachel along the edge where the mat met the polished wooden floor. Valerie sat next to him on his right and Sarah sat down next to Valerie. Elsa and Tina sat down next to Rachel on the opposite side.

Mary glared toward Lieutenant Michael and Rachel, saying, "Hey you two, don't get so comfortable with each other over there on the floor! I'm going to finish this real quick." Lieutenant Michael rolled his eyes and pretended he didn't hear what she said.

Giana moved her stance to a military martial fighting stance. She called out, saying, "Just so you know Mary, the other day Lieutenant Michael couldn't help but put his hands on me."

Mary shook her fists tightly and said, "What! He'd never do that!"

Lieutenant Michael called out saying, "Geez you two, stop taking things the wrong way. I was only brushing the dirt off of the back of her jacket."

Mary went into her own form of a fighting stance and pointed at Giana, saying, "You're totally taking things out of context! I bet you put dirt on your back on purpose too. I'm going to beat you into a pulp for that one!"

Giana said, "Well, come on then, you cow, bring it!"

Mary's eyes began to glow red again. Giana's eyes began to glow red as well. Red light also began to radiate from their hands and feet.

Mary ran at Giana and then leapt at her from across the room. She brought her right fist back and then plunged it toward Giana who then jerked out of the way. Mary's fist went through the floor causing a shower of wooden splinters. Lieutenant Michael yelled out, "If possible, try not to break everything again!" He shook his head as he thought of the repair cost.

Mary called back, saying, "It's her fault! She keeps moving away from me! Why don't you stand there and take it!" Mary leapt at Giana again who blocked her next punch with her own hand. As their hands of red light made contact with each other, a shower of sparks exploded from where their fists met and the smell of ozone began to fill the room.

Giana then tried to kick Mary in the stomach but Mary blocked it with her other fist. Another shower of sparks exploded from them. Mary then jumped, spinning over Giana's head, and landed behind her. She attempted to punch Giana in the back of her head but Giana spun around and blocked it again, causing another shower of sparks to appear.

Mary laughed and said, "What, you too afraid to punch back."

Giana replied, "Pfff ... I'm just not the mindless attack dog you are. I use a thing called stra-te-gy." She enunciated each syllable of the word strategy.

Giana jumped backward and then charged at Mary, throwing punch after punch, with Mary blocking each one of them. With each block another shower of sparks exploded from between them.

Mary, after blocking the last punch, grabbed onto Giana's arms and tossed her about thirty feet across the room. Giana straightened herself and landed on her feet in a squatting position. The momentum of the throw caused Giana to skid backwards a few feet along the floor. Black skid marks could be seen on the polished surface of the floor.

Mary then charged straight at Giana with a yell and Giana used her own power to leap back across the room. The two collided and Mary was finally hit and was knocked backward falling onto her butt. Giana then leapt at her again but Mary jumped up and over Giana as she fell downward with her fist just missing Mary by an inch. With Mary out of the way, Giana instead punched the floor, causing another shower of splinters. Wood fragments flew in all directions. There was now another hole in the floor. Lieutenant Michael shook his head again and winced at the thought of the cost of the damage.

With Giana's back fully exposed now, Mary brought her fist back and brought it down straight into her back between her shoulders. Giana cried out from the pain and fell flat on her face. Giana jumped up, recoiling from the pain in her back, saying, "Now you've gone and made me angry, trollop!"

Mary replied, "You're angry? After all you've done to me? I'm the one who's angry! I'm going to pound you so hard that not even Elsa will be able to put you back together!"

Mary ran at Giana, so Giana ran at Mary. The two of them collided with their fists flying at each other. Their fists moved so fast that Valerie could hardly see them move. With each strike and block a shower of sparks exploded between them. The shouts of frustration could be heard from both girls as they continued to stand there punching and blocking each other.

Finally, at the same time, they both slipped past each other's defenses and landed a powerful blow on each other's cheek. With the force of the blow both Mary and Giana cried out in pain. They both flew backward in opposite directions and landed flat on their backs with a loud thud. For a moment, Valerie thought the fight was over. But, to her surprise, both of them started to roll over and stand back up.

Mary stood there panting, her uniform full of rips and holes. Blood dripped down from the left side of her mouth. Giana also stood there panting, her uniform also full of rips and holes. Blood also dripped down from the left side of her mouth. Mary, still panting, said, "I ... I'm not backing down!" Giana, also panting, said, "Neither ... am ... I!"

Again, the two ran at each other and there was another shower of sparks as their fists collided together. Valerie began to worry that they would kill each other. Lieutenant Michael noticed the worry on her face and whispered into her ear, "Don't worry, they do this all the time, they'll be okay."

Valerie nodded and said, "I hope so."

Again, Mary slipped past Giana's strong defense and managed to land another powerful blow on the left side of her cheek. Much to Mary's dismay, that move allowed her own strong defense to go down as Giana managed to punch her straight in the gut. Giana was thrown sideways from the force of the blow to her face and landed with another thud on the floor. Mary was thrown backward and landed on her back gasping for air.

Lieutenant Michael stood up and said, "Okay, girls, why don't we just call it a draw again?"

Mary rolled over and stood back up, saying, "Hell ... no! I've ... got to teach ... this cow ... a lesson!"

Giana rolled over and then stood up, saying, "No ... way! Mary's ... gotta ... be put ... in her place!"

Both of them stood there breathing heavily with bruises forming on their body and blood dripping from the corner of their mouths still. They stood there staring each other down.

Finally, Mary leapt at her from where she stood. Giana also leapt at her from where she stood. Both of them raised their fists back as they flew in the air, hurling toward each other. They ended up colliding into each other in midair.

Without any thought of defense, Mary put the last of her strength into her right fist, and plunged it into the left side of Giana's face again. At the same time, Giana, who also did not think to defend herself, put the last of her strength into her own right fist, and plunged it into the left side of Mary's face again.

There was a loud smacking sound and the two girls flew in opposite directions of each other after they collided mid-air. There was a loud "umph" sound that came from both girls as they collided, but that was it. They both landed on their backs with a loud thud as they crashed onto the floor.

Lieutenant Michael and Rachel watched them for about twenty seconds but neither of them moved an inch. Lieutenant Michael got up and said, "You girls conscious?"

Lieutenant Rachel also got up and said, "Well, looks like the fights over in a draw again. Let's see if they're okay."

Lieutenant Michael walked over to Mary, whose body was lying sprawled on the floor. She was still breathing but she wouldn't wake up after he shook her. Giana was also lying sprawled on the floor and breathing. Both of them appeared to be unconscious.

Lieutenant Michael called over to Valerie saying, "Hey Valerie, come over here, and heal Mary."

Valerie walked over to Mary and looked over her sprawled out body on the floor. She couldn't help but laugh at the sight of it, saying, "She reminds me of a rag doll." Valerie's eyes began to glow with the yellow light and she held out her hands. Her hands began to radiate with yellow light and she knelt beside Mary, placing her hands in the middle of her torso. Yellow light began to spread over Mary's body until her body was entirely enveloped by it.

After a few moments of this, Mary began to cough and wake up. She sat up and said, "Did I win?"

Valerie and Mary looked back at Giana, who was also being healed by Elsa. Giana coughed and sat up as well, saying, "Did I win?"

Lieutenant Michael spoke loudly so that both of them could hear him, saying, "Both of you went unconscious at the same time, which means that today's fight was a draw." He laughed and said, "Looks like I don't have to go out with either of you today!"

Mary laid back down on her back and yelled out to Giana, "At least I kept you from going out with him!"

Giana also laid back down and yelled at Mary, "Don't get all cocky, you didn't win either!"

Lieutenant Michael bent down over Mary, put his hands under her back, and lifted her up by her armpits. The front of Mary's dress was torn enough to expose her bra underneath. Mary looked down and noticed this and wrapped her arms around her chest and started to blush.

Lieutenant Michael looked at her and said, "What's wrong, Mary?"

Mary stuttered and shyly said, "My ... My dress is ripped in front." She continued to cover her chest with her arms. She turned her face slightly downwards and to the side and said quietly, but loud enough for him to hear, "I don't know if I am ready for you to see me yet, Lieutenant."

Lieutenant Michael rolled his eyes and said, "Knock it off. Go upstairs and put on a new uniform. Geez, always with those stupid jokes."

Mary laughed and said, "Okay, I'll wait for you all upstairs."

Giana then also walked by holding the front of her tattered dress. Lieutenant Michael noticed her too and said, "You girls really did a number on each other."

Giana turned away from him and said, "Are you happy to watch two girls fighting over you?"

Lieutenant Michael rolled his eyes and shook his head, saying, "Girls, you both need to quit acting stupid like that. Head on up and change your uniform. Geez, I'm an adult you know. You both need to learn some respect."

Mary and Giana laughed as they got their jackets. Giana said, "Calm down Lieutenant Michael, we're just joking. Why do you always take it so seriously?"

Lieutenant Michael shook his head as he watched them leave the room, muttering to each other.

Lieutenant Rachel walked up to Michael, put her hand on his shoulder and said, "Those two are quite the handful, aren't they? Should I have another talk with them?"

Lieutenant Michael shook his head at the thought and said, "Well you can try, but, I don't think it would work. It didn't last time or the time before that. I think I'm just stuck with it till they get bored of it."

Lieutenant Rachel said, "So, we done here?"

Lieutenant Michael replied, "Well, I was hoping also that maybe Sarah and Tina would give a demonstration of their abilities. Would you mind?"

Lieutenant Rachel nodded her head and said, "That's fine with me if they want to?"

Lieutenant Michael then turned to Sarah and Tina, who were still sitting on the mat, and said, "Sarah, Tina, would you two mind giving Valerie a demonstration of your abilities?"

Sarah stood up and smiled, saying, "Sure, I don't mind." She turned to Tina and offered her a hand. Tina shrugged her shoulders and said in her melancholy tone, "Whatever." She took Sarah's hand and Sarah helped her to her feet. Tina brushed off her uniform and said, "What'd you want us to do, Lieutenant."

Lieutenant Michael replied, "Why don't you, Tina, erect a barrier, and we'll have Sarah shoot at it with her light spear."

Tina shrugged her shoulders again and said, "I suppose."

Sarah said, "Don't worry, I'll go easy on you."

Tina walked toward the center of the open area and said as she turned away from Sarah, "Gee, how thoughtful of you." When Tina reached the center of the open area, she turned around to face Valerie. Valerie sat there in excitement to see the next spectacle that was about to unfold.

Tina's eyes began to glow with her blue light. She placed her hands together in front of her chest and then moved them apart about two inches away from each other. Suddenly, a small blue orb appeared from out of her chest. Tina then stretched her arms out straight sideways and the glowing blue orb expanded until it had formed a large dome over her. Tina stood there waiting for Sarah to make her move.

Sarah stood there smiling from across the room. Her eyes began to glow with the blue light and then her hands also began to radiate with the same blue light. She placed her hands together and then stretched out her arms toward Tina. She held out her glowing hands with her palms facing her opponent. Suddenly, a beam of blue light flowed out of her palms and struck the barrier that Tina had formed. At the place of contact, there was a large shower of sparks. The same smell of ozone, which came during Mary's and Giana's fight, began to fill the room again.

Sarah began to repeatedly shoot the same spear of light over and over again at Tina. Tina stood there motionless, unaffected by the shower of sparks that exploded with each contact of their powers. The look on Tina's face seemed uninterested.

Next, there was a loud noise that echoed behind them. Lieutenant Michael, Rachel, and Valerie turned to see what it was. Mary and Giana, who were now in new uniforms, came bursting into the room yelling a war cry at the top of their lungs. Their eyes, fists, and feet were glowing with red light. Tina said in her melancholy tone, "Not again."

Lieutenant Michael said, "What are you two ..."

Before he could finish, Mary and Giana suddenly leapt together, side by side, from across the room, bringing their glowing fists back behind them. Together they landed right next to Tina and began smashing their fists into her barrier. There were more showers of sparks as the two of them, together, continued to smash their fists against the barrier.

Sarah, who began to laugh at the situation, lifted her palms back up and added to the mayhem by firing her spear of light at Tina's barrier again.

Tina, who began to show signs of anger, said a bit forcefully, "Geez, knock it off!" The three attackers ignored her and continued to smash at the barrier.

Cracks began to form in the barrier. Tina began to show signs of severe strain as she struggled to maintain her protective shell. At this sight, Sarah stopped firing her beam. Mary and Giana paused for a moment, smiled really big at each other, and then put all their strength into one last hit. Their fists smashed right through the barrier.

The momentum of their fists were so powerful that they could not pull it back in time. Their fists smashed right into Tina's chest. Tina gave a loud cry of pain and she was thrown back across the area. Her body smashed into the wall on the other side of the room. She then dropped to the floor with a loud thud. Her body lay motionless in a heap on the floor. A pool of blood began to form underneath her head.

Lieutenant Michael and Rachel stood there in shock for a second and then said together, "Holy crap!" Lieutenant Rachel and Elsa ran over to Tina. She was unconscious and the back of her head had a huge gash in it. Blood poured out of it and pooled on to the floor.

Valerie stood there in shock at the sight and began to cry. Lieutenant Rachel yelled out to her, "Valerie, please help us!"

Valerie overcame her shock and ran over to where Tina lay in the puddle of her own blood. Valerie said, "What should I do?"

Lieutenant Rachel said, "Activate your power and assist Elsa in the healing." Valerie activated her power. Her eyes and hands glowed with yellow light. She squatted down on the opposite side of Elsa and began to assist in the healing. Her feet stood in the puddle of blood.

Lieutenant Michael stormed over to Mary and Giana, who were standing there in horror at the spectacle of Tina lying in her own blood. He grabbed onto each one of their arms and spun them around to face him. Shock was still written all over their faces. Lieutenant Michael yelled at them, saying, "What the hell were you two thinking, doing that to one of your friends!"

Tears began to flow from their eyes and they avoided looking into his face. Lieutenant Michael spun them back around again and pointed at Tina laying on the ground in her own blood. He thrust his arm in between their two heads. Lieutenant Michael began to yell again, saying, "Look at her, she's lying in a puddle of her own blood. If Elsa or Valerie wasn't here, she could be dead. What the hell were you two thinking?"

Mary and Giana still didn't say anything. Lieutenant Michael grabbed Mary's shoulder and shook her harshly, while yelling once more, "I am your Lieutenant! I asked you a question!"

Mary turned around looked at Lieutenant Michael straight in his eyes. Tears rolled down her cheeks and her eyes were red not from her power but from her tears, "We … We … We wanted to show Valerie that the barrier can be broken with enough force, we … we didn't intend to hit her so hard."

Lieutenant Michael thrust his hands on his face and gave a loud sigh, he said, "Gee, great, I'm sure she'll definitely remember this for the rest of her life." He put his hands down from off his face and looked at Valerie, who had managed to stop crying in spite of the drama.

Tina gasped for air suddenly and her eyes opened. She began to cry deeply. Lieutenant Rachel put a hand on Tina's forehead and said, "Don't worry, you're okay now." She then walked over to Lieutenant Michael and the two culprits. She folded her arms across her chest, stared at the two of them intently, and shook her head. She finally said, "Geez, you two certainly are a handful."

Mary and Giana, said dejectedly, "We're sorry."

Lieutenant Rachel bumped each one of them on the head with her right hand and said, "Don't apologize to me, go apologize to her!"

Mary and Giana walked over to Tina and squatted down beside her. Lieutenant Michael stood next to Rachel and said, "I'm sorry about that. Like I've said before, Mary can be a little rough."

Lieutenant Rachel, still crossing her arms, shook her head again and said, "Giana is just as guilty as Mary. When those two are together … I swear!"

Lieutenant Michael said, "What do you think we should do?"

Lieutenant Rachel thought for a moment and then said, "Well, I can tell it wasn't intentional so I don't think we need to go through the hassle of reporting it. Tina's wound is fully healed and she doesn't have a concussion. I'd give 'em bathroom duty for two weeks."

Lieutenant Michael nodded his head and said, "That's fine with me, if that's good enough for you."

Lieutenant Rachel nodded her head and said, "Yep, that's good enough for me I think. Let them do both yours and mine together."

Lieutenant Michael nodded his head again and said, "That's what I was thinking."

Tina began to move again and she groaned.  Giana and Mary were still sitting there beside her.  Giana said, "Tina, I'm so sorry, I didn't think that I would hit you that hard."

Mary said, "Yeah, I'm sorry too.  I didn't mean to hurt you."

Tina sat up crying still and said, "You two can be real jerks sometimes.  I told you to knock it off but you just had to keep going." Tina then looked around to see Sarah standing there nearby.  She stood there watching them while biting the thumbnail on her right hand.  Tina pointed at her and said, "And you!  I can't believe that you actually helped them do this to me!  If you hadn't kept shooting my barrier I could have maintained my energy level!"

Sarah dropped her hand to her side and looked downward.  She said, "I'm sorry, I know what that's like, but at least I stopped when it cracked.  These two kept going."

Lieutenant Michael interrupted, saying, "And that's why Sarah's not going to get in trouble because she knows when to quit.  Mary and Giana, get over here."

Mary and Giana looked at one another, stood up, and then walked over to Lieutenant Michael.  Their faces were still downcast and their shoulders slumped.

Lieutenant Michael continued what he was saying, "Alright you two, we decided not to report this since Tina is okay.  But the both of you will be cleaning bathrooms together for two weeks.  Both the bathroom in our place and Lieutenant Rachel's place.  Is that fair?"

Giana and Mary nodded their heads and said in unison, in a depressed monotone voice, "Yes, that's fair."

Lieutenant Michael said, "Good.  To start with, I want you to clean up all this blood from your friend in here and then you and Giana can go upstairs and get started on our bathrooms."

Giana and Mary nodded their heads again and said in unison, "Okay." They turned away and walked out of the room without another word to get the things they would need to clean up the blood.

Lieutenant Rachel called out to Tina, saying, "Hey, Tina, can you walk?" Tina stood up and said, "I think so." Tina began to walk normally and walked toward her with Elsa, Valerie, and Sarah following her.  Her black hair was matted and covered in blood.  Her white uniform with blue strips was soaked along the back with the redness of her blood.

Lieutenant Rachel put her hand on Michael's shoulder and cheerily said, "Well, at least Valerie got in some practice healing today."

Lieutenant Michael shook his head and said, "Well at least you can still find the good in every situation."

Later that night, Lieutenant Michael sat at the dinner table, sipping a cup of herbal tea. The door opened and he turned his head to see Mary standing in the doorway. Her face was downcast and her uniform had blotches of water stains on it. She stood in the doorway hesitating to enter. Lieutenant Michael said, "Well hello, Mary, did you make the bathrooms shine?"

Mary nodded her head and said, "Yes, we just finished the other one." Mary lifted her face a little and slowly approached Lieutenant Michael. She cautiously slid herself next to him as he sat there in the chair. Her face became downcast again and she raised her right hand to his arm. She pinched onto the fabric of his jacket and held it there. He put down his cup of tea and looked up into her face. Her eyes began to turn red from tears that started to roll down her cheeks as she stood there. She said, "Michael, do you hate me now?"

Lieutenant Michael, confused, said, "What are you talking about, why would you think that I hate you?"

Mary said, still clinging on to his jacket, "Because you've never yelled at me like that before. I thought that I made you ..."

Lieutenant Michael jumped up from his chair, knocking it over backwards as he jumped up. He wrapped his arms around Mary and held her close to his chest. He whispered into her ear, "Mary, I could never hate you."

Mary began to sob into his chest, saying, "I couldn't live with myself if you hated me." Lieutenant Michael continued to hold her tight and rested his head on top of hers.

Sarah and Valerie came into the dining area after hearing the noise. They saw Lieutenant Michael holding Mary, who was still sobbing. Sarah said, "What's going on, Lieutenant?"

Lieutenant Michael said, "She thought that I hated her for what happened today." Mary turned her head to look at Sarah. Sarah looked back at her in pity and walked over to her. She began to stroke her head and said, "Don't worry. Nobody hates you here."

Lieutenant Michael let go of Mary, who had now stopped crying. Mary then hugged Sarah and said, "I'm sorry. I went too far. I promise that I'll never do that again."

Mary then turned to Valerie and said, "Are you scared of me now?"

Valerie shook her head and said, "Not really ... well, maybe a little. You threw that girl across the room as a prank. My shoes were soaked in her blood. What would you do to me if you were angry?"

Mary dropped to her knees and sat down on her feet, her face downcast again. She began to cry again so she covered her face with her hands.

Sarah came up beside her and knelt with her. She wrapped an arm around her shoulder. Mary spoke into her hands and said, "I ... I'm sorry Valerie. I just wanted to show you that you can't always depend on the barrier. I really didn't mean to hit Tina like that."

Valerie began to tear up. She walked up next to Mary and said, "Okay, I know you didn't do it on purpose. If you did, I don't think that it would eat you up inside this much." She also wrapped her arm around Mary's shoulder. Mary dropped her hands from her face and wrapped them around both Sarah's and Valerie's back, and said, "I'll do everything I can to protect you, so you don't need to worry. You can still count on me."

- 5 -

Lieutenant Michael ran through the crowded street. All he could hear were the screams of commotion and the cries of despair. He thought he heard the noise of a tank coming. Sure enough, a tank rolled passed a building around the corner. It halted its movement with a jerk and the tank's turret rotated to point straight down the street.

Lieutenant Michael turned around to see a giant Harvester in the distance. The tank's cannon roared as it fired its first volley. Another soldier stood behind the tank's fifty caliber machine gun. The gun echoed tat-tat-tat as it shot in short bursts at the Harvester over and over again to no effect. People dropped to the ground as the tank continuously fired as fast as it could. Another soldier yelled out, "Don't stop! Keep moving!" Most people got back up and ran past the tank. Others couldn't move paralyzed by fear.

A jet passed overhead and Lieutenant Michael could see it drop several pay loads as it passed over the area. After a few seconds, there were six explosions, one right after the other. A pillar of fire and black smoke could be seen rising behind them down the street.

Michael stood there staring at the familiar scene. "What was I supposed to be doing again?" he said to himself, "That's right I was looking for my mom." He cupped his hands over his mouth and yelled, "Mom, where are you!"

After he called out, there was suddenly silence. All the other people disappeared. The tank disappeared. He saw in the distance a woman running towards him, her hand outstretched toward him as if she could reach him from where she ran from afar. Behind her, a fully grown Harvester appeared and continued to chase her. "Mom! Is that you?" He yelled out.

The woman yelled back at him, "Michael, help me!" Michael ran toward her as fast as he could. The woman then suddenly tripped and fell flat on her face. She looked up as she lay there on the broken pavement of the street. She reached out toward Michael, her fingers clawing toward him, yelling, "Michael, save me!"

Michael was still too far away. The Harvester was right on top of her. She screamed and screamed as the Harvester pierced her chest with its foot. Blood began to pool beneath her. The Harvester then proceeded to dismember her legs and arms with its mandibles as if she were a paper doll. She continued to scream and scream as the Harvester continued its bloody harvest. Finally, the screaming stopped as the Harvester feasted on the sweet innards of the woman. She had died. All he could do was stand there and stare on in horror at the sight of his mother being devoured by the Harvester.

Another voice came from behind him. The voice of a girl. "Michael, why didn't you save me?" He turned around to see a fourteen year old girl with blond hair in twin tails wearing the yellow Spirit Wielder uniform standing before him. "Susan?" he said. Tears rolled down her face as she stared at him with a gloomy smile. Suddenly cracks began to form all over her body. Yellow light poured through the cracks. Then pieces of her body began to drop off one by one. Her body then exploded right in front of him in a flash of yellow light. Then she was gone.

Lieutenant Michael woke up with a start from his sleep. He was sweating and breathing heavily as he stared into the darkness of night. "It was only that dream again," he said to himself. He wiped his forehead with his hand and then rubbed it on the side of his mattress sheet.

Lieutenant Michael then looked at the clock, which said four-thirty on it. He sighed and rubbed his eyes. He then moved his arm over beside him to check if there was anybody else there again. He felt the familiar form of a girl there. It was probably Mary.

He sat up and stumbled in the dark toward his bathroom. Finding the door, he opened it and then closed the door behind himself. He turned on the light and stared at himself in the mirror. "It's okay, Mike, it was only a nightmare," he said to himself, "It is a dream that manifests from my past regrets." He told himself this every time he had a nightmare. It helped him to understand why he kept having those dreams. The image of his mother being devoured before him came back into his mind. It was the same image that he saw when he was sixteen years old. It continued to haunt him from time to time.

He washed his face and then dried it with a towel. He turned off the light and made his way back to his bed. He gently slid back in under the sheets and softly pulled the cover back over himself. A warm body gently rolled over to his side. An arm draped itself over his chest. A soft voice whispered into his ear. It was the voice of Mary, saying, "Don't worry, I'll make the bad dream go away."

Lieutenant Michael said, "I'm sorry, I didn't mean to wake you."

Mary then whispered into his ear again, "It's not your fault, Lieutenant."

Lieutenant Michael, confused, said, "If I didn't get up, then I wouldn't have woken you, so, technically, it is my fault."

Mary whispered into his ear yet again, saying, "No, I mean it's not your fault that you couldn't save them. There was nothing that you could have done to prevent it."

Lieutenant Michael, shocked, said, "How ... how do you know about my dream?"

Mary replied, whispering into his ear again, "Because I know you."

Another voice then spoke up, annoyed, saying, "Geez, it's too early to be making so much noise!" It was the voice of Sarah coming from behind Mary.

Lieutenant Michael reached over Mary and felt Sarah lying there, he said, "Sorry, Sarah, I didn't think you were there." He rolled over onto his side facing toward the door. Mary then let go of him and rolled over in the opposite direction with her back leaning against his. Neither of them said another word.

Lieutenant Michael closed his eyes. Surprisingly to him, her gentle words did make him feel better. The horror of his nightmare began to fade. *She's right*, he thought to himself, *there really isn't much that I could have done about it at that time.* He cleared his mind and quickly drifted back to sleep.

After what seemed like a moment, Lieutenant Michael heard some strange noises. He slowly opened his eyes to sudden brightness. He found the face of a little girl right in front of his own face. He leaned backward and sat up, rubbing his eyes. After blinking multiple times he looked back at the little girl in confusion and noticed the platinum blond hair fixed back with a butterfly clip. He yawned and said, "Good morning, Valerie, is something wrong?"

She took a step back from his bed and said, "We were worried that you might have died so they sent me to check in on you."

Lieutenant Michael said, "Huh?" He then reached for the alarm clock and noticed that it said seven-thirty on it. "Seven-thirty!" He shouted, "What happened to my alarm?" He looked over behind himself on the bed. Neither Mary nor Sarah were there. He thought to himself, *Did I forget to turn on the alarm?* He thought for a moment but clearly remembered turning it on.

Valerie, who seemed to understand what he was thinking, said, "Mary turned off your alarm clock. She said that you had a rough night and needed some extra sleep."

Lieutenant Michael shook his head, saying, "Geez, what if I had an important meeting today?"

Valerie patted him on the shoulder and said, "Don't worry, Lieutenant, we've already started making breakfast. So why don't you get into your uniform, and then we can eat it together."

Valerie then walked out of the room and Lieutenant Michael continued to sit there in a confused stupor. Valerie started to close the door behind her, but stopped half way through. She smiled at him and said, "You should be happy. It's not every day that a pretty girl wakes you up." She then giggled and shut the door behind herself.

Lieutenant Michael shook his head and thought to himself, *Great, are you going to make those kind of jokes too?* He mustered up the strength to get out of bed and headed to the bathroom to get ready for the day.

Valerie returned to the kitchen where Mary and Sarah were standing in front of the stove. Valerie stood in the entryway and said, "I got him up."

Mary turned her head to look at her as she held a spatula in her right hand, saying, "Great ... did you say what I told you to say?"

Valerie nodded her head and said, "Yep, I said it."

Mary then asked, "What did he do?"

Valerie thought for a moment and said, "I think he just rolled his eyes at me." Sarah giggled, listening from behind Mary.

Mary replied, saying, "Yeah, that's normal. He acts like he doesn't like it, but secretly he loves the attention. What guy wouldn't?" Mary then turned back to the frying pan and flipped the pancakes that were in it. She then said, "Val, can you please set the table? These are almost done."

Valerie nodded her head and began to rummage for dishes. She placed them on the table and then returned to the entryway of the kitchen. Sarah handed her a bowl of scrambled eggs, which she put on the table.

Mary said, "All done!" as she picked up the last pancake, putting it onto a plate. Mary put the plate of pancakes on the table. As she was doing so,

Lieutenant Michael came into the dining area breathing in the smell of breakfast. Mary, Sarah, and Valerie then sat down in their chairs at the table.

Lieutenant Michael stood there and half-heartedly glared at Mary. He then said, "Mary, please don't turn off my alarm. What if I had an important meeting this morning?"

Mary replied, saying, "But you don't have an important meeting this morning."

Lieutenant Michael said, "But what if I did?"

Mary replied, "Then I would have made sure that you got up on time."

Lieutenant Michael sighed and sat down at the table, saying, "Well, just don't do it again. Thank you girls for making breakfast anyway." He began to take some of the pancakes off of the plate and tossed them onto his own.

Mary clasped her hands together, put her elbows on the table, and then rested her chin on her clasped hands. She smiled at Lieutenant Michael, batting her eyes, and said, "Don't you feel special that three pretty girls made you breakfast this morning?"

Lieutenant Michael proceeded to eat his meal and said, with his mouth full of food, "Nof parficuaree." He then swallowed his food and repeated, saying, "Not particularly."

Mary replied, "But you should. I filled each pancake with my love and affection as I made it."

Lieutenant Michael spat out the pieces of pancake that he just put into his mouth, and pretended to cough and gag. He drunk a glass of water and said, "What did you put in my pancakes?"

Mary, offended, dropped her hands to the table and said, "I didn't put anything bad in them. I meant my 'love' metaphorically."

Lieutenant Michael nodded his head and said, "Oh, okay." He proceeded to return the food to his mouth.

Sarah then said, "I made the scrambled eggs, Lieutenant. They're filled with my love too!"

Lieutenant Michael then took a bite of the eggs, patted her on the head and said, "That's sweet, Sarah, I love you too." A very large grin appeared on her face as he patted the top of her head.

As Lieutenant Michael did this, Mary jealously said, "Humph! When I told you that, you spat out my food! I told you I loved you first!"

Lieutenant Michael paused from eating and said, "Mary, when you do it, you are just making fun of me. When Sarah does it, she means it. You make fun of me so much that it just kind of blows over my head now." He waved his hand over his head back and forth as he said it.

Mary didn't say anything but looked dejected as she began to eat her food. Lieutenant Michael looked at her and patted her head, saying, "I'm sorry, Mary. I was just teasing you. I love you too. Thank you for this wonderful meal filled with your 'love'." His fingers motioned in quotation marks as he said 'love'.

In spite of his sarcasm, Mary's mood perked up with his declaration but she still said, "Don't patronize me."

Lieutenant Michael then turned to Valerie and said, "What did you do for breakfast, Valerie?"

Valerie opened her eyes and put down her hands that she held up pressed together in silent prayer. She smiled and said, "I set the table and I woke you up."

Lieutenant Michael reached over and patted her on the head, saying, "Good job on setting the table. But, when you wake someone up, you are supposed to like shake them or something so that they, you know, like wake up. All you did was stand there."

Valerie blushed and looked downward, bringing her right hand to her mouth, her thumb to her lip, saying, "But when I saw you sleeping it was so cute. It was like watching a baby sleep and your face was in a puddle of your own drool. I couldn't help but stare at you." Lieutenant Michael rolled his eyes again and kept eating.

After breakfast, Lieutenant Michael took care of the dishes by himself to repay the girls for making breakfast without him. Today, they would officially begin training Valerie in her position. Since she was technically a support class, she did not require much combat training. They would still train her in combat techniques since it was still important to learn them. As a yellow Wielder, Valerie would focus most of her time on healing others instead of destroying Harvesters.

Inside the training room, Mary and Sarah stood at ease in a line. Their arms were squared behind their backs and their feet were slightly spread apart. Valerie stood next to Sarah and imitated her stance. Lieutenant Michael began to pace back and forth in front of them. He then stopped in front of Valerie, bent downward toward her and said, "This is called 'standing at ease'. When an officer tells you to stand at ease, this is what you do."

Lieutenant Michael stood up and began to pace again. He stopped and called out, "Attention!" Mary and Sarah brought their feet together and their hands down along the side of their bodies. Valerie watched them and then imitated them.   He said, "This is what you do when an officer calls out 'attention'." Valerie nodded her head.

Lieutenant Michael then said, "At ease girls." The three of them stood at ease together.  He then said, "That is all the military formation training that you need, Valerie. They don't expect more than that from you."

He then brought his hand to his chin, and said, "Well, thanks to Mary's and Giana's antics, we already know that you are an excellent healer."  Mary looked down toward her feet embarrassed.  Lieutenant Michael turned his head and gave her his annoyed look.  He then looked back at Valerie, saying, "Since you already seem to be really good at that I don't think we need to cover it.  The question I have for you is, can you pull the energy out of something living and use it yet?"

Valerie shook her head and said, "No, I've never been able to do that before."

Lieutenant Michael shrugged his shoulders and said, "That's okay, most can't do that anyway.  Only the most powerful yellow Wielders have been able to do that successfully.  There's no way to teach it either, so, if you have that ability within you, it will come out on its own one day when you really want it to. That's all we can say about that."

Valerie looked dejected and lowered her head.  She twisted her body side to side and said, "I'm sorry I'm not that strong."

Lieutenant Michael put his hand on her shoulder and said, "No, no, no, there is no need for you to be sorry.  Only a few of your type can do it.  For now, we will focus on exercise and combat techniques.  These things will help you get stronger."

The regimen that Lieutenant Michael had developed was one that he had trained all the other girls with.  Sarah and Mary were already familiar with it, but they endured the extra training for Valerie's sake.

To start with, he had the girls do exercises for an hour, which they would have been doing every day anyway with or without the training.  After that, he would show her common military hand to hand combat techniques for another two hours.  This part was harder for Valerie as she did not have a fighting disposition.  At one point, after a week, Valerie dropped to her knees from exhaustion and said, "What's the point of me learning all of these martial arts? It's not like I can kick or punch a Harvester like Mary can or shoot a beam of light like Sarah can."

Lieutenant Michael knelt down beside her, placed his right hand on her shoulder, and said, "Well, that's true, but there are three reasons we do this.  The first is so that, when you see your teammate in action, you can better predict what they are going to do. Working together like this helps you to learn to think together. The second reason is that it's good exercise. The third reason is that, in the field, you need to be able to be prepared for anything. You don't know what's going to happen so we prepare you with everything that you might need. If a situation arises and you need it then you got it. Does that make sense?"

Valerie nodded her head and said, "Yes, that makes sense."

Lieutenant Michael said, "Do you want to take a break for now or can you keep going?"

Valerie stood up, brushed off her dress, and said, "I can keep going."

Lieutenant Michael smiled and rubbed the top of her head, saying, "Excellent, that's my girl." Valerie then got back into position and continued to practice the technique that Lieutenant Michael had showed her.

When Valerie seemed confident in the basic moves that he had showed her, he paired her up with Mary who would then spar with her. Mary, who could be counted as an expert in hand to hand combat, showed her everything that she knew.

Sarah began to train Valerie in the use of sword techniques. Though she was not as much of an expert at swords as Mary was at hand to hand combat, she had acquired enough knowledge to be useful to Valerie.

After the first week of training, Lieutenant Michael added small firearms to the training regimen. After lunch one day, Michael walked into the apartment carrying a small case. He told the girls to sit back at the table and placed it in front of Valerie. Valerie looked at the case in wonder and he said, "Go ahead and open it."

Valerie opened that case and sat there staring at it in shock. Valerie slid back in her seat and stuttered, saying, "Tha-tha-that's a gun!"

Lieutenant Michael nodded his head with a smile and said, "That's right, this is your gun. Since your power is not really meant for combat, they give you the option of carrying these. It is officially called the UEDT3-21 submachine gun, but we tend to call it the "cattle prod" for short. It fires nine millimeter titan puncture rounds, which are the only type of rounds that have the capacity to break through Harvester shells. They're not really effective so they are more of a last resort kind of weapon. But, it still might save your life one day."

Valerie continued to stare at it and said, "I ... I don't think I'm big enough for a gun."

Lieutenant Michael placed his hand on her shoulder and said, "It seems that way, but, in reality, this gun was designed by our engineers to be usable by the Spirit Wielders who are your age.  You don't have to use it if you don't want too, but why don't we give it a try first before you decide, okay?"

Valerie nodded her head and said, "Okay.  I trust you."

The four of them then went outside to an area behind the Phoenix Guard complex.  There was a row of three targets in a chained off area.  Lieutenant Michael entered the area and hung a picture of a beetle on the center target and then returned to the firing line.  He picked up the gun and let Valerie see it again. He said, "Okay, Valerie, see this little switch here.  This is your firing mode selector.  See this little picture of a single bullet?"  Valerie nodded her head.

Lieutenant Michael then continued, "This picture represents single fire mode which means that if you pull the trigger you will only fire one bullet.  The other mode, which is represented by the picture of the three bullets right here, represents full-auto mode.  This means that if you hold down the trigger, it will keep firing bullets automatically until you let go."

Lieutenant Michael then showed her how to load bullets into the clip and also how to load the clip into the base of the gun.  He moved the firing mode selector to the single bullet mode, brought the gun to his shoulder, and fired at the picture of the beetle.  The gun made a heavy ku-thunk sound as it fired a bullet.

Valerie said, "Wow, that was a lot quieter than I thought it would be.  I was expecting a loud bang like in the movies."

Lieutenant Michael lowered the gun, removed the clip, and emptied the chamber, saying, "Well, first thing is to forget everything you've seen in movies about guns.  The second is that those guns use bullets that are explosion propelled.  This gun here fires bullets that are magnetically propelled.  But don't tell anybody about it because this gun is classified knowledge.  Want to try it now?"

Valerie looked at Mary who nodded her head.  She looked at Sarah, who also nodded, and patted her on the back as well.  Valerie stepped forward and held out her hands.

She stepped up to the firing line, loaded the clip into the base of the gun like Lieutenant Michael showed her, and double checked the firing mode selector. Lieutenant Michael stood behind her and helped her to line up the sight with the target.  He placed a hand on the butt of the gun and another hand right above where Valerie put her own hand.  He then said, "Okay, Valerie, pull the trigger when you are ready."

Lieutenant Michael could feel Valerie's little body tremble as she stared down the barrel of the gun.  She hesitated pulling the trigger.  He whispered into her ear from behind, saying, "It's okay, Valerie, it won't hurt you, I'm right here helping you."

Valerie sighed and said, "Okay, here I go." Again, she re-aligned her sight and stared down the barrel trying to focus on the picture of the beetle. She pulled the trigger and the gun pushed into her shoulder with a loud ku-thunk. The bullet completely missed the target and rammed into the brick wall behind it.

Lieutenant Michael let go of the gun and stood up, saying, "So, how'd you like it."

Valerie removed the clip and cleared the chamber, saying, "It was not as bad as I thought it would be. My shoulder feels funny, but it doesn't really hurt."

Lieutenant Michael said, "So, do you want to keep using it?"

Valerie replied, saying, "Well, like you said, I don't know what I'm going to need, so, I'll keep practicing with it in case I do need it." Valerie reloaded her gun and proceeded to practice firing at the picture of the beetle. With each shot, Valerie learned how to correct her aim. Lieutenant Michael would look at her form and give her a few pointers when he felt that she needed it.

In the third week of Valerie's training, they teamed up with Lieutenant Rachel's squad and performed mock battles against one another. It was more like a game of capture the flag then an actual battle, but things did tend to get heated between Mary and Giana again. At one point, they activated their powers and started to fight again until Lieutenant Michael yelled at them to stop, which they begrudgingly did.

On the Friday of the third week, after the day's training was complete, a knock came to the door. Lieutenant Michael went to open the door as the girls sat there watching TV. He opened the door and Captain Faust was standing there. He saluted the Captain, saying, "Good evening sir, would you like to come in?"

Captain Faust nodded and said, "Certainly, Lieutenant Snyder." He then shook his hand as he entered into the apartment.

Mary looked behind her to see who it was. She turned off the TV, jumped up, and said, "It's Captain Faust!" She rushed over to Lieutenant Michael's side and said, "Hello Captain."

Captain Faust patted her head and smiled, saying, "Hello Mary. You've had quite the vacation. Are you ready to go back to the field?"

Mary saluted him and said, "Yes, sir. I got a few scores to settle out there." She wrapped her arms around Lieutenant Michael's arm as they stood there chatting.

Sarah also got up and stood next to Mary, saying, "Hello Captain." She gave a slight bow and curtsy as she spoke. The Captain also patted her head and said, "Hello Sarah. Are you also ready to go back out in the field?" Sarah sighed and said, "I guess so." The Captain patted her on the back and said, "That's good to hear. We need you out there."

Valerie quickly followed behind Sarah and stood next to her in front of the Captain. Valerie said, "Hello Captain." She then gave an informal salute.

Captain Faust stepped forward and said, "Valerie, I've come to see you tonight, my dear. Can we sit at your table?" Valerie nodded her head and moved to sit at the table. Lieutenant Michael sat down next to her and the Captain sat down in front of her. Mary and Sarah moved to stand at ease behind Lieutenant Michael.

The Captain leaned forward and rested his arms on the table. He smiled at Valerie again and said, "Valerie, I heard that you went through your training very well. Do you feel that you are ready for field duty now?"

Valerie began to swing her legs in the chair. She held onto the seat with both of her hands, and said, "Well, I ... I guess I am. Lieutenant Michael said I got all the basics down good. I suppose I won't ever be truly ready till I actually get out there and try it."

Captain Faust then said, "Are you scared?"

Valerie looked downward as she thought for a moment, still swinging her feet in nervousness. After a moment she said, "Yes, I am. But I believe I can trust my life with the Lieutenant and Mary and Sarah."

Captain Faust nodded his head and said, "I'm glad to hear you say that. The trust that you have is what's going to keep you going out there. I learned that for myself as well. It's okay to be scared, but remember that your teammates will be there for you. Will you remember that for me?"

Valerie stopped swinging her feet and looked straight into the Captain's face and said with a nod, "I will remember, Captain."

The Captain sat up straight and placed his hands in his lap and said, "Good, starting on Sunday morning at midnight your unit will be on active duty again. I want you to always be alert in the field and I want you girls to watch out for each other. I don't want a single one of you lost to those monsters outside the walls. Since your unit is newly revived, I will also assign Phoenix Guard unit four as your backup unit until Valerie is situated in the field. For the time being they will go with you till Valerie is used to deployment."

Lieutenant Michael nodded and said, "Yes, sir. Thank you sir."

Captain Faust said, "Well that's all I have to say to you for today." He stood up and Lieutenant Michael stood up after him. Captain Faust walked over to Valerie and shook her hand saying, "Welcome to the Phoenix Guard as a full-fledged Wielder, Valerie." He then let her hand go and said, "Would it be alright if I hugged you?"

Valerie nodded her head and the Captain leaned over and hugged her saying, "I'm proud of you, Valerie. Keep doing a good job like you've been doing and you'll be okay." He hugged Mary and Sarah as well and said to each one of them, "Make sure you look after Valerie for me, okay." Both Mary and Sarah said together, "We will, Captain."

Captain Faust then shook Lieutenant Michael's hand again and said, "I'm counting on you Lieutenant Snyder!" Lieutenant Michael saluted him again and said, "You can count on me sir." He opened the door for the Captain and softly closed it behind him.

Lieutenant Michael looked at his watch and said, "Girls, Magical Girl Squad is about to start. Why don't you turn the TV back on again and watch it?"

Valerie began to jump up and down shouting, "It's time, it's time!" The three of them ran down to the couch and jumped on it. Mary took the remote and turned on the TV again, changing it to the right channel. She called out to Lieutenant Michael, saying, "Lieutenant, can we have some popcorn tonight?"

Lieutenant Michael headed into the kitchen and said, "Of course, it will be a few minutes, girls."

Mary then called out, "Since Valerie is now officially a Phoenix Guardian, we should celebrate with some beers."

Lieutenant Michael laughed and said, "Sorry, you girls are too young for beers."

Mary said, "Those rules shouldn't apply to us, we're never going to be old enough to drink beer."

Lieutenant Michael said, "Well, that may be true, but rules are rules. I will let you girls have some root beer though."

Sarah then said, "If we have vanilla ice cream, can I have a root beer float?"

Lieutenant Michael opened the freezer, pulled a bucket of vanilla ice cream out, and said, "Yes, we have it, do all of you want root beer floats?"

Valerie raised her hand from behind the couch and shouted, "I do! I do!"

Mary crossed her arms and said, "Well, if you won't let me have a beer, I guess I'll settle for a root beer float."

Lieutenant Michael said, "That's more like it. Even if I allowed you to drink beer, Mary, we don't have any since I don't drink it myself." He prepared three root beer floats without any other arguments as the popcorn was popping in the microwave.

TEARS
OF
DARKNESS

CHAPTER
# 02
TRIAL BY FIRE

- 1 -

The next morning, after breakfast, Valerie sat at the vidcom in the corner of the dining area. It had been three weeks since she had last seen her parents. She was afraid that, if she facetimed them, she would feel sad all over again. The first time was hard enough. She sat there for five minutes staring at a blank screen before Lieutenant Michael came over to her, saying, "Valerie, do you not know how to use a vidcom?"

Valerie shook her head and hid her hands between her thighs. She slouched forward and whispered, "I'm afraid that, if I facetime them, I'll feel sad like I did when I left them."

Lieutenant Michael nodded his head in understanding. Placing a hand on her shoulder, he said, "I can understand that. You don't have to facetime them if you don't want too. But, I think that it is important to do it even if it makes you sad. Think about how sad your parents would be if they never got to see or hear from you again. It's up to you, but I think you'll feel guilty if you don't."

Valerie, thought for a moment and then nodded her head, saying, "You're right, Lieutenant. I think I would feel worse if I didn't facetime them." She brought her hands up to the vidcom and turned it on. Lieutenant Michael rubbed the top of her head and walked away from her to give her privacy.

Valerie pulled a slip of paper out of her jacket pocket and unfolded it. On the paper was written, in the Lieutenant's handwriting, the number to her parents' vidcom. She closed her eyes and exhaled. She then re-opened her eyes and touched the numbers listed on the screen. It rang once, twice, three times, and then the screen came to life with the image of a woman, her mother.

In recognition, her mother called out, saying, "Valerie, hi … Dear it's Valerie on the phone." Shortly thereafter both her parents' faces were visible on the screen. Her dad said at the sight of her, "Hey Val, you sure look more mature now that you're wearing that uniform."

Valerie nodded her head and said, "Well, now that I'm complete with my training, I am officially a Wielder. I'd say the training has made me more grown up now."

Her mother said, "Those colors look really good on you, Hon."

Valerie ran her hands along the yellow stripes on the front of her jacket, and said, "Thanks, Mom, but we all wear the same uniform except for the color bars. So it's nothing special."

Her dad then said, "How is the military treating you?"

Valerie looked at Lieutenant Michael off screen and smiled. She then turned back to her parents, saying, "The Lieutenant is really nice to me. He makes sure that I got everything I need and he was the one who trained me. They gave me my own room and I've got my own toilet and shower. I even get an allowance!"

Her dad nodded and said, "Well, that's good then. I can't tell you enough how proud your mom and I are of you. We know that we're safer with you protecting us."

Her mother then said, "Are you making any friends?"
Valerie nodded her head with a smile and said, "Yes, I am. I'm friends with Mary and Sarah in my squad. It's really great because they like Magical Girl Squad too. Mary gave me that Asteria costume dress that I've always wanted. We train together and do exercises. We get to go places together too. We have lots of fun in our free time. How are you two doing?"

Her mother tried to hide the grief on her face and said, "Well, it's lonely without you. We're still getting used to the idea that you aren't here anymore. But, like your dad said, we're both really proud of what you're doing. You don't need to worry about us."

Her dad interrupted her and said, "Yes, that's right Val, don't worry about us at all. We're going to be just fine. Just focus on doing what you have to do. Feel free to facetime us whenever you want too."

Valerie said, "Okay, I'm not worried anymore. I was afraid of facetiming you because I thought it would make me sad to see you. But, Lieutenant Michael helped me to not be afraid. I do miss you still. Tomorrow is my first day on active duty. I can be sent out into the field now that my training is complete."

Her mother turned away from the screen so that her face could not be seen. Valerie assumed that she was hiding tears that she didn't want her daughter to see. Her dad put his hand on the screen as if to touch her and said, "Well, we've got to go now, we've got some business to take care of. But, just remember that we love you and are proud of you."

Her mother turned back around in spite of her red eyes and also put her hand on the screen, saying, "Yes, we love you Val."

Valerie put her hand on the screen between the images of their hands and said, "I love you too and I'll talk to you later." She tapped the vidcom hang up button and the screen went back to its homepage. She then leaned back in her chair and sighed, dropping her hands beneath the sides of her chair.

Lieutenant Michael walked back to her when he saw that she was done. He put a hand on her shoulder again and said, "Are you okay Valerie?"

Valerie stood up and wrapped her arms around his waist. He wrapped his own arm around her back and hugged her. She said, "I'm okay. I think it was actually harder on my parents than it was on me."

Lieutenant Michael replied, saying, "Well, I'm glad that you're okay. The first time is always the hardest, for both you and your parents. Next time it will be easier and now you know you can do it with no problem." Valerie let him go, so Lieutenant Michael released her as well.

Mary and Sarah were sitting in the two recliners in the living room waiting for her to finish her facetime call. Mary was rubbing her stomach as she digested the pancake breakfast that she had just finished eating. Sarah lay in the other recliner with her hands behind her head resting her feet.

Lieutenant Michael approached them. Valerie jumped onto the couch sitting down in the middle. Lieutenant Michael stood there with his hands squared on his hips, saying, "Well girls, since today is the last day of our non-active duty, why don't we go do some shopping. We can get stuff so we can have a dinner party tonight."

Mary and Sarah perked up. Mary sat straight up in the recliner and said, "Shopping!" Sarah sat straight up in her chair and said, "Dinner party!" Lieutenant Michael nodded with a smile, "That's right we can go shopping for a special dinner tonight."

Mary jumped out of her chair in front of him, clasped her hands together, and said with a large expectant grin, "Can we go shopping for swimsuits too?" Lieutenant Michael shook his head and said, "Well, maybe not today."

Mary pouted her lips and said with a sad face, "But it's almost summer and my swimsuit is getting too small for me."

Lieutenant Michael said, "Well, if that's true we can go swimsuit shopping at a later time. For now let's just go shopping for food."

Mary began to smile mischievously again. She stroked her chin and said, "Why not now? Would you rather I wear a swimsuit that's too tight on me? Is that what you really want to see?"

Lieutenant Michael shook his head and sighed, saying, "Mary, how many times do I have to tell you to not say stupid stuff like that before you'll listen?"

Mary shrugged her hands and said, "Don't get all mad, Lieutenant, I was just joking again."

Lieutenant Michael rolled his eyes and exhaled deeply with a sigh again, saying, "Anyway, should we have a pizza party or do you girls have something else in mind?"

This time Valerie jumped up from her seat, shouting, with both hands in the air, "Pizza! Pizza! I want pizza! It's for me anyway, right?" She jumped up and down where she stood.

Lieutenant Michael clapped and rubbed his hands together, saying, "Pizza it is! Let's get going then." He turned to Sarah and said, "Sarah, would you be so kind as to get our shopping bags for us please?"

Sarah nodded her head and went into the kitchen. She opened a cabinet underneath the sink and pulled out a cloth bag that had other cloth bags in it. She then handed it to Michael, who took it. He rubbed her on the head, saying, "Thank you, Sarah." Sarah gave a big smile and said, "You're welcome, Lieutenant."

As they left the apartment, Lieutenant Rachel, who was wearing only a bikini, and her three wielders, who were wearing long shirts over their swimsuits, opened up their own door and came out. Lieutenant Michael smiled at Rachel, saying, "Good morning, Lieutenant Rachel, I think you're forgetting something?"

Lieutenant Rachel shrugged her shoulders and said, "What? We're just going to the pool."

Lieutenant Michael held up his cloth bags and said, "Never mind. We're just going shopping for food."

Mary wrapped her arms around Lieutenant Michael's right arm and sneered at Lieutenant Rachel, saying, "The Lieutenant is going to take me to get a new swimsuit. I asked him to help me pick one out that looks good on me."

Lieutenant Rachel glanced at Michael and said, "How nice of you." Lieutenant Michael shook his head and said, "Mary, quit lying. I said we could get you a new swimsuit another day."

Mary began to pout her lips and to give him puppy dog eyes, saying, "But ... but, Lieutenant ..."

Lieutenant Michael shook his head again and said, "Don't be unreasonable, Mary."

Mary stood there and stared at him with a less sad face, but still looked disappointed.

Giana laughed and said, "Admit it, Mary. Your old swimsuit is just fine. You are just jealous of my new swimsuit."

Mary waved her off and said, "Who'd be jealous of a sea cow like you." She cupped her hands over her mouth and said, "Moooooo!"

Lieutenant Michael interrupted her, rolling his eyes, saying, "Geez, it's still too early in the morning for you two to get into a fight again. Come on, girls. Let's get going." He placed his hand on Lieutenant Rachel's bare shoulder and said, "Have fun at the pool. Next time, let's go together."

Lieutenant Rachel smiled and said, "Lieutenant, are you asking me out on a date?"

Lieutenant Michael ran his hand through his hair and shrugged his shoulders, saying, "Well, I meant with both our squads."

Lieutenant Rachel said, "Oh, I see. Well, that's fine too. See you later then."

Lieutenant Michael smiled and nodded saying, "Okay, see you later." He turned away and said to the girls, "Okay, girls. Let's roll!" He waved his hand in the direction of the stairway.

As Lieutenant Michael walked away with Mary holding onto his arm again, Mary turned her head around, stuck out her tongue at Giana, and blew a raspberry at her." Giana frowned at her. She raised her right fist and shook it at Mary.

Mary smiled with victory and turned her head forward again.

Giana crossed her arms across her chest and said, "That Lieutenant Michael is pretty dense isn't he."

A slight look of disappointment fell upon Lieutenant Rachel's face as she said, "Well, we've been friends for so long that he probably doesn't notice me like that anymore."

The Phoenix Guard Complex was located on a street nearby the local shopping district. It was about a twenty minute walk from the complex to the shopping district.

Mary continued to cling on to Lieutenant Michael's arm as they walked down the street. Sarah and Valerie walked behind them linking each other's arms together. Sarah hummed a tune as they walked.

Lieutenant Michael was lost in thought as Mary continued to babble on about what happened on the latest episode of Magical Girl Squad. He would occasionally mumble, "That sounds cool," and "Interesting." Mary said, "Hey, Lieutenant, are you really listening to me?"

Lieutenant Michael replied, "I am."

Mary said, "Don't you think that's a great plot twist? It turned out that the evil power was being controlled by the magic kingdom itself. The magic king was using the evil power to trick the good people of the kingdom. My mind was blown when I found that out!"

Lieutenant Michael dispassionately said, "Yes, I would never have thought of that before."

Suddenly Mary stopped and let go of Lieutenant Michael's arm. He stopped walking and turned to see what she was doing. Mary's face was plastered onto the glass pane of a clothing store. Her hands rested on the glass. Her breath fogged up the glass in front of her. She sighed heavily. Lieutenant Michael said, "Come on, Mary. You know we can't go in there today."

Mary turned around and pouted her lips, looking at him with even sadder eyes, saying, "But, but, but Lieutenant, we're already here. Can't we just take a moment to check out some new swimsuits? I promise not to take long. I already know what I want."

Valerie cupped her hand over Sarah's ear and whispered, saying, "Watch this." She let go of Sarah's arm and walked up to Lieutenant Michael. She tugged on his jacket arm, pouted her lips, and looked up at him with sad eyes. She said, "Lieutenant, to be honest, I don't have a swimsuit at all. I really want to go swimming, but, I can't, because I don't have one." Lieutenant Michael rubbed his forehead and exhaled loudly.

Sarah walked up to him next and put her hands up together. She gazed at him with sad eyes too, saying, "Please, Lieutenant. Can't we just get swimsuits today? We never know when our last time to swim together could be."

Valerie's eyes began to get teary and her lower lip began to quiver. She said, "But Lieutenant, I thought you said that we should do everything together as a team. We haven't gone swimming yet as a team."

Lieutenant Michael looked upward and rubbed his face in frustration with both of his hands. He then exhaled loudly again and looked back at them. They all stood there next to each other, clasping their begging hands together. Their faces smiled with hopeful expectation.

Lieutenant Michael gave in and said, "Alright, alright, alright! We can get you three some new swimsuits today. Please, just, for the love of God, stop with the puppy dog faces."

Lieutenant Michael opened the door of the store and the three girls walked in. The three of them put their hands together and jumped for joy with girlish squeals. As they passed him, he said, "I'm glad to see that you girls work so well with each other now."

Mary, Sarah, and Valerie ran off together to the swimsuit section. Lieutenant Michael slowly trailed behind them with his hands shoved into his pockets. Mary smiled big at Valerie and gave her a thumbs up. Valerie nodded in understanding, saying, "You're welcome."

Lieutenant Michael slumped down in a chair in the corner of the store. He tossed the cloth bag he was carrying underneath his seat. He crossed his arms over his chest and silently watched as the three girls began to rummage through the different swimsuits. He thought to himself, *Geez, those girls, three against one isn't fair.*

Mary searched through the two-piece bikini section. She stopped sliding hangers aside as her eyes fell upon a red and black swimsuit. She smiled and held it up in her hands to get a better look. It was a bikini top with a skirt bottom. The left cup was black and the right cup was red with matching strings that would tie behind the wearer's neck. The skirt was short with a red-black plaid pattern.

Mary ran to Sarah and held the swimsuit on the hanger in front of her own body, saying, "I found it! What do you think of this?"

Sarah looked at the suit and thought for a moment. She said, "I think that'd be really cute on you." Sarah then held up a light-blue one piece swimsuit with a short white skirt in front of herself, saying, "What do you think of this one?"

Mary looked at her for a moment, and then said, "That's really cute too! It matches your eyes."

While they were talking together, Valerie was still looking through swimsuits in her own size. While she looked, Mary and Sarah walked up to her with the swimsuits that they chose for themselves.

Mary and Sarah held up their selected swimsuits in front of their bodies. Valerie stopped looking at the swimsuit rack and looked at Mary and Sarah's choices. Valerie nodded and said, "Those look like a really good match for both of you."

Sarah said, "Do you want help looking for something?"

Valerie said, "I was hoping to find one with butterflies on it."

Mary and Sarah looked at each other and nodded, saying, "Leave it to us!" They each went to a rack and began looking for a swimsuit with butterflies on it that might fit her.

After a few minutes Sarah called out, saying, "I found one!" She ran over to Valerie and held it up. It was a regular one piece swimsuit. It was pure white and had images of rainbow colored butterflies rising along the front.

Valerie held it up and said, "Oh my gosh! This is exactly what I wanted!" She hugged Sarah with excitement.

Mary came over and looked at it too. She nodded, while stroking her chin, saying, "Yep, that definitely has Valerie written all over it." Mary said, "Let's try them on now!"

Together they walked over to the single dressing room that was in the store. It was empty. Mary said, "Why don't we all try it on together and see how we all look at the same time?"

Mary walked up to the lady attendant and said, "Hello, we'd like to try these on now together."

The attendant smiled and said, "Certainly, officer." She opened the door for them and the three of them walked into the moderately sized changing room.

Valerie stood there and stared at the door as Mary and Sarah began to take off their Wielder uniforms. She said, "She called you an officer?"

Mary continued to undress and said, "Of course. We are officers in the military. They also call us Guardians out of respect sometimes too."

Valerie said, "Wow, I wasn't expecting that." She began to undress and put on her swimsuit.

The three of them stood in front of the mirror and admired the new swimsuits. Mary said, "Well, I think it looks good on me."

Sarah said, "I agree, and on me as well."

Valerie said, "Yep, those match you two really well."

Sarah said, "That looks good on you too, Valerie."

Mary held out her fist with a thumb's up and said, "Yep, it's super cute. Now we need the Lieutenant's opinion." Mary opened the door of the dressing room and said to the attendant waiting outside, "We'll be right back. We need to show our Lieutenant." The attendant nodded and said, "Certainly, officer."

Mary ran ahead with Sarah and Valerie trailing behind her. She stopped running when she reached Lieutenant Michael. Sarah and Valerie stopped behind her. Sarah stood there with her arms behind her back. Valerie clasped her hands together in front of her chest and held them there in embarrassment. Mary lifted her head up in an air of pride. She placed her right hand behind her head, her other hand on her hip, and struck a pose, saying, "So, Lieutenant, What-cha think of this swimsuit?"

Lieutenant Michael took a quick glance at the swimsuit and dispassionately said, "It's fine."

Mary dropped her hands to her side and balled them into fists. With frustration she said, "Lieutenant, you're not supposed to tell a lady her outfit is just fine!"

Lieutenant Michael, in the same dispassionate tone, said, "Eh, whatever. What am I supposed to say then?"

Mary squared her arms on her hips and said in an arrogant tone, "You're supposed to say that the outfit is the most beautiful thing ever, or something like that."

Lieutenant Michael shrugged his shoulders, stood up, and said with fake passion, "Well girls, those are wonderful swimsuits. I think they match each one of you perfectly and they are very cute. Now go change back into your uniform and I'll buy them for you."

Mary turned her head to the side and said, "Humph." She stormed off back to the changing room relaxing her attitude as she approached the attendant again. Sarah and Valerie followed her into the changing room.

Valerie said, "I don't think the Lieutenant cared too much about our choices."

Mary took off the swimsuit and said, "Are you kidding me? He was acting aloof on purpose."

Valerie took off the swimsuit she chose and said, "Aloof? What does that word mean?"

Mary said, "Aloof means that you pretend to not care about something even though you do care."

Valerie put her dress on again and said, "Why would the Lieutenant pretend to not care?"

Mary finished buttoning her dress jacket and said, "Because he's trying to balance between being our protective guardian, with being our military commander too. You see, when Lieutenant Rachel hit on him this morning ..."

Valerie looked surprised and said, "Lieutenant Rachel hit the Lieutenant?"

Mary gave a frustrated laugh and rubbed the top of Valerie's head, saying, "Ah! You are sooo cuuute! I don't mean she really hit him, I mean that she tried to get him to think about going on a date with her."

Understanding fell upon Valerie's face and she said, "Oh, I see."

Mary continued and said, "The Lieutenant knew that I might get upset by what she said so he tried to play it off acting like it was nothing. That's the Lieutenant acting as a protective guardian. When I asked him about my swimsuit he acted like it was nothing. That was the Lieutenant trying to act like a military commander to try to balance what happened with Lieutenant Rachel."

Valerie looked confused and said, "I don't get it, but you seem to."

Mary shrugged her shoulders and said, "That's okay, I am an adult now ..."

Sarah butted into the conversation, saying, "You're only thirteen and a half."

Mary pointed at Sarah and said, "Hey, I'm almost fourteen and I'm as adult as any of us are going to be."

Sarah said, "Let me see if I can make this easier to understand, Valerie. The Lieutenant is afraid of getting too close to anyone so he pretends to not care about stuff. The truth is that he really does care though and wants us all to be happy. That's all you need to know"

Valerie nodded and said, "I think I get it now. He wants both Lieutenant Rachel and Mary to be happy."

Mary said, "Yep, that sounds good enough. Let's get these swimsuits to the Lieutenant so he can buy them." Sarah and Valerie nodded their heads in agreement and the three of them walked up to Lieutenant Michael with their new swimsuits in their hands.

Lieutenant Michael took the swimsuits and looked at the prices on the tag. His eyes opened wide and his mouth dropped open. He said, "Mary, how is this swimsuit one hundred dollars while Sarah's and Valerie's are about fifty dollars?! It has less fabric then both of them! I don't get how girl's clothing works."

Mary shrugged her shoulders and said, "I don't know. Maybe because it's meant for adults? I'm an adult now so I need an adult swimsuit."

Lieutenant Michael dropped his hands to his sides while still holding onto the swimsuits. He looked at Mary and said, "I know you know Mary that there is a hundred and fifty dollar limit on extra clothing. All of this together is going to be over two hundred dollars. They're not going to pay for this."

Sarah held out her hand and said, "That's okay, Lieutenant, I don't really need a new swimsuit."

Lieutenant Michael ignored her offer and said, "I'll tell you what, since you really seem to like it, I'll pay for this out of my own pocket. I'll charge Sarah's and Valerie's to the government and I'll pay for this one myself as a gift for you. It is a nice swimsuit after all."

Mary smiled big and threw her arms around his torso, saying, "Thank you, Lieutenant!" He patted her on the back and said, "Sure, no problem."

Lieutenant Michael went up to the register with the girls trailing behind him. Mary swayed side to side and smiled in glee as she waited for the transaction to finish. Lieutenant Michael then handed her a small bag with her new swimsuit in it. He stuck the other bag with the other swimsuits into the cloth bag he was carrying. He said, "Okay, girls! Let's get back on track."

They left the clothing store and continued on their way to the grocery store. Mary wrapped her arm around Lieutenant Michael's arm. She had a huge grin on her face. Sarah and Valerie linked arms with each other and followed behind Lieutenant Michael and Mary.

As they walked, Valerie began to notice that people were staring at her, not just her, but all four of them. She thought she could see a hint of fear in their eyes. *But why would they be afraid of us? I thought that Mary said they respected us?* She thought to herself. *Maybe we are a reminder of the constant danger over the walls?* Valerie looked into the distance to see the dark shape of the wall on the horizon that protected the city.

Valerie's thoughts were interrupted by Lieutenant Michael, saying, "Here we are, girls. Before we start, we should decide what kind of pizza we want to make."

Mary let go of his arm, raised her hands in the air, and loudly said, "Pepperoni!"

Sarah let go of Valerie's hand, raised her fists up to her chest excitedly, and said, "I want olives!"

Lieutenant Michael turned to Valerie and said, "Well, Valerie, looks like you can break a tie."

Valerie slumped her shoulders and began to look worried.  Lieutenant Michael said, "What's wrong?  Why'd you get so depressed?"

Valerie said, "I ... I ... I want mushrooms on my pizza."

Lieutenant Michael ran his hand over his head and said, "Well, I guess we're just going to have to make three pizzas now aren't we?"

Valerie straightened up and smiled, saying, "Really?"

Lieutenant Michael nodded his head and said, "Sure, it's not like I'm paying for it.  Plus, it's your welcome party after all.  Maybe we should invite Squad four to our little party too?"

Valerie nodded and said, "That sounds like a good idea."

Together they entered the store and headed down different isles picking up needed supplies.  Valerie watched the people around her.  Again, they appeared to be staring at her and the others.  She could sense fear coming from them again.  *Why would they be so afraid?*  This thought kept coming into her mind.  It began to bother her.

As Lieutenant Michael was picking up the last item, Valerie walked over to him and held onto the sleeve of his uniform jacket.  She continued to watch the people around her.  He looked down and said, "Valerie, what's wrong?"

Valerie looked up at him.  He could see the worry that was on her face.  She continued to look up at him in silence.  Sarah linked arms with her again and said, "What's wrong?"

Lieutenant Michael leaned over and said, "Remember, Valerie, you can tell me anything.  I won't get mad at you.  I promise."

Valerie spoke to him quietly so that other people couldn't hear her, "Lieutenant, why do lots of people look at us like they are afraid of us?"

A look of confusion fell on his face.  He stood up and looked around himself.  He scratched the top of his head and said, "Well, actually, I've never thought of that before."

Sarah said, "I've noticed that too, but I don't think they are afraid of us.  Underneath their respect toward us is a small layer of fear.  I think they are afraid of what we represent.  I think we are a reminder that there are monsters out there that want to kill them. "

Lieutenant Michael stroked his chin and said, "Well, that makes sense to me.  What do you think of that answer Valerie?"

Valerie let go of his uniform jacket and said, "That was my thought too."

Mary got into a fighting stance and held a fist up, saying, "Don't worry about them, Val.  If they give you any problems, I'll kick their butts for you!"

Lieutenant Michael waved his hand toward Mary and said, "Alright, calm down there Mary. We're all done here so let's go pay for these and then head back home." The three girls each nodded. Mary held out her arm and gave him a thumbs up.

As they walked up to the register, an old man in front of them turned toward them and smiled. He said, "Hello there, Guardians!"

Mary smiled and said, "Hello, sir."

The old man then said, "I just wanted to thank you girls for all your hard work. When the wall breach occurred last year you saved my family."

Mary said, "Oh yes, I remember that incident. You're welcome."

The man smiled again and went up to the register. Mary leaned over to Valerie and whispered into her ear, "See, Val. Most people appreciate us." Valerie nodded her head with a smile.

When they returned to the Phoenix Guard Complex, they began to walk up the stairs to their floor. As they walked up to the second floor, Lieutenant Michael stopped, and said, "While we're here, why don't we invite Squad four now. They did say that they'll be in the pool." Lieutenant Michael opened the door before anybody could answer him.

The indoor pool was built inside a raised platform that was four feet high. Beyond the pool, Valerie could see a small basketball court. On the other side there was a small area that had what looked like the older style arcade games.

Lieutenant Michael walked up to the edge of the platform. Giana noticed him first and raised her hand high, waving it, and yelling, "Hello, Lieutenant Michael!" Lieutenant Rachel, who was swimming in the opposite direction, stopped, and turned around to see him. She then swam toward him, lifted herself out of the water, and sat down on the edge of the platform. She ran her hands over her head and smiled, saying, "Did you decide to join us after all?"

Lieutenant Michael couldn't help but notice the olive green bikini that she was wearing. He awkwardly watched her body as she pulled herself out of the water. His eyes went to the familiar scar that ran across her stomach.

Sarah leaned over to Mary and whispered into her ear, "He's totally ogling Lieutenant Rachel again. Aren't you going to say something?"

Mary crossed her arms, scrunched her face, and quietly said, "He bought me this new swimsuit, so, I will let it go for today."

Lieutenant Michael composed himself and said, "Well, we're going to be having pizza for dinner tonight. Sort of a welcome party for Valerie. We just wanted to invite your squad too, since we're going to be working together after all."

Giana, Tina, and Elsa swam over. Lieutenant Rachel said, "You girls want pizza tonight?"

Giana gave her a thumbs up. Tina shrugged her shoulders and said in her melancholy voice, "I guess." Elsa nodded her head and smiled. Lieutenant Rachel then turned back to Michael and said, "Sure, sounds like fun."

Lieutenant Michael gave a quick nod and said, "Excellent, why don't you ladies come by around eighteen hundred tonight and we can have some fun with pizza."

Lieutenant Rachel smiled and said, "Sounds good!" She stood up, adjusted her bikini top, turned around, and dove back into the water. Lieutenant Michael watched her as she jumped off the platform. He then turned around and walked out of the room with Mary, Sarah, and Valerie following behind him back to their apartment.

Later that day, Lieutenant Michael and the girls made the pizzas together. Lieutenant Michael rolled out the pre-made dough and spread the sauce on them. Mary grated the mozzarella cheese. The three girls then put the toppings they chose on their own pizza. He put them in the oven and set the timer. Soon enough, the timer went off, and three freshly made pizzas were cooling on the table.

A knock came to the door. Mary ran to answer it and quickly opened the door. She bowed gracefully and said sarcastically, "Welcome to my abode. Please come in and enjoy yourselves."

Tina walked in first, shrugged her shoulders and said in her melancholy tone, "Hey." Elsa followed behind her and gave her a two-fingered salute, saying, "Thanks!"

Before Giana and Lieutenant Rachel could walk in, Mary slammed the door shut, and walked away. Lieutenant Michael said, "Mary, that was very rude! Let them in too."

Mary put a hand on her hip and held her hand out, saying, "Oh, I'm sorry. I didn't think they were invited." She went back to the door and opened it, saying, "I'm sorry. I didn't know you two were coming."

Giana stood there in the doorway. She had squared her arms on her hips and was tapping her foot with an annoyed look on her face. She said, "You're only mad because you wanted to pig all the food for yourself! You don't need to worry, you cow. I don't eat as much as you do."

Mary stepped aside and waved them in, saying, "Please, do come in and make yourselves at home."

Giana stormed passed her, while Lieutenant Rachel rubbed the top of her head and said, "Thanks, little girl."

Mary brushed Lieutenant Rachel's hand off of her head and said, "I'm almost fourteen. I'm a lady now, not a little girl."

Lieutenant Michael reached out toward Mary and said, "Please, Mary, that's enough joking around for tonight. Let's just have fun."

Mary shut the door and said, "Fine, I'll be good today since you bought me that swimsuit."

Lieutenant Rachel looked at Michael and said, "So, you ended up buying her a new swimsuit after all."

Lieutenant Michael shrugged his shoulders and said, "Eh, I bought all of them new swimsuits. They all ganged up on me with their puppy dog eyes and I just couldn't say no. It wasn't fair."

Mary ran into her room and came back holding her new swimsuit. She held it against her body and said, "I'm mature enough for an adult swimsuit now."

Giana was about to open her mouth but Rachel flicked her on the forehead and said, "Looks nice, Mary. It looks like it would suit you well."

Mary smiled and ran back into her room to put away her swimsuit. Lieutenant Rachel turned to Giana and pointed at her, saying quietly, "I don't want to hear any fighting tonight. Okay?"

Giana slumped her shoulders and said, "Fine, I won't get into it if she won't."

Lieutenant Rachel patted her on the head and said, "Great."

Mary returned bringing Valerie to the front with her. Mary stood behind her and placed her hands on her shoulders, saying, "Tonight, Valerie, is officially on active duty. So, I would just like to say to you, Val, welcome, and I look forward to fighting together with you."

Valerie began to look embarrassed and said, "Thank you everyone for being so welcoming to me."

Sarah gave her a thumbs up and said, "I'm glad we'll get to work together now too. Welcome to our unit."

Valerie smiled and said, "Thanks, Sarah."

Lieutenant Michael said, "Yep, we're all glad to have you with us, Valerie. Please everyone, help yourselves to pizza and soda. We can eat it in the sitting area."

As Lieutenant Michael motioned them toward the pizza, a chime began to ring in the room. A woman's voice said, "Attention, Lieutenant Snyder Third squad and Lieutenant Harris Fourth squad, please report to C.O. office. Thank you."

Lieutenant Michael dropped his hand to his side and sighed, saying, "Geez, perfect timing."

Lieutenant Rachel said, "I guess that means both of us."

Mary pointed at them and said, "What did the two of you do now?"

Lieutenant Rachel said, "We haven't done anything ... yet." She took Michael by the arm and started to pull him toward the door before Mary could respond. He let her drag him and he said as they left the apartment, "Mary, you're in charge till we get back."

Mary saluted and said, "Aye, Lieutenant!" Lieutenant Michael shut the door behind them.

Valerie stood there with a plate in her hands, holding it flat against her chest. She looked worried and said, "Do you think something's wrong?"

Mary waved the question off as she began to pile pizza slices on her plate, saying, "Nah, they're probably talking about your activation tonight. Since we'll be working with Squad four, they probably want to go over some details."

Sarah said, "Yeah, there's nothing to worry about. If there was a problem, the sirens would go off."

Valerie put some of the mushroom pizza slices on her plate and said, "Sirens? I haven't heard any sirens here before."

Giana said, "Yeah, it has been pretty quiet lately. I don't think the sirens have gone off once since you got here, Val."

Valerie looked at her and said, "What do the sirens mean?"

Giana said, "The sirens mean that we are being deployed to combat."

Mary said, "Yeah, they blow the siren and flash those red lights on the ceiling there." She pointed at a red light that sat above the door on the ceiling. Mary continued, "When the siren goes off, listen for the squad deployment request."

Sarah said, "They'll say 'Squad three deploy in ten minutes' or whatever time frame they say, but it will be like that."

Mary said, "Hey, Val, how you feel 'bout deploying?"

Valerie said, "Well ... I'm not as scared as I was when I first came."

Giana said, "You won't really know what it means to be scared till you deploy for the first time."

Valerie's face went pale and she looked down to her feet. Mary bopped Giana on the head and said, "Why'd you have to go and say that for?"

Giana held up her hands questioningly and said, "What? I'm just tellin' it like it is."

Valerie waved her hand at them to stop and said, "It's okay. I know that's true."

Mary spread her feet apart, placed a hand on her hip, and pointed toward herself with her thumb, saying, "Don't worry, Val. Just stick with me and I'll protect you so you don't need to be afraid."

Tina walked up behind Giana and smacked her on the back of the head, saying, "Quite being stupid, let's eat!"

Lieutenant Michael and Rachel walked down the stairs to the first floor where the Captain's office was located. The door was already open, waiting for them. Lieutenant Michael bowed slightly and motioned for Rachel to enter first. She walked in and saluted the Captain, saying, "Sir."

Lieutenant Michael followed behind her and then stood next to her and saluted, saying, "Yes, sir."

The Captain put down his pen and looked up at them, saying, "Thank you for coming. Please, have a seat." Lieutenant Rachel and Michael sat down in the two chairs in front of the Captain's desk. He continued, "Lieutenant Snyder and Lieutenant Harris, San Francisco sector is planning on running a wall breech drill. I have decided that this would be a good opportunity to help get Valerie situated in the field. At five in the morning, the sirens will go off and Squads three and four will deploy outside the San Francisco sector wall and defend that section."

Lieutenant Michael said, "Yes, sir. If I may ask, sir, should I tell them it is a drill?"

The Captain shook his head and said, "No, I want Valerie to feel that it is real. I want Squad three to stay in the vanguard as long as possible. Squad four will serve as rearguard. When Valerie can't take it anymore, I want Squad three to fall back behind the wall while Squad four covers your retreat. Then, when it is safe to do so, have Squad four pull out back behind the wall. Understood?"

Lieutenant Michael and Rachel said in unison, "Yes, sir."

Captain Faust said, "This may be a drill, but you will still be in danger so don't let your guard down. I don't want to lose anyone, especially on a drill."

Again, Lieutenant Michael and Rachel spoke in unison, "Yes, sir."

The Captain then said, "Okay, you two are dismissed. Have a good night, if you can."

Lieutenant Michael and Rachel stood up, saluted, and walked out of the office. As they walked back up the stairs to his apartment, Rachel said, "This is nice. It will help get Valerie used to fighting, without putting pressure on you to keep civilians safe."

Lieutenant Michael shrugged his shoulders and said, "That's true, but she'll still be in danger. There's no way around that."

Lieutenant Rachel playfully punched him in the back and said, "Don't worry, my team has you covered!"

Lieutenant Michael said, "I'm counting on it."

The rest of the evening was fun for all the girls as they ate pizza and joked around with each other. Lieutenant Michael tried to hide the heaviness that had formed on his mind. Again, he was putting these girls' lives in danger. He quickly swallowed that thought deep inside of himself and tried to hide it with a smile.

- 2 -

Valerie was sleeping soundly in her bed. She unconsciously held onto the butterfly pillow. At five in the morning, a siren began to go off. The noise of it startled Valerie out of her peaceful sleep. Valerie sat up in bed and tried to force the grogginess off of her mind. The klaxon blared for ten seconds and then went silent. A woman's voice then blared through the intercom, "Squad three, Squad four prepare for deployment, ten minutes."

Valerie jumped out of bed and quickly took off her pajamas, dropping them to the floor. She then changed into her uniform. *This is really it,* she thought to herself. The tension of her first deployment began to dawn on her.

She opened her door and saw that Sarah and Mary were already coming out of their rooms. *Of course they'd be more used to this than me,* she thought to herself.

Lieutenant Michael was at the dining table opening a pack that Valerie saw him put on the table. He said, "Okay, girls, come get your coms." Mary and Sarah walked up to him. Valerie followed their lead.

Lieutenant Michael handed Mary a small earpiece. Mary put it in her ear and pushed a small button on it. Lieutenant Michael then handed the same ear piece to Sarah, who also put it in her ear, and pushed the same button on it.

Lieutenant Michael then held up a third earpiece in front of Valerie and said, "This is your radio. It will allow you to hear everyone else and to talk to us.

Put it in your ear and push this little button." He pointed at a button that was on the ear piece.

Valerie took the earpiece and put it in her ear and pushed the button. She heard a fizzle noise and then it was clear as soon as it started.

Lieutenant Michael then put in his own earpiece and turned it on. He said, "Radio check."

Valerie heard him clear in her own earpiece. Mary said, "Red on." Valerie heard her clear in her own ear too. Sarah then said, "Blue on." Again, Valerie heard her as well. Following suit, Valerie said, "Yellow on."

Sarah then strapped on a belt that had what looked like two scabbards attached on it. Instead of swords the scabbards had straight metal sticks inside of them. Sarah pulled them out, examined them, and then put them back in the scabbard.

Lieutenant Michael held up an over the shoulder gun holster and held it up toward Valerie, saying, "Valerie, you want to bring the cattle prod?"

Valerie said, "Okay." She took the holster and put it on like a backpack. The butt of the gun rested behind her left shoulder where she could easily pull it out. Along the belt of the holster were three pouches filled with magazines for the gun affectionately known as the cattle prod. It was light and easy to carry.

Lieutenant Michael said, "Okay, girls, you ready?"

Mary and Sarah said, "Yep!" Mary shook her fist and added, "Let's go squash some bugs!" Valerie said, "I-I-I'm ready." Her voice trembled with nervousness.

Lieutenant Michael opened the door and the three girls followed him outside and up to the roof. When they got to the stairs they could see Squad four ahead of them upstairs.

On top of the roof, Squad three and four waited for a helicopter that was already approaching. Lieutenant Michael handed Mary, Sarah, and Valerie a small packet. When he handed it to Valerie, he said, "That's your breakfast." She took it and watched Mary and Sarah open the small packet and begin to eat.

Valerie opened the packet and smelled the contents inside. It smelled like a mix of cinnamon and maple syrup. She looked inside and could see that it looked like some kind of cake. It was hard to see the color as the sun had not risen yet and the lights on the roof created an odd discoloration. She bit into it and sure enough it was like eating a cake but it tasted like French toast. "It's good." She said.

The transport helicopter landed on the roof and the rear cargo door opened, lowering itself into a ramp. Inside the helicopter it looked empty except for a bench that ran along the sides.  In even spaces, seat belts were placed where they expected people to sit.

Mary sat down on the bench closest to the door and said to Valerie, "Come here and sit next to me Valerie."  Valerie nodded and sat down next to Mary.  Mary then showed her how to buckle herself in and then did the same for herself.  Sarah then sat down next to Valerie and buckled herself in.

Lieutenant Michael boarded the Helicopter and checked Mary's seat belt. He then checked Valerie's seat belt and Sarah's seat belt.  He then sat down next to Sarah and strapped himself in.

Valerie could see that Lieutenant Rachel was also checking the seat belts of the girls on her own team.  When Lieutenant Rachel finished, she sat down next to Elsa and strapped herself in.  She then gave a thumbs up to Michael who returned her gesture with his own thumbs up.

Lieutenant Michael then picked up what looked like a communication device that was attached to the wall with a cord.  He pressed a button and said, "P.G. Squad three, Squad four, ready for deployment."

A moment later the ramp of the helicopter began to lift up and a voice came over the intercom, saying, "P.G. Squad three, Squad four deployment San Francisco Sector.  Potential wall breach imminent.  Deploy outside perimeter while wall integrity investigated. ETA thirty minutes."

The lights inside the cabin of the helicopter switched to red and Lieutenant Michael spoke back into the intercom, saying, "Confirmed, Squad three, Squad four deploy San Francisco Sector.  Defend outer perimeter.  Deploy thirty minutes."

The rotors of the helicopters began to pick up speed.  The helicopter began to shake as it lifted itself off of the ground.  Lieutenant Michael spoke through the ear piece to his unit, saying, "Okay, girls, this is our first deployment. Watch each other and keep each other safe.  They want us to guard a sector of the wall while they check for a potential wall breech.  We've got to clear out the Harvesters in that area till the checks completed."

Mary and Sarah said in unison, "Understood."  Valerie followed their example and said, "Understood."

Valerie turned her attention to Squad four, who were sitting in front of her.  Giana sat next to the door and stared at Mary with an intense smile.  She balled a fist and began to pound it into her hand.  Mary gave her a thumbs up and then held up ten of her fingers.  Giana shook her head and held up five fingers. Mary then laughed and gave her a thumbs up.

It was too loud inside the helicopter to communicate effectively by speaking. So the girls on opposite teams, who could not communicate by earpiece, were forced to communicate by hand signs. Valerie looked at Mary and said, "What are you two doing?"

Mary said, "Oh we were just making a bet. No need to worry about it. We make bets like this all the time."

Another voice came over the intercom saying, "Deploy, fifteen minutes."

The nervousness that was already inside Valerie began to swell up. She gripped her hands together, placed them in her lap, and began to bounce her knees. She started breathing deeply.

Mary put a hand over Valerie's hands. Valerie loosened the grip on her own hands. Mary took one of Valerie's hands and held it in her own hand. Sarah then took the other hand and held it too. Mary spoke through the earpiece, saying, "Don't worry, Val. We're going to be with you the whole time. I'll protect you."

Valerie began to cry into the earpiece and said, "I'm sorry. I'm getting scared."

Lieutenant Michael's voice calmly came into her earpiece, saying, "It's okay to be scared, Valerie. We're going to help you through this. You're not alone. We do this all the time so we know what to do."

Valerie tried to stop crying and nodded her head, saying, "I know." She wiped the tears with her jacket sleeve. Mary and Sarah continued to hold her hands.

Another voice came over the intercom, saying, "Deploy five minutes."

There were no windows in the cargo hold. Valerie hoped that the sun was already rising. Her heart began to beat louder and louder; she thought she could hear it. Or, was it just the sound of the rotors beating? She wasn't quite sure.

Suddenly, she felt her body fall as the helicopter made its descent toward the ground rapidly. She heard the same voice say over the intercom, "Ready to deploy."

Lieutenant Michael said, "Okay, girls, this is it. Unbuckle now." Mary and Sarah said, "Roger." They began to unstrap themselves. Valerie quickly unstrapped herself. She could see the girls of Squad four talking but could not hear what they were saying.

Together both squads stood up from their seats. Lieutenant Michael said, "Okay, girls, activate." Valerie joined in unison this time, all three of them saying, "Roger."

Mary's eyes began to glow with the red light of her power. Her fists began to radiate with red light as she prepared for battle.

Sarah's eyes began to glow with blue light. She pulled out the two metal sticks that were attached to the belt on her waist. Her hands began to radiate blue light and the light covered the two sticks that she held.

Valerie activated her own power. Her eyes began to glow yellow as she felt power flow through her body.

Valerie turned her head toward Giana, Tina, and Elsa. She could tell that all three of them had activated their powers because their eyes were glowing with the light of their own colors.

A slight jolt rocked the helicopter and the cargo door ramp began to lower. When it stopped moving Lieutenant Michael motioned with his hand, saying, "Mary, scout!"

Mary and Giana walked up to the edge and stepped down the ramp. Mary and Giana stood there looking both ways. Mary's voice came into Valerie's ear, saying, "All clear."

Lieutenant Michael again motioned with his hand and said, "Squad three, deploy!" Sarah and Tina then stepped out of the helicopter, followed by Elsa and Lieutenant Rachel. Lieutenant Michael took Valerie's hand and said, "Okay, Valerie, our turn." Valerie nodded and allowed him to lead her down the ramp of the helicopter.

All eight of them stood there in a circle so that they could see around them in all directions. The helicopter ramp then lifted back up and the helicopter rose back into the sky. The sound of its rotor grew quieter as it faded away into the distance.

Together they stood there in silence. The blackened charcoal of previous fire clearings laid underneath their combat boots. The morning sun was already peeking over the hills that overlooked the wall of the San Francisco sector. There was not a Harvester in sight.

Mary said, "Looks like we're clear for now, thank goodness."

Lieutenant Michael said, "Squad four will maintain a rearguard here in this location. Squad three will move out east and act as vanguard."

Mary cocked her head and said, "What? Don't you think it'd be smarter to stay in the clearing where we can see more clearly?"

Lieutenant Michael shrugged his shoulders and said, "We got our orders, so we got to follow them."

Mary shrugged her shoulders and said, "Okay, Lieutenant, whatever you say."

Lieutenant Michael looked at Rachel and nodded his head with a smile. She nodded back and said, "Don't be gone too long. I bet the helicopter noise is going to bring some friends out real soon."

Lieutenant Michael turned eastward and said, "Mary on point. Sarah take rear position." Sarah and Mary responded saying, "Aye, Lieutenant." Mary began to walk in front and Sarah moved behind Lieutenant Michael.

Lieutenant Michael took Valerie's hand and said, "I want you to stay right next to me. Okay, Valerie?" Valerie nodded and said, "Aye, Lieutenant."

Together they began to walk away from the sector wall. Outside the wall was the ruins of a long abandoned city. The once paved roads were in bad disrepair. Huge cracks had formed in the asphalt and tall weeds and grasses grew through it. Skeletons of buildings lined the dead streets. This is what happens when a city is abandoned.

The four of them began to walk down what was once a street. Chunks of pavement were scattered all over the place and more weeds pushed through the broken streets. Valerie's eyes darted back and forth as she watched for movement among the old ruins. She could feel her heart pounding in her chest as if it would burst out.

As they continued to walk, Valerie noticed an old street sign that was once this city's welcome sign. It read, "Welcome to Fremont." The forgotten sign now lay in the rubble of asphalt. There was no one left there to welcome except for some small animals and, of course, the four of them entering the dead city.

The sun began to reach higher in the sky. Its light began to reveal the minute details of the city ruins. Birds began to fly and chirp their songs among the dead buildings. Valerie noticed a large rat scurrying over an abandoned vehicle. No one made a single noise, except for the sound of their footsteps, as they all listened for movement.

Suddenly Mary stopped in her tracks. She quickly held up a hand behind her and everybody stopped moving. Mary stood there motionless as she stared into the distance.

Lieutenant Michael whispered into the earpiece, "Mary, what do you see?"

Mary whispered back, "I think I see two half-sized bugs."

Valerie looked where Mary appeared to be looking but could not see anything. She squinted her eyes and tried to force herself to see what Mary was seeing.

Lieutenant Michael walked up beside Mary and looked in the direction that she pointed at. He could see two of the purplish-black shells that protected the back of the Harvesters.

Suddenly there was a crash and Sarah screamed, "Lieutenant!" Another half-sized Harvester crashed through the remains of a building to their left side and dashed out toward them. The beast screeched a deafening cry. The sound echoed through the ruins of the old city. In the distance, several more Harvester cries could be heard in response.

Mary, without hesitation, leapt toward the rushing Harvester. Valerie, in shock, stumbled backwards and tripped over some broken asphalt, falling onto her behind. Sarah moved in front of Valerie holding her two glowing sticks up in defense.

Mary landed right beside the Harvester's head and punched it with all her might in the side of its head. A shower of sparks erupted from where her fist hit the armored shell. The Harvester stopped rushing forward as it buckled to the side with even more loud screeches. Mary yelled out, "Let's pluck it!"

Mary then jumped in front of the Harvester again and grabbed it by the mandibles. Valerie watched Mary struggle with the Harvester as it tried to free itself from her grasp. Clear slime began to pour from its mouth as Mary held onto the mandibles.

The Harvester began pushing against Mary, whose feet started to be dragged along the ruined pavement. Sarah then ran to the side of the Harvester near the front leg on that side. She lifted her blue glowing stick and slammed it down on the leg with all her might. She grunted as she slammed the stick down on the leg over and over again until it broke off. One by one, Sarah broke off each one of its legs while Mary gripped its mandibles with her red, glowing hands.

The Harvester continued to scream in agony as it tried to shake off Mary. More clear slime dripped from its open mouth. With Sarah's work done, she ran back to be in front of Valerie. Mary let go of the now limbless creature that now struggled to rock side to side as its amputated limbs wiggled back and forth as if it could still walk with them. Mary then said, "Say hello to my thunder hammer!" She brought her right fist high up above her head and then brought it down with as much force as she could on top of the Harvesters head. Again, a shower of sparks erupted from where her red, glowing hand made contact. She repeated this attack several times until the head cracked open and yellow Harvester body fluid poured out of the cracks.

Mary brushed her hands together and turned to Valerie with a smile. She gave her a thumbs up and said, "How cool was that! I cracked it like a nut!"

Valerie stood there in shock, her body trembled from fear. Tears began to flow down Valerie's cheeks as she muttered, "I-I-I-I-I thou-thou-thought, I-I-I thought I-I-I was going to die." Valerie dropped to her knees, her head collapsed to the ground. She began to cry.

Lieutenant Michael picked her up and cradled her into his arms, saying, "It's okay, Valerie, you're okay now. We're not going to let you die." She stopped crying but her little body was still trembling in his arms. He held her for a moment.

After a minute Valerie said, "I-I-I think I'm okay now." Lieutenant Michael put her down and she stood there beside him. She composed herself and forced herself to stop trembling. She held onto Lieutenant Michael's arm for support.

Another Harvester screech could be heard nearby. The two half-sized Harvesters that Mary had spotted earlier were now running at full speed to their location after hearing the death cries of the first harvester.

Sarah put both of her sticks in her left hand and held up her right hand toward the closest Harvester. A blue spear of light poured out of her hand as she repeatedly fired it at the closest Harvester.

The Harvester tripped and rolled over on the ground. It got back up and stood there shrieking at Sarah. Sarah continued to shoot blue beams of light at the Harvester, which caused it to stop moving forward and, instead, began bucking up and down like a wild bull in circles trying to avoid the blue light beams. Mary ran toward the second Harvester that was still running toward them. She leapt up twenty feet into the air and managed to land on its back right behind its head. Mary wrapped her arms around its neck and pulled upward. The Harvester began to jump up and down as it tried to shake Mary off of its back.

Mary held on tight as it screamed and bucked up and down. Mary laughed, saying, "Hey look, Lieutenant, I'm a cowgirl now! Yee haw!" Sarah laughed as she watched Mary getting rocked back and forth as the Harvester bucked like a wild bull. Finally, Mary's hands slipped and she was thrown off of its back. She landed in a blackberry bush and yelled, "Damn it! That hurts!"

The Harvester quivered as it sensed that Mary had let go of it. It turned around in a circle a couple of times, turned toward Mary, and then began to stamp its two front legs on the ground as it made more screeching noises. Clear slime drooled from its gaping mouth.

Mary picked herself out of the blackberry bush and brushed off her dress that now had a few rips in it from the thorns. She pointed at the harvester and said, "You stupid bug! You put a couple of holes in my favorite dress!"

The Harvester ran toward her, so Mary ran toward it. Instead of crashing into each other, she jumped up into the air and landed behind it as it ran underneath her. It crashed into the ruins of a building causing the fragile structure to collapse on it. Mary then leapt at the first Harvester that Sarah was keeping at bay with her spear of light.

Mary landed on the back of that Harvester and wrapped her arms around its neck, pulling upwards. It began to screech again and rocked back and forth as it tried to shake Mary off.

The second Harvester dug itself out of the rubble it had crashed into and began to screech again. It looked at Mary who was still riding the other Harvester. It ran at the first harvester and crashed into it. Mary yelled, "Hey bug, you already had a turn. I'm playing with this one now." The second Harvester tried to climb onto the first Harvester but Mary kicked it with all her strength, causing it to fall over backward.

Mary said, "Time to finish this! This one's for Susan!" She began to pound her fist into the first Harvester's head repeatedly causing showers of sparks to fly. Finally, the armored shell cracked open and yellow Harvester goo began to spray out.

While Mary was finishing off the first Harvester, the second Harvester managed to roll over and get back on its feet. It stood there and screeched at Mary. Sarah began to fire her blue spear of light at it. It stumbled backward and shook its head from the pain.

Mary and Sarah could hear Lieutenant Michael talking to Valerie through the earpiece all of a sudden. They looked backward and saw Valerie sitting on the ground. Mary looked at Sarah and said, "Let's wrap this up before it happens." Sarah nodded and got ready to fight with her two sticks that she covered with blue light.

Mary jumped off the back of the dead harvester, squared her left arm on her hip, pointed at the living Harvester, and said, "I changed my mind, bug. I think I will play with you again!" She leapt toward the Harvester, landed next to its head, and slammed her fist against its face as hard as she could causing another explosion of sparks.

Sarah then ran up to it with her two sticks of blue light and slammed them down on top of its mandibles, which broke off in a clean cut. The Harvester began to move backward as it screeched and shook its head side to side, spilling yellow blood on the ground.

Mary said, "You want this one?"

Sarah said, "Sure, why not." Again she lifted her two sticks of blue light and slammed them over the head of the Harvester causing sparks to fly again. The hard shell cracked open revealing soft inner tissue. Again, Sarah raised her two sticks of blue light and slammed them into the opening of the shell. This time the two sticks of light sliced right through the head causing it to fall off. The decapitated Harvester ran backwards, tripped over itself, and began rolling as yellow goo poured out of its neck.

Mary and Sarah gave each other a high five as they celebrated over the severed Harvester head. Mary put a foot on top of its severed head and said, "Now that's how we do it, Val." Their celebration was interrupted by the screeching of another half-sized Harvester who had entered the scene. Mary glared at it and said, "Oh come on! Can't I take break?" Mary and Sarah moved to engage it.

Valerie watched the action from Lieutenant Michael's side. When the second and third Harvesters appeared, her knees started to feel weak. Her poor little legs began to tremble. Her body began to shake with fear again. The sound of their screeching was deafening to her. She felt like the sound of it could shatter her bones.

Tears began to flow down her cheeks again but she did not cry out. The sight of the Harvesters began to fill her with terror. The shriek of their cries was too much for her to bear. Her body lost all control of itself as she stood there and peed herself. The warm urine stained the front of her dress and flowed down her legs onto the ground. Her knees lost their strength and she collapsed onto the ground sitting on her feet. The sounds around her began to slow down and sounded as if they were far away. Then there was silence. Her vision went fuzzy and began to fade. There was nothing but darkness.

Lieutenant Michael stood there next to Valerie, as Mary and Sarah engaged the final Harvester. Out of the corner of his eye he watched her as he also kept watch over Mary and Sarah. Out of the corner of his eye he saw Valerie fall down sitting on her knees. He looked downward and said, "Valerie, can you hear me."

She sat there sitting on her feet, her hands draped on each side of her. Her face was stiff and looked expressionless. She looked like a rag doll that had been forced to sit up on itself. He could see the puddle of urine that had pooled beneath her.

Lieutenant Michael looked at his watch, put his hands on her shoulders, and said, "Valerie, can you hear me?" She remained unresponsive. He shook her and repeated, saying, "Hey, Valerie, you awake?" Again she did not respond.

Lieutenant Michael called out through the earpiece, saying, "Damn it! Girls we got black out, fall back!"

Mary and Sarah stood there watching the newest Harvester that stood there screeching at them. Mary said, "Sarah, help the Lieutenant, I'll deal with this small one quickly.

Mary stood there and watched the smaller Harvester run toward her. She braced herself and held out her hands to grab it. The Harvester ran right up to Mary and she grabbed it by the mandibles, causing her to slide along the ground a couple of feet till she steadied herself. Then, with all her might, she twisted her arms, causing it to roll over on to its back. Mary then stomped on the bottom side of the head with her foot till it cracked. Once again, yellow goo began to spill onto the ground. Mary spat on the dead Harvester and said, "That's what you get for wasting my time!" She then kicked its head again and jogged back to Lieutenant Michael.

Lieutenant Michael stood there holding Valerie in his arms. She continued to be in a catatonic state. Her eyes appeared lifeless. Sarah stood there next to him watching Mary to see if she would need back up. With the last Harvester defeated Mary jogged to Lieutenant Michael and said, "Is she okay?"

Lieutenant Michael said, "I'm sure she'll be fine, but let's get out of here before another pack comes."

Mary and Sarah said, "Roger, Lieutenant!"

Mary and Sarah followed behind Lieutenant Michael as the three of them ran back toward the wall where Squad four was waiting. They ran back down the broken street until they reached the burnt out clearing in front of the wall.

Lieutenant Rachel stood there with Giana, Tina, and Elsa as Lieutenant Michael came into the clearing with Valerie in his arms and Mary and Sarah following behind him. Lieutenant Rachel said, "How'd she do?"

Lieutenant Michael nodded his head in thought and said, "Well, she lasted eight minutes before black out so I think she did pretty well for a first day."

Giana slammed her fist in the air and kicked at the charred ground, yelling, "Damn it, eight minutes?"

Mary laughed and shook her fist in victory, saying, "Pay up, cow, she lasted more than five minutes and under ten minutes."

Giana began muttering to herself and reached into her jacket pocket, pulling out a folded paper bill. Mary held out her hand, cupped her other hand over her ear, and said, "What was that, Giana?"

Giana slammed the paper bill into Mary's waiting hand and sarcastically said, "I said fine, here you go."

Lieutenant Michael looked at them in shock and said, "I can't believe that you two made a bet on how long Valerie would be conscious in the field."

Mary unfolded the paper bill and began tugging on it, saying, "I won five dollars!" She then smelled the five dollar bill and wiggled it at Giana, laughing.

Lieutenant Michael said, "Okay, you two, save it for when we're on the other side of the wall. Let's go." He gently put the catatonic Valerie over his left shoulder and headed to the wall.

Lieutenant Rachel and her squad stood there watching to see if any Harvesters would come following Squad three. Lieutenant Michael led Mary and Sarah to the wall and helped them to climb up the small rungs that led up to the top of the wall. After the two of them were standing on the top, he, himself, climbed up as he continued to hold onto Valerie over his shoulder.

At the top of the wall the three of them stared back over the wasteland they had just come from. More packs of Harvesters were starting to approach the wall. Lieutenant Michael spoke to Rachel through the commander's channel on his ear piece, saying, "Rachel, we got several bands approaching, you better come on up here now."

Lieutenant Rachel responded to him, "Thanks for the heads up." Rachel, Giana, Tina, and Elsa began to climb up the wall one by one.

Mary, confused, said, "Don't we still have to guard the wall? I doubt they finished the check yet."

Lieutenant Michael nervously chuckled and said, "Well, to be honest, there was never any problem with this wall. It was just a drill. Captain Faust thought that this would be a perfect opportunity to start getting Valerie used to combat."

Giana's head suddenly popped up from the wall and she said, "You mean I had to get up at five because of some stupid drill?" She finished climbing up over the wall and joined them at the top.

Lieutenant Michael said, "I'm afraid so, Giana."

Mary said, "Geez, leave it to the brass to ruin our morning. Well, at least we got Valerie out here, and I made five dollars."

Tina and Elsa climbed up over the wall, followed by Lieutenant Rachel. When Rachel finished climbing over, she turned around to join everyone as they looked over the wasteland. A group of four Harvesters entered the clearing and began screeching at the people on top of the wall.

Mary pointed at them and laughed, saying, "Hey dummies, can't climb very well can you?" She then turned around, bent over forward, lifted the back of her dress up exposing her underwear, and waved her butt all the while taunting, "Stupid, stupid buggers, come on up and kiss my butt!"

Lieutenant Michael said, "You know, Mary, ladies don't expose themselves in public like that. You keep telling me you want me to think of you as an adult yet you act like you are five years old." Mary frowned and pouted her lips as she stood back up and lowered the skirt of her dress.

Giana laughed and pointed at Mary, saying, "Yeah, Lieutenant Michael, she's so immature."

Lieutenant Rachel swung her hand across the back of Giana's head and said, "Look who's talking. You're just as bad as she is."

Giana rubbed the back of her head and said, "Ow, Lieutenant, why'd you have to hit me like that."

Lieutenant Rachel replied, "Because, that's why."

Lieutenant Michael turned around and saw a military vehicle down below. The vehicle was an armored personnel carrier. It was painted in the standard olive green drab color. It looked like a cross between a tank and a van. The logo of the World Government was painted on the side in black.

Lieutenant Michael pointed at the vehicle and said, "Looks like our ride is here. Let's go home." He readjusted Valerie on his shoulder and then began climbing down the rung ladder on the inward side of the wall. Lieutenant Rachel then followed him down. The others then went down one by one.

A Private stepped out of the vehicle and walked over to Lieutenants Michael and Rachel. He saluted them and said, "Sirs, I have been asked to transport your units to the airfield." Lieutenant Michael and Rachel nodded saying, "Thank you," and then they returned the salute.

The Private returned to the driver's cab and a ramp began to be lowered in the back of the vehicle. Lieutenant Rachel said, "Okay, everybody, into the truck."

The inside of the vehicle was similar to the helicopter but it was much brighter inside. Mary and Sarah were the first to rush up the ramp. Mary plopped onto the seat and spread her limbs out saying, "That was exhausting. We took out four harvesters today." Sarah sat down next to her and said, "Well, you did do most of the work today. I'm just glad there were only four of them and they were the smaller kind."

Giana, Tina, and Elsa walked up the ramp and sat down on the bench on the other side of the cabin. As Giana walked by Mary, she intentionally kicked her foot, saying, "You were only out there for like twenty minutes."

Mary sat up and said, "Give me a break, it's been like five weeks since I had to go out there."

Elsa said "What did you do for all those weeks? Sit around and do nothing?"

Mary said, "No, I didn't do nothing. We did training together with Valerie."

Lieutenant Michael stepped inside the vehicle carrying Valerie in his arms. He sat down next to Mary on the bench. Lieutenant Rachel followed behind him and sat down next to Elsa.

Elsa said, "How long is she going to be out?" She pointed to Valerie as she spoke.

Lieutenant Michael said, "I'm sure she'll be awake very soon." As he said this the ramp began to lift back up. The engine of the vehicle then roared to life and they could feel the wheels begin to roll underneath them.

As the vehicle began to roll, Valerie suddenly began to gasp for air. Her gasping was soon replaced by crying as she began to wail at the top of her lungs. Lieutenant Michael sat her up on his lap and held her tightly against his chest. He rocked her back and forth and whispered gently into her ear, "It's okay now. It's all over. You're safe now."

Mary looked at her lovingly and placed her hand on Valerie's back. Sarah got up and moved to sit on Lieutenant Michael's other side. She placed her hand on Valerie's back as well.

Valerie continued to cry for about a minute and then she slowly began to stop. Her body still trembled in Lieutenant Michael's arms. He continued to hold her against his chest.

Valerie slowly began to stop trembling. When she finally stopped, she pressed her hands against Lieutenant Michael's chest so he loosened his grip on her. She sat up and looked around her surroundings. Her face was covered in mud from the dust mixing with her tears. She said, "Where am I?"

Lieutenant Michael said, "We are in a vehicle heading to the local airfield."

Valerie then said, "What happened to me?"

Lieutenant Michael said, "What's the last thing you remember?"

Valerie replied, "All I can remember is staring into the face of a Harvester, then, nothing."

Lieutenant Michael said, "You passed out so I had to carry you here."

Valerie began to get teary-eyed again and said, "I-I-I'm sorry, I-I-I tried to-to be brave, but ..."

Lieutenant Michael interrupted her and said, "Don't even worry about it. We knew that this would most likely happen to you and we prepared for it."

Valerie said, "Did I ruin the mission?"

Lieutenant Michael said, "Nope. Not at all. In fact the sector was never in any real danger, it was just a drill. We used this drill to get you some field experience without putting citizens in any real danger."

Mary said, "See, Val. I told you that I'd protect you." Valerie didn't respond.

Lieutenant Michael continued to let Valerie sit on his lap. She leaned sideways into his chest with her hands in her lap. She began to feel the wetness of the front of her dress and of her underwear. Forgetting that her coms system was still on, she whispered into Michael's ear, "I think I peed myself."

Lieutenant Michael said, "That happens a lot so don't be embarrassed about it."

Sarah said, "Yeah, Mary peed herself too when she was first out."

Mary said, "I did not."

Valerie began to blush and said, "You heard me?"

Lieutenant Michael tapped his ear and said, "Remember the coms in your ear?" Valerie remembered and realized everything she was saying could be heard by her whole squad. She hid her face in Lieutenant Michael's chest and said out loud, "I'm so embarrassed."

Sarah said to Mary, "You did too pee yourself. I also peed myself Val. You don't have to be embarrassed."

Lieutenant Michael said, "Come on, Mary, for Valerie's sake tell the truth."

Mary grabbed her twin tails and shook her head saying, "Fine! I peed myself the first time I went out too! So did Giana and Elsa." She quickly pointed at them on the other side of the vehicle.

Lieutenant Michael then said, "You see, Valerie. You're in good company. Just about everyone here peed themselves the first time too. There is no reason to be embarrassed by it."

Valerie lifted her face from Lieutenant Michael's chest and leaned back into his arm as she did before. Her face still had the look of embarrassment on it. She continued to sit there quietly.

Lieutenant Michael said, "You did very well for your first time in the field. You lasted a whole eight minutes. Most girls pass out around the four or five minute mark."

Mary pulled out the five dollar bill and waved it toward Giana again, as she spoke to Valerie, "Yeah, thanks to you lasting so long I won five dollars." Disgruntled noises came from Giana as Mary waved the five dollar bill at her.

Valerie pointed at Mary and said, "Since it was me who did the work, you owe me a soda."

Mary laughed and shoved the five dollar bill back into her pocket. She said, "Sure, no problem, Val. I can get a whole case of soda to share with you for five dollars. What type of soda do you like?"

Valerie said, "Root beer."

Mary replied, "Great, I'll definitely get you a root beer with Giana's five dollars."

Giana crossed her arms across her chest and said, "Geez, can you just let it go, you cow! You won, I lost. Get over it!"

Suddenly the vehicle came to a stop and the ramp started to lower. They could see a transport helicopter through the widening opening. Lieutenant Michael said to Valerie, "Do you want me to carry you or do you want to walk?"

Valerie said, "Can you please carry me?"

Lieutenant Michael nodded and said, "Sure, no problem." He stood up and carried Valerie down the ramp as they all got off together.

The ramp of the helicopter was already open and waiting for them to board. Lieutenant Michael placed Valerie on the bench and stooped down to buckle her seat belt. He then sat down next to her as Sarah and Mary boarded the helicopter as well. Valerie wrapped an arm around his arm and leaned up against it. She rested her head on his arm and closed her eyes, falling asleep quickly, even before the helicopter engine started.

Lieutenant Rachel smiled at the view and said, "She's so adorable."

Lieutenant Michael said, "Yeah, I can see that."

Mary clasped her hands together and raised them in hopeful expectation, saying, "Am I adorable, Lieutenant Michael?"

Lieutenant Michael chuckled and rubbed the top of Mary's head, saying, "Little kids are adorable. You're more of an awkward teen now."

Mary dropped her hands, looking confused. Sarah said, "Am I adorable, Lieutenant Michael?"

Lieutenant Michael said, "Yeah, I'd say so. You're still going to be adorable for another year, then, you're going to turn into Mary and be an awkward teen."

Mary cocked her head to the side and said, "What do you mean by awkward?"

Lieutenant Michael said, "I mean that teenagers are clumsy and are learning the ropes to being an adult so they make a bunch of stupid mistakes."

Tina spoke out in her melancholy voice, saying, "That describes Mary and Giana perfectly."

Giana slugged Tina in the arm. Tina rubbed her arm, saying, "Ow that hurt. I was just speaking the truth."

Giana slugged her in the arm again and said, "Who asked your opinion." Giana then smiled mischievously at Lieutenant Michael and said, "So Lieutenant Michael, if the little kids are adorable, and us teens are awkward. How do you think Lieutenant Rachel looks?"

Before he could answer, the rotors on the helicopter began to spin, and their noise filled the helicopter cabin so that they could not hear one another from across the cabin. Lieutenant Michael began to move his lips and pointed at his ear acting like he could not answer the question due to the noise.

-3-

Except for the noise of the helicopter, the ride back to the Phoenix Guard headquarters was quiet. Valerie had slid down from Lieutenant Michael's arm and was now sleeping with her head on his lap and her feet on the bench, her little body in fetal position. Sarah sat next to Valerie's feet and leaned back resting her head along the wall. Mary sat on the other side of Lieutenant Michael, next to the door, and swung her feet back and forth, making faces from time to time at Giana. Lieutenant Michael supposed that it took all her energy to not bounce off the walls so he let her sit there fidgeting.

Lieutenant Michael looked down at Valerie's sleeping face on his lap. The smeared mud had dried on her face and there were now stained trails of dirt where her tears had mixed with the dust. He began to rub her head and adjusted her hair behind her ear. Again, he began to feel a pain of regret gnawing in the pit of his stomach. *These poor girls shouldn't have to deal with this pain,* he thought to himself. A voice came over the intercom again, saying, "Landing, five minutes."

The noise of the intercom caused Valerie to stir and she sat up from laying on Lieutenant Michael's lap. Valerie said, "Are we home yet?"

Lieutenant Michael wondered for a moment if Valerie truly thought of this place as home yet. He said, "Yeah, we're almost there. You slept pretty hard."

Valerie yawned and said, "I feel exhausted."

Lieutenant Michael said, "Yeah, I bet you do. This sortie was pretty rough on you but I want you to know that you did very well for your first time."

Valerie looked down and quietly said, "Thanks." She began to swing her feet beneath her. She then said, "Are they going to make us go out again today?"

Lieutenant Michael shook his head and said, "They usually don't. They'd only call us again today if there was a serious emergency. You can expect to have a few days off as well, as they will tend to cycle between the squads so that they don't over use any one squad."

Valerie looked back up and smiled, saying, "Well, that's good. I really don't want to go out again today. Is there anything else that we need to do today?"

Lieutenant Michael said, "Not really. When we get home you can take a bath and then we'll get you checked out by the doctor."

Valerie, her voice subdued, said, "Okay."

The helicopter started to descend and Mary ended her own silence by yelling out, "Finally! When we get back I got a few words to say to that Captain of ours!"

Lieutenant Michael said, "What? You going to yell at the Captain now? Good luck with that."

Mary pushed Lieutenant Michael playfully and said, "I ain't going to yell. Just giving him a piece of my mind on this whole drill thing."

The helicopter rocked slightly and then touched down on the roof of the headquarters. The ramp slowly came down and they all could see Captain Faust standing on the roof with a couple of his aides.

Lieutenant Michael, with a sarcastic smile on his face, pointed at the Captain and said, "Look, Mary. Now you can give the Captain a piece of your mind."

Mary unbuckled herself and jumped up from her seat. She stormed down the ramp before anybody else could stop her and she marched up to Captain Faust.

Lieutenant Michael shook his head and then turned to face Valerie, saying, "Do you want me to carry you again or can you walk?"

Valerie slid off the bench and stood up on her feet with a faint-hearted smile, saying, "I think I can walk now." She then turned toward the ramp and began to walk down it. The others followed behind her. The ramp then lifted back up and the helicopter rose into the air. It sped off to its next destination.

Mary angrily marched up to Captain Faust. The Captain saw her and said with a smile, "Good morning, Mary. How did the mission go?"

Mary aggressively said, "I got a bone to pick with you, Captain!"

Captain Faust straightened up and said, "Oh, really? Again?"

Mary pointed at him with her right hand and squared her left arm on her hip, saying, "If you knew that this was all just a drill, why did you not tell us."

The Captain straightened his jacket and said, "Why did I not tell you that it was a drill? I wanted you to take it seriously. That's why."

Mary said, "You made me get up at five for a drill!"

Captain Faust said, "You're lucky I chose not to have the drill at three in the morning."

Mary dropped her finger of accusation and said, "Alright, Captain, you won this round."

The Captain then said, "Mary, I win every round. That's why I'm the Captain."

As Mary conceded defeat, Lieutenant Michael, Valerie and Sarah walked up behind her. Squad four was standing beside them at the same time. Lieutenant Michael grabbed Mary by the back of her collar and pulled her back in line with the rest of them. Mary made choking sounds as he pulled her backwards.

Captain Faust then turned toward Valerie and said, "So, Valerie, how did you do on your first day?"

Valerie clenched her fists together and raised them to her mouth in nervousness and said from behind her hands, "I-I hear I did well."

Lieutenant Michael put an arm around her shoulder and said, "She did very well. She lasted for eight minutes before blacking out."

Captain Faust rubbed Valerie on top of her head and said, "Eight minutes! That is pretty good."

Valerie lowered her clenched fists and nervously smiled from the praise. She slightly twisted her body from side to side as the Captain looked at her.

The Captain then said, "Alright, I'm glad to see all you girls back in one piece. You girls got the rest of the day off so go on down stairs and enjoy yourselves."

Mary saluted and said, "Aye, Captain!" She then took off running downstairs. Sarah began to follow her and she saluted the Captain saying, "Thank you, Captain!" Valerie then saluted the Captain and said, "Thanks, Captain!" She then ran after Sarah and Mary.

One by one, Giana, Tina, and Elsa saluted the Captain and ran off till only the Captain, Lieutenant Rachel, and Lieutenant Michael remained, with his aides. The Captain held onto Lieutenant Michael's arm, and said, "Lieutenant Snyder, how'd it really go today?"

Lieutenant Michael said, "Well, I thought it went pretty good. Like I said, she lasted eight minutes. She's not a fighter so I did not even try to get her to fight. No one was hurt so there was no problem there. I'm not sure yet if she'll black out again or not. Personally, I think she's going to do just fine. I don't have any worries yet."

Captain Faust nodded and said, "Well, that's good. I'll look forward to reading the after action report from both of you. You can go on down now with your squads."

Lieutenant Michael nodded and said, "Thank you, sir."

Lieutenant Rachel said, "Thanks, Captain.

Together they made their way down the stairs. As they walked down the stairs, Lieutenant Rachel said, "Is there anything I can do to help you with Valerie?"

Lieutenant Michael shook his head and said, "I don't think so. She seems pretty strong to me so I think she will handle it better than normal. I'll take her to see Doctor Lovecraft today and I'll hear what she has to say about it."

Lieutenant Rachel then said, "I was kind of interested in what you were going to say before the noise of the helicopter interrupted you."

An awkward look fell on Lieutenant Michael's face as he averted his gaze and said in an over-exaggerated tone, "I don't know what you're talking about."

Lieutenant Rachel, not believing him, said, "Oh, really? You know, when Giana asked you what you thought I looked like."

Lieutenant Michael said, "Oh that. I thought she was just joking."

Lieutenant Rachel replied, "Of course she was joking. But, I am a little curious myself. We've been friends for so long, I've been wondering if you can see me as a woman." She gripped her hands behind her back and perked up her chest a little bit.

Lieutenant Michael swallowed in his throat and looked embarrassed. His eyes, out of reflex, began to dart from Rachel's face to her bosom, then back to her face, and back to her bosom again. He said, "Wha-What are you talking about? Of course I think of you as a woman. Look at you! How could I not. You're very beautiful."

Lieutenant Rachel then smiled and leaned toward him a little closer, saying, "So you do think I'm beautiful. That's good at least. Do you think about me often?"

Lieutenant Michael rolled his eyes a little and rolled his head backward. He said, "Okay, I can handle it when Mary pretends to hit on me like this, but I don't think I could handle it if you started joking with me like that too."

Lieutenant Rachel laughed and said, "Don't worry, I won't tease you too much."

They reached the door of their floor and Lieutenant Michael opened the door for her. He jokingly bowed as his hand pointed the way for her. She smiled and said, "Thank you, kind sir." He followed behind her through the door.

Mary was the first one through the door of the apartment. She yelled as she opened the door, "Welcome home, I'm back!"

Sarah and Valerie nearly crashed into Mary who stopped suddenly in the doorway to shout out her line. Sarah said, "Isn't that something you say to someone when they come back?"

Mary began to spin around in a circle with her arms open wide and said, "But there's nobody home to greet me when I get back, so I got to do it myself. If only I could be Lieutenant Michael's house wife then I could wait for him to get back from work instead of me having to go to work." She stopped spinning in a circle and brought her hands together and held them up saying, "Then when he got back I could say, welcome home darling. How was your day?" She then smiled and rested her cheek on her clasped hands.

Sarah said, "Just give it up, Mary. There is no way you will ever get to marry Lieutenant Michael in the future. If anybody is going to marry Lieutenant Michael, it's Lieutenant Rachel. Haven't you seen how much he stares at her?"

Mary's shoulders drooped and her hands dropped to her side. She said in a depressed tone, "There's always hope."

Sarah said, "Yeah, there's hope that I can find a million dollars, but I'm not counting on it."

Valerie chuckled and said, "Yeah, I might find a million dollars too!"

Mary's face began to pout and her lower lip began to quiver. She folded her arms across her chest and said with sorrow in her voice, "Why are you two trying to ruin my dream?"

Suddenly the door opened and Lieutenant Michael walked in to see Mary pouting with her arms crossed and Sarah and Valerie laughing at her. He said, "What's going on now?"

Sarah and Valerie stopped laughing. Mary turned around and ran toward Lieutenant Michael with her arms out stretched to him. She ran into him and threw her arms around him, saying in a fake crying tone, "They're makin' fun of my dreams."

Lieutenant Michael patted her on the back and said, "Well, that's okay. You can dream about whatever you want. All that matters is that it's your dream."

Mary, still pretending to cry, said, "So you want my dream to come true?"

Lieutenant Michael said, "Of course, if it's something that you want, I'd be very happy if it came true for you."

Sarah and Valerie could hold back no more. They began laughing at the top of their lungs. Sarah dropped to her hands and knees and began to pound on the floor with her fist. Valerie leaned over and grabbed her own stomach.

A look of shock fell upon Lieutenant Michael's face as he stood there watching them. He said, annoyed, "Why are you two laughing so hard?"

Sarah got up and tried to speak in between bouts of laughter, "Her ... her dream ... is to marry you!" Slowly she began to gain composure over herself as she wiped a tear from the corner of her eye.

Mary looked up at Lieutenant Michael as she continued to cling to him. Her lips began to pout again. He looked down at her and rolled his eyes, saying, "Come on! Not this again. I'm sorry, but you know that there is no way that dream can ever come true, Mary."

Mary said, "But ... but, it's okay to have hope, right?"

Lieutenant Michael said, "I think it would be better if you just gave up on that entirely. I think you'd be a much happier person."

Valerie said, "Like we told her. You're far more likely to marry Lieutenant Rachel."

Lieutenant Michael pried Mary off of his body and said, "That's not true either. Lieutenant Rachel and I are just friends. I have no plans to get married and I probably never will."

Valerie cocked her head to the side and looked at him questioningly, saying, "How come?"

Lieutenant Michael said, "Because I don't want to bring children into a world like this one." He paused for a moment and looked upward. His cheeks began to blush slightly and scratched his cheek with a finger saying, "Besides, you three girls are all the family I need right now."

Valerie said, "So, we're like a family?"

Lieutenant Michael rubbed the top of her head and said, "Yep, I think of you three as if you were my own daughters, or at least as close as I'll ever get to having daughters."

Valerie looked up at him and smiled with a big grin, then she began to blush a little in embarrassment and looked downward.

Lieutenant Michael then said, "Okay now, why don't you three give me your com units and then you can go take a bath. Don't forget to leave your gear on the table first. And, Valerie, after your bath and breakfast, you and I are going to see Doctor Lovecraft." He opened the palm of his hand and held it up to receive the com units.

Valerie took out the com unit that was in her ear and placed it in the palm of his hand. She then unstrapped the holster on her back and put it on the table.

Sarah then took out the com unit in her ear and placed it in the palm of Lieutenant Michael's hand. She then took off her belt with the two scabbards and metal sticks, and she placed it on the table as well.

Mary then took the com unit out of her own ear and placed it into Lieutenant Michael's hand. As she put it down, she said, "I'm happy being your daughter too."

Lieutenant Michael smiled at her and rubbed the top of her head, saying, "Alright, go take a bath and then you're free to relax the rest of the day. While you're taking a bath, I'll make us a late breakfast."

The girls agreed and ran off to the bathroom. Lieutenant Michael looked at his own clothes and saw that they were dirty too. He then went into his own room to change his uniform and take a quick shower.

Valerie entered the bathroom first, followed by Sarah and then Mary. Valerie was anxious to get her pee stained uniform off of her body. Mary and Sarah could sense Valerie's embarrassment as they watched her trying to hide the stains on her uniform.

Mary said, "Don't worry, Val, we're not going to tease you about what happened. After all, we're like sisters now." She wrapped an arm around Valerie's neck and rubbed the top of her head with the knuckles of her fist.

Valerie struggled and jokingly said, "Hey, knock it off sis."

Sarah said, "That was really sweet that he thinks of us as his daughters. I kind of wish that he really was my dad."

Mary said, "The Lieutenant can be really sweet at times, dense at others."

Valerie quickly turned on the water in the bathtub and watched the steam rise from the hot water. The sound of the rushing water brought back the recent memory of the noise of the helicopter. Then an image of a Harvester popped back into her mind. Its jaws twitched at her and the sound of its screeching echoed in her head. Instantly, Valerie squatted down on the ground. She raised her hands on top of her head and covered her face with her arms. She began to cry again as she squatted there next to the bathtub.

Mary and Sarah, who had also taken off their dirty uniforms, rushed over to Valerie. Mary dropped to her knees and wrapped her arms around Valerie and said, "It's okay, it's okay. You're safe here."

Sarah said, "Should I get the Lieutenant?"

Mary said, "Not yet, I think she's okay."

Valerie leaned into Mary and said, "I'm sorry, I-I-I just started thinking about the Harvesters again and got scared. I'm okay."

Mary said, "You sure? 'Cause we can get the Lieutenant if you want."

Valerie shook her head and said, "No, that's okay. I'll be fine."

Mary let go of her and Valerie stood back up. Mary said, "Don't try to force yourself. If you feel like crying, cry. If you feel like screaming, scream. If you feel like punching somebody, punch Sarah."

Sarah interjected, saying, "Why can't she punch you."

Mary waved her question off and said, "You're the one with the body shield. What are you worried about?" Mary then focused back on Valerie, saying, "We're all in this together and we're going to support each other. With all of us working together we can accomplish anything because we're a team."

Mary held her arm out, palm facing downward. Sarah then put her own hand on top of Mary's and said, "We're a team and together we can accomplish anything!"

Valerie stared at Mary's and Sarah's hands. She then put her own hand on top of Sarah's hand and said, "Together we can do anything!" Mary smiled and put her other hand on top of Valerie's hand. Sarah then put her other hand on top of Mary's and Valerie put her other hand on top of Sarah's hand.

Mary said, "Let's make a promise to always watch out for each other and protect each other. I promise!"

Sarah said, "I promise."

Valerie said, "I promise."

Together they dropped their hands and then put their arms around each other in a circle, bringing their heads together.

Lieutenant Michael took off his dusty uniform and tossed it into his laundry basket. He ran the shower and let the warm water run down over his body. The water now laced with his sweat would be captured, recycled and redistributed to the inhabitants of the city sector. *Let them drink the sweat I produced protecting them today,* he thought to himself. As the water ran over his body, he began to examine scars that were the remnants of previous battles against the Harvesters. Each one of them was a sign of his past bravery.

The one scar that can never be seen are the emotional scars left on all the little girls who were forced to fight by the World Government. He recalled the look of absolute terror on little Valerie's face as she wept in his arms. That look of sweet innocence would soon be replaced with a harsh look of reality that she will probably try to hide with jokes and giggles. Her sweet dreams would be replaced with vicious nightmares. Yet, there was nothing that he could do about it, except be there for her. For them.

Anger began to well up inside of him again. He slammed a fist against the wall of his shower. *If only I had the power to fight,* he thought to himself, *then those girls wouldn't have to.*

Valerie, Sarah, and Mary sat in the bathtub. Mary began to rub shampoo into Valerie's hair and to lather it up. Valerie said, "Did I really do good today out there? You're not just saying that to make me feel better are you?"

Sarah said, "Yeah, for your experience level you did good today."

Mary said, "Look at it this way, Val. Did you run away? No. Did you make things worse? No. All in all, you did what was expected of you. You even lasted a little longer than the average four minutes. Give yourself some credit."

Sarah said, "If you did something wrong, the Lieutenant would have told you. He wouldn't just say something to make you feel better. If you were doing something wrong, he'd tell you because it might get you or somebody else killed."

Mary said, "That's right, Val. The Lieutenant said you did good, so, you did good." She paused and then said to Valerie, "Do you think you can go out and face the Harvesters again?"

Valerie looked down into the water, watching her reflection, and said, "I think I can. I just hope that I'm not as scared next time." Valerie then dropped her head underneath the water and rinsed her hair out. She then lifted her head back up out of the water and wiped the water off of her face with her hands.

Mary said, "Do you trust us Valerie?"

Valerie said, "Yes, I do."

Mary then smiled and wrapped an arm around Valerie's shoulder, saying, "Great. Next time you get scared, just remember that you trust us and the fear will go away. Remember, we promised one another that we would protect each other. That means we won't let anything happen to each other so there's no need to be scared."

Sarah said, "Yep, we're going to protect each other so you don't have to be afraid."

Suddenly the klaxon scream of the emergency siren began to wail. Mary, Sarah, and Valerie sat up straight in the water in silence as they stared back and forth at each other. The siren stopped and a voice followed saying, "Fifth squad, prepare for deployment, ten minutes."

Mary, Sarah and Valerie relaxed and leaned back against the walls of the bath tub. Mary laughed and said, "I knew it wasn't for us, but still, twice in one day?"

Sarah said, "To be fair, our deployment was just a drill so it's still only one real one."

Valerie said, "Sure felt real to me."

Mary said, "Yeah, we still had to go out and fight so it sure felt real to me too."

Sarah put her hands up in surrender and said, "I was just saying that there was no real danger to the citizens this time."

Mary said, "I bet our sortie stirred up a nest of them. Now Squad five has to finish off our work. I wish you could have seen it Val. We squashed four bugs today!"

Valerie looked downward as she tried to remember the fighting. She said, "I remember some of it. I can't believe you held down a Harvester."

Mary flexed her arms and said, "I know, right? I'm just too strong."

Valerie then said, "And the way Sarah cut off the legs was awesome too. I wish I could fight like you two do."

Sarah said, "Even though you can't fight like us, you still do something that is even more important than fighting. You're a healer. If Mary or I get hurt, we're counting on you to fix us."

Mary then said, "You're just a beginner. For all we know you might be one of those super rare yellow Wielders that can pull the life energy right out of a Harvester. Then you'd be able to fight like us too. For now, though, we're just glad that we got you to heal us."

Sarah's head lifted up as she began smelling deeply the scent of food wafting underneath the door. She said, "I smell pancakes. Let's get out and eat breakfast. I'm starving!"

Sarah jumped out of the bath and tried to run to her towel. The steam from the bath had distilled onto the floor and the added moisture from the water running off of her body had made a perfect condition for a fall. Sure enough, Sarah slipped and fell right onto her butt, sliding across the floor.

A roar of laughter erupted as Mary and Valerie carefully stepped out of the bath. Sarah carefully got back up and rubbed her posterior saying, "Come on, you guys. That really hurt."

Mary held up her hands in innocence and said, "Don't look at me. That was entirely you."

Valerie walked over to her and held up her hands, saying, "Do you need me to heal your butt?" Valerie could hardly hold back the laughter that kept slipping from between her lips.

Sarah rolled her eyes and said, "No, I think I'll be okay." She then gave Mary a spiteful glance and carefully walked over to her towel. She wrapped the towel around her body and then walked out of the bathroom shutting the door behind herself.

Mary and Valerie stood there and watched her leave. When she left, they looked at each other and started to snort in laughter. This only led them to begin to roar with laughter again as they remembered Sarah slipping across the floor on her butt.

Lieutenant Michael peaked his head around the corner to see an embarrassed Sarah walk down the hall to her room in a towel. He could hear a roar of laughter coming from the bathroom. He said, "Is everything okay?"

Sarah, still embarrassed, said, "I slipped and fell on my butt."

Lieutenant Michael chuckled and said, "Oh, I see. Do you need Valerie to heal your butt?"

Sarah blushed with embarrassment and said in an annoyed tone, "Geez, why did everyone say that?"

Lieutenant Michael put up a hand from around the corner and said, "Calm down, I wasn't making fun of you. Pancakes are ready so get dressed and come eat."

Sarah frowned and pouted her lips. She then walked into her room. As Sarah entered her own room, Mary opened the door and started to come out of the bathroom with a towel wrapped around her body. When she saw Lieutenant

Michael standing there, she backed up into the bathroom and then stuck her head out of the doorway, saying, "What are you doing, Lieutenant? Were you waiting just to see me come out of the bathroom in my towel?"

Lieutenant Michael rolled his eyes and sighed out loud, saying, "No, you were making so much noise I ..."

Mary then interrupted him and said, "I'm just kidding, Lieutenant. You know I don't care." She then walked back out of the room and smiled at him as she walked into her own room.

Behind her followed Valerie. As she stepped out of the bathroom, she looked left and right at the other doors, and then hurriedly walked to her own room, clasping her hands together underneath her chin.

Lieutenant Michael, confused, shook his head and returned to putting the rest of the breakfast he made on the table. He then sat there at the table waiting for the girls to come out.

Valerie was the first to come to the table. She sat down at the table across from Lieutenant Michael. She rested her arms on the table and then focused her attention on him.

Lieutenant Michael raised a hand and pointed toward the food and said, "You can start now if you want to. You don't have to wait for the others if you don't want to wait."

Valerie nodded her head and said, "Okay." She took three pancakes off the serving platter and placed them on her own plate. She then took the syrup bottle, carefully opened the top, and began to squeeze syrup onto the plate in large quantities.

Lieutenant Michael watched her intently as Valerie spilled large amounts of syrup on her plate. He said, "Geez, Valerie, would you like some pancakes with your syrup?"

Valerie put the bottle down, cocked her head to one side, and gave him a look of confusion on her face. She batted her eyes and said, "What?"

Lieutenant Michael supported his head with his hand, while his elbow leaned on the table. He sighed, saying, "Oh, nothing. Don't mind me."

Valerie then placed the palms of her hands together and said a silent prayer. As she prayed, Sarah came to the table, and sat down next to Valerie. Sarah grabbed some pancakes off the serving platter and waited for Valerie to finish praying. When Valerie opened her eyes, Sarah said, "Val, that's a lot of syrup."

Valerie began to shovel food into her mouth and said, "I like sweet things."

Mary suddenly came out of the hallway and said, "Are you talking about me?"

Lieutenant Michael said, "You sure took your time Mary."

Mary raised her head and said, "Of course, it takes me longer to get ready because I'm a lady now."

Lieutenant Michael rolled his eyes and said, "Yeah, sure, whatever."

Mary sat down at the table next to Lieutenant Michael and began to take pancakes off of the serving platter. As Mary did this, she said, "Hey, Lieutenant, while you and Valerie are seeing Doctor Lovecraft, can Sarah and I go to the convenience store?"

Lieutenant Michael thought for a moment and said, "That's fine with me, but what do you need to go for?"

Mary reached into her pocket and pulled out a five dollar bill. The same five dollar bill she had won from Giana. She began to wave the bill in the air and said, "I got to use Giana's money to buy a case of root beer like I said I would."

Lieutenant Michael nodded and said, "Sure, that's fine with me. After breakfast, let's do the dishes together and then we can go our separate ways."

Mary raised her fist high in the air and said, "You bet, Lieutenant!"

After breakfast they cleaned the dishes together. Lieutenant Michael then took Valerie's hand and led her down the staircase toward the first floor. As they walked down the steps, Lieutenant Michael asked, "This is your first time seeing Doctor Lovecraft, isn't it?"

Valerie nodded and said, "Yeah, I only heard about her today. I never had a reason to see a doctor here before. I hope I'm okay."

Lieutenant Michael said, "I wouldn't worry about it. We just want to make sure that everything is fine. If you ever get sick or hurt you can see Doctor Lovecraft. You can also talk to her if you are too embarrassed to talk to me about something. She's a little weird but she's really smart too."

A look of confusion fell on Valerie's face and she said, "How is she weird?"

Lieutenant Michael said, "Oh, really smart people sometimes have quirks about them. You'll just have to wait and see."

At the bottom of the staircase, Lieutenant Michael opened the door to the first floor. The exit of the Phoenix Guard complex was right next to them. Across the way was another hallway that had rooms in them. As they walked toward it, Valerie saw that the first room in the hallway had a sign on it that read, "Captain Faust, Phoenix Guard Wielder Company." Other doors had name plates on them that Valerie didn't recognize. There were also words and letter arrangements that she did not understand. At the end of the hall was another door with the name plate on it reading, "Megan Lovecraft, Major, M.D."

Lieutenant Michael, still holding Valerie's hand, knocked on the door. Valerie stood there in anticipation to finally meet the mysterious Doctor Lovecraft. After a moment, the door flung open and an energetic, short woman opened the door. She had dirty blonde hair wrapped into a bun with a pen sticking through it. She wore black square rimmed glasses that rested awkwardly on her nose. They seemed to be held together in the middle with duct tape.

The woman looked up at Lieutenant Michael with wide eyes and then looked down at Valerie with a look of surprise. She then hollered in excitement, shouting, "Oh my God! Oh my God! Oh my God! There's a new one!" She then grabbed Valerie and picked her up off the floor. She embraced Valerie in a tight hug and spun around in a circle. Valerie's limbs flailed as if she were a rag doll being shaken in a dog's mouth.

Lieutenant Michael took a step back to avoid getting hit by Valerie's flailing limbs. He said, "Hey, Doctor Lovecraft. This is Valerie, my new team member."

Doctor Lovecraft stopped spinning and then held Valerie up by her armpits, lifting Valerie above her head. She said, "So this is Valerie. She is just so adorable, I can hardly contain myself!"

Valerie, looking both dizzy and horrified at the same time, hung in the air motionless as her mind tried to figure out what was going on. She said, "Please try."

Doctor Lovecraft, still holding her up, turned around and entered into the examination room. Lieutenant Michael followed behind her. Doctor Lovecraft then sat Valerie down on a padded examination table and said, "Lieutenant Michael, how could you keep this cutie away from me for so long?"

Valerie stared at Lieutenant Michael with a confused look of betrayal that Michael interpreted as her saying, "How could you bring me to this crazy person?" Lieutenant Michael replied to her look with a silent chuckle and a shrug of his shoulders. Valerie interpreted this as him saying, "I told you she was weird."

Valerie looked around the room. On the wall, next to Lovecraft's desk, were rows of pictures of young girls. She saw the two pictures of Mary and Sarah in the lineup. Next to Mary's picture was an empty space that had the residue of old tape that had left a mark. Valerie thought to herself that this must be where Susan's picture once hung.

Valerie focused again on Doctor Lovecraft as the Doctor began to poke her in various places on her body. She lifted Valerie's arm and began tickling her in the armpit, saying, "Cuchie cuchie coo." Valerie ripped her arm out of the Doctor's hold and tightened her limbs together as she laughed and squirmed from the tickle. The Doctor said, "Her reflexes seem normal."

The Doctor then pulled out a small flashlight that looked like a pen. She began to flash it into Valerie's eyes, and then said, "Seems normal." The Doctor then said, "Open your mouth, please." Valerie opened her mouth and the doctor shined the light down her throat and said, "Looks good too, though I detect the faint odor of pancakes."

Doctor Lovecraft then turned the light off and swiveled in her chair to face Lieutenant Michael. She said, "Where's my pancakes?"

Valerie began to poke herself in the stomach with both hands and said, "I put them all in here."

Doctor Lovecraft then swung back around to face Valerie and said, "That's okay, I got to maintain my womanly figure anyway. So, Valerie, tell me how you feel?"

Valerie looked at Lieutenant Michael and then back at Doctor Lovecraft. She said, "I feel fine. For a little while I felt really tired but then I took a nap and felt better."

Doctor Lovecraft then said, "That was scary wasn't it. You had to face the Harvesters."

Valerie looked downward in embarrassment and said, "Yeah, I was scared."

Doctor Lovecraft said, "Yeah, I'd be really scared too. It's okay to be scared. That's just a normal part of our brain telling us that something can hurt us. Do you have a way to help you not be so scared?"

Valerie, still looking down, said, "I remember that Mary and Sarah will help me, so I don't have to be afraid anymore."

Doctor Lovecraft put her hand on Valerie's knee and said, "Friends can definitely help us not be scared. Talking about it can also help you not be scared. If something bothers you, you can tell your Lieutenant Michael about it. Or, you can even come see me and talk to me about it. If you have bad dreams you can come talk to me and I'll help you to understand them. Okay?"

Valerie nodded her head and said, "Okay, Doctor Lovecraft."

The Doctor then jumped up and grabbed a camera from off her desk and said, "I like to collect little girls on my wall. Is it okay if I take your picture and put it on my wall?"

Valerie lifted her head but still looked embarrassed as she nodded and said, "Okay."

Doctor Lovecraft lifted the camera up and pointed it at Valerie. Valerie looked straight into the camera and began to blush as she half-smiled in embarrassment. The Doctor said, "Cheese," and then snapped a picture with a bright flash. She then said, "I'm going to put you right on my wall."

The Doctor put the camera back on her desk and said, "Well, Valerie, you seem to be in good health so I'm going to let you go. I hope that you'll come see me once in a while even if you feel great."

Valerie nodded her head and said, "Okay, Doctor Lovecraft."

Doctor Lovecraft then said, "Is Lieutenant Michael giving you your shot every week?"

Valerie nodded her head and said, "Yep, the Lieutenant gives me a shot every Friday night before I go to bed."

The Doctor said, "Good, those shots were developed by some of our greatest scientific minds to help you girls be strong against the Harvesters. That's why we have to make sure that you get your shot every week."

Lieutenant Michael said, "Don't worry, Doctor Lovecraft. I make sure they get it every week."

Doctor Lovecraft then stood up and picked Valerie up by the armpits and placed her feet down on the floor. She then hugged her again and said, "Okay, Valerie, you're good so I'm going to let you go. Don't forget about me."

Lieutenant Michael extended his hand toward Valerie. Valerie walked toward him and took his hand. She said, "Goodbye Doctor!"

The Doctor opened the door for them and they walked out. Doctor Lovecraft stood in the doorway waving goodbye with a large grin. When Valerie and Lieutenant Michael got to the other side of the hallway, Valerie said, "She is weird. I definitely won't forget about her. She does seem really nice though." Lieutenant Michael smiled at her and said, "See, I told you so."

Five minutes after Lieutenant Michael and Valerie left to go see Doctor Lovecraft, Mary and Sarah left the apartment to go to the convenience store across the street. After Sarah shut the door to their apartment, Mary walked over to Squad four's door.

Sarah looked at her weirdly and was about to speak when Mary held a finger to her own mouth and hushed her. Sarah stood there waiting and Mary cupped her hands over her mouth. She then shouted, "Lieutenant, we're going to go spend Giana's five dollars now!"

There was a loud crash beyond the door to Squad four's apartment and then there was an eruption of laughter from inside.  Mary began to quietly chuckle.  Sarah placed a hand over her mouth to hold back a laugh.  Mary walked over to Sarah and said, "Okay, now we can go."

The convenience store was a small place that stood by itself.  Due to gasoline shortages caused by the Harvester invasion, most people did not have gasoline cars.  Gas rations were usually reserved to the very wealthy and the government, which includes the military.  Well-to-do people had the option of solar powered cars, but they were not that good.  Most people either walked or rode bikes.  Each city sector was generally self-contained so that it had everything an average citizen would need.  There were still streets but they were not really used for cars anymore, though an occasional military patrol drove by, or, a well-to-do person who could afford a solar energy car drove by.

Sarah and Mary reached the street corner, looked both ways and then crossed the street.  There were a few loafers sitting down in front of the store.  As the two girls approached the store, the people turned to look at them.  Mary and Sarah ignored them.

Mary opened the door for Sarah and then went in after her.  Together they went into the back where the cold cases were kept.  Mary began to look through the glass doors till she found her favorite brand of root beer.  She opened the glass door and pulled a case of it out.

Mary and Sarah went to the cashier and the attendant said, "Hello girls, where's your Lieutenant?"

Mary said, "He's busy right now so we came on our own."

The cashier nodded and took her money and said, "Okay, girls.  You have a good day."

Mary and Sarah, in unison, said, "Thanks!"  As they left the store, Sarah turned back around and waved goodbye to the man with a smile.

As they left the store one of the loafers had stood up and said, "Hey there little girls, aren't you too young to be drinking beer?"

Mary stopped in her tracks and looked at the man with disgust, saying, "Uh, are you talking to me?"  She then shook off her agitation and continued heading for the street.

The man, slurring his speech, began to follow after them and said, "Hold on there, little girl, can you spare some change for a drink."

Mary said, "Sorry, I'm all out."

The man stumbled over to her and put his hand on her shoulder. Mary stopped in her tracks and stared right into his face, her eyes glowed red with the activation of her power. She said, "Do you have any idea who I am?"

Mary handed Sarah the case of soda. Sarah then backed away from the man and held her nostrils shut with her hand, saying, "He reeks of alcohol."

The man would not let go of her shoulder, so Mary grabbed the man by the collar of his shirt, and forced him to the ground. She then lifted him up and tossed him effortlessly as if he weighed nothing. The man flew about twenty feet through the air and crashed on the sidewalk. He rolled over a few times and then lay there silently.

Mary brushed off her shoulder and said, "Humph! That'll teach you if you're sober enough to remember." Mary held open her hands and Sarah gave her the case of soda back.

Sarah said, "So, after seeing that, do you still want to drink beer like an adult?"

Mary said, "I was just joking about that. I don't really care about drinking beer. Let's go before someone else wants to try something."

As Sarah and Mary walked through the front door of the complex, Lieutenant Michael and Valerie stepped out of the back hallway. All four of them stopped and stared at each other in surprise. Lieutenant Michael said, "Oh, perfect timing."

Mary jogged over to Lieutenant Michael and pointed toward the convenience store, saying, "Some drunk out there tried to grab me!"

Lieutenant Michael looked out the glass doors and said, "Are you okay?"

Mary said, "Yeah, I sent the drunk flying."

Lieutenant Michael looked her over to see if she was really okay and said, "Do you want me to go over there and take care of it? I know you're much stronger than me but I still can help in this situation."

Mary said, "No, that's okay. It just pissed me off." Mary then held up the case of root beer towards Valerie and said, "Look, Val. Root beer just like I promised. Let's go up and have a drink on ice!"

The three girls ran up the stairs with Lieutenant Michael jogging behind them. When they reached their door, Valerie stopped and walked over to Squad four's door, cupped her hands over her mouth, and shouted saying, "Wow, look how much root beer Giana's five dollars bought!" Beyond the door there was another crash, followed by an eruption of laughter within. Mary and Sarah then busted out laughing.

Suddenly the door flung open and an angry Giana stood huffing in the doorway. Mary and Sarah stopped laughing. Giana pointed at them and yelled, "You girls are jerks!" She then slammed the door and Mary, Sarah, and Valerie erupted into laughter again. Valerie pointed her thumb at the door and said, "She's too easy."

Lieutenant Michael waved at them to calm down and said, "Okay, girls. I think that's enough teasing Giana for today. We don't want a repeat of what happened last time."

Once inside their own apartment, Mary set out four glasses of ice and filled each one with root beer. Together they sat at the table and enjoyed their drinks. Mary held up her glass to Valerie and said, "This is for Valerie doing so well on her first sortie." Sarah held up her own glass and said, "To Valerie!" Lieutenant Michael joined in and said, "Good job Valerie!"

Valerie slumped forward and lowered her head in embarrassment. Her cheeks began to blush and she wiggled in her seat, saying, "Thanks everybody, for helping me. I know I still have a long way to go before I can be like you."

-4-

Later that night, Valerie was sleeping soundly in her bed. As she slept, another siren went off in the apartment. Valerie sat up in bed and waited for the siren to stop so she could hear the call to action for the next assigned squad. Much to her surprise, the alarm did not cease.

A deep sense of dread began to form in the pit of her stomach. She pulled back the covers off of her legs and rolled out of bed. She made her way in the dark to her door and turned on the light. The alarm continued to blare.

She cautiously put her hand on the door knob. She slowly turned the knob and carefully opened the door. The lights in the hallway were already on. As she stepped into the hallway, the alarm finally ceased. There was nothing but silence. There was no call to action.

The silence made her even more uneasy. She ran over to Lieutenant Michael's room and knocked on the door. There was no answer. She knocked again and called out to the Lieutenant. There was still no answer. *Did he leave me behind?* she thought to herself.

Valerie cautiously opened the door and looked inside his room. The bed was not only empty, but was neatly made as if no one had slept in it. Valerie looked inside his personal bathroom and found it empty as well. She stood in the middle of his room and yelled out, "Lieutenant Michael, are you here? I'm really scared!" Still there was no answer.

Valerie ran out of his room and ran to Mary's door. Without knocking, she opened it, and saw that, not only was it empty, but the bed was neatly made too.

Valerie then ran over to Sarah's room and it was empty as well with the bed neatly made   Valerie ran into the dining area and yelled out, "Is anybody there?" She began to cry.

She remembered that Fourth squad was just across the hall and decided to see if they were still there.  She ran out of the apartment and began to pound on Squad four's door.  She yelled as she pounded, "Is anybody there!"  There was no answer.

As she stood there crying, she heard the horrifying screech of a Harvester down the hallway.  She turned toward the sound.  There was nothing there in sight but a shadow began to move from around the corner.  It bore the familiar shape of a Harvester.  Valerie stood there and her legs began to tremble like before.   She backed up a few steps and then started to quickly move backwards.

The Harvester screeched again and she turned to run but tripped over something soft.  She turned to see what it was.  To her horror she saw Mary lying there in a pool of her own blood.  Valerie looked at her hands and they were covered in blood   Valerie screamed in horror.  She crawled over to Mary and began to shake her but Mary would not wake up.

The shadow of the Harvester became larger and larger.  Valerie got back up and ran toward the stairway.  She opened the door to the stairs and ran inside the stairwell, slamming the door behind her.  She turned to run down the stairs and another body was lying at her feet in a puddle of blood.  Valerie rolled the body over and saw that it was Sarah.

As Valerie stared at Sarah's lifeless body, there was another Harvester screech echoing.  This time the sound came from down the stairs.  Valerie looked over the railing and saw a large shadow coming up the stairs.  She knew she was trapped.

Not knowing what to do anymore she sat down in the corner of the stairwell.  She buried her face into her knees and covered her ears with her hands to block out the screeching.  She began to chant to herself, "It's not real.  It's not real.  It's not real.'

Valerie suddenly felt something grab her shoulder.  She woke up with a start in her bed.  Tears were pouring down her eyes.  She looked up to see Lieutenant Michael standing over her in the dark of the night.  His hand was gently shaking her awake.

Valerie looked around her room in the dark trying to understand what was going on. She began to stutter, "I ... I was running and I ... I couldn't ... I..."

Lieutenant Michael's voice came to her gently in the dark of the night, saying, "You were just having a bad dream. Everything's alright."

Valerie sat up in her bed and began to cry even more. She reached out to Lieutenant Michael. He gently picked her up. She wrapped her arms around his neck and her legs around his waist. He supported her with one arm beneath her bottom and another arm around her back. He could feel his shoulder being soaked with tears.

Valerie quickly tried to compose herself. She stopped crying and said, "I dreamed that I couldn't find you."

Lieutenant Michael said, "I'd never leave you. I'll always be there for you."

Valerie said, "Can ... can I sleep in your bed tonight?"

Lieutenant Michael said, "Sure, why not. Everyone else does anyway even without asking me." He carried her back to his room and put her down in his bed. She rolled over and he then crawled in. He pulled the blankets over them and wrapped his arm around her. She gently rested her head onto his pillow and leaned into his chest.

Valerie said, "Lieutenant, I want to get stronger. I don't want to be afraid anymore."

Lieutenant Michael said, "If that's what you want to do than you can do it. You can always make yourself stronger. You can choose not to be afraid."

Valerie said, "Lieutenant, did you really mean it when you said you think of me as your daughter?"

Lieutenant Michael said, "Of course. You, Mary and Sarah are a precious part of my family now."

Valerie said, "I love you, Lieutenant."

Lieutenant Michael kissed her on the top of the head. She yawned and didn't say anything else. He lay there waiting for her to fall back to sleep. Slowly her body relaxed and she began to breathe deeply in sleep. When he was sure she was fast asleep, he too closed his eyes, and drifted off to sleep.

The alarm went off at six-thirty in the morning. Lieutenant Michael quickly reached over and tapped the alarm with his free arm. He then looked at Valerie who was still sleeping next to him. Her head now gently rested on his arm. One of her little hands gently clasped onto his shirt.

Beyond Valerie, he saw someone else. He sat up and saw two other heads poking out from underneath the covers. He got out of bed and rolled his eyes. He then threw back the covers revealing a sleeping Mary and a sleeping Sarah. He spoke loudly, "Okay, girls! It's time to wake up!"

Valerie, confused, sat up and looked around her not recognizing where she was. A line of morning drool stained her chin. Then, remembering what happened in the night, said, "Oh, yeah, I slept here tonight. Good morning, Lieutenant."

Mary, who was sleeping on her side, rolled over onto her back and stretched out her arms and legs as she groaned. Her belly button poked out from under her button pajama shirt. She then scratched her visible stomach and said, "Good morning, Lieutenant!"

Lieutenant Michael said, "You know girls, it never ceases to amaze me how you can sneak into my bed from time to time. I'm a trained soldier so stuff like this should wake me up."

Sarah sat up and yawned, saying, "You don't sense us because you're trained to sense danger. We're not dangerous, so you don't notice it."

Lieutenant Michael cocked his head to the side and raised his eyebrow in thought as he stroked his chin with his fingers. He then dropped his hand and shrugged his shoulders, saying, "Well, that's as good an explanation as any other one I suppose. Hopefully, I'm not losing my skill as a warrior."

Mary rolled over and sat on her knees, saying, "If you want, Lieutenant, I can do some extra training with you."

Lieutenant Michael quickly shook his head and said, "Are you kidding me? You'd kick my butt. I wouldn't stand a chance."

Lieutenant Michael then motioned his hand for them to get out of his bed and said, "Okay, girls. Time for you to get dressed and then we'll make some breakfast."

Mary, started to slide across his bed, and stopped short of pummeling Valerie, saying, "Welcome to the Good Morning Lieutenant Club. Did you have a bad dream?"

Valerie slid off of the bed. She looked up at Mary and said, "Yeah. I had a bad dream so the Lieutenant said that I could sleep in his bed."

Mary put her hands on Valerie's shoulders and said, "Isn't his bed comfy and warm?"

Valerie nodded her head and said, "Yeah, it was comfy and warm."

Mary then said, "But the most important part is that at night it's the safest part of the world. Lieutenant Michael has the ability to chase bad dreams away."

Lieutenant Michael looked up at the ceiling awkwardly and scratched the top of his head. He then walked over to them and said, "Okay, girls. It's my turn to get dressed, so I need you all to go to your own rooms now."

The girls left the room and Lieutenant Michael shut the door behind them. He turned back toward his bathroom and said to himself, "I can chase bad dreams away, huh? I thought I was helping to cause them."

Lieutenant Michael, got dressed and then walked into the dining area. Mary, Sarah, and Valerie were already sitting at the table. He thought he didn't take that long, but, apparently, they all beat him today. *Well, that's good too,* he thought to himself. He walked up to the table and said, "Good morning everybody. Let's start the day with some oatmeal." He raised his hands high in the air as if he had just won a race.

Mary's head collapsed on the table. She sighed loudly and said in exaggeration, "Oatmeal! That's so boring!"

Lieutenant Michael said, "It's good for growing girls like you." He went into the kitchen and began to make oatmeal on the stove. After a few minutes, the oatmeal was ready and they began to eat it together at the table.

As they were nearly done eating, an alarm began to sound. The four of them froze in place as they waited for the deployment announcement.

Mary said as they waited, "It can't be us. Not this soon."

Sarah hushed her and said, "Don't jinx it!"

The alarm finally silenced and a woman's voice came over the intercom saying, "Squad one, Squad two, Squad three, Squad four, deployment ten minutes."

Mary slammed her hands on the table and yelled, "Four squads!"

Lieutenant Michael jumped up from the table and said, "You heard it, girls. Let's get ready!"

Sarah pointed at Mary and said, "Darn it, Mary! You jinxed it!"

Mary held up her hands in surrender, shrugging her shoulders. She said, "Who'd know there'd be a four squad deployment!"

Valerie said, "Is it rare that they deploy this many squads?"

Lieutenant Michael walked over to a cabinet in the wall and said, "Yeah, it's rare. It means there's probably a major Harvester infiltration." He opened the cabinet, pulled out a box that contained the communicator units. He then pulled out Valerie's gun case and Sarah's scabbard belt.

Sarah took the scabbard belt and fastened it around her waist. She pulled out her metal sticks and examined them before putting them back in their sheath.

Valerie took her gun holster and strapped it to her back like last time. She double checked the cartridges on her belt to make sure they were loaded properly.

Lieutenant Michael opened the box of com units and put his device in his ear first. He twisted the button and the device activated with a crackle in his ear. He then handed a com unit to Mary, who stuck it in her ear, and twisted the button on. Next, he handed Sarah a com unit and she stuck it in her ear. She twisted the button on. Finally, he handed a com unit to Valerie, who was now familiar with it. She stuck it in her ear and twisted the button to make it turn on. It crackled to life in her ear.

Lieutenant Michael said, "Radio check." His voice came clearly in their ears.

Mary said, "Red, on."

Sarah said, "Blue, on."

Valerie said, "Yellow, on."

Lieutenant Michael smiled at them and nodded, saying, "Okay, girls. Let' go!"

Mary said, "Hold on one second!" She stretched out her arm and held out her hand like before, saying, "Okay, team! Remember our promise. We're going to protect each other." Sarah put her hand on Mary's hand and then Valerie joined in by putting her own hand on Sarah's hand. Lieutenant Michael, understanding what was going on, waited for a moment and then said, "Okay, girls. Let's go!" He knew that Mary was trying to help Valerie not be afraid anymore.

As they left the apartment, Sarah said, "Well, at least we got to eat first this time."

Mary said, "This better not be another drill, Lieutenant."

Lieutenant Michael waved his hand in denial and said, "If this is a drill they didn't tell me about it this time so please take it seriously."

Mary jogged up to Lieutenant Michael's side and wrapped an arm around his arm, saying, "Don't worry, Lieutenant. I always take killing Harvesters seriously."

Lieutenant Michael said, "Don't worry, Mary. I know you always do a great job in the field."

A huge grin appeared on Mary's face and she said, "I know, right? I'm awesome. Oh, and I guess Sarah's not bad either."

Lieutenant Michael said, "Don't worry, girls, you both do an excellent job in the field. I've learned that I can always count on you."

Valerie ran over to Lieutenant Michael's other side and grabbed onto his hand. He opened his palm and held her hand back. Valerie said, "This time I'm not going to be afraid and I'm going to make myself stronger."

Sarah said, "Don't worry, Valerie. We believe in you."

Mary said, "Yep, we think you're going to be great out there too. I think you have the potential to be the strongest yellow wielder out there!"

Valerie blushed in embarrassment and said, "I don't know about that, but I'll do my best."

When squad three entered onto the roof, the helicopter was not yet there. They were also the first squad to show up for duty. Lieutenant Michael had them stand in a line from oldest to youngest and they stood at ease as they waited. He, himself, stood next to Mary.

Soon enough, Fourth squad came through the door next. Giana was already complaining, saying, "This better not be another drill. I went out just yesterday."

Lieutenant Rachel said, "Don't worry, I think this is the real deal. They didn't tell me anything about a drill."

Lieutenant Rachel waved hello to Michael. She then joined them in standing in the line. Lieutenant Rachel stood next to Valerie, followed by Giana, Elsa, and Tina.

Lieutenant Michael turned his head to look at Rachel. He said, "Have you heard anything about this yet?"

Lieutenant Rachel shook her head and said, "Nope, I'm in the dark."

Lieutenant Michael said, "Well, that makes two of us."

As they were speaking, the door opened and two squads that Valerie had yet to see came on to the roof. She watched the new girls walk in front of her as they passed. A few of them smiled at her as they joined the line.

The man who led them appeared to be the officer of one of the squads. He stood in front of the line so that everyone could see him from where he was standing. The man spoke saying, "Captain Faust just informed me that there is a major Harvester movement in the Reno sector." Valerie's eyes went wide and her jaw dropped. She spoke out loud saying, "That's where my mom and dad live!"

The man then continued speaking, saying, "The Harvesters are attempting to breach the wall. First squad, Second squad, and Fourth squad will go over the wall and hold back the Harvesters while the repair crew reinforces that section. Third squad will hold back on top of the wall as back up. If the wall is breached, third squad will block the breech. Fourth squad will hunt down Harvesters that made it inside the wall. First and Second squads will continue to block harvester advances outside the wall. Any questions?"

The other officers answered, "No" and the man walked back to his own squad and stood at the head of the line.

Valerie leaned forward to look at all the other new people she had not seen before today. She spoke into her com unit, saying, "Lieutenant Michael, who was that man who was speaking just now?"

Lieutenant Michael replied to her, saying, "That's Lieutenant Steven Lloyd. He's the Lieutenant for First squad."

Valerie looked confused and said, "If he's a Lieutenant, doesn't that mean that you and him are the same rank? How come he's giving you orders?"

Lieutenant Michael said, "We call it the chain of command. Even though we're the same rank, when we work together like this, our squad number represents our command level. So First squad is first, then the Second squad is second in the command line, then there's me as third and Rachel as fourth."

A light went on in Valerie's face and she said, "Oh, I get it Lieutenant." The look of understanding began to be replaced with a look of dread as she returned to thinking about her parents still living in Reno Sector. She said, "Do you think my mom and dad are going to be okay?"

Sarah said, "They haven't breached the wall yet so I wouldn't worry about them."

Mary shook her fist and said, "Yeah, don't worry about it. Even if they make it through, we'll stop them!"

The transport helicopter began to grow larger in the distance. Its duel rotors could be heard far off. The helicopter quickly made its approach to the roof and then landed. The rear door ramp lowered and the squads began to enter in according to their number. The odd numbered squads sat on the right side while the even numbered squads sat on the left side of the helicopter.

Lieutenant Michael sat down next to the red wielder of first squad. The young girl looked up at him and smiled. He said, "If I remember correctly, your name is Leslie, right?" She smiled at him and nodded her head.

Valerie sat down next to Lieutenant Michael. He turned to her and watched her buckle in correctly. He could still see a look of worry in her face. She caught him looking at her and looked up at him with a grim smile on her face trying to hide the worry behind it. She didn't fool him.

Sarah sat down next to Valerie and wrapped an arm around her shoulder. Mary sat down next to Sarah and started swinging her feet in the air.

Across from them, on the other side of the helicopter, Squad four sat. Lieutenant Rachel looked at Michael and smiled. He smiled back at her. Mary, watching, rolled her eyes, sighed, crossed her arms, and leaned backward along the wall of the helicopter. Giana stuck her tongue out at Mary. Mary returned the gesture, followed by an added shaking of her right fist.

With all of the squads loaded, the ramp of the door began to rise. The voice of a woman came over the intercom saying, "Squad one, two, three, four ready for deployment, Reno sector. ETA one hour. Deploy outside main wall."

Lieutenant Steven Lloyd picked up the intercom radio, saying, "Squad one, two, three, four ready for deployment, Reno sector, outside main wall."

Suddenly, the rotors of the helicopter picked up speed and the noise of their rotation increased. The helicopter shook and lifted up off the ground. It quickly sped to its destination.

Every ten minutes, the voice of the pilot gave an updated time estimate. With fifteen minutes left to go, the pilot's voice prematurely began another announcement, "Attention, wall breach has occurred. Redeploy within sector wall."

Valerie's eyes widened and she looked up at Lieutenant Michael, sitting beside her. She said, "Oh no! My mom and dad!"

Lieutenant Michael looked down at her as she sat next to him. He put a hand behind her back and said, "Try not to worry. We're going to do everything we can to save them. You just got to focus on the mission. Okay?"

Valerie gave a nod of her head and held her hands over her heart. She said, "Okay, Lieutenant. I'll try my best." She closed her eyes and looked to be praying.

The pilot announced that there was five minutes left to deploy. The time seemed to last for an eternity within Valerie's mind. Gunfire could be heard over the noise of the rotors. No doubt the sector's defenders were trying to put up a valiant fight. Valerie knew, though, that without the Wielders, their fight would not last long.

The door of the helicopter started to lower even before they landed. The pilot's voice spoke, "No landing zone, prepare for drop."

Lieutenant Lloyd said, "Blue Wielders, create a drop zone." Sarah, Tina, and two of the other girls stood up and walked over to the opening door. All the girls activated their powers so their eyes started to glow. As the door ramp opened, the screeches of the Harvesters could be heard below them.

When the door finished opening, the four girls jumped out of the helicopter, cushioning their fall with their blue shields. They landed among a group of Harvesters that were scattering from the helicopter above them. The four of them formed a square and created a shield around themselves that touched each other's shield, leaving a space in the middle open.

When the Harvesters overcame the initial shock of the four girls landing in the middle of their swarm, they began to ram the blue shields with all their might. With each strike of their powerful mandibles, a shower of sparks flew into the air.

With an acceptable drop zone created, Lieutenant Lloyd said, "All units, begin deployment!"

Squad four dropped first. Giana wrapped an arm around Lieutenant Rachel and Elsa. Then, together, they walked off the ramp. Giana used all her power in her feet to endure the jump and helped to cushion their landing.

Squad three was up next. Valerie followed Squad four's example and went to one side of Mary. Mary wrapped an arm around her and Lieutenant Michael and said, "Okay, let's jump." As they approached the edge of the ramp, Valerie looked over to see that the area was swarming with Harvesters of all different sizes. Some were smaller like the ones she fought before. Others were twice as large. Some looked like baby ones. She had never seen so many Harvesters together. She said, "Is it going to hurt when we land?"

Mary said, "You'll find out." She then yelled, "Geronimo!" as the three of them walked off the ramp. Mary's arm held tightly around Valerie's waist as they plummeted to the ground. The shock of the landing hurt a little but it could have been far worse if Mary did not take the full impact for them. Mary let them go and they watched Second and First squads land in the opening behind them.

Lieutenant Michael spoke to Sarah through the com unit, saying, "How you holding up?"

Sarah, her arms outstretched maintaining the shield, said, "Still good, Lieutenant."

Lieutenant Lloyd yelled out, "We got to plug that hole first. I want Third and Fourth squads to plug that hole. First and Second squads will clean up here first. Then we'll proceed as planned."

Lieutenant Michael looked around him and said, "There's got to be at least thirty in here!  I would suggest that we send the reds out first to scatter them.  Then the blues can keep formation as we make our way to the breach."

Lieutenant Lloyd said, "That's what I was thinking too."  He motioned to the four red wielders and they nodded their heads.

Lieutenant Michael said, "Don't worry about killing them, just distract them for now.  We can kill them after the breach is plugged."

Mary saluted him and said, "Leave it to me, Lieutenant!"

Mary, Giana, and the two other red Wielders jumped over the shields created by the blue Wielders.  They began jumping around in random directions landing on top of the fully grown Harvesters.  The Harvesters stopped attacking the shields and began to chase the red Wielders around as they jumped from space to space.

Lieutenant Lloyd said, "Okay, girls, now's our chance!"  Together, while maintaining their protective shield in that formation, they walked cautiously toward the breach in the wall.

Lieutenant Michael said, "Okay, Sarah, when we get to the breach, redo your shield to plug up the hole."

Sarah nodded her head and said, "Aye, Lieutenant!"

As they walked to the wall breach an occasional Harvester would ignore the red Wielders and run up against the shield causing a shower of sparks to fly.  Valerie began to smell the same smell of ozone that appeared when she saw the fight between Mary and Giana.  She began to whisper to herself, "I'm not going to be afraid.  I'm not going to be afraid.  I'm not going to be afraid."  Valerie's words could be heard in the com unit by the rest of her squad.  No one said anything to her as they focused on plugging the wall breach.

As they approached the breach another swarm of smaller Harvesters entered the sector through the opening and began to chase the red Wielders too.  Beyond them a larger group of fully grown Harvesters could be seen coming in the distance.

Lieutenant Michael said, "Sarah, do you think you can run and plug the breach now?"

Sarah looked left and right to see if the area was clear.  It was.  She said, "I think I can."

Lieutenant Michael looked at Lieutenant Lloyd for confirmation.  Lieutenant Lloyd nodded his head.  Lieutenant Michael said, "Okay, go Sarah!"

Sarah dropped her shield and sprinted with all her might toward the opening. The other blue Wielders adjusted their shields to engulf the group inside their shield barrier.

Sarah ran faster and faster toward the breech. Valerie watched her in anticipation. A baby sized Harvester stopped and turned to watch Sarah run. It then began to run toward her.

Mary, who happened to be nearby, standing on the back of a fully grown harvester watched the little one run for Sarah. Like a bullet, she jumped with all her might to intercept the running Harvester. Mary managed to land in front of the Harvester's path and she skidded to a stop. She grabbed the little one by the mandibles and began to swing around in a circle with it. When she picked up enough speed, she hurled the Harvester, sending it rolling down the way.

As Sarah ran past Mary, she said, "Thanks!" and kept running. She ran right into the middle of the breach and quickly extended her hands, forming a shield inside the breach. She said, "Okay, Lieutenant. Breach is blocked!"

Lieutenant Michael spoke to Lieutenant Lloyd, saying, "Breach is blocked."

Lieutenant Lloyd nodded his head and said, "Good. Okay, everyone. When I say go, you three girls drop your shields and start blasting at them. Reds, time to start slaughtering these bugs!"

Valerie watched Lieutenant Michael pull a smaller version of the cattle prod gun off of his belt and he held it in his hand. He nodded at her as a sign to get ready. She moved to stand next to him.

Lieutenant Lloyd held up his hand and then dropped it, yelling, "Go!" Tina and the two other blue Wielders dropped their hands and began shooting blue beams of light over and over again at the Harvesters that remained on the inside of the wall.

With the need to distract the Harvesters no longer there, Mary shouted out, "Hell yeah! Stomping time!" She leapt back into action by propelling herself into the midst of a group of baby Harvesters. With her hands and feet glowing red she began to punch and kick at the little ones, quickly bringing them down.

With five of the little ones killed, she leapt to an older one. She grabbed it by the mandibles and began to kick it in the mouth. As she kicked, one of the Harvester claws stabbed into her leg, tearing a large gash along her thigh.

Mary grunted in agony, but forced herself to endure the pain. She ripped off one the mandible sections in her right hand and shoved it inside the Harvester's mouth and up inside its brain. The harvester began to jump around in circles and then fell over on its side as its legs twitched.

Mary jumped out of the battle and landed next to the circle of blue wielders, who were keeping Harvesters back with their blue spears of light. She limped over to Valerie and said, "Okay, Val. Your turn."

Valerie saw the blood spilling down Mary's leg. Mary lifted her skirt to reveal her injured thigh. A deep gash had been cut from the top of the knee to the middle of her thigh.

Valerie looked at the gash and felt sickened by it. She winced at the thought of it but quickly activated her power into her hands. Her hands glowed yellow and she placed them over the gash on Mary's thigh. Yellow light began to cover Mary's thigh. The wound began to close up until there was not even a mark of it left.

When the wound had completely healed, Mary smiled, and punched her fist into her hand, saying, "Back to the fun!" She then turned around and eyed the battlefield. She saw Giana trying to push back a fully grown Harvester by herself. Mary shook her head, saying, "Idjit!"

Mary then leapt toward Giana twice, landing on the back of the Harvester, saying, "You look like you could use a hand."

Giana, whose feet were now slowly being dragged back by the strength of the Harvester, said, "Don't just stand there! Give me a hand!"

Mary said, "Sure, no problem." She then began to slowly clap her hands together.

Giana yelled at her, "Stop goofing around! This is serious!"

Mary jumped onto the Harvester's head and began to stomp onto it with her foot. The Harvester began to screech as her foot slowly began to crack its hard shell. With each strike, a shower of sparks sprayed into the air.

Finally, the hard shell cracked and yellow Harvester goo began to spray out of the dying Harvester. It sprayed right into Giana's face. With the creature now dead, Giana let go of its mandibles, wiped the yellow goo off of her face, and flung it on the ground. The front of her uniform jacket was stained as well.

Mary, standing on top of the corpse, pointed at her, and laughed, "Hey Giana! You're supposed to shower after the mission, not during it." She then dropped down from off the corpse next to Giana.

Giana wiped her hands on the front of Mary's uniform jacket and said, "Thanks for the help."

Mary looked down at her own jacket in disgust and wiped it with her own hands, saying, "Don't mention it."

Together they assessed the situation. All the little Harvesters were already easily killed off. The other two red Wielders were currently battling their own fully grown Harvester. That left just three fully grown Harvesters left. Mary said, "Let's take these three out together!"

Giana nodded her head and together they jumped toward the nearest fully grown Harvester. Mary, this time, grabbed onto the Harvester's mandibles and began to brace herself to stop it from moving. The Harvester screeched at her as drool spilled from its mouth. A look of disgust fell on Mary's face and she said, "Why are you so ugly?"

After Mary had stabilized the Harvester, Giana jumped onto its back, and began to stomp her own foot onto its head. Again, a shower of sparks sprayed into the air. Finally, the tough shell cracked and yellow Harvester goo sprayed out of the opening. Mary's face was now covered in Harvester goo as well as the front of her uniform jacket.

With the second Harvester now dead, Mary let go of its mandibles and wiped off her face with her hands, flinging the goo onto the ground. Giana laughed at her and said, "Serves you right!"

Mary wiped her hands on her skirt and said, "Yeah, yeah. Why does it have to stink so bad?"

While Mary and Giana were killing off the second fully grown Harvester, the three blue Wielders had managed to concentrate their spear of light ability on the next Harvester, killing it from afar. The other two red Wielders were already jumping to the last fully grown Harvester. Mary dismissed it with a wave of her hand and said, "Ah, they can have the last one." They watched as the other team killed the last Harvester.

After the last Harvester died, Mary ran toward Lieutenant Michael with her hands outstretched toward him. She ran up to him and tried to hug him. Lieutenant Michael saw her coming and quickly stopped her by outstretching his hand onto her forehead. He said, "Uh, not with bug goo all over you." He then leaned forward and sniffed the air, saying, "You stink too."

Mary put her arms down and said, "I can't help it! I killed a gusher."

Lieutenant Michael put his arm down and noticed that his hand was slimy with Harvester goo. He wiped his hand on Mary's arm sleeve. Mary moaned and said, "Don't make it worse, Lieutenant!"

Mary then began to jump up and down, shouting, "Did you see me, Val? Wasn't I awesome?!"

Valerie nodded her head and said, "Yeah! That was amazing!"

Mary then pointed at Valerie, saying, "And you, Val. You didn't pass out at all this time. You're becoming stronger!"

Valerie nodded her head with a huge grin on her face. She brought her arms up in victory, saying, "Yeah, I even helped today! We were really a team!"

Mary said, "That's right! When we work together, nothing can stop us!"

As Mary was celebrating her victory, Fourth squad took off running down the street into the city. Valerie said, "Where are they going?"

Lieutenant Michael said, "They're going to hunt down any other Harvesters that might be in the sector still."

First and Second squad had already gone over the wall to distract the Harvesters from attacking Sarah. All that was left to do was to wait for the repair crew to show up. While they were waiting, they would have to defend this section.

Valerie and Mary stood on both sides of Lieutenant Michael as they kept an eye on the city. It was unknown how many Harvesters had made it inside the sector. Lieutenant Michael could hear Rachel reporting kills over the command channel on his com unit. Mostly there appeared to be young ones that had scattered first inside the city.

As they waited, a fully grown Harvester appeared from behind a building. It stared at them from afar and began to screech. It then ran toward them as fast as its legs could move.

Mary said, "Great, a straggler." She then leapt toward it, held out her hands, and braced her feet to absorb the impact of the Harvester.

Sarah said, "Lieutenant, should I help Mary?"

Lieutenant Michael said, "No, you got to hold the breach."

Mary said, "Don't worry, Sarah. I got this."

The Harvester did not slow down as it crashed into Mary. Mary held onto its mandibles and tried to stop it from moving. Her feet began to be dragged along the ground. Mary stomped her foot into the pavement, leaving an indent in the street, trying to force the Harvester to stop moving. In spite of this, Mary continued to be slowly dragged backward.

Lieutenant Michael spoke over the commander's channel, saying, "Lieutenant Rachel, we got a fully grown harvester at the breach. We could use some help."

Lieutenant Rachel replied, "Okay, we're clear here so we'll be there as soon as possible."

Mary continued to struggle with the Harvester. Suddenly, she began to scream in pain and the Harvester managed to push her down onto her back on the ground.

Sarah said, "Lieutenant ..."

Lieutenant Michael stopped her, he shouted, "Hold your position!" He held his gun up and pointed it toward the Harvester.

Valerie watched on in horror as Mary tried to keep the mandibles from cutting into her stomach. She kicked with one foot at the Harvester's mouth.

Valerie continued to watch this spectacle in horror. She shook her head and said, "I got to help her! I promised!" She took off running toward Mary and pulled her cattle prod gun out of the holster on her back.

Lieutenant Michael realized what was happening and he began to run after Valerie, saying, "What are you doing?" She ignored him and ran up to the side of the Harvester's head. She held up the gun, switched to full-auto and began to fire into its head. Lieutenant Michael ran up right beside her with his own gun and joined her in firing at the Harvester's head.

The Harvester stopped focusing on Mary. Mary let go of its mandibles and began to slide on the ground backwards away from it. With Valerie and Lieutenant Michael distracting the Harvester with their cattle prod guns, the Harvester lost interest in Mary, and began to jump around in a circle in confusion.

The Harvester stopped spinning and began to screech at Lieutenant Michael and Valerie, who were standing side by side. Valerie dropped the second clip in her gun and shoved in the third clip. It was her last one. The Harvester trembled in agitation and looked directly at them. It focused its attention on Valerie, who stared back at the Harvester. The Harvester charged at Valerie. Valerie began to fire the last clip in her cattle prod gun.

Lieutenant Michael dropped his gun and was about to pick Valerie up and run, when, suddenly, Giana came spinning like a bullet through the air. She smashed into the side of the Harvester causing it to roll over onto its side. Giana repositioned herself as the Harvester rolled back over onto its feet. She jumped in front of it and held onto its mandibles. Tina came running, swinging a metal stick that glowed blue with her power. She smashed it over the already weakened head of the Harvester. Its head cracked open and yellow goo began to spill out. The Harvester stopped moving and was now a corpse.

Valerie stood there still pointing her gun at it. Her whole body was frozen stiff but her finger still clutched onto the trigger, which made a repeating clicking sound indicating that the clip was now empty.

Lieutenant Michael pried the gun out of her hands. Valerie slowly came out of her stillness and looked at Lieutenant Michael in shock. He said to her, "Are you okay?"

Valerie just stared at him for a moment with her eyes blinking and then said, "Yeah." Slowly her body began to unfreeze itself.

Lieutenant Michael said, "I don't want you to do something like that without first telling me, okay? It could have killed you."

Valerie, looked down at the ground and said, "I...I said I'd protect everybody. I...I had to do something."

Mary was still sitting on the ground. Lieutenant Michael turned his attention to her and said, "Mary, you okay?"

Mary said, "I think my left leg is broken."

Lieutenant Michael said, "Really?"

Mary lifted her left leg and her lower leg sagged like a wet noodle. Lieutenant Michael winced and said, "Okay, Valerie. Heal her leg."

Valerie ran over to Mary and again activated her power. Her hands glowed with yellow light. She gently placed her hands on the broken part of Mary's leg. The yellow light moved over the broken part of her leg.

Mary said, "Thanks for helping me back there. You saved me this time."

Valerie said, "Well, we promised to protect each other and that's what I'm going to do."

Lieutenant Rachel came over and said, "You and Valerie stared down a fully grown Harvester yourselves. I'm impressed."

Lieutenant Michael said, "Well, Valerie jumped the gun, literally. I was planning on waiting a few moments later before doing it by myself, but then Valerie ran out there so I ran after her."

Lieutenant Rachel said, "Well, I'm glad you're all okay. We think we found all of them in the sector. Mostly small ones. That big one slipped by us though. I'm sorry about that."

Lieutenant Michael said, "No worries. Everything turned out okay. I'm just glad that Giana showed up when she did otherwise Valerie and I might have been toast."

As Lieutenant Michael finished speaking, several helicopters with large stone blocks came. Sarah let down her shield and moved out of the way. The helicopters set the stones in the breach. Workers then came to cement them in place and fill in the gaps with smaller stones and cement.

There were no more Harvesters in the area so First and Second squad climbed back over the wall to join Third and Fourth squad. The Harvesters probably would not return for a few days as new ones would migrate to this area.

Valerie approached Lieutenant Michael and tugged onto the sleeve of his jacket. He looked down at her and she said, "Lieutenant Michael, is there any way to check to see if my parents are okay?"

Lieutenant Michael nodded his head and said, "Of course, we can all go together to the evacuation center. After all, they might need our help with healing people."

Valerie smiled and said, "Okay. Thanks, Lieutenant."

Together, the four squads began to walk down the street toward the chosen place for the evacuation command center. Valerie could see the ruined buildings and objects along the street where Harvesters had stampeded. She was not prepared for what came next though.

As they walked on, they came across a section where dead bodies lay in the street. To be more accurate, it was a section of the street where parts of dead bodies were haphazardly scattered on the ground.

As they began to move through the remains of arms, legs, heads, and internal organs that had spilled out of torsos as Harvesters feasted on them, Valerie became overwhelmed by the sight. The smell of blood only added to the problem. She ran to the side of a building, bent over forward, and vomited on the pavement.

Lieutenant Michael, Mary, and Sarah ran over to her. He placed a hand on her back as she remained bent over staring at the puddle of vomit at her feet. She began to cry and said, "I... I can't see... I can't see any more of this. What if my mom and dad are dead like this?"

Lieutenant Michael said, "Okay, I can carry you. Just keep your eyes closed, okay?"

Valerie said, "Okay." She closed her eyes and turned around. Lieutenant Michael picked her up and carried her through the section of the street where the people did not have enough time to evacuate.

After ten more minutes of walking, they reached the front line where the soldiers had managed to cut off the Harvester advance. Lieutenant Michael said, "Okay, Valerie, we're here. Can I put you down now?"

Valerie said, "Okay, there's no more dead bodies, right?"

Lieutenant Michael said, "That's right. No more dead bodies." He put her down and she opened her eyes to see all the people still alive. She began to see people that she recognized. She walked among the crowd, looking left and right. Then she saw her parents standing together.

Valerie yelled out, "Mommy! Daddy!" She began to cry again and ran toward them. Her parents, recognizing her voice, turned in surprise to where they heard her and saw her running toward them. Her mom opened her arms and Valerie ran right into them. Her mom picked her up and began crying as well.

Valerie began to speak through her crying, "I...I helped to save you. I did my very best to save everyone I could."

Her mom put her down and Valerie hugged her dad next. He picked her up and held her, saying, "Thank you. Valerie, you did a really good job."

Lieutenant Michael, Mary, and Sarah stepped through the crowd to find Valerie. They watched her as her parents hugged her and talked to her. Lieutenant Michael walked up to them and said, "Hello again."

Valerie turned her head to face Lieutenant Michael and said, "Look, my parents are okay!" Her dad set her down.

Lieutenant Michael said, "See, I told you they'd be okay. Considering everything, there appears to be very few casualties this time."

Valerie then saw Mary and Sarah and said, "Mom, dad, these are my new friends: Mary and Sarah." Mary and Sarah waved at them as they stood next to Lieutenant Michael.

Her mom said, "Hello there, thanks for looking after our Valerie."

Mary said, "No problem, she's an awesome member of our team."

Sarah said, "Yeah, we love being with her."

Lieutenant Michael said, "I'm sorry to do this, but we got to head to the trauma center so that Valerie can help to heal the injured that survived."

Her dad said, "We understand." Both her mom and dad hugged Valerie as they said their goodbyes again.

Lieutenant Michael then held out his hand to Valerie. Valerie took his hand and together they headed for the trauma center. Valerie's parents watched her as they left.

Valerie helped the other three yellow Wielders heal those who had been injured. Fortunately, there were not that many injured so it did not take long to heal everybody.

According to the battle report, there were only twenty human deaths and thirty-three injuries. There were a total of seventy-four Harvesters eliminated in this action.

The helicopter ride back to the Phoenix Guard headquarters was quiet. Everyone was exhausted from the battle. Most of the girls fell asleep on the way back. Mary leaned on Lieutenant Michael's shoulder as she slept. Sarah leaned over on Mary's shoulder as she slept. Valerie rested her head on Sarah's lap as she slept. Lieutenant Michael watched them sleep and he said to himself, "I got a really good team. I hope they can keep it up."

-5-

The helicopter landed on the roof of the Phoenix Guard complex. Lieutenant Michael shook Mary awake, saying, "We're back." She sat up, looking confused and said, "Huh?" As she sat up, Sarah woke up from the movement. She looked down to see Valerie still sleeping on her lap. Sarah shook Valerie awake and said, "We're home."

Valerie sat up and stretched saying, "I'm so tired."

Lieutenant Michael stood up and said, "I bet you're tired. That was a long mission."

Mary stood up. She placed a hand on her stomach, saying, "My stomach doesn't feel so good."

Lieutenant Michael said, "Do you want to see Doctor Lovecraft?"

Mary shook her head, saying, "Nah, I'm probably just tired and hungry. It's not quite dinner time and way past lunch time. It's, it's dunch time." She laughed at her own joke.

Lieutenant Michael rolled his eyes and said, "Dunch, huh?"

They exited the helicopter together and stood in a line again according to their squad number. Captain Faust was waiting for them again. He smiled at them and said, "I've already heard the report of your actions today. I'm very proud of how you girls handled the wall breach. The World Government has noted that you were able to, not only save a sector, but managed to keep casualties of civilians low. Now I know you're all tired and hungry so I won't take up your time. I have already taken the liberty to order you all dinner and it is waiting for you in your apartments. You are dismissed."

The girls gave him a tired salute and then shuffled down the stairway. As Lieutenant Michael followed them, Captain Faust touched his arm and pulled him aside, saying, "How did Valerie do today?"

Lieutenant Michael nodded his head and said, "Oh, she far exceeded my expectations today. She even managed to save Mary with the cattle prod. I don't think we have to worry about her anymore. I'm sure she's going to do just fine now."

Captain Faust said, "That's good to hear. Make sure you write about that in your report for me to read. We'll probably keep you teamed up with squad four one more time to make certain of it. Then you'll be free to run independently. As always, I'm glad that you are a reliable guardian. It makes my job so much easier." He said with a chuckle.

Lieutenant Michael said, "Thank you, sir." He then saluted and turned back toward the stairway to go back to his apartment.

Mary opened the door to the apartment. The smell of fresh pizza caused her to sniff into the air. She smiled and looked toward the table to see two pizza boxes sitting on the table. Mary said, "Pizza! Nice!" She ran toward the table and lifted up the top flap of the box.

Sarah sniffed the air and said, "You smell pizza. I can only smell bug juice." She winced her face in disgust and plugged her nose.

Mary sarcastically said, "Geez, I'm sorry. I can't help it since I got sprayed by bug guts."

Lieutenant Michael walked in through the open door and said, "Oh, I can smell pizza," he paused for a moment and then said, "and ... I can also smell bug juice."

Mary threw her hands down in frustration and balled her hands into fists, saying, "Come on you guys! You know that the fully grown Harvesters spray their guts when I bash 'em!"

Lieutenant Michael chuckled, saying, "Calm down, Mary. I was just joking with you. You girls can take a quick shower first before we eat."

Mary sighed and said, "I was going to do that any way." She pointed at the stains on her uniform. Her jacket was stained with yellow Harvester goo and her skirt was stained with blood from her thigh injury. Mary then turned and stormed down the hallway toward the bathroom.

Valerie and Sarah looked at each other with worried faces and then followed after her. When they entered the bathroom, Mary was already taking off her uniform. Sarah walked up to her and said, "Are you okay? You seem really angry."

Mary shrugged her shoulders and said, "I don't know. I just kind of feel frustrated and I don't know why. I'm probably just tired and my stomach hurts too. That's all." Again, she placed a hand over her stomach.

Valerie stood next to Sarah, with a look of worry on her face, and said, "Are you frustrated because I helped you?"

Mary reached out and held her on the arms, saying, "Are you kidding me? That was so awesome how you and Lieutenant Michael came running to help me when I broke my leg. Who knows what would have happened to me if you two hadn't done that. I owe you big time for that."

Sarah nodded her head and said, "Yeah, Valerie. My jaw dropped when I saw you running to help her. That was amazing. It was only your second mission."

Valerie began to blush and looked embarrassed. She scratched her cheek with a finger and said, "Well, we all promised to protect each other so I just couldn't stand there and watch. I thought I would be too scared to do anything but I was more scared of losing you."

Mary reached out again and took Valerie into her arms, hugging her. She rested her head on Valerie's head and said, "Thanks Valerie. Next time it's my turn to protect you."

Valerie returned her embrace and started to cry a little, saying, "I don't want to lose any of you."

Mary let her go and then Valerie hugged Sarah. Sarah said, "As long as we're together, we can protect each other."

Mary finished taking off her uniform and she pulled out her hair bands. Her hair was stiff from dried Harvester goo. She quickly turned on the water to the shower and waited for it to warm up. Valerie and Sarah quickly got undressed and turned on their own showers.

While the girls were in the bathroom, a knock came to the door. He opened the door and Lieutenant Rachel was there. She smiled and said, "Hey Michael, we're going to go swimming tomorrow again. Do you want to come with us this time?"

Lieutenant Michael's eyes lit up and he said, "Sure, I'll have to ask my squad, but I'm sure they'll want to try out the swimsuits we got recently. What time?"

Lieutenant Rachel said, "Oh, how about thirteen hundred?"

Lieutenant Michael nodded and said, "Yeah. That would be great. I'm pretty sure they'll go for it. Just assume it's a yes and if they don't want to then I'll let you know."

Lieutenant Rachel then nodded and said, "Okay, I'll see you tomorrow then."

Lieutenant Michael said, "Great, I'll see you tomorrow." Lieutenant Rachel turned away and headed into her own apartment across the hall. Lieutenant Michael watched her leave and then slowly shut the door. He then headed into his own room to shower and change his clothes.

Lieutenant Rachel entered into her own apartment. Giana, Tina, and Elsa stood there waiting for her to return. Lieutenant Rachel shut the door behind her with a smile.

Giana stepped forward with her arms squared on her hips, saying, "So, are they coming?"

Lieutenant Rachel nodded and said, "Yeah, seems that way."

Giana gave her a thumbs up and said, "Great! This means we can begin Operation Cupid. We'll help you catch that dense Lieutenant Michael." She stretched out her right arm and held up two fingers in a V sign.

Lieutenant Rachel's smile faded and she looked depressed, saying, "Thanks, girls, but that just might be an impossible mission."

Elsa said, "If we all work together, we can do anything!"

Tina shrugged her shoulders and spoke in her melancholy tone, "I guess I could help. I don't know what I could do though."

Lieutenant Rachel smiled again and said, "Thanks girls. Being in a relationship in the military is really hard so I don't have much hope. But, I'll do my best."

Valerie and Sarah came out of their rooms wearing their uniforms. Mary came out of her room wearing her red and black pajamas. Lieutenant Michael looked at her and said, "Mary, it's only fifteen hundred hours and you're already in your pajamas?"

Mary stretched out her hand and held up her palm, saying, "Lieutenant, there's no way we're getting called out again today. I'm going to eat my pizza and then I'm going to lay down on that couch and watch TV until I pass out." She pointed at the couch as she stood there.

Lieutenant Michael held up his hands in surrender and said, "That's fine with me. You've earned it."

Mary then walked up to the table, pulled out a chair, and sat down. She slumped her shoulders and looked down cast, saying, "I'm so tired." She then flipped open a pizza box and took a slice of pizza. She ate it in silence.

Valerie, Sarah and Lieutenant Michael joined her at the table and began to eat with her. Sarah said, "Two missions in two days is rough. We usually can go several weeks without a mission."

Lieutenant Michael said, "You know, I just want to say that I'm really proud of how well you girls did in this mission. It could have been so much worse but you all did your best and it really showed."

Mary gave him a thumbs up as she shoved more pizza into her mouth. Sarah smiled and said, "Thanks, Lieutenant." Valerie started to blush again and she slumped her shoulders forward, swinging her feet in her chair.

Lieutenant Michael's face lit up as he remembered his conversation with Rachel. He said, "Oh yeah, before I forget again. While you were in the shower, Lieutenant Rachel came over and invited us to go swimming with her squad tomorrow at thirteen hundred hours. I told her that we'd go but I'd have to ask you first. We haven't gone swimming yet in your new swimsuits. Do you three want to go?"

Valerie perked up and nodded her head, saying, "Yeah, that'd be fun!"

Sarah, clapped her hands together and said, "Yes, I've been wanting to go swimming but we've been too busy."

Mary nodded her head and said, "Excellent, now I can make Giana jealous in my new swimsuit."

Lieutenant Michael said, "Great! That will be our big plan for tomorrow. You girls definitely deserve some relaxation and fun after all your hard work today."

After dinner, Mary was true to her word. She laid on the couch and started to watch movies that she liked. Sarah and Valerie changed into their own pajamas. They each sat in one of the recliner chairs.

As the girls enjoyed themselves, Lieutenant Michael cleaned up the place and then wrote up his after action report for the Captain. As he went to deliver his report, he smelled a pleasant smell in the hallway. He thought that maybe Squad four was baking something good. He submitted the report and then decided to join the girls in their movie watching.

Lieutenant Michael walked around to Mary's feet and said, "Do you mind if I join you?"

Mary, who looked really tired, sat up and patted a spot on the couch next to her. He sat down where Mary's feet had been. Mary then laid back down but leaned over the other way. She rested her head on Lieutenant Michael's lap. He rubbed the side of her head and brushed her hair back with his hand. She smiled.

TEARS
OF
DARKNESS

CHAPTER
**03**
TRAGEDY AND HOPE

- 1 -

Lieutenant Michael prepared breakfast by himself the next morning before the girls got up. He woke up a little early on purpose so that he could have it ready for them when they came out of their rooms. He prepared scrambled eggs and tater tots. A special breakfast for their hard work.

One by one, the girls began to come into the dining room. Sarah came in first, sniffing the air. She said, "I smell eggs and tots!"

Lieutenant Michael, who was finishing up in the kitchen said, "Good morning, Sarah. That's right. You sure know your food."

Sarah gave a huge grin, rubbed her stomach with both of her hands, and said, "Good morning, Lieutenant! I can't help it. I love food!"

Sarah skipped her way to the table. She pulled out her chair and sat down. She started to hum a tune as she waited.

Valerie came out next. She had put her monarch butterfly clip in her hair again. It held the hair on her right side back behind her ear. She also sniffed into the air and said, "Good morning, Lieutenant! I smell potatoes!"

Lieutenant Michael smiled and said, "Good morning, Valerie. That's right, I made tater tots and scrambled eggs for breakfast."

Valerie walked up to the table and pulled out her chair. She sat down and said, "I love tots!"

Lieutenant Michael set two bowls on the table.  One was filled with scrambled eggs and the other filled with tater tots.  He said, "I'm glad you love them."  He then put a bottle of ketchup on the table.

Valerie grabbed the bowl of tater tots and began to shovel them onto her plate.  Sarah grabbed the bowl of scrambled eggs and shoveled them onto her own plate.  They looked at each other, giggled, and then switched bowls, shoveling the contents onto their plates.

Lieutenant Michael said, "Mary is sure taking her time this morning."  He then took the bowls of food from the girls and began to serve himself.  As he did so, Mary finally came out of the hallway.  Immediately he saw that she looked like she had been crying.  A look of despair filled her face.  He had not seen such a look on her face except when Susan had died about two months ago.  Her hair hung freely without her normal twin tails.

Mary stopped for a moment in the entryway of the hallway and stared back at him.  She continued on and walked right up to him instead of taking her seat.  She reached out and held onto the sleeve of his jacket and said, "Lieutenant, can I please talk to you alone in my room for a moment."

Sarah stopped shoveling food into her mouth and stared at Mary, saying, "What's wrong?"  Mary ignored her and continued to look to Michael.  Valerie stopped eating and watched Mary with concern on her face.

Lieutenant Michael's eyes grew wide.  He set his fork down on his plate and stood up, saying, "Of course, Mary."  He followed behind Mary as she escorted him toward her room.  Sarah turned her head to watch them leave.  Valerie watched them turn the corner from where she sat.

Mary opened her door and allowed Lieutenant Michael to enter in first.  She then came in and shut the door behind herself.  She stood there and brought her hands together, rubbing them.  She stared at her hands silently.

Lieutenant Michael stood there and waited for her to speak, but, she said nothing.  He said, "What's wrong, Mary.  If there's something bothering you, I want to know about it so I can try to help you.

Mary continued to stand there silently.  Her hands began to tremble.  Tears began to form in her eyes.  Lieutenant Michael said, "Mary, you're scaring me.  Please talk to me."

She continued to stare at her trembling hands, but she managed to speak.  She said in a tone that was near crying, "It happened."

Lieutenant Michael shook his head in confusion and gently said, "What happened?  What do you mean?"

Again, Mary continued to stare at her hands. She held them together to try to stop them from trembling; it was only moderately successful. Again, she spoke in the same tone, "IT happened." She stressed the word 'it' as she spoke.

Lieutenant Michael reached out to her and put his hand on her shoulder. He gently squeezed it and said, "Please, Mary. I need you to help me to understand what you are talking about."

Mary reached into her pocket and held a crumpled up piece of white fabric in her hand. It had a red mark on it. Lieutenant Michael looked at it in confusion for a second and then realized what it was. He realized that it was her underwear and that the red mark was her blood. Mary said, "I...I had...I had my first period."

Lieutenant Michael began to relax as understanding replaced the tension of ignorance.

In spite of his sudden relief, Mary suddenly began to cry deeply. She dropped the underwear she was holding onto the ground and fell to her knees. She covered her face with her hands.

Lieutenant Michael immediately dropped to his knees and embraced her, holding her against his chest. She wrapped her arms around his back and buried her face into his chest. He spoke out gently to her, saying, "Mary, it's going to be okay. This is just another part of life, this ..."

Mary cut him off and said, "Except when this happens to one of us, it's just a timer telling us that we're going to die soon. No wielder has ever lived past a year of their first period!"

Lieutenant Michael held her tighter and said, "That's true, Mary. I can't lie to you."

Mary said, "I don't want to die! I don't want to die like Susan and Cheryl. I want to finish growing up. I want to be a wife and a mother! I want to grow old and die next to the man I love! But...but...but that's never going to happen because I was born like this, and I'll die like this!"

Michael couldn't contain his composure anymore. The tears he had been forcing back began to roll down his cheeks. He said, "I...I...I don't know what to say to you, Mary. I don't know what I could do to comfort you. If it was within my power I would make sure that you would never have to fight again. I would take away this burden you're forced to carry if I could."

Mary locked up at his face. He looked down at her. The white of her eyes were red from crying. Tear streaks stained her cheeks. She looked up into his eyes and said, "Michael...just...just...just tell me...tell me that you love me. Even if you don't mean it. That will be enough."

Lieutenant Michael shut his eyes, he used his hand to turn her head to the side and held her head against his chest. He said, "I don't have to lie to you. I love you. I love you with all my heart. Not a day goes by that I don't think how lucky I am to have been the one to select you for my team."

Mary stopped holding up her own weight. She began to sob again. He held her up to support her weight against his body. She said, "Thank you, Michael. Please, just let me stay like this for a little bit."

Lieutenant Michael began to stroke her back and said, "Okay. That's okay." He leaned back onto his feet and gently began to rock her in his arms. Slowly, she stopped crying.

After about ten minutes of silence she began to push herself away from his chest. He let her go and said, "Are you okay now?"

She looked up at him and forced a smile on her face. Behind the smile though, he could still see the despair on her face. She wore a smile as if it was a mask. She said, "I'm better. Do I have to tell the others about it?"

Lieutenant Michael shook his head and said, "No, you don't. But, I think it would be better if you did tell them. You shouldn't have to hold this all in yourself. We've been here for a while now and they are probably really worried about you."

Mary nodded her head and said, "Okay, Lieutenant. I trust you. I'll tell them." She stood up and brushed her uniform and wiped her face with her hands.

Lieutenant Michael stood up and said, "Do you feel up to eating breakfast?"

Mary nodded and said, "Yeah, I think I can eat."

Lieutenant Michael said, "Okay, after breakfast, we will go see Doctor Lovecraft. She'll help you get set up with all the things you will need. Do you want to go alone or do you want me to go with you?"

Mary nodded her head and said, "Please go with me. I don't want to be alone."

Lieutenant Michael put a hand on her shoulder and said, "Okay. Are you ready?" Mary nodded her head. He then reached for the door knob, twisted it, and opened the door.

Sarah and Valerie continued to sit at the table while Lieutenant Michael and Mary were in the room. Valerie said, "Do you think something is wrong?"

Sarah said, "Obviously something is wrong."

Valerie said, "Do you think we should check in on them?"

Sarah shook her head and said, "No, they'll tell us about it when they're ready too."

After about five more minutes had passed, they began to become even more worried. They could not continue to eat. Sarah got up out of her chair and began to pace back and forth with concern. She gripped her hands together in frustration. Valerie got up and walked over to her. Sarah stopped pacing and took Valerie's hand and held it tightly in her own.

As they were standing there holding hands, Mary and Lieutenant Michael came out of the hallway. Sarah and Valerie looked up at them; their faces were full of concern.

Mary stepped forward and said, "I'm sorry for worrying you. The truth is I just had my first period."

Sarah gasped. She dropped Valerie's hand and brought her hands together, covering her nose and mouth. She closed her eyes and said, "Oh God! I knew it." She paused for a moment but then began to cry. She covered her face with her hands. Mary walked over to her and wrapped her arms around her. Sarah buried her face and hands into Mary's shoulder.

Valerie, not remembering, said, "I don't get it. What does ..."

Lieutenant Michael stopped her and said, "Remember? No spirit Wielder has ever lived past a year of their first period."

Understanding fell upon Valerie's face as she connected the knowledge together in her head. She remembered what she was told by her parents and by a doctor. She said, "Mary's going to die within a year?"

Valerie covered her mouth with her hands as reality began to sink into her mind. She too began to cry. Mary quickly reached out to Valerie. She wrapped an arm around her neck and pulled her against her own body. Mary said, "It'll be okay  It's not like I'll be dead in a week. We still got lots of time together." This did not comfort them. She held Sarah and Valerie until they stopped crying on their own.

Sarah lifted her face and let her go and said, "Is...is there anything I can do for you?"

Mary said, "Yeah, let's have lots of fun together and continue to do our best."

Sarah nodded her head and said, "Okay, I'll try."

Valerie let Mary go and clasped her hands together over her heart. She said, "I...I knew about this, but it never seemed real, but I guess it is."

Mary said, "Try not to worry about it. Let's just focus on what we got to do. Right now I'm hungry so let's finish eating."

Mary went over to the table, sat down and started to shovel food onto her plate. Lieutenant Michael sat down next to her, he stared at his plate and no longer felt like eating. But, for Mary's sake, he forced himself to put food into his mouth.

Sarah and Valerie sat back down at the table. Sarah began to eat again but then she started to cry. She shoved the plate of food away from herself and said, "I'm sorry. I can't do this." She then got out of her chair and ran into her room.

Mary watched Sarah as she left and then started to get up to go after her. Lieutenant Michael reached his hand out to her and touched her shoulder, saying, "Let me take care of this." Mary nodded her head and sat back down. She held her head up on the table with her hand and started eating again.

Lieutenant Michael stood and walked into the hallway toward Sarah's room. He stood in front of her door and knocked, saying, "It's me, Sarah. Is it okay if I come in?" There was no reply. He put his hand on the door knob and said, "I'm coming in Sarah. Okay?"

Lieutenant Michael turned the door knob and slowly pushed the door open. He stuck his head inside and saw that it was dark. He flipped the light switch on and saw Sarah lying face down on the bed; her face was buried in a pillow.

Lieutenant Michael walked up to her bed and sat down on the edge. He placed his hand on her back and began to rub her back in a circular motion. He could feel her body tremble from silently crying. He said, "Do you want to talk about it, Sarah? I'm here to help you."

Sarah slowly rolled over on her back and covered her eyes with her arm. Lieutenant Michael could see the streaks of tears that still rolled down the sides of her face. Sarah then used her arm to wipe her eyes and sat up, looking at Michael through teary eyes. She said, "I... I can't... I can't get the image of how Susan died out of my mind. I...I thought I was okay now but it's all come back. Instead of seeing Susan's face, now I see Mary's face. I see her body fall apart right before my eyes. I...I...I..."

Lieutenant Michael wiped her cheeks with his hands and said, "I understand how you're feeling, Sarah. I see Susan in my dreams too. I see her when I'm awake. I see the same thing you see, her body collapsing in on itself. It's one of the most horrible things I've ever seen and I've seen a lot of messed up crap. But you're not alone Sarah. I'm right here with you. I'm sure Mary would say the same thing. Before you came, there was Cheryl. Mary watched both Cheryl and Susan die, just like I did. I've watched a total of four girls die. Each one of them I've loved like a part of my family. This here is the hardest thing you'll ever have to go through. Losing your friends, your sisters."

Sarah crawled over to Michael and sat on his lap. Lieutenant Michael wrapped his arms around her and held her. He said, "If I knew a way to make it so that you wouldn't have to go through this, I would do everything in my power to fix it. But, all I can do right now is be there for you."

Sarah said, "I wish that you were my dad."

Lieutenant Michael kissed her on top of the head and said, "Let's think about Mary now. How do you think she feels? I think the best way to help yourself, is to help Mary deal with her situation now. Mary's really good at covering her fear with humor. Despite her giggles and smiles she is scared of dying. We need to help her get through this. Can you help me, help her, Sarah?"

Sarah nodded her head against his chest and said, "I'll try, Lieutenant."

Lieutenant Michael stroked her hair and said, "That's all I ask. Are you ready to go back out there?"

Sarah lifted her head up and slid off of his lap, saying, "Yeah, I'm ready." Lieutenant Michael smiled and nodded his head. He stood up, took her by the hand, and together they went back to the dining room.

When they returned, Sarah let go of his hand, and went back to her chair. She pulled her plate back toward her and said, "I'm sorry, Mary. I just started thinking about Susan again. That's all."

Mary nodded her head and said, "That's okay, I understand." She took another bite of food and chewed it in exaggeration. Then she said, "Now Susan, she died because her time limit expired. That's not how I want to go. I want to go out in a blaze of glory. I want my death to be the most epic battle of all time. I want it to be so glorious that the World Government puts up a monument of me so that future generations can remember my sacrifice."

Sarah then said, "I'll tell them to set it up the way you lived, with your feet up on a chair and a finger in your nose." Sarah shoved a finger up her own nose and pretended to pick it. Valerie started to laugh. They all stopped what they were doing and stared at her. Valerie stopped laughing and covered her mouth with a hand.

Mary laughed at Valerie and said, "Well, if I had to design a statue of Sarah, it would be her naked butt sliding along the bathroom floor!" Valerie, still cupping her mouth with her hand, started to laugh again. Mary joined her in laughing.

Lieutenant Michael said, "Okay, girls. That's enough playing. We have got to finish eating so we can get on with our day. Mary and I have got to go see

Doctor Lovecraft. While we're dealing with that, why don't you two take care of the dirty dishes?" He pointed at both Sarah and Valerie.

Sarah and Valerie nodded their heads. Sarah said, "Okay, Lieutenant, leave it to us!" Valerie said, "Sure can do!" She then gave him a thumbs up like Mary would have done.

After breakfast, Lieutenant Michael and Mary walked down the stairs together. She held his hand as they walked to Doctor Lovecraft's office. Mary was unusually silent. Normally at times like this she would talk about things, anything so that it would not be quiet.

Lieutenant Michael said, "How come you didn't put your hair in twin tails today? You always wear twin tails."

Mary said, "I looked in the mirror and I thought it looked too childish. I think it looks more feminine this way. Maybe now you will see me as a lady and not a little girl, hmm." She chuckled.

Lieutenant Michael said, "I'm sorry, Mary. No matter what, I will always see you as my little girl who I first met when she was just nine years old."

Mary smiled and said, "I was really cute then wasn't I."

Lieutenant Michael nodded his head and said, "Yes, you were."

Mary said, "But you don't think I'm cute now?"

Lieutenant Michael said, "Now, you've become a beautiful young woman." Much to his surprise, Mary started to blush and she looked awkwardly downward.

Mary changed the subject and said, "Is Sarah okay?"

Lieutenant Michael said, "Yeah, she's okay. This whole thing just brought back Susan to her mind."

Mary's voice became somber, "Yeah, I can see that. I see her too from time to time. At the time, she was my best friend. Now, I am to Sarah as Susan was to me."

Together they reached Doctor Lovecraft's door. Lieutenant Michael knocked on the door three times and waited. The door soon opened. Doctor Lovecraft awkwardly looked out through the opening of the door. She looked at Mary and said, "Mary, you've changed your hair."

Mary nodded and said, "Yeah, Doctor Lovecraft. Don't you think it's more feminine this way?"

Doctor Lovecraft opened the door wide and said, "I guess so." She motioned for them to enter into her office and the examination room. Mary let go of Lieutenant Michael's hand and walked over to the examination table. She turned around facing them and then jumped up onto the table, sitting down on it.

Doctor Lovecraft said, "Okay, Mary. What's troubling you today?"

Mary glanced over at Lieutenant Michael nervously and then turned her attention back to Doctor Lovecraft, saying, "Well, Doc. I had my first period this morning."

Doctor Lovecraft adjusted her glasses and walked over to her, saying, "I see. This is big news." She motioned for Mary to lie down on the table. Mary complied.

Doctor Lovecraft then said, "Do you feel any pain?"

Mary said, "Yeah, off and on. It hurts in my lower stomach." She lifted up her uniform jacket, and rubbed her hand over the area she was talking about.

Doctor Lovecraft then said, "Do you feel any bloating?"

Mary said, "Well I guess I do feel kind of fat today." She lowered her jacket back down over her belly and rested her hands over her stomach as she lay there.

Doctor Lovecraft said, "Well, all of those symptoms are normal for your menstruation cycle. I can give you some medication that can lessen the pain if you want."

Mary said, "Nah, that's okay. I want to feel the pain so I know I'm still alive. I already know that no Wielder lives a year past their first period."

Doctor Lovecraft adjusted her glasses again and said, "Yeah, the World Science Council is working on ways to correct it, but the real problem is that we don't understand how it all works. I mean, we are not even sure how you girls get your abilities except that it's passed on through the XX-chromosome. We also have no idea why your hormones have a negative reaction with your ability. It's mind blowing."

The Doctor then shook her head and said, "I'm going to give you some supplies to take." She walked over to a cabinet and opened it. She began to pull out some boxes. She then turned to Lieutenant Michael and said, "I'm going to have to ask you to please wait outside now, Lieutenant. I'm going to explain to Mary how to use these, and you're getting in the way."

Lieutenant Michael said, "Sure, I understand." He turned around, opened the door, and left the room. He shut the door behind himself and leaned against the wall, crossing his arms across his chest.

After Lieutenant Michael left, Mary sat up and the Doctor began to explain to her the differences between pads and tampons. She explained how to use each one, and gave her a box of each.

Mary then said, "Doc, we were supposed to go swimming today. Can I still go swimming?"

Doctor Lovecraft nodded her head and said, "Yep, but if you do, make sure you use the tampons. You can pretty much do anything that you want to do as long as you feel up to it. If there's something that you don't feel up to doing make sure you tell your Lieutenant."

Doctor Lovecraft then handed Mary a third box and said, "If you start feeling frustrated, make sure you take one of those."

Mary opened the third box and looked inside. There were rows of chocolate bars lined up inside. She picked one up and said questioningly, "Chocolate? For real?"

Doctor Lovecraft smiled and nodded her head, saying, "Yep, for real. Trust me it will help every time. Okay then, if you don't have any more questions, then you are free to go."

Mary nodded and said, "Thanks, Doctor Lovecraft." She slid off the table holding the three boxes of supplies she was given.

Lieutenant Michael continued to wait patiently. He knew that they would be done when they were done. Suddenly, the door opened and Mary stepped out holding the familiar three boxes. She said, "Okay, Lieutenant. I'm all ready to go. Now, we just have to wait till it's time to swim."

Lieutenant Michael looked at her confused and said, "Swim ... oh yeah. With all that happened this morning I completely forgot about swimming today. Are you sure you feel up to it?"

Mary nodded her head and said, "Yeah, I feel much better right now. Besides, I want to show off the swimsuit that you bought for me. I also don't want to be the one to drag everybody down. I want everyone to have fun."

Lieutenant Michael nodded his head, and said, "Well, if that's what you want. But, I'm leaving it up to you if you want us to cancel."

Mary smiled and said, "Thanks, Lieutenant. But, I think it will be fine." She wrapped her arm around his arm and together they walked back to their apartment.

- 2 -

Giana stood in the mouth of the hallway, waiting for Lieutenant Rachel to come out of her room. She crossed her arms and tapped her foot with impatience. Finally, Lieutenant Rachel came out of her room wearing her olive drab colored bikini with her hair in a ponytail.

Giana uncrossed her arms and squared them on her own hips, saying, "What do you think you're doing?"

Lieutenant Rachel looked down at her and said, "Uh, I'm getting ready for the pool?"

Giana pointed at her chest and said, "You need to put a shirt on over those things!"

Lieutenant Rachel shrugged her shoulders and said, "Why? It's not like we're leaving the building."

Giana said, "Geez, I thought just Lieutenant Michael was dense. You're just as dense as he is. The key is in the reveal. You wear the shirt down to the pool. This will cause him to wonder what's underneath it. Then, when Lieutenant Michael is watching, you slowly take it off revealing your womanly assets. Instead of dropping the shirt on the ground, you slowly bend over like this and place it on the ground." She imitated the movements as she described them.

Giana then continued, "If your body is always revealed to him, he'll just get used to it. Then it won't matter to him anymore. You have to tease him a little."

Lieutenant Rachel then slumped her shoulders and said, "But, he's already seen me naked, so it's probably too late for that."

Giana threw her arms down in frustration, yelling, "What! When did this happen?"

Lieutenant Rachel said, "Calm down, it was during the academy. We sometimes had to shower together. It was like five or six years ago."

Giana sighed in frustration. She rubbed the temples on the sides of her head and said, "Okay, okay, it's been a while so this just might still work. Maybe we can bring up old memories."

Lieutenant Rachel looked depressed and said, "I feel really silly doing this."

Giana pointed at her and said, "What are you talking about? You're a soldier. You should know that the best offense is to, you know, actually go on the offensive. It's called stra-te-gy." She enunciated each syllable as she waved her index finger in the air.

Lieutenant Rachel sighed and said, "Okay, you win. I can't believe I'm getting dating advice from a thirteen year old."

Giana then pointed at her hair and said, "I'd also suggest that you take off that hair band and let your hair hang freely. It will make you look more feminine."

Lieutenant Rachel reached up and pulled off the hair band that kept her hair in a ponytail. She then shook her hair and said, "How's that?"

Giana gave her a thumbs up and said, "Beautiful!"

Lieutenant Rachel turned around and went back into her room. She dug around in her drawer until she found an old T-shirt she had in the back of the drawer. She pulled it over her body and went back out for Giana's inspection. Giana looked her up and down, while stroking her own chin. She held up her thumb again and said, "Great. I'd say you're all ready for Lieutenant Michael now."

Lieutenant Rachel followed Giana into the dining area. When Rachel entered into the dining area, she saw that they were all in their swimsuits. Giana wore a two-piece swimsuit that was green and black. The top part consisted of a green spaghetti strapped tank top that extended slightly over the top of her stomach. The bottom portion looked like a tight pair of black shorts. Tina wore a one piece standard swimming suit that was pitch black. Elsa wore a one piece standard swimming suit that was pink with white edging, covered in flowers.

Tina and Elsa smiled as they looked at Lieutenant Rachel. Together, they started clapping their hands. Elsa said, "I'm sure Lieutenant Michael is going to notice you today."

Lieutenant Rachel said, "Thanks, girls, for all your support but don't be too angry if it doesn't work out the way that you think it should."

Giana picked up her towel and slung it over her shoulder, saying, "Don't worry, we're not expecting too much, but we've got to get the ball rolling sometime."

Lieutenant Rachel said, "Okay, girls. Let's get going."

Giana pointed at the door and added, saying, "Let Operation Cupid commence!"

Lieutenant Rachel picked up a basket that was on the table and together they left the room.

Lieutenant Michael sat at the dinner table wearing his swim trunks and a white tank top. His towel rested around his neck. He leaned back in his chair and rested his hands behind his head. His face could not hide his frustration from what happened this morning.

Valerie came out of the hallway wearing her new white swimsuit with the ascending rainbow colored butterflies. She had wrapped her towel around her body like a blanket. Lieutenant Michael couldn't tell if she was embarrassed or cold. She walked up to him and said, "I'm ready, Lieutenant!"

Lieutenant Michael nodded and said, "Great! Now we got to wait for everybody else."

Sarah soon came out of the hallway after Valerie. She wore her new swimsuit, a light blue one-piece with a short white skirt. She hung her towel around her neck and smiled, saying, "I'm ready! Don't I look cute?" She spun around so that her skirt lifted up by the motion.

Lieutenant Michael said, "Yeah, very cute." He put his arms down on the table and sat up forward.

Mary came out of the hallway last, wearing her new red and black two-piece swimsuit. It had a bikini top with the left cup being black and the right cup being red. It had matching strings that tied around her neck. The bottom portion was a red and black plaid short skirt. She held her towel in her hand.

Mary ran up to Lieutenant Michael. She did a spin in front of him, causing her skirt to be lifted up by the motion. She then stopped and struck a pose, with her right hand behind her head and her left hand squared on her hip. She said, "Lieutenant, don't I look lovely in my new swimsuit?"

Lieutenant Michael dispassionately said, "Yeah, yeah, you look lovely in your new swimsuit."

As Mary stood there posing, a knock came to the door. Lieutenant Michael said, "That's probably them." He got up and opened the door. Lieutenant Rachel stood there with Giana, Tina, and Elsa. He said, "Just in time."

As Mary stepped forward she saw Giana. Giana saw Mary. Mary pointed her finger at Giana and said, "Where's your swimsuit? That's a track suit!"

At the same time, Giana said, "Who the hell are you? What've you done with your hair?!"

Mary said, "I'm just letting my hair hang freely today."

Giana said, "What are you talking about, this is totally a swimsuit. By the way, Mary only wears twin tails. So if you don't have twin tails, then you ain't Mary!"

Mary waved her hand in the air and said, "Uh, that is the ugliest swimsuit I've ever seen, but I suppose it makes sense being on you, because, if you knew what a good swimsuit looked like then you might also realize that the reason I let my hair down is so that I'd look more feminine." Mary ran her fingers through her own long hair.

Lieutenant Rachel smiled at the thought; it was the same as Giana had said. She kept looking back between the arguing girls and Lieutenant Michael.

She could not help but stare at his well-toned body. She started to blush, but, nobody noticed as they were focused on Mary and Giana arguing.

Lieutenant Michael started looking annoyed as he glared at the two of them arguing.

Giana said, "Oh my gosh! You are so ..."

Lieutenant Michael suddenly spoke up angrily, "Can't I have one day where the two of you don't start fights! Don't you two know that our days together are limited?" He spoke more forcefully than he had intended too.

Mary stopped immediately and looked down cast, saying, "I'm sorry, Lieutenant. I won't argue anymore today."

Giana was a little surprised by Lieutenant Michael's reaction. He always intervened but his tone sounded more angry then annoyed this time. Giana said, "I'm sorry too. This is just how we communicate with each other."

Mary and Giana wrapped an arm around each other's back. Giana said, "We're friends, see?"

Mary said, "Yeah, we're just friends teasing each other. We don't really mean it."

Lieutenant Michael wiped his face with his hand and sighed, saying, "I'm sorry, I didn't mean to speak in that tone. I guess I'm still frustrated from earlier." Depression once again filled Sarah's and Valerie's face. They looked down toward the ground to try to hide it.

Lieutenant Rachel said, "What happened earlier?"

Lieutenant Michael looked at Mary and said, "Is it okay, if I tell them?"

Mary let go of Giana, nodded her head, and said, "It's okay."

Lieutenant Michael said, "Well, Mary had her first period this morning. So you all know what that means."

Mary said, "Yep, my life timer has started ticking ... so, I got to enjoy what time I got left."

Lieutenant Rachel looked toward the ground and said, "Oh, Michael, I'm ... I'm so sorry to hear that. Mary, I'm sorry ..."

Lieutenant Michael tried to cheer everyone up so, with as much excitement that he could muster, he said, "Well, let's try to not think about that and just have fun at the pool today. It's been a while since we've gone swimming together." He put on a fake smile.

He started to walk toward the stairwell. Mary, Sarah, and Valerie followed after him. Giana and Lieutenant Rachel looked at each other with shock on their faces. Tina, with her melancholy voice, said, "Life is death. All our clocks are slowly ticking away toward nothingness."

Elsa looked at Tina and said, "That was deep."

Giana said, "I'll probably be next. I am only a couple of months younger than Mary."

Lieutenant Rachel said, "Well, let's use our time together to help them through this. They lost Susan only two months ago and now this." She then followed after Lieutenant Michael. Giana, Tina, and Elsa followed her down the stairs.

When Squad four entered the pool area, Lieutenant Michael was already sitting at a table, and Mary was sitting on the edge of the pool kicking her feet in the water. Valerie and Sarah were already in the water splashing at each other.

Giana, Tina, and Elsa climbed up to the deck of the pool. Giana sat down next to Mary. Elsa jumped in the water and started helping Valerie splash Sarah. Tina slid into the water, rolled over on her back, and pretended to be dead.

Lieutenant Rachel walked up to the table that Michael was sitting at. He was staring at the top of the table in deep thought. She placed the small basket she had been carrying in front of him and said, "I made you these peanut butter cookies last night."

Lieutenant Michael did not change his glance but said, "I thought I smelled something good last night." He reached his hand into the basket and said, "Thanks a lot!" He took a bite and looked up at her, saying, "These are really good."

She held her hands behind her back, perked up her chest, and smiled at him, saying, "Really? I'm glad." She pulled out the chair next to him and sat down. He took another cookie and ate it. She said, "Are you okay?"

He looked at the basket of cookies and said, "Not really. This is just so soon. Just two months have passed since Susan's death. Everything was going so well, so of course I had to be pulled back into the reality of it all."

Rachel put her hand on his arm and said, "I know. It's always hard to lose one of your girls. I've had my team for some time now, which means that it'll happen to us soon too."

Michael reached out and took her hand in his. He held her hand gently, he felt the warmth of her hand. He said, "I wish I knew why all of this was happening to us ... to them. I wish I knew why the first aliens wiped out our large cities for no apparent reason. I wish I knew why the girls developed the powers that also murder them. I wish I knew why the Harvesters came. If I knew why and how, then, maybe, just maybe, I could stop it. Then they wouldn't have to fight anymore. Maybe we could even find a way to stop their bodies from being destroyed."

Michael then shook his head and closed his eyes, saying, "This is why I don't want to have children. If I had a daughter like this, it … it would break me. I … I can hardly take it with these girls that aren't even mine." A tear escaped out of his closed eyes.

Rachel got out of her chair and walked over to his side. She placed a hand on the side of his face and pushed his head onto her chest. He did not push her away. He breathed in her scent as he rested his head on her bosom. She held his head and stroked his hair, saying, "I believe we'll win. I believe that humanity will win. We'll stop the Harvesters. So long as we have people like you, who are willing to sacrifice everything they have, even your own sanity, we can't lose. We won't lose."

Michael moved away from Rachel's hold on his head. He wiped his eye and said, "I believe that too. That's why I don't give up. No matter how many times my heart breaks, I'll keep going. If we give up, we will lose, and all their suffering, all our suffering, will have been in vain."

Mary sat on the edge of the pool, allowing her feet to dangle in the water. She sat there with her hands in her lap. She watched her legs move through the water.

Giana climbed up the ladder to the deck of the pool, following Tina and Elsa. She saw Mary sitting there on the edge of the pool, with her feet dangling in the water.

Giana walked up to Mary and sat down beside her. She dropped her legs into the water and slowly moved them back and forth to stir up the water too. She said, "Are you okay, Mary?"

Mary said, "I'm mostly okay. At first I cried. I was really scared but I've been prepared for this. I saw what happened to Susan and Cheryl and what they went through. I'm not as afraid as I was earlier."

Giana said, "It will probably be my turn next. I'm thirteen now too. Naomi was almost twelve when it happened to her. She died six months later. If you don't use your full power you could last closer to a year."

Mary said, "Does it scare you?"

Giana said, "Of course. I've seen what happens too."

Mary leaned back and supported herself by placing her hands on the deck behind her. Giana copied her. Mary said, "Is there anything that you really want to do before it's your time to go?"

Giana looked up at the ceiling and thought for a moment, saying, "Well, I've always wanted to see Italy. That's where my grandparents came from. Before

I was taken by the World Government, I would always listen to my grandpa's stories of his village in Italy. I would love to see it. Not likely to happen since it's unlikely we'll be deployed to that region. How 'bout you?"

Mary looked at her with a half-hearted smile and said, "I want to get married. I'd wear a beautiful all white dress. He'd wear a black tuxedo with a cute bow tie. We'd exchange our vows and then he'd take me into his arms, kissing me passionately. Afterwards, we'll dance in front of everyone."

Giana said, "Well, that's even less likely to happen then mine."

Mary shrugged her shoulders and said, "I know. But, it's my dream."

Giana looked at Elsa, who had joined with Sarah and Valerie. Together they fought a splashing war against each other. Tina continued to float there pretending to be dead. Giana said, "Kids sure do love splashing in the pool."

Mary nodded her head and said, "Yep."

Giana then said, "You want to join them?"

Mary shrugged her shoulders and said, "Okay, why not. We're still kids after all I guess.' Mary and Giana then slid into the pool and began splashing water at them as they swam toward them.

Rachel sat back down next to Michael and watched in silence as Mary and Giana joined in the splashing fight. Rachel then looked back at Michael, who was biting on another cookie. She said, "You want to jump in the pool with them?" She stood back up and began to take off her T-shirt in front of Michael.

He shoved the rest of the cookie into his mouth as he watched her take off her T-shirt. As her body began to be revealed, his eyes followed behind the ascending T-shirt. His eyes were then drawn to the scar that was on her stomach. Rachel placed her shirt on the table top and said, "Come on, Michael. Swimming together might help you feel better."

Lieutenant Michael nodded and stood up, saying, "Yeah, you are right. It probably would." He stood up and took off his tank top and put it on the table. As he took it off, Rachel's eyes were drawn to his well-toned chest.

Rachel walked over to the ladder that led up to the pool deck and Michael followed behind her. They both put their hands on opposite sides of the ladder and then looked at each other. They nervously smiled and chuckled.

Rachel brushed her hair back behind her ear and said, "Go ahead."

Michael said, "Oh no, ladies first, please." He motioned for her to climb up first.

Rachel gave a slight nod and said, "Okay, then." She started to climb the ladder. Michael could not help staring at her as she made her way up the ladder.

After she made it to the pool deck, Michael then climbed up, and, together, they stood on the pool deck.

Sarah waved at them and said, "Come on in!" Michael and Rachel then jumped into the water causing a giant splash that sprayed everybody.

Valerie doggy-paddled over to Michael and Rachel. She swam around Lieutenant Michael and jumped onto his back. She wrapped her arms around his neck. Lieutenant Michael said, "Hello, Valerie."

Valerie looked at Lieutenant Rachel and said to her, "You're very pretty."

Lieutenant Rachel said, "Thank you, Valerie. That's very sweet of you."

Valerie then said, "I think Lieutenant Michael thinks you're pretty too because he's always looking at you."

Lieutenant Michael quickly ducked underneath the water, while holding onto Valerie. He then rose back up and said, "Uh ... sorry about that. Kids don't know what they're talking about. Valerie, you shouldn't speak for other people." He nervously laughed.

Lieutenant Rachel laughed and said, "That's okay. So you don't think I'm pretty then?"

Lieutenant Michael began to look back and forth to try to avoid making eye contact with her. All the other girls in the pool suddenly stopped splashing and focused their attention on Lieutenant Michael. Even Tina, who was still pretending to be dead, sat up and joined the others in staring at him.

Lieutenant Michael scratched his cheek with his finger. He glanced at Lieutenant Rachel and said, "Uh, no ... no ... I ... I think you're pretty."

Mary then glared at him in disapproval and said, "Lieutenant Michael, do you think I'm pretty too?"

Lieutenant Michael said, "Yes, yes, you're pretty too. Can we just drop this topic now? It's making Lieutenant Rachel uncomfortable."

Giana leaned over to Elsa and whispered into her ear, "I think he's the only one who's uncomfortable."

Sarah joined into the conversation, saying, "Lieutenant, am I pretty too?"

Lieutenant Michael rolled his eyes and said, "Yes, Sarah, you're pretty too. All of you are pretty, adorable little girls."

Valerie then said, "Lieutenant Rachel, can I ask you a question?"

Lieutenant Rachel nodded her head and said, "What do you want to know?"

Valerie pointed at the scar on her stomach and said, "How'd you get that scar? I thought yellow Wielders could heal scars?"

Lieutenant Rachel ran her hand along the scar and said, "Oh, this? Well, if a wound is not closed quickly it can still scar even if a yellow Wielder heals it. What happened is that when your Lieutenant and I were in the academy, we were on a training mission beyond the wall. I got left behind. I got attacked by Harvesters and thought that I was going to be killed. Suddenly, out of nowhere, Michael comes running up to me like a hero with a cattle prod in his hand. He unloads a clip in the Harvesters face causing it to run away. He bandaged up my wound and then carried me all the way back to the wall by himself. That's why I'm still alive and that's why I have this scar."

Lieutenant Michael shrugged his shoulders, while Valerie hung on them. He said, "Well, when I noticed you were missing, I just couldn't leave you behind. I didn't want to break in a new best friend yet."

Valerie then said, "Is that why you love Lieutenant Michael, because he saved you?"

Lieutenant Michael dropped down into the water again and then stood back up, saying, "Valerie, didn't I just tell you to stop speaking for other people."

Valerie's voice became whiny, saying, "But, Lieutenant, my mom says that you only make cookies for people that you love."

Lieutenant Michael rolled his eyes and said, "Come on, Valerie, that's enough. Look, you're embarrassing Lieutenant Rachel."

Giana stood there in shock next to Mary as the two of them watched the exchange between Lieutenant Michael, Valerie, and Lieutenant Rachel. Giana flinched and said, "I ...I can't tell if Valerie is like some super genius, or, if she is just childishly cute."

Mary stuck a finger in her mouth and pretended to gag. She said loudly, "You two flirting is making me sicker!"

Lieutenant Michael pried Valerie off of his back and tossed her into the water, saying, "We're not flirting. We're just really good friends, and that is how it's going to stay."

Giana sighed and slapped her hands on the water while rolling her eyes. She then dove under the water and screamed as air bubbles climbed to the surface. Her scream was muffled by the water.

When Valerie resurfaced, Lieutenant Michael said, "And Valerie, what did I just say about speaking for people."

Valerie began to pout and looked depressed. She said, "I'm sorry, Lieutenant."

Lieutenant Rachel said to Michael, "Go easy on her, Michael, she's very observant." She then turned her attention to Valerie and said, "Yes, Valerie, that's part of the reason why I love Lieutenant Michael because he's always there for me. We're best friends so of course we love each other."

Tina went back to pretending to be dead on top of the water. As she floated by Giana, she said, "See, I told you he's too dense."

Giana glared at Tina and said, "It just wasn't the right time. He's too distracted by what happened this morning."

Tina then said, "Looks like your Operation Cupid has become Operation Stupid." Elsa began to laugh at the joke.

Giana pushed Tina into the water and held her there as she struggled to return to the surface. Giana then let her go and she floated back to the surface of the water, pretending to be dead once again. Giana rolled her eyes and pushed Tina in the opposite direction.

Mary swam over to the edge of the pool and climbed out. She sat back on the edge of the deck and once again let her feet hang in the water. She placed her right hand over her stomach and looked uncomfortable.

Lieutenant Michael watched her and said, "Mary, are you okay?"

Mary shrugged her shoulders and said, "I'm not feeling good again. I don't think I can swim anymore."

Lieutenant Michael said, "That's okay, Mary. If you want to, you can go back upstairs. He then turned to Sarah and Valerie, saying, "Do you girls want to keep swimming or do you want to go back upstairs."

Valerie said, "I want to keep swimming."

Sarah said, "Yeah, I still feel like swimming too."

Lieutenant Michael turned to Rachel and said, "Would you mind watching them for me? I should probably help Mary."

Lieutenant Rachel nodded and said, "Sure, that wouldn't be a problem for me."

Lieutenant Michael looked back toward Sarah and Valerie, saying, "Okay, girls, I'm letting you two stay with Lieutenant Rachel, so make sure you do what she tells you."

Sarah and Valerie in unison said, "Okay, Lieutenant!"

Lieutenant Michael waded toward Mary and said, "Okay, Mary, I'll go back with you."

Mary looked downcast and said, "Are ... are you sure that you want to go with me? I don't want to spoil your fun."

Lieutenant Michael pulled himself out of the water and held out his hand to Mary, saying, "Don't worry about that. I don't want you to be alone right now."

Mary shyly smiled at him and took his hand. He lifted her up on to her feet. He let her hand go and walked over to the ladder. She followed behind him.

As they disappeared beyond the door, Giana swam up to Lieutenant Rachel, saying, "I'm sorry, Lieutenant. This was just really bad timing. Don't give up though. We'll definitely have another chance later."

Lieutenant Rachel shrugged her shoulders. She ran her fingers through the water and stared at the motion of the ripples she made. She said, "You think so?"

Giana nodded her head and said, "Yep, you both already love each other. We just need to get him to think about a relationship. It will happen. I can sense it."

As Lieutenant Michael and Mary walked up the stairs together, Mary followed behind him instead of running up beside him. Again, Lieutenant Michael noticed that she was unusually quiet. *This must be so hard for her,* he thought to himself. He wasn't sure if he should just let it be or if he should try to say something to cheer her up. *What could I possibly say?*

As he was thinking about this, Mary decided for him, saying, "Lieutenant Michael, do you like my hair in twin tails better or do you like it better when I let it hang freely like this?"

He stopped climbing the stairs and turned toward her. She looked up at him with expectant eyes as she waited for his reply. He looked down at her and said, "Well, I don't really think either way is better. I'm used to you in twin tails but I can get used to this way too. What I think is more important is what you think about it. I think you should do what makes you feel like yourself the most. I'll be happy with whatever you choose to be. I just want you to be you."

Mary began to look embarrassed as she blushed. She looked downward and said, "Thank you, Lieutenant." She went back to walking up the stairs herself.

Lieutenant Michael turned around and continued onward up the stairs. Mary was now walking beside him on the left. He watched her out of the corner of his eye. She was opening and closing her right hand. She kept moving her hand toward his arm, then, she would withdraw it.

Lieutenant Michael said, "This must be so hard for you, Mary. I can sense that you are holding yourself back. I guess that you are trying to be strong for the other girls. I can understand that. When Susan and Cheryl died, I felt like I had to hold myself back for your sake. When we are alone, you don't need to hold yourself back if you don't want to. I'm right here with you."

Mary didn't say anything. He turned his head to watch her. He saw a tear roll down her cheek. Then another one followed behind it. She wiped her cheek with her hand and then started to cry even more. She wiped her cheeks again.

Lieutenant Michael took hold of her hand as she started to compose herself. Mary said, "You're right, Lieutenant. I know I need to be strong for Sarah and Valerie. I'll ... I'll do my best. But ... but in my heart, I'm really scared. Of ... of losing them ... of losing you."

Lieutenant Michael nodded his head and said, "Remember what we kept telling Valerie? It's okay to be scared."

Mary nodded and said, "Yes, I remember. It's the same thing that Susan kept telling me."

Lieutenant Michael said, "And what did Susan say to help you not be scared?"

Mary replied, "She said to trust her, to trust one another, and to trust you. I trust you, Lieutenant. I really do."

Lieutenant Michael smiled at her again and said, "I trust you too, Mary. I'm going to help you through this the best I can. Okay?"

Mary, who had stopped crying, nodded and said, "Okay, Lieutenant."

Back inside the apartment, Mary went straight to the bathroom. She took off her swimsuit and left it on a hanger to dry. Next, she got into the shower and let the water run over herself to cleanse her body of the smell of chlorine. Another wave of pain fell upon her. She groaned and rubbed her stomach, saying to herself, "Ugh ... why do I have to go through this."

Mary turned off the water and reached out for her towel. She wiped her face off and then wrapped the towel around her body. She stood in front of her mirror at the sink and looked at herself. She looked at her small bust and sighed, "I guess I will never be like Lieutenant Rachel after all."

Mary sighed as she pulled out a brush and began to brush her hair. She then pulled a blow dryer out of her drawer and began to dry her hair. The heat of the blow dryer felt good on her skin.

After her hair was dry, she again looked at herself in the mirror. She observed how her hair ran over her shoulders. She then pulled her hair up into twin tails and held it there with her hands. Lieutenant Michael's voice came back to her from her memories, "I just want you to be you."

She smiled at herself and let go of one of her twin tails. She reached into the drawer and pulled out a hair band and tied her hair up on one side. She then grabbed another hair band and tied her hair up on the other side of her head. She wrapped her hands around each twin tail and ran them over her tied up hair. She said to herself, "This is who I really am."

Mary nodded at herself in the mirror and went to her room to change into her uniform. After dressing herself, she opened her top drawer, and pulled out a small box. She opened the box, revealing a stack of money. She picked up the money and counted it. There was still five hundred dollars there. She placed the money back into the small box and put it back into the drawer.

Mary left her room and went into the dining area to find Lieutenant Michael sitting at the table with a tea pot and a cup in front of him. She walked up to him and stood next to him.

Lieutenant Michael picked up the cup of tea and blew over the top of it. He took a sip and turned to face her, saying, "What's up?"

Mary brought her hands together and interlocked her fingers, while twirling her thumbs. She said, "I've ... I've been saving some money to buy a dress. I finally have enough money, so, would it be alright if we go to the shopping district tomorrow so I can buy that dress?"

Lieutenant Michael put down his tea cup and said, "Well, that's fine with me, but why do you want a dress? We're supposed to mainly wear this uniform."

Mary said, "I know that, but, I've always wanted to wear a fancy dress before I die. My timer is ticking so I want to do as many of those things as I can before I ... you know ... before I die."

Lieutenant Michael nodded his head somberly, saying, "I can understand that. Well, it's your money so you can do what you want with it. I don't see any problem with going to the shopping district tomorrow."

Mary smiled and said, "Thanks, Lieutenant." She then walked over to the couch and laid down, turning on the television.

An hour later, as Lieutenant Michael sat reading a book at the table, the door opened up. Sarah and Valerie stood in the doorway. Behind them was Lieutenant Rachel with Giana, Tina, and Elsa.

Sarah stood there with a huge grin on her face as she held Lieutenant Rachel's basket in her arms. She said, "Lieutenant, you forgot the cookies!"

Lieutenant Michael looked up and put his book down on the table. He said, "Oh, I'm sorry Rachel. I was so distracted that I forgot."

Valerie held up a white tank top, saying, "You also forgot your shirt, Lieutenant."

Lieutenant Michael nodded his head and said, "You're right, I did. Thanks for bringing it to me." He stood up and walked over to them. He took the basket in one hand and the shirt in the other. He looked up at Rachel and said, "Thank you, again, Rachel. It was rude of me to forget them. They are very good. My mind has been really distracted today."

Lieutenant Rachel jokingly said, "Yeah, it was very rude of you to forget. I put in a lot of work there you know."

Michael nodded his head and said, "I know. I don't deserve a friend like you. Thanks again for watching Sarah and Valerie too."

Lieutenant Rachel said, "I'll forgive you ... this time. I know you got a lot going on today." She then pushed Sarah and Valerie forward, saying, "Alright, I'll let you get back to your day."

Sarah and Valerie walked up to the table. Sarah waved goodbye at Squad four and said, "See you girls later!"

Valerie also waved and said, "Thanks! I had a lot of fun."

After Squad four said their own good byes, Lieutenant Michael shut the door and said, "Alright, you two. Go take a shower and I'll start thinking about dinner."

Valerie and Sarah nodded at him and together they said, "Okay, Lieutenant!" Then they ran off toward the bathroom together.

- 3 -

That night, Sarah woke up with a start from the nightmare that frequently tormented her. She rolled over onto her back and stared at her ceiling in the darkness.

It was the same type of dream every time. She would be fighting the Harvesters and then she would realize that she's alone. No matter where she looked, she could never find anybody. The loneliness is what scared her the most.

She contemplated whether she should sneak into the Lieutenant's bed again. She turned her head to the clock and saw that it was one hundred hours. There was still lots of time to sleep.

Sarah rolled out of bed and stumbled through the dark to the door. She walked across the way to Lieutenant Michael's room and opened the door. She quietly snuck up to his bed and softly crawled into it. The Lieutenant rolled onto his other side but he did not wake up. She felt around to see if Mary or Valerie was there. They were not.

As she was laying there trying to go back to sleep, she heard the door open. A figure made its way through the darkness and climbed onto the bed. She felt a hand touch her foot. She felt a body climb over next to her and it slid underneath the sheets.

Sarah quietly whispered into the dark, "Is that you, Mary?"

A voice quietly replied, "Yeah, it's me."

Sarah said, "Did you have a nightmare again too?"

Mary replied, "Yeah."

Sarah waited for a moment and then whispered again, saying, "How come you never tell me about your nightmares?"

Mary said, "Because I don't want to think about them."

Sarah reached over to her and draped her arm over her. She said, "You're my best friend."

Mary replied, "You're my best friend too." Mary then also draped an arm over Sarah. The two of them quietly held each other in the darkness.

As they were falling back to sleep, the door opened a third time. A small figure quietly made its way toward the Lieutenant's bed. It then awkwardly climbed onto the bed. Mary let go of Sarah and scooted over, whispering, "Come on over here between us Valerie."

Valerie whispered in the dark, saying, "Okay." Mary opened up the blanket and allowed Valerie to crawl over to her. When Valerie was carefully snuggled between them, Mary folded the blanket back over herself.

Sarah said, "Did you have a nightmare again?"

Valerie said, "Yeah, I got scared."

Mary said, "It's okay to be scared. We're there for you so you don't need to be scared anymore." She put her arm over Valerie.

Sarah said, "Yes, we're here with you." She also put her arm over Valerie and held her gently.

Lieutenant Michael, who had been awoken by Valerie's clumsy movements, said, "More nightmares?"

Mary said, "Yeah, we're sorry to wake you."

Lieutenant Michael said, "That's okay. Try to go back to sleep though." Together, in the darkness, the four of them slowly drifted off back to sleep. Lieutenant Michael laid there waiting for the three of them to go back to sleep first. He thought about how much they all relied on each other. It was the only way they could deal with the fear that each one of them kept in their hearts. Not only the fear of the Harvesters, but the fear of losing each other, the fear of losing themselves. He reached over and touched each one of their sleeping heads in the darkness. *I wish I could take their fears away from them,* he thought to himself, *even if I had to carry it by myself.*

The alarm went off at six-thirty.  Lieutenant Michael sighed as the alarm clock blared.  It seemed that he had only blinked his eyes and it was morning.  He wondered how long he had laid there awake before finally going back to sleep.

Lieutenant Michael reached over and turned off the alarm.  He then sat up on the edge of the bed and turned his head to see if the girls were still there. Like three sardines in a can, they were snuggled up against each other.

Sarah had been the closest to him this time.  Little Valerie was in the middle with her back towards Sarah.  Sarah's arm rested over Valerie's chest. Mary laid down next to Valerie, facing her.

Mary was already awake and laid there watching Lieutenant Michael. When he noticed that she was awake, she sat up and said, "Good morning, Lieutenant.  Don't forget what you promised."

Lieutenant Michael yawned and scratched his stomach, saying, "Don't worry, Mary.  I haven't forgotten."

Sarah spoke as she lay there holding Valerie, "Don't forget about what?"

Mary said, "I asked the Lieutenant if I could go and buy a dress today with my own money."

Sarah said, "Really?  Can I come too?"

Mary said, "Of course!  I'll need your opinion."

Valerie suddenly sat up from in between Mary and Sarah, saying, "I want to go too.  Where are we going?"

Lieutenant Michael said, "Don't worry, girls.  We'll all go together so it'll be more fun."

Valerie said, "What are we going to do?"

Mary replied, "I want to buy a dress with my own money, so today, we're going to go to the dress shop."

Lieutenant Michael stood up and said, "Okay, girls.  Let's get dressed and have breakfast.  Then we'll do our morning exercises.  After that, the stores should be open by then so we'll go check them out."

One by one, the girls slid off of his bed, and went into their own rooms to change.  He shut the door behind them and began taking off his pajamas to change into his uniform.

After changing into their uniforms, the girls filed into the bathroom one by one.  Valerie was first this time and she went up to her mirror to brush her hair.  Sarah came in next, followed by Mary.

The three of them stood in front of their mirrors as they brushed their hair. Valerie put her butterfly clip in her hair on the right side, pulling her hair on the right side behind her ear. After she was done, she turned to Mary and said, "Sarah and I talk about our nightmares, but I never heard about your nightmares. How come you don't talk to us about them?"

Mary shrugged her shoulders as she parted her hair into twin tails, saying, "They're just dreams."

Valerie said, "I know they're just dreams. But they're a part of who you are, and I want to know all there is about you."

Mary smiled as she put the last hair band in her hair, saying, "That's sweet. I'm sorry. I just don't like talking about them, but I promise that one day, when I'm ready, I'll be sure to tell you all about my dreams."

Valerie said, "You promise?"

Mary nodded and held out her pinky finger. Valerie wrapped her own pinky finger around Mary's pinky finger. Mary said, "I promise." Valerie put a big grin on her face and, together, they shook their fingers.

Sarah finished putting her hair into a ponytail and said, "I want in on this promise too. I've been trying to learn about your dreams for a long time."

Mary said, "Okay." She extended her pinky finger to Sarah. Sarah wrapped her pinky finger around Mary's pinky finger and, together, they shook on it. Mary said, "I promise you too."

Sarah gave a nod and smiled, saying, "That's good enough for me."

Valerie changed the subject, saying, "What kind of a dress do you want, Mary?"

A thoughtful expression came upon Mary's face and she said, "I want a beautiful white dress that I can twirl in." She spread her arms out and began to spin where she stood. After a moment, she stopped spinning and placed her hand on her stomach with a groan.

Sarah watched her and said, "Are you still feeling bad?"

Mary sighed and nodded her head, saying, "Yeah, but it's a little better than it was yesterday. I'm finally turning into the lady that I always wanted to be. But, now that I know how it feels, I kind of wish I could go back to the way it was."

Sarah's face showed her depression as she said, "Yeah, I wish we could be like this forever."

Tears started to form in Sarah's eyes. Her lower lip began to quiver. Mary reached out to her and pulled her body next to her own. She held her tightly as Sarah began to cry again.

Valerie rushed over to Sarah and Mary, saying, "I know it's hard, but we can go through this if we work together." She then wrapped her own arms around Mary and Sarah.  Mary and Sarah opened up their embrace and added Valerie into it.  The three of them held each other till Sarah stopped crying.

Lieutenant Michael sat at the table waiting for the girls to come out.  He had already made oatmeal and it was now sitting on the table getting cold.  The girls were taking a little longer than normal.  He sat there wondering if he should check in on them.

As he was about to get up, the three girls came around the corner of the hallway.  Sarah's eyes were red like she had been crying.  He said to her, "Sarah, are you okay?"

Sarah pulled out her chair and said, "Yeah, I'm okay.  I just got a little sad in the bathroom, but I'm all better now."

Mary pulled out her own chair and sat down, saying, "Yeah, we could smell the oatmeal in the bathroom.  Sarah smelled it first.  She covered her face with her hands and said, 'Not oatmeal again' and then she started crying."

Lieutenant Michael rolled his eyes and said, "Come on, girls.  Give me a break.  I felt a little tired this morning."

Valerie pulled her own chair out and sat down next to Sarah.  She pressed her hands together, bowed her head, and closed her eyes for a moment as she said a silent prayer.  When she opened her eyes she stuck her spoon into the oatmeal and said, "Not only have we had oatmeal two out of three days, but this time it's cold like a frisbee."

Lieutenant Michael sighed and said, "You girls took longer in the bathroom than I thought you would."

Mary chuckled and said, "Sorry, Lieutenant, we had to gather the courage to come out and face your oatmeal."

Lieutenant Michael held up his hand and said, "Courage to face oatmeal? Just a couple of days ago you all faced some fully grown Harvesters."

Sarah said, "Harvesters are nothing.  I could deal with them in my sleep … I often do, but this cold frisbee oatmeal.  I don't know what to say?"

Lieutenant Michael shoveled the last bit of his oatmeal into his mouth, then he rested his elbows on the table, and hid his face in his hands.  He said, "You three sure know how to kick a man when he's down."

Mary said, "Calm down, Lieutenant.  We're just kidding around.  See. It's not all that bad."  She put a spoonful of oatmeal into her mouth, swallowed it, and then pretended to gag.

Lieutenant Michael leaned back into his chair and said, "Okay, girls. Since you can't stand my breakfast, you three can make something for breakfast tomorrow and I'll sit here and make coughing noises from the smoke of burning food."

Mary turned to Valerie and said, "See, what did I tell you, Val. He made crappy food so that I would feel obligated to make it next time. Don't worry, Lieutenant, tomorrow I'll make you the best breakfast I've ever made by myself. Then you can sit there and enjoy it while remembering this crappy breakfast that you made for me.'

Lieutenant Michael shrugged his shoulders, saying, "That's fine with me, as long as I'm not the one making it."

When he said this, all three of the girls started to laugh in unison. Lieutenant Michael watched them and then joined in the laughter.

In spite of their complaints, the girls finished their breakfast and helped with the dishes. Mary stood at the sink with her jacket off and her hands were scrubbing dishes with a scrub brush. After she scrubbed a dish, she would hand it to Sarah, who rinsed it in clean water. After rinsing, Sarah handed the dish to Valerie, who wiped it with a towel till it was dry. Valerie then handed the dish to Lieutenant Michael, who put it away in its appropriate spot.

As Mary scrubbed the next dish, she sighed and looked up with longing in her eyes. Sarah said, "What's wrong now?"

Mary replied, "Oh, it's nothing. Just doing stuff like this makes me feel like I'm a young housewife."

Sarah said, "Really? You think so?"

Mary replied as she handed Sarah the last dish, "Oh yes, it does. Don't you ever wonder what it would be like to get married?"

Sarah said, "Not really."

Mary opened the drain on the sink and the dirty, soapy water began to run down the drain. She rinsed her hands and said, "Well, I guess you're still a little kid, so, of course, you wouldn't think about that kind of stuff. I am an adult after all." Lieutenant Michael rolled his eyes. Mary looked at him and said, "What?"

Lieutenant Michael waved his hand and said, "Oh, nothing. Don't mind me. Please continue."

Sarah handed the newly rinsed dish to Valerie and said, "Well, I figured I wouldn't worry about something that will never happen."

As Valerie wiped the dish off, Mary said, "How about you, Val? You ever think about getting married in the future?"

Valerie handed the last dish to Lieutenant Michael and said, "Not really. But, I saw pictures of my mom in an all-white dress that was really pretty. My mom told me that it was her wedding dress. I always thought it would be nice to wear a wedding dress like that."

As Lieutenant Michael put away the last dish, Mary said to him, "So, Lieutenant, do you plan on getting married?"

Lieutenant Michael shrugged his shoulders and said, "Well, I'm not against the idea of getting married. But, I just don't think it's going to happen."

Valerie said, "But what about Lieutenant Rachel? She loves you. I know it because she made you cookies."

Lieutenant Michael said, "Well, I don't think that will happen either since we're just friends. She said that too. Plus, if something goes wrong, then it might ruin our friendship. I'd regret that too much."

Mary wiped her hands off with a towel and said, "Don't worry, Lieutenant. It will happen when it happens."

Lieutenant Michael shrugged his shoulders and said, "Eh, I'm not worried about it at all. Besides, this job takes up all my time and energy. I'm happy with the way things are now."

Valerie looked up at Lieutenant Michael as he said this. He looked down at her with a smile and rubbed the top of her head, saying, "Well, we're all done here. So, let's go to the training room and get our daily exercises out of the way."

Sarah wiped her hands on a towel and said, "Okay, let's go!" She raised her fist high into the air.

Valerie nodded her head with a smile and said, "Okay, Lieutenant!"

Mary put her hands on her stomach and said, "Ug...how long is this going to last?"

Lieutenant Michael placed a hand on her back as she walked past him, saying, "Up to a week generally."

Mary sighed and said, "This sucks." She then stopped walking and turned around to face him, saying, "Would it be alright if I take it easy during exercises today?"

Lieutenant Michael put his hand on her shoulder and gently squeezed it, saying, "Sure, you're plenty strong already. Just do what you feel up to doing."

Mary put her hand on top of Lieutenant Michael's hand that was resting on her shoulder and said, "Thanks, Lieutenant." She put her hand down and he let her shoulder go. Together, they all went down to the training room.

After doing stretches, Mary mostly sat and watched them exercising. After Lieutenant Michael, Sarah and Valerie ran around the open area, they went off on their own to do their own personal choice exercises.

Valerie went off to do more work with the dumbbells. She had managed to increase her weight limit from ten pounds to fifteen pounds. She was really happy about that and said, "Look, Lieutenant, I'm getting stronger!" He had congratulated her and rubbed the top of her head, saying, "Good job! Keep this up and you'll be super strong."

Mary stood up and walked over to where Valerie was. She sat down on a weightlifting bench and watched Valerie struggling with the fifteen pound dumbbells.

Valerie noticed her and said, "What's up, Mary? You going to do more lifting too?"

A strange look fell on Mary's face that she had not seen before. It looked like she was embarrassed. Valerie said, "What's wrong?" She put her weights on the ground and sat down next to Mary. She wrapped an arm around Mary's arm, saying, "Is there something bothering you?"

Mary sighed and said, "You always pray to yourself over meal time. Do you really believe that there is a god?"

Valerie nodded her head and said, "Oh, yes, I do."

Mary said, "How do you know that there is a god?"

Valerie cocked her head and looked upward in deep thought. She brought her finger to her lips and then said, "Well, I first believed in God because my parents taught me all about him even though the World Government discourages it a little."

Mary said, "So you only believe in God because your parents taught you to believe in a god?"

Valerie said, "Not exactly. It may have started out that way but the reason I believe in God is because when I pray, I feel a feeling of love fall on me. It helps me to feel better when I am sad or scared. I believe that feeling of love comes from God."

Mary said, "I see." She paused for a moment and looked downward.

Valerie said, "Is there something else you want to ask me?"

Mary shyly said, "So ... do you believe that we go to heaven when we die?"

Valerie nodded her head and said, "Good people go to heaven and bad people go to hell."

Mary clasped her hands together and began to twirl her thumbs. She said, "Do you think that when I die, I'll get to go to heaven?"

Valerie let go of Mary's arm and wrapped her arms around Mary. Tears began to form in her eyes as she said, "Of course. You're a good person so of course you would go to heaven. Is that what you are worried about?

Mary said, "I wouldn't say I'm worried about it, but I never had a friend who really believed in that before so it's just making me think is all. Would you mind showing me how to pray?"

Valerie said, "Sure, first you bring your hands together like this." She put her hands up and brought the palms of her hands together.

Mary said, "How come you got to put the palms of your hands together?"

Valerie cocked her head and looked upward in deep thought again, she said, "Actually, I don't know why, but that's what my parents taught me and that's just what I do."

Valerie then said, "Then you say 'Dear God' or 'Dear Heavenly Father.' After that, you thank him for things and then you tell him what is in your heart. When you're all done praying then you close in the name of the son Jesus and say 'Amen.' Then you're done."

Mary said, "Who's the son Jesus?"

Valerie said, "My parents tell me that Jesus is the son of God. He gave up his life and died to save all people so that we can go to heaven."

Mary nodded her head and said, "That kind of sounds like us, we're born only to die to save people too."

Valerie nodded and said, "Yeah, I didn't think of that before but you're right."

Lieutenant Michael suddenly called out, saying, "Alright, everyone. That's enough exercising for today. Let's get some lunch and then we'll go out shopping."

Valerie let go of Mary and stood up. Mary stood up and rubbed Valerie's head, saying, "Thanks for helping me, Val."

Valerie looked up at her and smiled, saying, "You're welcome!"

After lunch, they walked together to the shopping district. Mary wrapped an arm around Lieutenant Michael's arm and walked beside him. Sarah and Valerie linked arms and walked behind them. They finally reached the clothing store. It was the same place that they went to get their latest swimsuits.

Lieutenant Michael found the same chair he sat in last time. He sat down, leaned back, and rested his hands behind his head. He watched them as they worked together.

Mary stood there with her hands on her hips as she began to scan the area with her eyes. Her eyes were intently focused.

Sarah stood next to her and said, "What kind of a dress are you looking for?"

Mary said, "I want a white dress." Her eyes finally caught a section of dresses that were white. She skipped over to the rack of white dresses as Sarah and Valerie followed her.

As Mary searched, Sarah began to search too. She held up a short white dress with spaghetti straps, saying, "This would look cute on you."

Mary stopped searching and looked at the dress that Sarah was holding up. Mary glanced over it and said, "It's cute, but I'm looking for something specific"

Sarah shrugged her shoulders and put the dress back on the rack. Mary said, "I'm sorry, I don't mean to sound rude. This is just something that I have to find on my own."

Valerie said, "You're looking for something that reminds you of a wedding dress aren't you."

Mary nodded her head and sighed, saying, "Geez, Val. You spoiled my surprise."

Valerie said, "I'm sorry, I didn't know it was supposed to be a secret."

Sarah said, "Ah, now I get it. Well, this makes sense since you like to talk about stuff like that all the time."

Mary said, "Don't worry, girls. When I find what I'm looking for I'll definitely want your opinion, so be honest."

Sarah and Valerie patiently waited behind her as she continued looking through the rack. Suddenly, Mary gasped, and said to herself, "I think this is it." She looked toward Lieutenant Michael, who was sitting on a chair, and appeared to be sleeping, or, at least faking it. He would probably make a joke later about how long it took to select a dress.

She sneakily took the dress off the rack and folded it up. She said, "Come with me to help me try it on." Valerie and Sarah followed her to the attendant at the dressing room area.

Mary spoke to her, saying, "Hello, I'd like to try this dress on now."

The female attendant nodded and said, "Certainly, officer." She opened the door to the dressing room and allowed the three of them to enter.

Sarah and Valerie stood there in anticipation as they waited to see what Mary had selected for herself. Mary took off her uniform and dropped it to the floor. She then slipped the new dress on over her head and tied it in the back. Sarah and Valerie stood there with mouths agape as Mary's dress was revealed to them.

The white dress went down to the middle of her calf in an A-line style. The skirt had three layers that were lightly ruffled. The bodice was perfectly formed to Mary's body. It had capped sleeves and a small V-neck line. From the shoulders to just above the bust there was see-through lace. Laced up along the back were white satin ribbons that ended in a bow. It was a very beautiful dress.

Sarah stood there in amazement and said, "Oh my gosh! That is such a pretty dress!"

Mary looked at herself in the mirror and said, "I know, right?"

Valerie said, "You definitely look like a bride in that dress."

Mary started to spin where she stood, saying, "Thanks!" The skirt of the dress began to expand like a bell. She stopped spinning and the dress shifted back and forth before quickly coming to a stop.

Sarah noticed the tag on the hem of the dress. She bent over and turned the tag over to see how much it cost. Sarah shouted out in surprise, "Three-hundred dollars?!"

Mary said, "Don't worry. I got enough."

Sarah said, "Are you sure you want to be spending all that money on a dress. Sure, it's cute, but you won't really be able to wear it much."

Mary sighed and shrugged her shoulders, saying, "I know, but this is something I've always wanted to have. Since my timer is counting down, I got to make sure I do everything I want to do so that when I die, I won't have any regrets."

Sarah slumped forward and looked downcast, saying, "I understand. I want to help you to do that too."

Valerie joined in, saying, "Me too. I'll help!"

Mary began to slip off the dress, saying, "Thanks! I knew I could count on my friends. After this, I want to go to the gelato ice cream place and buy a strawberry gelato cone. I'll buy one for you all too, so help me convince the Lieutenant. Okay?"

Sarah and Valerie began clapping for joy. Sarah said, "Of course we'll help with that."

Valerie said, "Yay, I love ice cream cones!"

Mary put her uniform back on. She ran her fingers over the red bars on her jacket as she looked at herself in the mirror. *Red is the color of blood,* she thought to herself, *the redness that flows from me is a warning that my life is almost over.*

Sarah watched her and saw the forlorn look that had fallen on her face in the mirror. She said, "Is something wrong?"

Mary smiled at her in the mirror, shook her head, and said, "No, just admiring my beauty in the mirror."

Sarah didn't believe her but let it go. It was the same look that Susan had after she started getting her period. *I'll probably get that look too when it happens to me,* she thought to herself, *best thing I can do is to just help her to keep strong like she wants to be.*

Mary folded up the dress and hugged it in her arms. She left the dressing room with Sarah and Valerie following her. As she stepped out of the dressing room she looked toward Lieutenant Michael, who was still sitting in the chair. His eyes were opened and he was looking directly towards her. She lowered her gaze and tried not to smile in embarrassment.

She continued to hug the dress over her heart and brought it to the woman at the register. After hearing the full price, including taxes, Mary pulled a stack of money out of her pocket. Valerie's eyes went wide as she noticed the large stack of cash, saying, "Wow, that's a lot of money!"

Mary chuckled and said, "When you're wealthy like me, wads of cash naturally flow out of your pockets." She lifted her head and closed her eyes arrogantly as she spoke.

The woman gave her some change and placed the dress in a bag, saying, "Thank you, Guardian." Mary smiled at her and took the bag in her hands. She held the bag with both hands and hung it in front of her skirt.

She walked up to Lieutenant Michael, who was watching her come up to him. He brought his hands down from behind his head and sat up in the chair. She walked up to him, still holding the bag in front of her skirt. She said, "Okay, Lieutenant, I'm all ready to go."

Lieutenant Michael looked at his watch and said, "Are you sure you're ready? You only took an hour. He laughed and said, "I think I even fell asleep waiting."

Mary smiled at him and said, "Thank you for being so patient with me."

Lieutenant Michael stood up and stretched, saying, "I thought that you would want to get my opinion on your dress before you bought it."

Mary turned away and looked toward the entrance of the shop. She hesitated a moment and then said, "I didn't want you to see it yet."

Lieutenant Michael said, "You don't have to show me if you don't want to. It's just that I'm used to you running up to show me."

Mary turned back to him and smirked at him, saying, "And I'm used to you saying 'eh, whatever, it's fine.'" She tried to imitate his voice as she quoted him. She pointed to Sarah and Valerie, saying, "Now those two are far more qualified than you at telling me what they think of a dress."

Sarah nodded her head and said, "It is a very beautiful dress."

Valerie spun in a circle and said, "Yeah, it's a beautiful dress, perfect for dancing in." She attempted to strike a ballerina's pose that she had seen once. It didn't go as planned. She tripped over her feet causing Sarah to reach out and catch her. Valerie gave a shy smile and said, "Thanks for catching me." Sarah giggled and said, "No problem."

Lieutenant Michael stuck his hands in his pockets, looking dejected. He said, "That's fine. Whatever. Let's get going." He walked toward the entrance. Mary ran up to him and wrapped her arm around his, while carrying the bag with the other. Valerie and Sarah linked arms again, following them out the door.

Lieutenant Michael started to turn back toward the Phoenix Guard headquarters but Mary pulled on his arm. He stopped and looked at her in surprise. He said, "Is there something else you wanted while we're out?"

Mary lowered her gaze and smiled shyly. She said, "I ... I promised Sarah and Valerie that I would buy them gelato ice cream next. It's thanks for helping me with my new dress."

Lieutenant Michael looked toward Sarah and Valerie, who were staring back at him with hopeful gazes. They waited to see if they needed to help convince him to let them go. He shrugged his shoulders and said, "Eh, that's fine with me." He turned in the opposite direction and started walking toward the gelato ice cream parlor.

Sarah and Valerie clasped their hands together. They started jumping for joy and shouted out, "Ice cream! Ice cream!"

The gelato shop was just down the street from the dress shop. It was a small shop with a couple of small tables inside and there was a patio outside that was stocked with even more tables and chairs.

As they walked up to the shop, they could see that there were several couples already there. Lieutenant Michael sat down at a table outside, nearest to the door. He said, "I'll wait here, while you girls get whatever you want. Okay?"

The three of them nodded their heads and said in unison, "Okay, Lieutenant."

Mary opened the door and allowed Sarah and Valerie to enter first. An old man with grey hair and an apron greeted them from behind the counter. He spoke in an Italian accent, saying, "Welcome, Wielders! How are you girls doing today?"

Mary spoke up for them, saying, "We're fine. Our friend told us about this place so we thought we'd check it out."

The old man said, "Oh, are you talking about Giana?"

Mary nodded her head and said, "Yeah, she said that we should check it out if we wanted to try real gelato."

The old man smiled and said, "That Giana is such a nice girl, a nice girl. Yes, my gelato is made right in my shop the traditional way. Do you know what makes it different?" The three girls shook their heads.

The old man continued, saying, "It has a lower fat to milk ratio, this makes for a denser more, intense flavor. You'll love it! For you girls, I'll give you an extra scoop free."

Mary said, "Thanks, mister!" She then pushed Sarah and Valerie forward, and said, "Okay, girls. Get whatever you want!"

Sarah brought her index finger to her lips as she slowly examined the different flavors. Valerie pressed her hands against the glass as she looked through the different flavors.

Valerie's eyes were drawn to a light yellow gelato. She read the sign and it said, "Banana." Valerie pointed at the banana flavor and said to the old man, "I want the banana flavor!"

The old man said, "You got it!" He took a waffle cone and scooped in the gelato, topping it with an extra scoop of gelato. He wrapped the cone in a napkin and handed it to Valerie. She accepted it with a big grin, saying, "Thanks!"

Sarah stood there agonizing over the decision. There were so many flavors that she wanted to try. Finally her eyes were drawn to a green colored gelato. She read the card that said, "Pistachio." She pointed at it and said, "I want to try the pistachio flavor!"

The old man grabbed another waffle cone and said, "You got it!" He scooped in the gelato and topped it with an extra scoop. Sarah watched in anticipation as the man wrapped the cone in a napkin and handed it to her. She took it with a big grin on her face, saying, "Thank you, mister!"

The old man then turned to Mary. She said, I want two strawberry cones. One for me and one for our Lieutenant."

The old man nodded and said, "Certainly!" He prepared each waffle cone individually and then handed each one to Mary as it was ready, each one with an extra scoop. Mary handed a cone to Valerie and to Sarah. She then pulled out the stack of money that was left in her pocket and paid the man what he asked for.

The old man smiled and said, "Thank you, girls! Make sure that you tell Giana that Alfonso said hi, and I hope to see you here again soon too!"

The girls smiled back at him. Mary said, "Don't worry, we'll definitely come back!"

Sarah nodded and said, "Yeah, I got to try more flavors next time!"

Valerie smiled shyly and said, "Thanks!" as she walked by.

Mary rested the bag handle on her arm and then took the two strawberry gelato cones in her own hands. Sarah opened the door for them. Mary walked up to Lieutenant Michael, saying, "I got one for you too."

Lieutenant Michael accepted it and said, "Wow, thanks, Mary. That was nice of you."

She sat down in the chair across from him and started to enjoy her gelato. Sarah and Valerie sat down in the two other chairs.

Sarah began licking the pistachio gelato and chewing on the broken nuts that topped it. She said, "This is amazing! I'm glad I started with this one."

Valerie licked her own gelato cone and took a bite of a chunk of frozen banana that was mixed in with the ice cream. She said, "Mmmm...this is so good!"

As they ate their gelato cones together, Mary would occasionally look up at Lieutenant Michael. She would then look back down at her cone and it looked like she was blushing. He said, "Is there something you want to ask me, Mary?"

Sarah and Valerie looked toward Mary, she lowered her gaze even more and looked even more embarrassed. Her cheeks turned red. She shook her head, saying, "Oh, no. I was just thinking how it's nice having a really good Lieutenant."

Lieutenant Michael sat up straight and scratched his head, saying, "So you think I'm a good Lieutenant?"

Sarah nodded her head and said, "Oh, yes. You are a very good Lieutenant. We know that you care about us."

Valerie said, "Yeah, we love you lots too!"

Lieutenant Michael looked down at his cone and said, "Gee, thanks a lot, girls. I don't know what to say. I'm just happy that we get along so well with each other. You girls make it easy for me to be your Lieutenant."

After they finished their gelato, they went back to their apartment. Mary took Sarah and Valerie into her room, saying, "Come with me, girls." Lieutenant Michael watched them leave and then sat at the table. He began to read the news report on his laptop.

After all three of them were in Mary's room, Sarah said, "What's up?"

Mary replied, "I'm going to put on my new dress now and show it to the Lieutenant."

Sarah said, "Okay, but why do you need us?"

Mary replied, "I was hoping that you could help me to do my hair." She reached into her desk and pulled out a picture from a magazine. It was a picture of a woman with the hair on her temples braided and pulled back behind her head. The rest of her hair freely hung down.

Sarah looked at the picture and said, "Yeah, I guess I can do that." She left the room to get a brush from the bathroom.

Valerie said, "What do you want me to do?"

Mary said, "I want you to go to Lieutenant Michael and make sure that he doesn't do anything that he would have to be too involved in."

Valerie looked confused but said, "Okay, I'll try."

Mary said, "I trust you."

Valerie left the room and went into the dining area. She walked up to the table and sat down next to Lieutenant Michael, who was still reading the news reports on his laptop. He looked at Valerie and said, "What's up, Valerie?"

Valerie shrugged her shoulders and said, "I'm not too sure what's going on, but Mary told me to make sure that you don't get too involved in anything while she puts on her new dress. I think she is ready to show it to you now."

Lieutenant Michael looked even more confused than Valerie did. He said, "So ... you just want me to sit here till Mary comes out wearing her new dress?"

Valerie nodded her head and said, "I think so."

Lieutenant Michael rolled his eyes and said, "Okay, whatever. I was just going to keep reading these news reports anyway."

Valerie said, "Is something going on in the news?"

Lieutenant Michael said, "Well, in the Los Angeles sector, it is being reported that a large group of Harvesters are starting to gather. It looks like they are going to attack the wall."

Valerie said, "Are we going to have to go down there to fight them?"

Lieutenant Michael leaned back in his chair and said, "Probably not. Leviathan Wielder Company is headquartered down there so they should be fine. Of course, they can always request our assistance if it gets serious."

As he finished talking, Mary and Sarah came around the corner. Mary stood there, her right arm hung down in front of her new dress, her other arm held her elbow. Lieutenant Michael noticed her and turned his attention to her. Mary stood there embarrassed and said, "What ... what do you think of my dress, Lieutenant?"

Lieutenant Michael looked at her and said, "That is a very nice dress. It looks really good on you."

Mary walked up to him clasping her hands together over her heart. She said, "You really think so?"

Lieutenant Michael said, "Yep, I really think so."

Mary took another step forward and took hold of his jacket with her right hand. She held the fabric between her fingers, saying, "I know this is a lot to ask of you, but I was wondering if you would please show me how to dance?"

Lieutenant Michael said, "You mean now? Well, the truth is, I don't really know how to dance much either, Mary."

Mary looked dejected, her hand dropped from his jacket, and she said, "Oh, really? That's okay then. I knew that it was probably too much to ask for." She joined her hands together and started twirling her thumbs.

Lieutenant Michael sighed and said, "Well, I guess there is one thing I could show you as long as you are not expecting too much from me."

Mary's face perked up, she clapped her hands together and said, "Anything is fine, Lieutenant!"

Lieutenant Michael stood up from the table. Sarah then sat down at the table next to Valerie and the two of them watched to see what would happen.

He took Mary by the arm and brought her to a more open area away from the table. He then put his left arm behind his back and he leaned forward. He held his right hand up, offering it to her and said, "May I have this dance?"

Mary said, "What do I do?"

Lieutenant Michael said, "Give me your left hand." She offered him her left hand. He took it and placed it on his right shoulder. He then took her right hand and held it up in his own left hand. He placed his right hand on the side of her stomach. He said, "This is what we call slow dancing. I used to do this back when I was in high school. You slowly sway and turn in a circle." He started to sway and guide her with his hand.

He turned with her in two complete circles. He then let her hand go and dropped his right hand from the side of her stomach, saying, "Okay, now you know everything that I know about dancing."

Mary said, "Thanks, Lieutenant. Would ... would it be alright if we dance to a song that I like? I want to try it out?"

Lieutenant Michael sighed and said, "I guess, but after this I got to get started on dinner."

Mary ran to her room and pulled out her digital music player from her desk. She then ran back out and began to slide her finger across the screen. A song began to play. She put the device on the table.

The song started out light with an electric guitar but got heavier with more instruments joining in as it continued. Lieutenant Michael recognized it as being a light 'metal' type of song, but, instead of it being fast paced, it was slow paced, perfect for slow dancing.

Lieutenant Michael took her by the hand again and got into the slow dancing position   Together they began to sway back and forth and slowly turn. Lieutenant Michael said, "I'm surprised you like this type of music."

Mary said, "It's an old song. When I lived with my dad he would listen to it a lot. It became one of my favorite songs. I've always wanted to dance to it."

Lieutenant Michael said, "I've never heard it before."

Mary said, "It's a really, really old band."

As they continued to dance, Sarah stood up and held out her hand to Valerie and said, "Would you like to dance?"

Valerie nodded her head and said, "Sure!" She took Sarah's hand and the two of them went near Lieutenant Michael and Mary. They started to dance together with Sarah leading her.

Mary looked up into his face. She hid her bottom lip underneath her top lip. She looked both happy and embarrassed at the same time. Her gaze looked like she wanted to ask him something more but was afraid to. As she looked up at him she started to blush but she didn't look away.

He shifted his gaze away from her face and began to stare at the walls around him. He began to feel a little silly, or, maybe, even a little uncomfortable. He endured it for Mary's sake; it seemed to be important to her.

Finally, the song ended and he let her go. She wrapped her arms around his torso and said, "Thank you, Lieutenant, for teaching me to dance, and for letting me dance to my favorite song. It means a lot to me."

Lieutenant Michael patted her on the back and said, "Sure, no problem. Guess I'll get dinner started. Tonight is Wednesday, so I suppose you girls will want to watch the re-run episode of Magical Girl Squad tonight?"

Mary walked over to the table and picked up her digital music player. She somberly walked back to her room. Sarah noticed the look on her face and started to follow her down the hall. When Mary opened the door to her room, Sarah said quietly, "Are you okay?"

Mary paused, but didn't look at her. She said, "Yeah, I'm okay. I just want to be alone right now. Let me know when dinner is ready, okay?"

Sarah nodded and said, "Okay, I will. If you need me, just let me know. I'm here for you."

Mary smiled and said, "Thanks, but I'm fine." She went inside and shut the door behind her, leaving Sarah standing outside her door a little confused.

Mary returned her digital music player to her desk and then took off her new dress. She put it on a hanger and hung it in her closet. She then began to dress herself in the uniform she was previously wearing before. She undid the braids that Sarah had made and returned her hair to the standard twin tails that she always wore.

Mary then sat down on the edge of her bed. She took one of her pillows and hugged onto it tightly. Tears began to fall out of her eyes. She buried her face into her pillow and then laid down on her side as she silently cried.

- 4 -

During the night, Mary woke up from a nightmare. She laid there with tears in her eyes as her mind started to process what was going on. It was the same nightmare that she always had. The nightmare that she refused to talk about.

She wiped her eyes and then looked at the clock next to her bed. It was almost two-thirty in the morning. She pulled the covers off of her bed and sat up. She sighed as she stood up expecting to feel pain in her stomach again, but, there was none. *Maybe it's over for this month,* she thought to herself.

She cautiously walked through the dark to the door of her room. She quietly turned the door knob and softly closed the door as she left. She tiptoed across the way to Lieutenant Michael's room and quietly turned his door knob. She softly stepped through the doorway and pushed the door till it lightly tapped against the frame. She did not close it completely.

Mary tiptoed to his bed and softly crawled onto it. She gently lifted the blanket and slid under it. She scooted herself over till she was right next to his sleeping body. She gently picked up his arm and wrapped it over her own body.

Lieutenant Michael woke up at this and said, "Are you okay?"

Mary said, "I had another nightmare and I was scared."

Lieutenant Michael said, "It's okay to be scared. I'm here for you."

Mary put her hands onto his chest. She said, with her voice on the edge of crying, "Would ... would you please hold me ... like you did when I was nine?"

Without answering, he wrapped his arm tighter around her back and pulled her closer to himself. As he held her, tears started to stream out of her eyes in the darkness of the night. He could feel her body trembling. He kissed her on the top of her head and said, "I know it's hard for you, Mary. I'm going to be with you all the way to the end. You are not alone." Slowly, she gained composure over herself and stopped crying. She fell back to sleep. When he was sure she was sleeping, he shut his eyes and fell back to sleep as well.

In the morning, the alarm went off at six-thirty as usual. Lieutenant Michael woke up and saw that Mary was still sleeping. His arm wrapped over her body still. He moved his arm off of her, rolled onto his back, and turned off the alarm. Mary stirred and woke up as he moved.

Mary sat up and smiled at him. She cheerfully said, "Good morning, Lieutenant!"

Lieutenant Michael sat up and said with a yawn, "Good morning, Mary. You seem to have a lot of energy this morning." He shook his head awake and then looked beyond her to see if any of the other girls had snuck into his bed. There was nobody else there.

Mary scooted up next to him and let her legs hang over the side of the bed. She bounced her legs off the side of the mattress. She looked up at him and smiled, saying, "I think my cycle is over for now. I don't feel any pain anymore."

Lieutenant Michael stood up and rubbed her on top of the head, saying, "That's good, Mary."

Mary jumped up and threw her arms around his torso and said, "Thanks, Lieutenant, for helping me."

Lieutenant Michael patted her on the back and said, "Of course, anytime. Why don't you go change into your uniform and make sure that everyone else is awake. Then we'll have breakfast."

She nodded her head in excitement and ran toward the door. She flung it open and then ran out to her room. Lieutenant Michael smiled and thought to himself that she seemed to be back to her old cheerful self. He was happy for her. He walked over to the door, shut it, and then locked it. He then got out of his pajamas and changed into his uniform.

As he left his room, Sarah came out in her uniform, rubbing her eyes. She looked at him with a sleepy face and said, "Mary has too much energy this morning."

Lieutenant Michael nodded his head in agreement and said, "I noticed."

Valerie came out of her room with an even sleepier looking face. She stood there in the doorway and wobbled a little. She held onto the door frame and said, "What's for breakfast?" as she rubbed one of her eyes.

Lieutenant Michael said, "What do you want?"

Valerie said, "I want pancakes."

Sarah said, "Oh, yeah, let's go with that."

Lieutenant Michael nodded and said, "Sure, we can do that today." He turned and left the hallway towards the kitchen. Valerie and Sarah went into the bathroom to brush their hair.

Valerie stepped inside the bathroom first and saw Mary standing at the mirror, she had just finished putting her hair up into twin tails. Valerie said, "Good news, Mary! The Lieutenant is going to make pancakes this morning."

Mary turned around, and much to Valerie's surprise, looked angry. Mary balled her fists and threw them down to her side, saying, "That idjit, I said I was going to make it today!"

Mary stormed past Valerie and Sarah. Valerie looked at Sarah with her face full of surprise and confusion. She said, "Did I do something wrong?"

Sarah waved her hand dismissively and said, "Who knows, I doubt it."

Mary stormed into the kitchen where Lieutenant Michael was already gathering the items that he needed to make pancakes. She stood in the entryway with her hands on her hips and an angry look on her face.

Lieutenant Michael stopped what he was doing and stared at her, saying, "What's wrong?"

Mary pointed her right index finger at him and said, "What do you mean, 'what's wrong?' I told you yesterday that I was going to make you breakfast this morning! Did you forget?"

Lieutenant Michael stood there and reached back into his memory. A look of remembrance fell upon his face and he said, "Oh, I guess I thought we were just joking around yesterday."

Mary said, "Geez, you never take me seriously!"

Lieutenant Michael said, "That's because you're always joking around."

Mary dropped her hands to her side and said, "Well ... well ... this is me trying to be serious now." She walked around behind him and started pushing him out of the kitchen, saying, "Just get out and I'll take care of it. Go sit at the table and wait for me."

Lieutenant Michael took the hint and walked over to the table and sat down. He said, "Try not to burn it."

He heard Mary blow a raspberry at him and then she said, "I'll have you know that I'm actually a better cook then you."

Lieutenant Michael shrugged his shoulders and said, "Whatever, it's fine. I'll just take the day off today and let you deal with everything."

As Mary started cooking the pancake batter she mixed, Sarah and Valerie came into the dining area. They saw Lieutenant Michael sitting at the table with his arms folded over his chest. He looked slightly agitated.

Mary looked at the girls and said, "Sarah and Valerie, could you please set the table for me, except for plates. I want to plate these myself."

Valerie's hands dropped to her side, she slumped forward and frowned, saying, "What's going on with my pancakes?"

Lieutenant Michael said, "Don't worry, Valerie, Mary is still making them. You'll still get some form of pancakes."

Valerie perked up and said, "Oh, that's fine then." She went into the kitchen and started gathering the things she needed to set the table.

Sarah went into the kitchen and said, "Is there anything you want me to do?"

Mary shook her head and smiled at her, saying, "Oh, no, I don't think so. I got it. You look tired so just sit at the table and wait. Make sure the Lieutenant doesn't try to help."

Lieutenant Michael interjected, saying, "Don't worry, I said I'd let you do it by yourself, so I'm just going to sit and wait like you want me to."

Mary didn't reply to him. She continued the process of making pancakes. As she waited for the next batch to finish, she started peeling some bananas and cutting them into thin slices.

When all the pancakes were done, she put some on a plate for Valerie and Sarah. She spooned some banana slices on them. She then carried them out and set them on the table in front of Valerie and Sarah. Valerie put her hands together and said a silent prayer before she started eating.

Mary returned to the kitchen and put more pancakes on a plate for Lieutenant Michael. Instead of randomly spooning banana slices on them, she neatly arranged them into the shape of a heart. She carried the plate out to him with a shy smile on her face. She placed the plate in front of Lieutenant Michael who stared at it in confusion. She anxiously stood beside him waiting for him to comment on it. She held her hands together and twirled her thumbs as she waited.

Lieutenant Michael stared at it and then looked back up at her. He saw the expectant look on her face. He gave a slight sigh and said, "It's cute. Thanks."

That was apparently good enough for her. She turned and went back into the kitchen with a big grin on her face. Lieutenant Michael cut up his pancakes and poured some syrup on them.

Valerie looked at his plate and said, "How come I didn't get a heart on my pancakes?"

Mary walked out carrying her own plate with banana slices randomly piled onto her plate. She replied, "Because I did it for the Lieutenant to thank him for teaching me how to dance."

Valerie said, "Oh, I get it." She then continued to shovel food into her mouth.

Sarah stopped eating for a moment and watched Mary. When Mary sat down at her plate, she brought the palms of her hands together like Valerie usually did, and closed her eyes for a moment. When she did this, everybody else stopped eating and watched Mary as she silently prayed.

When Mary opened her eyes and put her hands down, Lieutenant Michael said, "Did you just pray over your food?"

Mary shoved a piece of pancake into her mouth and said, "Yeah, so what? Is there something wrong with that?"

Lieutenant Michael said, "No, there's nothing wrong with it. It's just that you've never shown an interest in it before."

Mary shoved more food into her mouth and said, "Well, now I am. Last night, before I went to bed, I was thinking about what Valerie was telling me earlier about God and stuff. I decided to try it. So, I prayed before I went to sleep. And you know what? I think I did have that feeling of love fall on me like Valerie told me she feels when she prays."

Lieutenant Michael said, "Well that's great. I'm happy for you. I hope it helps you." Everyone went back to eating again.

As they were almost finished eating, a chime sounded over the intercom and Captain Faust's voice said, "All Lieutenants, please come to the briefing room immediately. Thank you."

Lieutenant Michael quickly shoved the last few bits of food into his mouth and stood up from his chair, saying, "Great, now what." He reached over and rubbed Mary on top of her head, saying, "Thanks for making breakfast this morning. It was really good." He then headed to the door and said as he was leaving, "Stay right there, we might have to deploy."

As he left, Mary slammed her elbow on the table and dropped her face into her hand, saying, "Geez, what's going on? How many times are we going to have to deploy this week!"

Sarah finished the last piece of pancake on her plate and said, "Do you think it's about deployment?"

Mary, still resting her face in her hand, said, "Of course, because I wanted to have a nice relaxing Thursday today."

Valerie, with a worried look on her face, said, "Yesterday, before we learned how to dance together, the Lieutenant was reading the news reports. It said that a large Harvester force was gathering near Los Angeles sector."

Mary sat up and shoved the last piece of pancakes into her mouth and said, "See, what did I tell you! I bet that's it!"

As Lieutenant Michael shut the door behind himself, Lieutenant Rachel opened her own door. He stopped and said, "Good morning."

Lieutenant Rachel smiled at him and said, "Good morning, do you know what's going on yet?"

Lieutenant Michael shook his head and said, "Not really, but last night I read a report that a large Harvester force was gathering near the Los Angeles sector. I believe it has something to do with that."

Together, they walked down the stairs to the briefing room on the first floor. Inside the briefing room, Captain Faust was already sitting at the conference table. His shirt and tie was loose, something that Lieutenant Michael had never seen him do. He looked like he had been awake all night and seemed very agitated. A cold cup of coffee sat beside him on the table.

The Lieutenants for First and Second squad had already arrived before them and were sitting at the table. Lieutenant Rachel and Lieutenant Michael sat down next to them in the order of their squads. As they sat down, the Lieutenant for fifth squad came in and sat down next to Lieutenant Rachel.

Seeing that all the Lieutenants had gathered, the Captain dropped his hands to the table loudly and said, "Thank you for getting here quickly. There's a major event going on outside the Los Angeles sector. A very large force of Harvesters have gathered on the outskirts of the sector. We believe they are going to breach the wall. Leviathan Company has asked for reinforcements. We are the closest so we are responding first. Two other companies are on the way but it will take up to six hours for them to get there. We can be there in about two hours."

Lieutenant Lloyd of First Squad said, "How large of a force are we talking about here?"

Captain Faust wiped sweat from his forehead with the palm of his hand. He wiped the palm of his hand on his pants and said, "There's an estimated number of about one thousand fully-grown Harvesters." The room filled with gasps. Rachel and Michael looked at each other. Another Lieutenant said, "One thousand?"

Captain Faust raised his hand and said, "Let me continue: there's a total estimate of five thousand Harvesters, a fifth of them are estimated to be fully grown."

Lieutenant Lloyd stood up out of his chair. His hands were shaking. He said, "There's no way we can stop a force like that."

Captain Faust waved his hand and said, "Calm down, we're not trying to stop them, just slow them down. There are about fifteen million people shoved into the Los Angeles sector. They have already begun evacuating people, we just need to slow them down so we can get more people out."

Lieutenant Michael said, "How ... how many people do they think they can get out?"

Captain Faust said, "Five percent."

Lieutenant Rachel said, "Only five percent! What is the World Government doing?"

Captain Faust replied, "The best they can, just like we will. We got a transport helicopter already on the roof waiting. It is dedicated to our use. It will take us there and wait for us to fall back. Okay, everyone. I know that there has never been any Harvester movement like this before. But ... but we got to stand up against them because if we don't ... if we don't then humanity is done for."

Lieutenant Davenport of Fifth squad said, "Don't worry, sir. We'll give them hell for as long as we can."

Captain Faust said, "I know you will. When you get there you will deploy in a half-circle around the Sector. You will alternate between Phoenix Guard Company and Leviathan Company." He handed each one of them a map, saying, "Here is the order. Now get on up to the roof with your girls and let them know about it. Dismissed."

All the Lieutenants stood up together and saluted. They then ran out the door and ran up the stairs to their floors and apartments.

Lieutenant Michael flung open his door. Mary, Sarah, and Valerie were still sitting at the table waiting. He hurriedly opened the wall cabinet and began pulling out equipment.

They saw the worry on his face. Mary spoke for them, saying, "What's wrong, Lieutenant? Are we deploying?"

Lieutenant Michael tried to calm down but he just could not do it. He spoke with great agitation, saying, "Yeah, we're all deploying to Los Angeles sector!"

The three girls stood up, Mary said, "What do you mean by all of us?"

Lieutenant Michael dropped the com unit case on the table and said, "I mean all of us ... the entire Phoenix Guard Company. We're going to support Leviathan Company in Los Angeles sector."

Mary said, "Ten squads! What the hell is going on down there?!"

Lieutenant Michael put a com unit into his ear and said, "There's a Harvester force of about five thousand Harvesters trying to breach the wall."

Mary yelled out, "Five thousand! There's never been a force that large!"

Sarah gasped and covered her mouth with her hands. Valerie's mouth dropped and her eyes went wide.

Lieutenant Michael said, "Don't worry, we just have to slow them down for the evacuation, not stop them." He handed a com unit to Mary who took it and put it into her ear. She twisted the button on. Sarah took a com unit next and put it into her ear. She twisted the button on. Valerie took the last com unit and stuck it in her ear. She twisted the button on and heard it crackle to life.

Lieutenant Michael said, "Radio check." They heard his voice through the com unit.

Mary said, "Red on."

Sarah said, "Blue on."

Valerie said, "Yellow on."

Lieutenant Michael handed Valerie her cattle prod holster. She strapped it over her shoulder and checked the magazines. He then handed Sarah her scabbard belt and she checked her two metal sticks. Lieutenant Michael put on his own holster belt that held his own cattle prod gun. Then they ran out the door and ran up to the roof.

As they ran, Squad four caught up to them from behind. Giana yelled to Mary as they ran, "This is nuts!"

Mary yelled back, "Yeah, if you die out there I'm going to kill you!"

Giana shouted, "Yeah, same to you!"

Fifth squad was already inside the helicopter. Third and Fourth squad joined them inside and sat down in their usual formation. A moment later First and Second squad came in and sat down.

Lieutenant Lloyd of First squad reached up and grabbed the intercom, saying, "Phoenix Guard Company is all loaded and ready for deployment to Los Angeles sector."

A man's voice came over the intercom and replied, saying, "Roger, ready to deploy. ETA two hours."

The rotors started to move and the ramp of the door started to lift. The helicopter shook as it lifted off of the ground.

Valerie sat in between Mary and Sarah. She lifted her gaze to Mary and then turned to Sarah. Mary took her hand and held it with a smile, saying, "Don't worry, we can handle it just like last time."

Sarah took Valerie's other hand and said, "Yeah, as long as we work together we can overcome anything. We're going to go out there and protect each other."

Valerie nodded her head with a smile and said, "You can count on me, I'm going to do my best!"

Lieutenant Michael turned his attention to Lieutenant Rachel. The two of them sat there staring at each other. Both of them had a grim expression on their face. He could tell what she was thinking because it was probably the same as he was thinking: This was going to be their toughest mission ever.

Time seemed to drag on forever inside the helicopter. Since there were no windows, they could not see what was going on outside. Every fifteen minutes the pilot would give them an update of an estimated time of arrival. The pilot also briefed them on any updates to the situation as they occurred.

Finally, the two hours were up. The helicopter landed next to the wall on the outside. The girls activated their powers. Their eyes glowed with red, blue, and yellow light.

The ramp of the helicopter started to descend. The pilot's voice came over the intercom again and said, "After deployment, we're going to sit on just the other side of the wall in sector three. When you're ready to retreat, come on over and get in. We'll leave the ramp open for you so we can take off in a hurry."

Lieutenant Lloyd picked up the com unit and said, "Copy that. Don't forget to leave the porch light on for us too!"

The pilot responded with a laugh and said, "Will do."

Lieutenant Lloyd then turned to all the girls and said, "Who's ready to squash some bugs?" All the older girls lifted a hand and said, "Yes, sir, we'll squash 'em." The newer girls, like Valerie, copied their teammates by raising their right hand in the air."

The ramp finished lowering and the five squads filed out. They began to run to their assigned sectors. Leviathan Company had already deployed to their areas before Phoenix Guard arrived. Squad three rushed over to their area next to the wall in sector four. They stood looking at the landscape that lay beyond the burned out ground that was next to the wall.

The landscape was already thrashed from the years of neglect since humanity now only resided behind the walls. There were old rotting cars that lined the broken streets. Grass and other weeds poked through the broken cement and asphalt.

The Harvesters continued to swarm back and forth. It was a chaotic scene that they had never seen before. It seemed like the Harvesters were acting as an organized unit instead of acting independently of each other. This was not normal behavior. If this behavior kept up, it would be disastrous for humanity. Humankinds only advantage was their intelligence.

Lieutenant Michael spoke into the com unit, saying, "Please, girls. Be extra careful today. This is nothing we've ever dealt with before. I don't want any of you to get hurt today."

Valerie said, "Don't worry, Lieutenant. If anybody gets hurt, I'll just heal them, and then they'll be okay."

A detachment of Harvesters broke off of the main body and started to move closer and closer to the wall. They moved in such a way to keep their formation even instead of rushing blindly at them. Again, this was unusual behavior.

Lieutenant Michael spoke over the commander's channel, saying, "Are you noticing their behavior? It seems too organized."

Other Lieutenants began to respond to him in agreement. Several Lieutenants noted that there appeared to be Harvesters that looked fully grown but seemed to be oddly shaped. After hearing that, Lieutenant Michael looked forward again and noticed it too. There appeared to be a new class of Harvester. This new Harvester might be the reason they were acting differently.

Another Lieutenant said over the com unit, "I don't like this at all. This is something we've never seen before. There's no way we can predict what is going to happen."

Several air force jets passed over head. They dropped their payloads and a wall of fire erupted among the Harvesters. Lieutenant Michael pointed at it and said, "Look at that, girls, hopefully they can reduce their numbers for us."

Behind them, on top of the wall, there were artillery guns that kept a constant barrage of fire at the location of the main Harvester body. The sound echoed over the land.

The detachment of Harvesters kept coming closer to the wall as they walked through the wall of fire as if they were tanks. The fire seemed to have no effect. Mary, Sarah, and Valerie stood in front of Lieutenant Michael and watched them approach. Mary then held her hand out like before. Sarah and Valerie formed a circle and put their hands on hers.

Mary smiled at them and said, "Don't forget, we're going to protect each other!"

Sarah nodded her head and said, "Yeah, together we can do anything!"

Suddenly, behind them, there were sounds that sounded like hundreds of jars smashing on the ground. It was a sound that none of them had ever heard before. They all turned toward the wall to see what had happened. All over that section of the wall, hundreds of blackish-purple thorns were sticking out of the wall and even were sticking out of the ground around them.

Sarah's voice spoke out, saying, "Lieutenant, I ... I ..."

Lieutenant Michael, Mary and Valerie turned around to look at Sarah. A line of blood began to trickle out of the corner of her mouth. They looked down at her stomach in horror as they noticed that a thorn had impaled her through the stomach.

Sarah's hands gripped the bloody thorn that was sticking out of her stomach. Her hands were covered in her own blood. Blood began to spill down the front of her skirt. She dropped to her knees and fell over on her side.

Lieutenant Michael said, "Oh my God, Sarah!" He rushed over to her side, held her in his arms, and touched the thorn that was sticking through her body.

Mary jumped over them to block them from anything else that might come at them.

Valerie rushed over to Sarah's side. Tears started to stream out of her eyes. She took Sarah's hand and held it in both of hers. She said, "Sarah! Sarah! What should I do, Lieutenant?"

Sarah looked up at Lieutenant Michael, tears streaming down her cheeks that had lost their color and were pale. She said, "Daddy, I'm scared. Don't let them kill me, daddy." As she spoke blood splattered out of her mouth. She began to cough and to gag on the blood.

Lieutenant Michael said, "Don't worry, Sarah. I'm going to do everything I can to help you!" Sarah's body then went limp in his arms. The blue light of her eyes dimmed and then was gone.

Valerie, her voice shaking, said, "Is ... is she dead?"

Lieutenant Michael put his hand under her nose and said, "Calm down. No, she's still breathing. But we got to do this quick or she'll drown in her own blood."

Valerie said, "Should we pull the thorn out now?"

Lieutenant Michael shook his head and said, "No, if we just pull it out, her guts are going to spill all over the ground and then she will be dead."

Valerie said, "If … if we can't pull it out, how can I heal her?"

Lieutenant Michael sat Sarah up in his arms to help keep her lungs clear of pooling blood. He said, "I'm going to pull it out a little and then you are going to start healing her. Then I'm going to pull it out some more and then you're going to keep healing. We'll keep doing that till it's done. Okay?"

Valerie nodded and said, "Okay."

The detachment of Harvesters started to run at them. Mary said, "Lieutenant, we got smaller ones rushing. I'm going to distract them while you deal with Sarah."

Lieutenant Michael said, "Okay, Mary, but if it gets too dicey, fall back to us, okay."

Mary saluted him and said, "Aye, Lieutenant." She then turned to Valerie and said, "I'm counting on you, Val. You're our healer!"

Mary ran toward the detachment of junior sized Harvesters and began to kick and punch at them with all her might. One by one the smaller Harvesters were killed as they tried to bring Mary down.

Lieutenant Michael began to slowly pull the thorn out of Sarah's gut. As he started to pull, blood started to flow out of the wound again. Blood began to spill on his and Valerie's uniform. Valerie put her power into her hands. They began to glow with yellow light and the wound stopped bleeding and slowly closed. Lieutenant Michael then pulled the thorn out some more. Again, more blood spilled out, and Valerie continued to heal the gaping hole in Sarah's stomach. The hole closed even more.

Mary continued to slaughter the charging Harvesters. She yelled out at them, saying, "How dare you hurt my best friend!" She leapt toward the next line of junior harvesters and continued to kick and punch them until they were also dead. Another detachment of slightly bigger Harvesters charged toward her from the main line. As they ran, another wave of thorns shot out at the wall like arrows. The sound of shattering glass echoed over the area. The wall was impaled again causing severe damage to the wall.

Lieutenant Michael continued to pull the thorn out of Sarah and Valerie continued to heal the wound. As they continued to work together, a voice came over the commander's channel, saying, "Wall breach has occurred in sector two."

Lieutenant Michael said to his own squad, "Wall breach happened in sector two. We're in sector four."

Mary replied, "I copy, Lieutenant. Orders?"

Lieutenant Michael said, "Continue as currently operating."

Mary replied, "Aye, Lieutenant." She continued fighting the smaller Harvesters that rushed at her.

Another voice of a Lieutenant came over the commander's channel in Lieutenant Michael's ear, saying, "There's too many of them! We're being overrun. Ashley fall ...." Then it went dead silent.

Another voice came over the commander's channel shouting, "Oh God, we're not ..." That voice went silent as well.

A third voice started screaming over the same channel, "They're tearing us apart. Oh God, help us! We .... Ahhhh! No! Argh!"

Lieutenant Michael tried to ignore the death groans that were echoing in his ear over the commander's channel. He focused his mind on Sarah and pulled out the thorn all the way out of her body. Valerie closed up the wound fully on both sides of her body. Sarah still did not wake up. Valerie put her hands on Sarah's stomach again and tried to put more energy into her hands but her hands lost their yellow light. Valerie looked at her hands in shock and tried to put her power back into her hands again. She held up her hands and said, "I ... I can't use my powers anymore? It won't turn on. What's going on?"

Lieutenant Michael shook his head and said, "You're depleted. Healing Sarah this much took all your energy. We're going to need another yellow Wielder to finish."

Suddenly, another shower of thorns rained down upon the wall. The sound of smashing glass echoed again over the area. The wall was torn open by this last barrage of thorns. The sound of smashing glass was replaced by the sound of crashing stones as the wall began to break up and fall over.

Lieutenant Michael shook his head again and said, "Damn it! We just got breached too!" He switched to the commander's channel and said, "This is sector four, we've got wall breach!"

A voice came back to him saying, "Sector two and sector four is breached. Leviathan units no contact, Phoenix squad five no contact. Presumed killed in action. All units fall back and retreat, we can't hold any more. They're already overrunning the city."

Lieutenant Michael spoke to Mary in the com unit, saying, "We've just been ordered to retreat so fall back."

Mary waited a moment and then replied through the com unit, saying, "I can't do that Lieutenant. If I don't stay and distract them, they're going to overrun you. If I don't hold them back, you, Sarah and Valerie will all die."

Lieutenant Michael lifted Sarah up and laid her head on Valerie's lap. Valerie placed her hands on Sarah's cheeks and held her face. Her pale cheeks felt cold to the touch, but she was still breathing. Valerie began to say over and over again, "Please wake up! Please wake up! We need you!"

Lieutenant Michael stood up and said, "What do you mean you can't? I just gave you an order!"

Mary stood her ground and said, "You know that we can't outrun these Harvesters. I'm not going to let you all die with me. I'm going to hold them here as long as I can to give you time to get out."

Lieutenant Michael became angry and ran out to meet her. She saw him running and jumped toward him. He grabbed her arm and said, "Damn it, Mary! I said come on, we might make it if we work together. We can make it together if we just try."

Mary said, "Sarah can't move, you're going to have to carry her. Valerie's out of energy. There are millions of people trying to flee the sector. If I leave now, more people are going to die, you are going to die!"

Valerie spoke into her com unit, saying, "Come on, Mary. Please, we can all make it if we work together. We promised to protect each other! You can't do this alone!"

Lieutenant Michael pulled on her arm and said, "Come on, Mary, you're going to come with me now."

Mary pulled back against his pull and said into the com unit, "I'm sorry, Val. It's up to you to get Sarah to safety. Remember, I said next time is my turn to protect you? This is how I'm going to protect both you and her. Only I can do this. This is goodbye. Tell Sarah goodbye for me too."

Valerie began to scream and cry into the com unit, "Come on, Mary! Please come with us!"

Lieutenant Michael pulled on Mary's arm again, his eyes began to water from tears. He said, "Please, Mary! I ... I don't want to lose you."

Mary's hands glowed with red light. She reached up and grabbed Lieutenant Michael by the collar of his jacket. She used her power to force him down on his knees. He looked up at her face in shock, he stared at her face without knowing what to say. She had never once used her power on him before like this. She smiled down at him with tears flowing out of her own eyes. Valerie was still crying into the com unit and pleading for Mary to come. Mary pulled the com unit out of her ear and stuck it into his jacket pocket. The red light of her hands and eyes turned off.

He looked past her and saw another red Wielder in the distance. She was too far to hear but he could imagine her screaming. She had been caught by two fully grown Harvesters, who were playing tug of war with her arms. One

Harvester won as the other arm broke off and the poor girl fell limp. The two Harvesters then tore her body apart as she laid there. They would soon overrun this area too.

Mary put both her hands on the sides of his face. He focused back on her eyes. She smiled at him and looked lovingly into his eyes, tears rolling down her cheeks. She lowered her forehead until her forehead was touching his forehead. Her nose touched his nose. Mary then spoke softly to him, her voice shook with the weight of her emotions. She said, "Michael, I ... I ... I love you. I'm in love with you. I love you with all my heart and with all my soul. I don't want you to die. My life is already over. If my death means I can save you then it is worth it to me. If my death can save Sarah and Valerie too, I am okay with it."

Lieutenant Michael said, "Mary, I ..."

Mary stopped him from speaking by pressing her lips onto his. She began kissing him. He felt her warm lips press against his. He did not know what to do. He was so shocked that he knelt there frozen, unable to move or say anything back to her.

Mary lifted her head, still holding onto the sides of his face. He stared at her blankly in confusion. She ran her right hand through his hair and said, "If you let them die, I won't forgive you! Now, get going." She let go of his face and grabbed on to his shirt. Her hands and eyes began to glow with red light again. She lifted him up and then flung him toward where Valerie sat with the unconscious Sarah.

Lieutenant Michael landed five feet from them with a loud thud. He sat up and looked at Mary. The Harvesters were now in a full run toward their position. He jumped to his feet, ran over to Sarah and Valerie, and picked Sarah up, tossing her over his shoulder.

Valerie, who was still crying, said, "What are you doing?"

Lieutenant Michael said, "We're getting out of here."

Valerie pointed at Mary and said, "What do you mean, we can't leave without Mary!"

Lieutenant Michael grabbed Valerie and tossed her over his other shoulder. He started to run toward the breach in the wall. Valerie began to scream, "Mary! Mary! Lieutenant what are you doing! We have to get her too! Don't just leave her behind!" Her legs began to flail and she pounded on his back with her arms.

Lieutenant Michael ignored her and kept running. Valerie stopped hitting him and flailing her legs. Her arms dropped motionless as she stared towards Mary with tears still flowing down the sides of her cheeks.

Mary smiled at her in the distance, her smile could not hide the grim look she was trying to hide. She waved goodbye to Valerie as Lieutenant Michael kept running. A look of confusion and betrayal was on Valerie's face as she stared back at her.

After they had disappeared beyond the wall breach, Mary leapt a couple of times till she stood in front of the breach. Her hands and feet glowed bright red. She raised her fists in a fighting stance and said, "Okay, bugs, if this is my last dance, I'm taking as many of you as I can with me!"

A line of fully grown and half-sized Harvesters were rushing toward her. When they got close enough, Mary leapt at them with all her might. She landed in front of a half-sized Harvester. She grabbed it by the mandibles and tore them off. She then kicked it in the face and smashed her fist on top of its head with all her might. There was a shower of sparks and the head split right open.

Mary jumped again and threw herself like a bullet toward a fully grown Harvester. The Harvester was knocked back and rolled over on to its back. Mary jumped onto its overturned body and smashed its head open with her foot. Yellow Harvester goo sprayed onto her legs.

Mary ignored it as she leapt toward the next Harvester that was also fully grown. She landed on its back and began smashing its head with her foot. Showers of sparks flew in all directions until the head finally cracked open. Mary's distraction worked. The Harvesters stopped focusing on the open wall breach and focused on Mary who kept jumping all around them.

Lieutenant Michael ran as fast as he could toward the landing zone where the helicopter was hopefully still waiting. Mary was right, if she had not distracted them there would have been no way for them to outrun the rushing onslaught.

The voice of Lieutenant Lloyd came into his ear, saying, "Squad three, what's your status?"

Lieutenant Michael responded over the commander's channel, saying, "In route to the Landing Zone. One dead, one critical, one depleted."

Lieutenant Lloyd replied, "Copy, you're the last squad out still, we'll wait for you as long as we can but you better get her soon. This whole area is about to be overrun."

Lieutenant Michael said, "Copy, we're almost there. I can see the helicopter now." He ran faster and faster. His legs began to feel like they were going to break off. His feet began to feel like lead. The combined weight of Valerie and Sarah began to weigh on him.

Lieutenant Rachel stood on top of the ramp and waved toward him.  He ran up the ramp and dropped to his knees inside the helicopter.  He was panting heavily.

Lieutenant Lloyd spoke into the intercom, saying, "We're clear, go now!" Even before the ramp started to lift, the helicopter rose into the air.  As it rose, the ramp slowly lifted till it was sealed.

Lieutenant Michael let Valerie slide off of his shoulder and then he gently laid Sarah down.  Valerie began to pound her fists onto his chest and said, "How ... how could you just leave her like that!"

Lieutenant Michael looked straight into her eyes.  His eyes were filled with pain and regret.  Tears began to form in the corner of his eyes.  He said, "She sacrificed herself so we could make it out."

Valerie began to cry again as she pounded her fists on his chest, "We could have made it out together if we just tried!"

Lieutenant Michael pulled a small injector needle off of his belt.  He then grabbed Valerie in an embrace and stuck her arm with the needle.  She struggled for a moment in his arms and then fell asleep from the tranquilizer.  He laid her down next to Sarah.

Lieutenant Michael looked up and noticed a girl that had managed to survive from Leviathan Company.  Her dark wavy hair was caked in Harvester goo and human blood.  Her caramel skin was covered with patches of mud and dried blood.  Her red stripped uniform was torn and had blood stains and Harvester goo on it.  She looked like a rag doll leaning against the wall of the helicopter.  A blank look was upon her face that showed the intense pain that was in her heart.

Lieutenant Michael still kneeled on the floor.  He looked up at Rachel who was sitting on the bench next to him.  He looked up at her, anguish filled his eyes.  He rested his arm on her lap.  He buried his head on her thighs and said, "She's gone, Mary's gone."

Mary continued to jump from Harvester to Harvester, inflicting as much damage as she could.  She spoke to herself, saying, "I need more power!" She began to release more of her power, a thing she had been too afraid to do since it can cause her body to fall apart.  That didn't seem to matter to her anymore.

Her limbs started to grow brighter and the light moved further up her wrists and calves.  She struck a half-sized Harvester crushing its head in one blow.  She said, "This is for you, Michael, for every time you comforted me!"

She leapt at another Harvester, a fully-grown one, and smashed its head open after a couple of kicks. The light of her hands and feet began to extend further up. She said, "This is for you, Michael, for every time I was scared at night and you held me in the dark."

Mary leapt at another Harvester and crushed its head in one blow. Again the light of her hands and feet began to climb up her arms and legs. She said, "This is for you, Michael, for every time you made me feel special."

Mary's body began to feel lighter. She leapt at another fully-grown Harvester and managed to crush its head in one blow. Her body began to feel more powerful then she had ever felt before. Her hands and feet changed from glowing with light and now looked like a burning red fire. She said, "And this is for you, Sarah, for being my best friend and sister. I love you with all my heart."

Mary leapt toward another fully-grown Harvester and she used her new power to tear off its head in one strike. A crack that glowed with red light began to open on her arm, she realized that her time was almost up. She had used too much power. She said, "And this is for you, Valerie, for helping me to believe in God. I love you with all my soul too!"

Mary leapt at another fully-grown Harvester. With her new power she easily tore right through its shell and bored all the way through it. Again more cracks of red light appeared on her arms and, now, even on her legs too. She thought to herself, "How could this power that makes me feel so good now, be the same power that kills me? It doesn't make any sense? I feel so alive!"

She leapt at another Harvester and tore right through that one as well. The cracks of red light were now opening up on her biceps and thighs. She felt even lighter than before. She imagined Lieutenant Michael's smiling face looking down at her. She said, "I love you, Michael. I love you! I love you!"

Mary leapt toward another Harvester and tore through its body with her power. The cracks in her body began to open even wider. Light poured out of them. It was uncontrollable now. The cracks began to cover her entire body. They opened wider and wider. Then, in an explosion of red light, her body reached its limit and exploded. She was gone. With Mary out of the way, the Harvesters rushed forward into the breach. They began to overrun the city, slaughtering those who were unfortunate enough to not be lifted out to safety.

Inside the helicopter, three of the surviving yellow Wielders had activated their power and were finishing healing Sarah. Sarah began to breathe deeply. She coughed and opened her eyes. Lieutenant Michael was leaning over her. She sat up and looked at the hole that was in her jacket. She saw the blood that covered her skirt and jacket. She then saw Valerie laying down next to her. She stared at her and said, "Is she okay."

Lieutenant Michael said, "Yeah, she's okay. I just gave her a tranquilizer shot. She'll wake up in a few hours."

Sarah looked around again and said, "Where's Mary?"

Lieutenant Michael hugged her and said, "She's dead. She sacrificed herself so that we could escape."

Sarah began to cry, her tears fell onto his jacket. She said, "I ... I didn't even get to say goodbye."

Lieutenant Michael said, "I know, she knew you loved her, that's why she sacrificed herself. She wanted us to live because she loved us. She said that our lives were worth it to her."

Sarah clung to him with all her might. She buried her face into his shoulder and cried until there were no more tears left in her.

- 5 -

Two hours later, the helicopter landed back on the roof of the Phoenix Guard Headquarters. The ramp slowly lowered. Captain Faust stood nearby with Doctor Lovecraft at his side. There were two other medics there with her as well. When the ramp finally lowered the two medics ran inside and began to look over all the girls.

Valerie was still sleeping on the floor. One of the medics asked Lieutenant Michael if she needed any medical attention. Lieutenant Michael shook his head and said, "No, I just gave her a tranquilizer shot to calm her down."

The medic nodded his head and then looked over Sarah. A small scar had formed down the length of her stomach. It was the only evidence that a thorn had pierced through her. They poked at her and determined that she was going to be fine. They proceeded to check the rest of the girls.

Lieutenant Michael knelt down and picked Valerie up off the floor. He cradled her in his arms. Sarah wrapped her arms around his arm and leaned her head against his arm. They walked down the ramp together. Doctor Lovecraft looked at Valerie and said, "Is she hurt?"

Lieutenant Michael shook his head and said, "No, I had to tranquilize her to calm her down. Sarah was badly injured but the yellow Wielders fixed her."

Doctor Lovecraft looked down at Sarah's torn uniform. Dried blood stained her jacket and the skirt of her dress. A large tear was in her jacket and dress over her stomach.

As Doctor Lovecraft looked over Sarah, one of the medics walked past them cradling the girl from Leviathan Company in his arms. Her seemingly lifeless body was limp in his arms. Her red eyes still stared blankly into nothingness. It was at that time that Lieutenant Michael noticed that in her right hand she clasped onto an adult's severed hand. It was most likely her Lieutenant's hand. She didn't let go of it.

The survivors hobbled into a line in front of Captain Faust. His intense emotions were held back by years of training. Despite that, his eyes looked like they were on the verge of tears too. He said, "I'm still going over all the reports of what happened. I will also read your own reports later when you turn them in. We haven't had losses like this since the Salt Lake sector collapse. That girl that they carried off is the only survivor of Leviathan Company. All the members of our Fifth squad are dead. Leslie of First squad is dead. Mary of Third squad is dead. About fourteen million people are presumed dead. Squad three's sector had the most rescues. I don't know what happened, but whatever you did, Lieutenant Snyder, they were able to rescue two thousand additional people from that area."

Lieutenant Michael stood there, still cradling Valerie in his arms. He said, "Mary volunteered to hold the Harvesters back so that the rest of our squad could retreat. If she didn't do that, we would have been over run. Those two thousand people were saved because of her self-sacrifice."

The Captain walked over to Lieutenant Michael. He put his hand on Michael's shoulder and squeezed it. He said, "That Mary is one of the bravest girls I've known. I will miss her. We'll always remember her as a hero who gave her life for the sake of the people. In all, a total of about eight hundred thousand people were successfully rescued. The World Government decided to nuke the region. The Los Angeles sector is now scorched land."

Captain Faust covered his eyes with his hand and wiped the tear that had finally formed. He dropped his hand, composing himself, and said, "We're going to find out why this happened so that we can make sure it damn well never happens again. I know you're tired and hurting from this loss. Believe me, I feel this loss too. Get some rest, mourn our comrades, and get yourselves ready to strike back. We won't give up till every last one of those damned creatures are destroyed! You are dismissed."

Slowly the tired Wielders made their way down the stairs to their apartments. Squad three and four entered their floor together. They walked in silence to their doors.

As they stood in front of the door, Giana hugged Sarah and said, "I'm sorry about Mary." Sarah, her face dejected, said, "Thanks."

Elsa hugged Sarah and said, "If you need me, I'll be there for you." Sarah tried to smile and said, "Thanks."

Tina hugged Sarah and said, "I'm sorry too." Sarah again said, "Thanks."

Lieutenant Rachel hugged Michael and said, "I'm so sorry. We're here for you."

Lieutenant Michael said, "Thanks. That means a lot to us. For now we're just going to rest and talk about it."

Squad four stood there and watched as Lieutenant Michael carried Valerie inside the apartment. She was still sleeping soundly from the drugs. Sarah followed behind him and closed the door behind herself. She looked back toward Squad four as she closed the door. Her face expressed her deep pain.

Lieutenant Michael laid Valerie on the couch by the television. Sarah looked down at the hole in her uniform and the blood that stained it. Lieutenant Michael, his uniform also stained with her blood, sat at the dining table. Sarah walked over to the table and sat down next to him. She said, "Tell me what happened to Mary. I want to know everything."

Lieutenant Michael clasped his hands together. He began to explain everything to her. How Mary distracted the Harvesters while he and Valerie worked to heal her slowly. He told her that when they received the order to retreat, Mary refused to retreat. He told her how he ran up to her and tried to force her to come but that she used her power to force him to the ground. He told her that Mary understood that they would be overrun by the Harvesters if someone didn't distract them long enough. He told her that he knew that Mary was right so he accepted her decision. He didn't tell her what Mary confessed to him, nor what she did after that.

Sarah leaned back in her chair and listened to everything he said. As she listened tears began to roll down her already stained cheeks again. Sarah said, "It's my fault. If I ... If I hadn't gotten injured, then I could have helped her." She covered her face with her hands and began to cry again. Her body was shaking.

Lieutenant Michael reached over and wrapped his arm around her. She slid her arms around his back and hid her face in his chest. He picked her up and let her sit on his lap. He gently said, "No, Sarah, it's not your fault at all. Don't even think that way. This all happened because we were unprepared for those new Harvesters. We've never seen that before. They taught us a lesson that we should never have forgotten. We should always expect something new."

Sarah began to compose herself. She said, "I wish I could have told her goodbye."

Lieutenant Michael said, "She knew you would have said it if you could have. She wanted you to live on for her."

As they were speaking, Valerie finally started to wake up from being tranquilized. She began to moan and said, "What? Why ... why am I so dizzy?"

Lieutenant Michael picked Sarah off of his lap and set her feet on the ground. He walked over to Valerie. He said, "I'm sorry, Valerie. I gave you a tranquilizer shot for your own good so that you would sleep."

Valerie sat up and began to remember what had happened. She started to yell again. She stared at Lieutenant Michael, her face showed her feelings of betrayal. Lieutenant Michael tried to approach her. He started to put his arm around her. She shoved his arm away and jumped up from the couch. She yelled, saying, "This is all your fault! All you had to do was get her! Instead, you ran away like a coward! I trusted you! She trusted you! You're a monster! I hate you!"

Lieutenant Michael lowered his arm and looked down toward the ground. His lips quivered as if he was trying to say something but there was no sound coming out.

Sarah watched from where she stood next to the table. Her face became full of anger. She stormed over to the couch. She stood in between Valerie and Lieutenant Michael. A deep look of disgust was on Sarah's face. She lifted her hand high into the air and then slapped Valerie across the face with as much force as she could.

Valerie was unprepared for this. She fell over and landed on the couch. A red hand mark began to form on her face. She brought her hand up to her cheek and placed it over the place where she had been slapped. Valerie looked up in surprise at Sarah. Tears started to roll from her eyes down her cheeks. She couldn't say anything as she sat on the couch staring back at her.

Still angry, Sarah picked up Valerie by the dress jacket and began to shake her, yelling, "You think you lost more than me? Do you think you lost more than me? Mary was my best friend! She was like an older sister to me! You've only known her for like two months, I've known her for years! You didn't love her as much as I did! She's a hero! She sacrificed herself so that the rest of us could survive! Her death saved two thousand people's lives! Why do you think we're here? To have fun all the time? Is that why you were taken away from your parents? We're soldiers, remember? We fight to save as many people as we can!

When we win, they die. When they win, we die! We lost big time! Mary's dead. Fourteen million people are dead. I ... I didn't even get to say goodbye to her!"

Lieutenant Michael reached out and put his hand on Sarah's shoulder. He was surprised at Sarah's outburst because he had never seen her act so violently to another person before. He said, "Sarah, take it easy on her. She never dealt with this before."

Sarah began to cry again, Valerie lost the will to stand on her own two feet. She remained standing only because Sarah was still holding her up by the jacket. Sarah stopped shaking her and pulled her against her own body. She held Valerie in a tight embrace and said, "If ... if you knew how much Mary loved Lieutenant Michael, you would never have said those disgusting things! If you knew how much he suffers each time one of us dies, you wouldn't say that! He didn't abandon her! She volunteered to stay behind to save us and you know it! What you said cheapens her death, her self-sacrifice!"

Valerie hung there in Sarah's embrace like a doll. Sarah finally stopped speaking and just held her. Sarah dropped to her knees and Valerie was forced down on her knees as well.

Valerie could feel Sarah's body trembling around her. She finally spoke out, her voice shaking, saying, "Sarah, I ... I'm sorry. I ... I didn't mean it. I know it's not his fault. It's really my fault. If ... if only I had been stronger, then I could have completely healed you and then maybe Mary would still be alive. I ... I killed her." Valerie started to weep even louder, she said, "I'm ... I'm not strong enough! I killed her because I'm not strong enough!"

Lieutenant Michael dropped to his knees beside them. He wrapped his arms around both Sarah and Valerie. He held them and said, "Valerie, it's not your fault either. You didn't kill her or cause her death. Neither of you are to blame. This happened because the Harvesters had a new trick that we've never seen before. Now that we know about it, we can prepare for it. We can make sure it doesn't happen like this again."

Sarah's grip on Valerie loosened. She reached over and clung to Lieutenant Michael. Valerie reached her arms out to Lieutenant Michael too. She took hold of him. She said, "I'm sorry I said those mean things to you. I didn't mean it."

Lieutenant Michael said, "Don't worry, it's okay. I know you didn't mean it. We're all really upset over this. You're not alone. All of us are in pain right now."

Sarah began to speak again. She said to Valerie, "All we have is each other. Don't forget that, all we have is each other. Mary knew that and made a choice. I'm going to honor it by living and by fighting so that Mary's sacrifice won't be in vain. That's what you're supposed to do now, Valerie. Will you help me do that?"

Valerie said, "Yes, I won't let Mary's death be in vain. I'll keep living and fighting for her."

Lieutenant Michael leaned his back against the couch. He shifted his legs and straightened them on the floor. Sarah and Valerie sat there on both sides of him. Their faces were buried into his chest. He held them tightly. The girls cried until they had no more tears left. They laid there together silently. Valerie and Sarah fell asleep in his arms. He let them sleep.

Lieutenant Michael thought to himself, *"It's not your fault girls. It's really my fault. If only I had been stronger, then Mary wouldn't have had to die; she wouldn't have had to fight."* He could still feel her warm hands on his face, her soft touch on his lips. He laid there in silence as he strived to push his grief to a place where it could not be seen. The girls slept. Their clothing still stained with Sarah's blood. He could feel their rhythmic breathing as they continued to sleep.

The girls slept for about two hours. Sarah started to wake up first. She started to move and Lieutenant Michael lifted his arm off of her. She sat up and looked around at her surroundings. She then looked at Lieutenant Michael and said, "How long was I out?"

Lieutenant Michael reached up and brushed the side of her head with his hand, saying, "It's been about two hours."

Sarah looked down at her uniform and saw the gaping hole that was torn open by the Harvester thorn. She looked at the stains of her own blood.

Valerie was awoken by Lieutenant Michael's voice. She sat up and looked up at Sarah. Sarah's handprint was still somewhat visible on her face. She brought her hand to her cheek and gently caressed it.

Sarah looked at it and said, "I'm sorry I hit you so hard."

Valerie, looking dejected, said, "No. It's okay. I deserved it for saying those things. I really didn't mean it. I just was so angry that I had to lash out. I'm really sorry, Lieutenant."

Lieutenant Michael rubbed Valerie on top of her head and said, "Like I said before, don't worry about it. When we're really sad we sometimes do things that we don't mean to do. Mary is now the fifth girl that I've lost in this war. Sarah has now lost two comrades. Mary also lost two comrades. That's not counting girls we know in other squads. It's horrible. It never gets easier too. I love each one of them. I miss them so much. We just push those feelings down and keep moving forward. We have got to keep going forward so that we can win this war. If we don't win, then all their deaths will be for nothing. All our pain and suffering will be for nothing. I won't let that happen. We have to win."

Valerie said, "What do we do next?"

Lieutenant Michael said, "We're going to be assigned a new teammate. That's how we got you on our team. We're going to get a new teammate and we're going to go out and fight. We'll give the Harvesters hell for taking Mary away from us."

Sarah said, "We're going to make ourselves stronger too so that they won't take another friend away from us."

Lieutenant Michael rubbed both of their heads at the same time and said, "We're all really dirty. Let's get out of these clothes and shower. Then we can get into our pajamas and take the rest of the day off."

Sarah stood up first. She reached her hand out to Valerie. Valerie took her hand and allowed Sarah to lift her up. As she pulled Valerie up, she brought her up close to her and wrapped her arms around her. Sarah said, "Thank you for saving me."

Valerie wrapped her arms around Sarah too. She said, "Mary told me to tell you goodbye for her."

Sarah began to tear up a little and said, "Thank you for telling me that. I wish I could have told her goodbye myself."

Valerie said, "Me too. All I did was yell at her."

Sarah chuckled and said, "Well, she is pretty stubborn, you can't help but yell at her."

Sarah released her hold on Valerie and Valerie then let her go. Sarah took Valerie's hand and they left to the bathroom. Lieutenant Michael then stood up and headed for his own room.

Inside the bathroom, Sarah removed her ruined uniform. She then walked over to the showers and turned one of them on. Valerie looked down at her own uniform and looked at the blood stains that were on the skirt of her dress. She took off her jacket and then pulled her dress over her head. She tossed them in her basket. She went to the shower stall next to Sarah and turned on the water. Together, the two girls rinsed the dirt and the blood off of their bodies.

Lieutenant Michael entered into his room and began undressing. He pulled Mary's com unit out of his pocket and placed it on the desk next to his bed. He angrily tossed his jacket, shirt, and tie on the floor in frustration. He kicked his pants off and left all his clothing sitting in a pile on the floor. He went into the bathroom and turned on the water to his shower.

As he waited for the water to get warm, he stared at himself in the mirror. The sight of his face began to disgust him. The words that Valerie had carelessly uttered, "You're a monster!" reverberated in his mind. She claimed that she did not mean them, but it was something that he had already felt inside his heart. *If only I was stronger. If only I could fight for these poor girls. If only I could take their place.* He knew that he would soon have to choose a new girl and the cycle would begin again. He would have to put another girl in this horrible position. A position that he could never fill himself.

After their showers, Sarah and Valerie joined each other at the mirrors. The two of them stood there brushing their hair in silence. They looked over at the mirror that Mary would have stood at.

Sarah finished brushing her hair. She put her brush away and then began to go through Mary's drawers. Valerie said, "What are you doing?"

Sarah replied, "I want to see if there is anything that belonged to Mary that I want to keep to remember her. Anything we don't take gets thrown away to make room for the new girl that will be coming within a couple of weeks."

Valerie walked over to the drawer too and began to look through it with Sarah. There wasn't too much in there. What interested them most was a small box that was shoved in the back. Sarah opened it up and it was full of mostly hair bands. Sarah took one of the hair bands and put it on her wrist. She said, "I'll wear this one for Mary." Valerie took a hair band too and put it on her wrist as well.

At the bottom of the box was a small glass bead ring. Sarah held it up and smiled, saying, "I remember when Mary got this ring. There was a festival and the Lieutenant took us there, I mean myself, Mary and Susan. The Lieutenant won this as a prize, he won all of us prizes, but this is the prize that he won for Mary. She called it her 'engagement' ring."

Sarah put the ring on the counter and said, "We should offer this to the Lieutenant." With nothing else to look at in the box, Sarah put it back in the drawer. She shut the drawer. She picked the ring back up and the two of them went to change into their pajamas in their own rooms.

Lieutenant Michael finished showering. He quickly dried himself off and hung up his towel. He left his bathroom and picked up the clothes that he had tossed angrily on the floor. He shoved them into his laundry basket and then put on his pajamas.

As he stepped out of his room, he saw Valerie and Sarah standing next to Mary's door. They appeared to be waiting for him. When they heard his door open they turned to him. Lieutenant Michael said, "What's up?"

Sarah said, "We were waiting for you so we can go through her room together."

Lieutenant Michael said, "Are you sure you want to do this now? It can wait till tomorrow."

Sarah shook her head and said, "No, I want to do this now while my heart is under control. If I do this later, I'm going to start crying again."

Lieutenant Michael nodded and said, "I understand. We can do this now if you really want to."

Sarah then held her hand out and opened it. Lieutenant Michael stared at her palm and saw the ring. He picked it up and looked it over. He said, "Oh, I remember this. This is the prize I won for Mary at that festival."

Sarah said, "I think she would have wanted you to have it. If you remember, she called it her engagement ring."

Lieutenant Michael smiled and put the ring into his pocket. He said, "Yeah, she ... she is ... she was always jo ... joking about that." He clenched his jaws and struggled to keep back tears that wanted to come out. He maintained his composure and pushed the feelings back down inside of him.

Lieutenant Michael put his hand on her door knob and opened it. He turned on the light. Together they entered. Sarah and Valerie began to look through her drawers together. Whenever either of them saw something they wanted, they took it.

Lieutenant Michael started to clean up the room by stripping the blankets off of Mary's bed. He would have to wash everything to get it ready for the new girl that would fill her position. He picked up one of the pillows and took off the pillow case. He reached for the other pillow and as he picked it up he saw a small book sitting beneath it.

Lieutenant Michael reached for it. On the cover of the book, written in black permanent marker, was the phrase, "My Diary." He sat down on the bed and held the book in his lap. Sarah and Valerie noticed him. Sarah said, "What is it?"

Lieutenant Michael stared at the cover and said, "It looks like Mary kept a diary." Sarah and Valerie stopped looking through Mary's drawers and went to sit down on each side of him.

Lieutenant Michael opened the cover and inside the cover was a sealed envelope with Mary's handwriting on it, which read, "For Michael." There was a heart drawn around his name.

He picked up the envelope and carefully opened it. He pulled out a letter that was neatly folded inside, written on two pages in Mary's sloppy handwriting. He unfolded the pages and began to read it to himself. Valerie and Sarah read it with him as they sat next to him on both sides:

Dear Michael,

If you are reading this letter then that means I am probably dead. I am writing this letter because there are things I want to tell you. First, I know how much you have suffered since both Cheryl and Susan have died. I know that you will feel the same way over me. I want you to know that I know that it was not your fault that I died, so please don't feel too bad. If I died it was because it could not be helped so please don't feel it was your fault.

Second, I want you to know that I love you. I know that when I say stuff like that you think of it as a joke and brush it off. It's not. I love you with all my heart and soul. I know you can't love me that way and you can only love me like family. I am happy with that. It makes me feel special. If I died to save you then I am even happier. If I died saving you, it was because I know that if you keep on living, a part of me will always live inside your heart. As long as you are alive, I will keep living inside of you and I will be alive with you wherever you go.

The third thing I want to tell you is that I want you to live your life. I want you to fall in love and to get married. You will be a really great dad. I want you to have children and to grow old together with someone you love. These are all the things that I want to do but I can't because of the way I was born. I'm not angry though. If I could be given a choice to either be born normal, and to have a normal life, or, to be born this way, I would chose to be born this way again so that I could meet you. Being with you and my teammates have made me so happy and I would never change that for anything. If there is a heaven I will watch over you from there. When you've lived a full life, and it is your turn to die, I want you to tell me what it was like to do all those things that I couldn't do. I'll be waiting for you there.

Love,
Mary

Lieutenant Michael's hands began to shake as he finished reading. He could no longer hold the pages in his hands. He dropped the paper on the floor. He lost control of the emotions that he had been suppressing. He started to cry like he had never cried in front of any of the girls before. He slid off of the bed and collapsed onto his knees. He buried his face into the carpet.

In shock, Sarah dropped down beside him and began to stroke his back with her hand. The sight of him crying made her start to cry again too. Valerie slid off the bed and kneeled next to Lieutenant Michael as well. She put her hands on his back and began to caress it too.

Sarah said, "It's okay, Lieutenant. Mary's right. It's not your fault either. She knew you would have done anything to prevent this. She loved you and wanted you to live for her too."

Lieutenant Michael sat up and began to quickly compose himself. He pushed the emotions that he had let slip out back down inside of himself. He said, "I'm sorry, girls, I just lost control of myself for a moment. I'm okay now."

He picked the diary back up and opened the cover again to see the first page. Sarah and Valerie again looked over his shoulder to read it with him. On the first page, she wrote at the top, "Things I want to do before I die." Underneath it, she wrote out a list. Next to each line she drew a box and most of the boxes had an 'X' drawn in it, which probably meant that it was completed:

☒ Stay up all night with Cheryl and Susan telling ghost stories.
☒ Buy an Asteria dress.
☒ Eat a whole pizza by myself.
☒ Go to a festival.
☒ Eat a whole bag of cotton candy.
☒ Beat Giana in a fight.
☒ Fall in love.
☒ Buy the same ice cream and it eat with the one I love.
☒ Wear a white wedding dress.
☒ Learn to dance.
☒ Dance to my favorite song with the one I love.
☐ Make the one I love breakfast by myself.
☐ Tell the one I love that I love him.
☐ Kiss the one I love.

Valerie looked at the list and said, "It's a good thing that Mary finished her list before she died. Now she can go to heaven happy."

Sarah looked confused and said, "What are you talking about, Valerie? She didn't do the last two."

Valerie said, "But she did, even though she took out her com unit I could still hear what she was saying. She told the Lieutenant that she loved him. Then, I saw her kiss him."

Sarah looked at Lieutenant Michael for confirmation. Her face was full of shock. He looked embarrassed and said, "It's true. It shocked me so much that all I could do was stare at her blankly and then that is when she tossed me over to where you two were."

Sarah started to blush and looked downward embarrassed. She looked toward her feet and said, "Well, I guess she did finish it then."

Lieutenant Michael flipped the pages into the center of the diary. He opened it to a page randomly and started to read it out loud:

"Susan and Sarah are angry at me because I won't tell them about my nightmares anymore. I want to tell them but I'm afraid because it is stupid. I think they will laugh at me about it. Maybe one day I will tell them but for now I am going to write it. When I first started fighting the stupid bugs, I used to dream about the Harvesters trying to kill me like everyone else. Then I started to get closer and closer to Lieutenant Michael and my dreams changed. I stopped dreaming about the Harvesters. Instead I would dream about Lieutenant Michael. He would be walking down the street, or, some other place, and I would start to follow after him. I would call out to him to stop, but he would ignore me. I would run after him, calling out to him but he would still ignore me. When I catch up to him, I try to grab onto his arm but my hand goes through his body like I'm a ghost. It is a stupid nightmare but it really scares me. It scares me because I'm afraid that he will forget about me or abandon me. But, when I wake up, I remember that the Lieutenant cares about me. I sneak into his bed and he makes me feel safe. I'm not scared anymore. I know he won't forget about or abandon me."

Lieutenant Michael closed the journal and hugged it against his heart. He said, "Yes, Mary, we won't ever forget about you."

Sarah chuckled and said, "Yeah, that is kind of a stupid dream, but it makes sense to me why it would make her scared. I knew she was afraid that you would forget her."

The next morning there was a memorial service. All the members of Phoenix Guard would gather on the rooftop to celebrate the lives of those who had been lost.

Right before the beginning of the service, Lieutenant Michael put a black arm band on his left bicep. He handed a black band to Sarah, who also put it on her own left bicep. Lieutenant Michael then handed a black band to Valerie and said, "It's a tradition that we wear a black band if we have lost a comrade or friend in battle. You wear it on your left arm until Mary's position is filled." Valerie took the black band and wrapped it around her left bicep.

Lieutenant Rachel, Giana, Tina, and Elsa walked up and stood beside them. They all wore the black band on their arm in remembrance of Mary. As more of the squads came, Valerie could see that they all had the black bands on them.

Together, they celebrated the memory of all those who died. Several girls, including Sarah, stood up to tell stories about their lost friends. They committed themselves to continue the struggle in their place.

After the memorial, Lieutenant Michael, Sarah and Valerie returned to their apartment. They ate lunch together and continued to talk about their fun memories of Mary.

After lunch a knock came to the door. An officer handed Lieutenant Michael a folder and then left. Sarah said, "Are those the new Wielders?"

Valerie said, "What does that mean?"

Lieutenant Michael said, "These are red Wielders that are ready to be added to our team."

He opened the folder and there were four pages inside. The first page had a picture of a girl named Kotoko Ikari. She just turned nine years old and was living in the San Francisco sector.

The second page had a picture of a girl named Farah Saad. She had also just turned nine years old and was living in the Denver capitol sector.

The third page had a girl named Heather Davis. She was also nine and was living in the San Francisco sector.

The fourth girl looked familiar to him. He read her name, which was Jennifer Gonzales. She was previously recruited by Leviathan Company. He remembered her face as the girl that was the sole survivor of Leviathan Company. It was the same poor girl who was sitting in the corner like she was a rag doll in the helicopter. The same girl who clung to her dead Lieutenant's severed hand. She was still nine but would be ten in two months. She was currently being held in the Sacramento sector where they lived at the military hospital.

Lieutenant Michael held up Jennifer's paper and said, "I think it would be best to take her. She's already been trained. She's lost all her friends so we can all better relate to her having lost one of ours. We can help each other heal. Since she's already been trained, we can start paying back the Harvesters sooner too."

Sarah looked at the paper and said, "I agree. Let's have her be our new partner."

Valerie took the paper and read it over too, saying, "Yeah, let's get Jennifer on our team. I think that is a good idea."

Lieutenant Michael nodded his head and smiled, saying, "Alright, then we are agreed. We'll ask to have this Jennifer assigned to us. Then we'll go out there and get some payback. We'll make sure they can't do this to us again."

Sarah stood up from the table and walked over to Lieutenant Michael's side. She took one of his hands and held it silently. Valerie followed suit. She held onto Lieutenant Michael's other hand. The three of them then looked back at Jennifer's picture laying on the table. Soon the struggle would begin again.

## Afterword

Thank you so much for reading my first book! I hope that you enjoyed reading it as much as I enjoyed writing it. I also want to give special thanks to my artistic niece, Veronica, who helped with all the artwork. I also want to thank all the people who helped read and edit my novel; I greatly appreciate all your hard work on my behalf.

In this first volume I really wanted the reader to feel what it was like to be one of those girls from the beginning to the end. I wanted the reader to feel all their hopes, dreams, fears, joy, sorrow, friendships, and loneliness. Tears of Darkness will have at least two or three more volumes. I have it all planned out already. I like episodic stories but I don't like stories that don't have a conclusive end, so you can be sure that all the mysteries will be solved by the end of the third or fourth book.

When I first tried to publish it, I brought them my manuscript, which was quickly rejected. Next, I unbuttoned my blouse a little, tilted my head cutely, and batted my eyes at the man, saying, "Pretty please." To which he flatly said, "No, that's not going to work Sophia." It was at that time that I got down on my hands and knees, tried to curl up on his lap, and purr like a kitten. In response, he called security, and two really big guys picked me up by my armpits and legs. They carried me to the front door, tossed me out on the street, and tried to spray water at me while shouting, "Scram, you stray cat!"

Well, none of that actually happened, but, it can be hard to get officially published. I'm hoping that this book will lead me to getting noticed. Till then, I will keep doing my best to write and provide you with good stories.

If you want to keep updated on the progress of the next volume, check out my blog at:

sophialiddellbooks.webs.com

See you next time in:
TEARS OF DARKNESS, Volume 2 -
THE WALLS OF JERICHO

www.ingramcontent.com/pod-product-compliance
Lightning Source LLC
Chambersburg PA
CBHW031322170626
46807CB00002B/528